KU-657-715

Wayward

PRAISE FOR THE AUTHOR

"An impressive novel from Hannah Mathewson. Rich and intricate world-building evokes a London that is both familiar and unfamiliar. The reader is swept into a world that is sometimes unsettling, sometimes terrifying, but always exciting."
JODI TAYLOR, AUTHOR OF *JUST ONE DAMNED THING AFTER ANOTHER*

"Witherward is catnip for fans of complex characters and delightfully messy worlds. It delivers on a world of intricate factions and intrigue, without ever losing track of the vividly written living, breathing characters that are at the heart of it. This book broke my heart in the best ways."
A.J. HACKWITH, AUTHOR OF *THE LIBRARY OF THE UNWRITTEN*

"*Mathewson has delivered a dazzling, fantastical adventure where magic awaits you on every page, and nothing is ever quite what it seems. With a magnificent world I'd love to get lost in, intriguing magic, and a wide cast of dynamic characters you can't help but love,* **Witherward** *is a phenomenal and immensely fun debut that will leave readers wanting more.*"

ADALYN GRACE, AUTHOR OF *ALL THE STARS AND TEETH*

"*Street-smart and wounded, Ilsa is a protagonist to cheer on as she navigates two Victorian Londons, both familiar and strange.*"

MARIE BRENNAN, AUTHOR OF *A NATURAL HISTORY OF DRAGONS*

Also by Hannah Mathewson and available from Titan Books

Witherward

Wayward

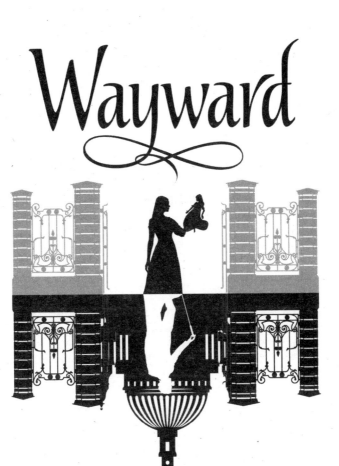

HANNAH MATHEWSON

TITAN BOOKS

Wayward
Print edition ISBN: 9781789094459
E-book edition ISBN: 9781789094466

Published by Titan Books
A division of Titan Publishing Group Ltd
144 Southwark Street, London SE1 0UP
www.titanbooks.com

First edition: May 2022
10 9 8 7 6 5 4 3 2 1

This is a work of fiction. All of the characters, organisations, and
events portrayed in this novel are either products of the author's
imagination or are used fictitiously. Any resemblance to actual persons,
living or dead (except for satirical purposes), is entirely coincidental.

© Hannah Mathewson 2022

Hannah Mathewson asserts the moral right to be
identified as the author of this work.

No part of this publication may be reproduced, stored in a retrieval
system, or transmitted, in any form or by any means without the prior
written permission of the publisher, nor be otherwise circulated in any
form of binding or cover other than that in which it is published and
without a similar condition being imposed on the subsequent purchaser.

A CIP catalogue record for this title is available from
the British Library.

Printed and bound in the UK by CPI Group Ltd.

In loving memory of Uncle Matt

THE WHISPERERS
Whitechapel

LEADER: LORD JERICHO VOSS
MILITIA: THE STEWARDS

THE ORACLES
The Docklands

LEADER: THE SEER
MILITIA: THE ACOLYTES

THE WRAITHS
The North

LEADER: LADY JOSAVIE WRIKE
MILITIA: THE BLADES

THE SORCERERS
The Heart

LEADER: HIGH SORCERER FISK
MILITIA: THE ENFORCERS

THE CHANGELINGS
Camden Town

LEADER: ALPHA HESTER
MILITIA: THE WOLVES

THE PSI
The Underground

LEADER: THE TRINITY
MILITIA: THE CLOAKS

I

Ollivan was fired from Pendergast's Occult Emporium at ten past nine in the morning, which he thought was leaving it a bit late.

The shop had been open for over an hour, but a persistent autumn rain was keeping the customers away. Mr Holt had retreated to the back room to manage his stock, or possibly to avoid Ollivan's cheerful whistling, when the bell above the door finally chimed.

"She said it was a very old technique from Malaysia, used to bring one in closer communion with the spirit world," the lady in green was telling her companion as they folded their umbrellas. "Before our very eyes, she put Louise in a trance. Just by touching her shoulder!"

At the counter, Ollivan went back to scribbling in the sales ledger, having determined that the women would not know real magic if it reached out and swept them into a waltz. The morning paper lay beside it, the front page similarly defiled. An illustration of Queen Victoria on some public duty that weekend now bore the note *but where is the rat???* across it.

He was working on an *unravelling* – a spell used to undo another spell – for a particularly tricky ward he needed to put to rest. Get it wrong, and Ollivan would suffer gravely unpleasant consequences. Get it right, and the last few touches were finally falling into place.

"Hello there?"

It was the lady in green. She summoned Ollivan with a polite wave, and he put his pen down and weaved between the tables and shelves to join them.

"Beautiful day," he said in greeting.

The customer turned her curious gaze to the window. Ollivan watched rivulets of rainwater roll down the glass, and his mind filled unstoppably with the scent of daffodils, and the unspoiled green of new leaves. It *was* a beautiful day; with any luck, his last on this hellish grey plane.

"I've been told," the lady in green said, visibly preening, "that I have a true aptitude for precognition and that I could encourage it by burning sage or mugwort. Which would you suggest?"

Ollivan didn't know where to start. "Precognition?"

"The talented medium Madam Rosalie told her so," said the woman's companion, and they exchanged satisfied smiles.

Ollivan looked at the woman in green again. Her eyes were brown, the pupils wide in the 'atmospheric' dimness of the shop; Mr Holt said the darkness gave the place an air of mysticism. If the customer was truly capable of precognition – a real Oracle – Ollivan would be able to tell from her eyes. And even if she was, no herb would help her. Only a Sorcerer, and not an Oracle, was capable of drawing out the magical properties of a substance, and he doubted the woman was one of those either.

"And how much did this medium charge you for knowledge of your gift?" he said.

"Well I—"

"Since you have the gift of precognition, perhaps you ought to have foreseen this charlatan spending your money with a swindler's grin on their face."

The woman started to turn red. A shuffling at the office door said Mr Holt had emerged into the shop.

"What a rude man you are," her friend exclaimed. "It is none of your business how Fiona learned of her gift. She merely asked your advice on herbs."

"Herbs." Ollivan cast an eye over the shelves of bundled dry herbs and sticks of incense. "The only herb we stock with any magical properties to speak of is rosemary, and that won't help except to counteract a nightmare tonic or encourage snow to stick, and either way you could buy it at a grocer's for half the price."

"Sage!" Mr Holt put a hand on Ollivan's shoulder and pressed him to the side. The women continued to stare at Ollivan in open bewilderment as Mr Holt reached up and collected a bundle of sage from one of the shelves. "For clarity, ma'am. It ought to clear the obstacles of your gift and bring you stronger visions." He handed the sage to the woman in green, who eyed what Ollivan knew to be nothing but overpriced seasoning suspiciously until Mr Holt added, "Consider it a gift."

The women left.

"Ollivan." Mr Holt sighed. "I'm letting you go."

"I'm fired?" said Ollivan mildly.

Mr Holt ran a hand down his face. He was not skilled in confrontation. That much Ollivan had deduced from the fact he had kept a job there for the past year. "You are simply not suited to this type of salesmanship. Perhaps you are a sceptic about these matters" – Ollivan objected to that characterisation; it suggested faith and mystery and other things that had no place in the practice of magic – "but you've cost me too much business by not being able to put your own feelings aside."

Ollivan couldn't argue with that. The lady in green had only been the most recent of many. Last week Ollivan had almost brought a patron to tears in an argument over astrology. And before that, the man who had tried to lecture *him* about how a glamour was performed. Something about faeries and mind control, Ollivan couldn't remember. He had glamoured the man's shoes to appear tied together and watched him hobble needlessly down the street when he couldn't unknot them.

Ollivan beamed his widest smile at Mr Holt and clapped him on the shoulder. "I'm sorry it had to end like this, Mr Holt. All the best in your future endeavours."

Mr Holt blinked stupidly as Ollivan fetched his coat and hat from the hook by the door; he had forgotten his umbrella that morning, but it was alright. He was tearing his notes out of the sales ledger and tucking them away when his former boss came to his senses.

"Wait," said Mr Holt, shuffling towards the back room. "Your pay."

"No need," Ollivan cut in. "I'm an undisciplined liability who has defaced nearly every page of your ledger and cost you good business at every chance I've had since you hired me. Keep your money. Buy some more herbs. You could make a nice stuffing."

Mr Holt glanced warily at the sales ledger, then the shelves of bundled herbs, as Ollivan tipped his hat to the old man and stepped out of Pendergast's Occult Emporium for the last time.

*"You must write and tell me everything about Sorcerer magic,"
says Fyfe. His voice is muffled by the shoulder of your coat. His
skinny, too-long arms squeeze you tightly. You've promised him
he'll grow into them. You realise for the first time that you won't
be here to see it.*

*When Fyfe lets go, Aelius shakes your hand and beams his
winning smile. "Knock them dead, my dear."*

"I will," you promise.

*And then you've said goodbye to everyone, and you're certain,
just for a moment, that this is a terrible mistake. Your friends
assemble behind you, their warm, melancholy presence a magnet
drawing you back.*

But you don't go back. You go forward.

2

THREE DAYS EARLIER

Cassia was furious with herself.

She had been standing before the gap in the hedge – the one that led to the rose garden – for nearly three minutes, waving her hands in front of it as she willed it to do her bidding.

But it wouldn't.

Jasper had chosen this exercise for her because the intention behind the glamour was clear and visual: make the gap invisible. Make the hedge appear as one unbroken wall of new green, flush with spring. She didn't need to work that hard to visualise it.

But her intention wasn't the problem.

"What are you asking the glamour to do?" said Jasper from behind her. His voice was soft. Cassia had heard him draw breath to speak several times before braving the question. "You're right to say the intention under your breath, it's good control, but tell me in the exact wording."

She let her arms fall to her sides in defeat. "*Close the gap.*"

"Good." His tone was too positive; so infused with praise that Cassia's frustration with herself must have been blindingly obvious. "Your intention is perfect. It couldn't be simpler."

Cassia flinched at his choice of words. Her shoulders grew heavier. It really could not be simpler.

Jasper was only trying to help, as always. In fact, he was one of the better tutors Cassia had had. He had never shown surprise at how rudimentary her skills were, having known she spent most of her childhood outside the Sorcerer quarter of London and without the influence of her own people. And he was patient, unlike her last tutor; an older man who, when all else failed, had threatened to encourage her progression with a strap.

But at the same time, studying with Jasper was torture. He was eighteen, only a year older than her, and yet his confidence in his magic emanated from him the way spellwork did from his fingers. He was, in Cassia's grandfather's words, a jewel in the crown of the Society of Young Gifted Sorcerers.

A society that had refused Cassia entry a year ago, and in three days' time, would have an opportunity to turn her down again.

Not for the first time, she wished she wasn't a Sorcerer at all. Changeling magic – the power to shift form – surely wasn't this hard. Oracle magic was impossible to fail at, technically; they Saw the past, present, and future almost uncontrollably. Their first lessons in using their magic were in blocking it out. Wraiths had to learn how to pass through solid objects, but their heightened physical abilities came naturally to them, as did a Whisperer's ability to read minds. And the Psi's power was psychokinesis; the ability to move and control objects without touching them. Cassia wasn't sure how one learned *that*, and it was probably very difficult at a high level, but it was still a single skill; the equivalent to a Sorcerer mastering just one spell.

She could have belonged to any of six incarnations of magic, and she belonged to the one who channelled and tamed raw power; who shaped something stronger and more wilful than themselves; gave form to something formless. Sorcerer magic was the most complex of the six, that was well known. And Cassia was starting to fear she just wasn't talented enough to wield it.

Compulsively, she looked up at the townhouse looming above them, afraid that her progress – or lack thereof – was being seen from within. But she would never know if her mother watched her lessons and judged her progress, as every pane of glass in every window was enchanted to reflect a pink and perfect sunset, regardless of the weather or the time of day. It was one of the subtler magical adornments on their street. The house on their left vanished at certain angles. The one on the right had the crown of a colossal oak tree in place of a roof. On the mornings when Cassia awoke from dreams of giant wolves and transforming wings – the trappings of an altogether different magical childhood – all she had to do was look out of her window to be reminded that she was in the Sorcerer quarter of London now.

As if she could ever forget.

"The problem isn't the intention," she said, glowering at the gap in the hedge.

"I'm sure you're right."

"If I *intended* to give this up and find a cup of tea, do you think I'd have more luck?"

Jasper grinned. "Not on my watch. Describe how it feels. Does your magic answer when you call it?"

"Yes." Just to make sure, Cassia called it again. It took no more than a thought, and she felt it bloom in the centre of her abdomen, strong and eager.

Jasper hesitated. "And you're directing it to your throat?"

"*Yes*," snapped Cassia. She caught herself, meeting Jasper's sharp blue eyes in apology. "I know how to perform a glamour."

Magic was channelled in one of several ways; through the body, through an object or substance, or in words. Because a glamour only *acted* on a thing, rather than imbuing it with magic, the intention was grounded with the latter, and to do so, the Sorcerer directed their power to their throat.

Five-year-olds knew these principles of how to perform magic; it was the first thing a Sorcerer learned, prioritised over even their letters and arithmetic. Cassia had learned it herself, and had been chagrined by every tutor in the last two years who had asked her to recite her magical theory aloud.

Jasper, thankfully, did not, but Cassia could tell what he was thinking. Her intellectual grasp of Sorcerer magic was solid, her intention flawless. So what was wrong?

She hadn't always been this hopeless. Before returning to the Heart – the name given to the Sorcerer quarter of London – she had cast spells more or less at will. Nothing complex, as she was untrained; her parents had arranged for a visiting tutor for years, but Cassia had been reluctant to practise and made very little progress. But since applying herself, it was as if the more her theory advanced, the less her magic showed itself. Occasionally, she could still pull off an enchantment without a hitch, but she was unable to predict or replicate it when it mattered. She had no idea what she was doing wrong.

"Would you mind just… turning around?" she said. "I can feel you watching me."

Jasper smiled and cocked his head. "Of course I'm watching you. I'm your tutor."

"I know, but it's distracting. Please."

Jasper quirked an eyebrow, but turned around.

"No peeking."

"Cross my heart."

Cassia watched him a moment to see if he would sneak a glance, then turned her attention back to the hedge. She raised her arms, aiming her open palms at the entrance to the rose garden. It wasn't how the magic would act upon the hedge, but using one's hands still helped guide the spell in the right direction.

She drew a deep breath and banished her previous frustrations, then she called her magic to rise. It did so obediently, pooling just below her ribs to be directed where she willed it. So far, so good. With the intention at the forefront of her mind – *close the gap* – she encouraged the warm, effervescent power to rise through her chest and into her throat.

Don't let me down this time.

Cassia felt some resistance as her lips formed the spell, but she pushed through it, focusing on growing the sensation as she started murmuring the words.

"Close the gap," said her mouth. *Do it, do it, do it*, implored her mind.

The magic left her lips as she repeated the mantra, a thinner, slower trickle than she had hoped for. *No.* She pushed uselessly with her hands, and then remembered that would do nothing. The intention slipped down under her anxiety; the clear image in her

20

mind of an unbroken, lustrous hedge flickered, and a humiliating alternative forced its way in.

I can't fail at this again, she pleaded, but her magic took no notice. Leaving a taste in her mouth that was vaguely vindictive, her magic began to work the glamour. The gap shimmered. Dead, black vines studded with thorns stretched across it and immediately started to crumble. As Cassia lowered her hands, she was hit by an irrational certainty that Jasper would tell his fellow Society members about this. About how weak she was.

"You can turn around now," said Cassia weakly.

Jasper turned. She expected to see that unfailing patience, the hint of sympathy that made her cringe, but before he could stop himself, he laughed.

At that, Cassia chased the last of the magic inside her away with an angry internal hiss. She almost threatened it against ever coming back. Her hands balled into fists.

"Well, you've cast a glamour," said Jasper, ceasing his laughter at the look on Cassia's face. "It's progress."

"Progress." She shot him a look. "You must be so proud."

"It's not that bad," assured Jasper. He tried to lay the tip of an index finger against a thorn and watched it pass straight through, clearly without the impression of having injured himself. A good glamour acted upon *all* the senses. Cassia's monstrosity was just an ugly mirage. "Well, the visual rendering is really quite convincing, if you ignore the… flaking."

"Jasper, they could be the deadliest-looking thorns the gardener's ever seen, and she still would never believe this was anything other than a glamour," said Cassia, gesturing at the lush

21

green hedge on either side. "Please let's try something else. Won't you teach me to *ward* the rose garden instead?"

"Wards?" Jasper scratched at his russet hair. "That's, ah…"

Too advanced for you That was what he didn't want to say. And he was probably right; wards protected against intrusion, interference, or magic, or alerted the spellcaster to any of the above. If they were not sturdy, they were useless. "Never mind, then," Cassia said tonelessly.

"But why don't you try unravelling a glamour instead?" he said hastily. "I think you can do it."

She couldn't. Jasper explained the correct intention for removing glamours, and even demonstrated it for her on a lilac he glamoured a vivid orange, but Cassia's magic still refused to cooperate. Before she could inflict any will whatsoever on the mess of black thorns, they disintegrated entirely.

"Let's call it your practice assignment, then. For tomorrow." Jasper gave her a reassuring smile, the single dimple on one side wrinkling his pale cheek. "How is the spell for your initiation coming along?"

Anxiety tightened Cassia's chest. Her second attempt to be initiated into the Society of Young Gifted Sorcerers was in three days' time. She and the other hopefuls would demonstrate an enchantment of their choosing in front of the entire assembled Society who, if they were adequately impressed, would accept their new member with a vote of 'ayes'. Those whose enchantments underwhelmed earned a cheer of 'nays', were awarded a children's book of basic spells as a consolation prize and invited to try again in a year.

It was all supposed to be good fun, a sort of ice-breaker for new members. Only, if you were the only member of your family to have failed their first initiation, there was nothing fun about it.

High Sorcerer Fisk – the ruler of the Heart – would be there, of course, because Cassia's luck dictated so and because this season's initiation ceremony happened to be taking place on the same night the Society would vote in its new President.

She had been working herself to death not to embarrass herself. She had designed a beautiful spell; straightforward in intention but complex enough magically, just as Jasper said all the best spells were. It would be a crowd-pleaser, a signature people would remember when they saw her in the common room of the Wending Place, the Society clubhouse.

If it worked.

When Cassia thought forward to the night of the initiation test, she saw it going one of two ways. In the first, the spell plays off as she intends. She breathes a sigh of relief, gently, so they won't guess she ever had a doubt, and smiles at her new brothers and sisters as the President calls for their votes and a chorus of 'ayes!' ring out across the ceremony hall.

In the second, the spell fails. The moment she knows all is lost stretches on as if she'll be stuck in it forever. The hall is quiet for that endless moment; the one in which Cassia knows she's failed and everyone else is about to know it too. It's so quiet she can hear someone shuffle impatiently at the back of the crowd, near the fireplace. And then understanding seeps through the watching crowd like laughing gas. From the corner of her eye, she sees the Society Secretary, Jan Lenniker, whisper behind his hand to Iwan Goff, who covers his own mouth in an attempt to hide his smirk, but fails. Her heartbeat pounds in her ears.

Heat rises in her cheeks. Everything they think of her is suddenly obviously true.

The details were sharper in the second scenario, the feelings more compelling when her mind wandered onto the night of the test. She had lived it before, after all.

"Fine," lied Cassia in answer to Jasper's question. "The spell's coming along just fine. In fact, I think I'm almost ready."

Jasper looked unconvinced and Cassia couldn't blame him. "You'll be brilliant, Cassia. I have every faith in you. You're from a strong magical pedigree."

A *strong magical pedigree* who had sent her away when she was five. She hadn't been brought up among her own people, let alone enjoyed the influence of her family's magic. And if the tutors they sent to train her were enough to make up for it, there was no way to know. Cassia's magic made her different, so she had shunned it.

Jasper must have seen from the look on her face that it was the wrong thing to say.

"Listen," he said hastily, "I don't think here is the best place for you to practise. There's a room at the Wending Place that's become a junk room of sorts. Full of props left over from games, equipment for the summer festival, things like that. I cleared a proper space in there a few years ago and I use it as a sort of practice room when I'm trying something new. No one's ever disturbed me there. It's a complete secret."

Cassia shook her head. Only the Society members – known to each other and wider society as the Successors – were allowed inside, unless by express permission of the President. "But I'm not a Successor."

"*Yet.*"

"I'm not allowed in the Wending Place."

"I can sneak you in," he said, his lopsided grin widening. There was glint of mischief in that smile that Cassia had never seen before. Jasper was always perfectly sensible in their lessons, but perhaps that was only because he was working. "I think it would do you some good to have some real privacy when you practise, not just an overbearing tutor trying to stare at a fountain instead of at you."

Cassia smiled. "You're not overbearing, Jasper." She said nothing of the comment about staring at her. She was worried he meant it exactly as it sounded.

She was fond of Jasper. She enjoyed spending time with him in their lessons, but she had always suspected he had other ideas when he had answered her mother's advertisement for a tutor. Was it real affection that had made him want to see more of her? Or was it all an attempt – a *second* attempt – to ingratiate himself with their faction's most powerful family?

She wanted Jasper as a friend. Too many of her peers were gracious to her face, then shot her sidelong glances when they thought she wasn't looking. But Jasper existed on the fringes of them all. He moved through social circles as much as was expected of him, but never within them. He was studious, and somewhat solitary; well-spoken-of when he was spoken of at all. In short, she would never suspect him of gossip, and that was priceless to her. Cassia was the subject of such volumes of gossip that she feared she would get used to it.

Was she imagining that the way he was looking at her now threatened to ruin their friendship? If she gave him too much opportunity or confidence to do something neither of them could take back, could they still be friends? He had called the junk room a secret; *his* secret that he was sharing with her. It felt too... intimate.

And yet, the allure of a place to practise without fearing that her mother watched was too good to pass up.

She returned his smile. "It sounds perfect."

3

If Ollivan hurried on his way to the boarding house, it was not because of the rain; he was in too good a mood to feel it. The only thing quickening his step was anticipation.

He paused only once, before the free library on Brompton Road. He was banned from entering, as he was banned from a great many places. But that was about to change.

"Nice coat, mister."

Ollivan looked round. The street urchin on the step behind him was eleven or twelve, and covered in grime. He was tensed from head to toe from the chill.

"Have it," said Ollivan, slipping the coat from his arms and handing it to the boy. He could feel the rain now, but it only made him want to chuckle.

The boy didn't dare hesitate. He reached for the coat with both hands and darted away lest Ollivan change his mind.

He took the rest of the walk at a brisk stride, but he was still soaked through by the time he reached the boarding house. Mrs Flint, the owner, offered to dry his clothes in front of the kitchen range, but Ollivan cheerfully declined; he was changing into his best suit anyway. He forced his key into the rusty lock and kicked the base of his door as he pushed it open, as was his method to make the aged, warped thing budge. The room looked out on nothing but a brick wall across a narrow alley. It had never caught a glimpse of the sun, and was all the colder for it. The hairs on Ollivan's arms stood on end as he swapped the buckets under the leak in the roof, and emptied the rainwater into the alley. He had promised himself not to fix the leak, or the lock, or the door. Settling in would be defeat, and Ollivan had not been defeated. He saluted to the door, the bucket, the miserable brick wall outside the window, and thought of how the months of discomfort had all been worth it.

Then he took his good suit from the wardrobe and beat the dust from the lapels, all the while whistling the tune still stuck in his head; a folk song he'd learned as a child about a woman who became a whale and ate all the people who'd wronged her.

When he was dressed, Ollivan stood before the dusty mirror and admired the effect. He was thinner than he'd been a year ago. Shop work earned him enough to keep a roof *mostly* over his head and feed him thrice a day, but it wasn't the fare he had grown up with. He wondered what his family were dining on tonight. He wondered if it was duck.

Then he tidied every trace of himself out of the tiny room, left his final week's rent on the bed, tucked his umbrella under his arm and the pages from Mr Holt's sale ledger into his notebook, and left the boarding house, all the while whistling off-key.

4

TWO DAYS EARLIER

Cassia stood at the corner of Drusella Square, looking up at the forest of blackened turrets growing from the gothic mansion the Successors called their clubhouse. The building below was shrouded in enchanted ivy. Each dark leaf was a butterfly, their wings closing and opening in lazy synchrony, so that they shivered across the brickwork like ripples on a pond. It made the whole house appear alive.

And perhaps it was. The enchantment on the Wending Place was one of the oldest and least understood pieces of magic in London. It was said that the spell had outlived not only those who had cast it, but their entire ancestral lines, and in reward, had been granted dominion over itself.

If Cassia knew anything about magic, such a thing wasn't possible, but generations of Successors had been swayed by the legend. The house played practical jokes. It was known as the Wending Place partly because the corridors had a habit of taking you to unexpected locations. It echoed with inexplicable noises, lost rooms, found them again on a different floor. It rearranged paintings, changed locks, cast shadows of doorways that weren't there. In the entrance foyer was a famed record of every Successor who had gone missing and never been seen again, including one name crossed through; Juniper Henry had eventually stepped out of the water closet eighty-five years after going in, still nineteen years old and with no recollection of where she had been for decades.

But it was also called the Wending Place in reference to the journey of those who occupied it. The Society of Young Gifted Sorcerers was the avenue one walked between adolescence and adulthood, along which its members acquired the wisdom and self-confidence to go forth and conquer. In real terms, it was where the next generation of wealthy, elite Sorcerers made connections and built a reputation. Anybody who was anybody had been a member before they turned twenty-two and aged out of the Society and on to bigger things: politics, business, the old, esteemed institutes of learning on the continent. The nickname of the members, the Successors, was supposed to invoke coming into adulthood and taking the mantel from the previous generation. It was a little too on the nose for Cassia. She had grown up among the ruling family of Camden, who inherited their power and status in a way that was even harder to ignore than it was among the Sorcerer elite.

Cassia had a place in this world carved by her birth, and yet she was struggling to fit in to it. Staring down the Wending Place from the other side of Drusella Square was the Chambers of Alchemy, the offices from which High Sorcerer Jupitus Fisk reigned over the Heart. The Chambers was a veritable palace, built to Fisk's liking when he first came to power fifty years previously. Unlike most of the buildings in the Heart, there was no obvious aesthetic enchantment on the façade, and yet the black marble had an uncanny *depth*; like looking down into a well and seeing nothing, but sensing a chasm that could swallow you whole.

They said looking the High Sorcerer in the eye carried the same feeling. Cassia could confirm this was true.

The square itself was crowned with an opulent fountain, the white paving stones cleaned almost to a shine, the streetlamps finished with gilded embellishments. The High Sorcerer liked his people to be reminded of how wealthy he had made them each time they returned to the Sorcerer quarter.

For on the western edge of Drusella Square, Westminster Bridge stretched across the Thames, the divider between factions. On one side, Cassia's home quarter of the Heart, territory of the Sorcerers. On the other, Camden Town, the Changeling quarter. Militia of both factions – Heart enforcers and Camden wolves – attended the bridge, each with a guard point on their own bank.

From where Cassia waited, fifty paces away, the Sorcerer guard point did not look like much. One needed to be moving across the square to notice how the ward refracted the light, so that the bridge beyond appeared to hover, disconnected from the bank. Sorcerers could pass straight through it without feeling a thing, but Londoners of other magics would find themselves trapped in the ward like flies in a spider's web, unless the enforcers at the border commanded the spell to let them pass. On the far bank, the Changelings accomplished their security with sand bags, a wooden barrier, and their own magic; half a dozen militia wore the forms of wolves with maws the size of Cassia's head.

So it was all over the city. Six peoples occupied London – Sorcerers, Changelings, Wraiths, Whisperers, Oracles, and Psi

– not as one community, but as isolated factions divided along brutal, ever-shifting borders. Everything west of Hyde Park and most of what lay south of the Thames was the Sorcerer territory. It met the Docklands, the Oracle territory, east of Tower Bridge. Just across the river from where Cassia stood, Camden Town came to a point, but widened as it stretched towards its northern border before Hampstead Heath. To Camden's east lay Whitechapel, the Whisperer quarter, and above them both, the Wraiths occupied the territory of the North. Invisible on a street map of the city was the territory of the Psi; dozens of staircases across every quarter led below the cobbles and foundations, past the sewers and long-buried ruins, to the cavern known as the Underground.

It had been more or less the way in London since the Sorcerer empire of Callica had founded the city two thousand years ago. Then, they had tried to maintain power with a hierarchy of magical castes, sowing tribalism and mistrust among the four other factions as a means of control.

It had lasted until the celestial event known as the Shift; the advent of the Changelings. The sudden existence of a sixth people in London had thrown the city into chaos and led to widespread slaughter, and the fall of the Callicans. But the entrenched divides between the factions could not heal, only deepen. For centuries, the city navigated the ebb and flow of perilous peace and outright war.

A third age in the battle for London had begun around the time Cassia was born, when the faction leaders had agreed a set of rules known as the Principles. It was these accords that mandated the passing from territory to territory by way of the guard points, and threatened punishment to those who used their magic beyond their own people's quarter. It was the faction rulers who enforced the

Principles, and they who paid the cost if one of their own was caught breaking them.

Cassia had not crossed a guard point into Camden in nearly two years, not since the day she was collected from the home of the Changeling's ruling family and brought to the Heart to receive a proper Sorcerer's education, somewhere where she wouldn't mark herself as *different* for doing so; where she could embrace her magic as she had always feared to while trying to be a Changeling.

She squinted at the opposite bank to see if she knew any of the wolves at the guard point. Were any of them among those who used to watch her with suspicion, or turned a blind eye if a Changeling cursed her on the streets of Camden? Were any of them the friends she never wrote to? Cassia had thought she had more chance of belonging in the Heart, among her own people, so she had put all the good of her life in Camden behind her with the bad. But it hadn't worked out that neatly. At seventeen, she was a Sorcerer of seven years, but a Changeling of ten… and a true member of neither.

But she was not ready to give up. She would master her magic, she would join the Successors, and she would shed the mantle of 'outsider'. She would become the person everyone expected High Sorcerer Jupitus Fisk's granddaughter to be.

With her gaze turned to the Camden militia, Cassia was late to notice that someone had crossed the bridge and was on a collision course with her. With his nose in a newspaper, it seemed he hadn't noticed her either. They were close enough to touch – Cassia stepping one way and then the other in an effort to anticipate his movements – before Virgil Pike looked up and jerked to a stop.

The blood drained from his face as he folded the paper. Virgil was two heads taller than her, with dark eyes, sharp cheekbones, and deep brown skin. His long fingers fumbled as he tucked the paper under his arm, beneath his jacket, where it sat nestled against a book.

"Good morning, Virgil." She suppressed the urge to ask about his trip to the neighbouring quarter, because then he might ask why she was hovering outside the Wending Place. *Waiting for Jasper Hawkes to sneak me in* wouldn't go over well with another Successor. It might even get her banned from joining.

"Cassia," said Virgil in greeting. He didn't meet her eye, his gaze roaming around them instead. Cassia recognised that look; she had seen it the first time she'd tried to talk to a Sorcerer her age, and many times since. It was her mother who had tactlessly informed her that many in the Heart thought her some kind of spy from Camden, or else just too inclined to sympathise with Changeling causes and Changeling concerns. The Heart enjoyed a good relationship with Camden, but it was not that good, and two thousand years of history had taught the people of London how volatile these alliances could be.

It was to be expected, yet every time it happened, Cassia's heart sank. She and Virgil did not know each other well, and though he always came across as reserved – sullen even – she had heard people say that's how he was with everyone. He had a handful of boisterous older sisters, which gossips liked to point to as the cause.

Then he fumbled the book tucked into his jacket, revealing a peek at the title, and the knot in Cassia's chest released. Laughter burst from her.

"Goforth's *History of the Heart*," she said, and the whites of Virgil's eyes expanded. Cassia waved a hand. "Oh, no. Please don't fear, Virgil. I'm not going to tell my grandfather."

Goforth was one of the histories that delved unreservedly into how Jupitus Fisk came to power; it had involved the disappearance of the previous High Sorcerer, and the unsolved murder of two of his advisors. The work was not explicitly banned in the Heart, but it wasn't sold, and Cassia suspected those known to have read it crossed the militia on their way to work more often than usual. Jupitus preferred the histories that focused on his masterful trade deals and spun the signing of the Principles as his own great plan for peace.

So it was understandable that Virgil still assessed her warily. "One must consult a range of sources to get a balanced view of things," he said, his tone probing.

"I agree," she said, offering a smile. "And I've read it too."

Virgil drew up in surprise. "You have?"

"It's not quite so scandalous where I grew up." Cassia regretted reminding him of it the second it left her mouth – as if the people of the Heart ever forgot – but if Virgil was put off, it didn't show. He drew closer, and looked about them again.

"Have you also read Martinez?" he said quietly. "Because I think some of her insights regarding Fisk's coup are uniquely—"

He looked up, gaze catching on something over Cassia's head that made him frown. A beat later, she heard footsteps.

Jasper had rounded the corner and was slowing as he got closer. He stopped beside her, and Cassia thought she saw the muscles in his jaw tense and release. "Pike," he said with forced cheer. "Good morning."

Virgil returned no greeting, but the look he gave Jasper surpassed his usual sullenness. It promised venom. Jasper had the High Sorcerer's favour, and it was wise not to continue their conversation in front of him, but this was more. He dragged his gaze back to Cassia, and drew breath to speak before settling on a nod and striding away, his arm curled protectively over the cargo under his jacket.

Jasper watched him go.

"I'm going to go out on a limb and say he doesn't like you," said Cassia, and Jasper grinned.

"I think you might be right."

"What was that all about?"

But Jasper was already shaking his head and taking her hand. "Come on. We can sneak in through the servants' entrance."

He took her around the side of the building, where a short set of steps led down to a nondescript door. Cassia paused.

"Is this a good idea?" Jasper frowned in question. "If I'm caught sneaking in, won't it affect my chances to join?"

"You're not going to get caught. Trust me." He squeezed her hand, and Cassia wanted to. He was doing a kind thing for her. "All the members inside are far too occupied to notice us. You'll see."

The door led to the kitchens, which smelled tantalisingly like pastries; the breakfasts members were served at the Wending Place were whispered about among hopefuls as often as the prestige of being initiated. A young kitchen maid watched them cross to the interior door, but she only blushed and smiled when Jasper winked and tugged Cassia onwards.

Then they were in a main corridor, and Cassia tried to contain her awe. It wasn't that the Wending Place was beautiful, though it was: the walls were panelled in dark wood carved with curling leaves and blooming flowers. The floorboards were ancient and worn, but polished to a liquid finish. But it was the atmosphere of ancient, living wonder. Her nose tickled with hallowed magic. A Sorcerer could sense any significant spell, but this was like swimming through champagne; the same feeling that rose in her when she called her magic, but flitting through the corridors and clinging to the walls. Even in the silence, it seemed to Cassia that she could hear the old place breathing.

And then a shriek went up, and a round of cheering. Cassia looked at Jasper, wide-eyed. He nodded towards the staircase and rolled his eyes.

"Come on."

In a common room on the first floor, two dozen or so rowdy Successors crowded around, watching something on the floor. Cassia and Jasper stood half-hidden behind a heavy velvet curtain in the archway leading from the hall.

"What are they doing?" Cassia whispered.

"Wasting their youth?" said Jasper. "Dulling the misery of their empty lives?"

She couldn't read his tone, but the smile he shot her rang false. Was this what Jasper thought of his peers?

Cassia craned around the curtain and started to piece together the game. The players had enchanted paper frogs to leap in some kind of race, while others magicked obstacles into their way. There were heats, and – most importantly, it seemed – a drinking component; the loser in every race was handed a glass of brown liquid to down in one.

Something squirmed in Cassia's belly, but she wasn't sure if it was anticipation or anxiety. She didn't much like to drink, and she always felt a little lost in crowds, though she attributed that to not having found *her* crowd in the Heart yet. Once she made friends, drinking games and boisterous behaviour might not intimidate her so much. Besides, she was sure plenty more went on at the Wending Place than this. She understood they had a library, and visiting lecturers who gave talks on magic and history, and the virtues of future careers and pursuits.

She was aware of Jasper watching her watch the Successors, so she gave her best impression of mild intrigue, then told him to lead on.

He took her to a narrow corridor on the mansion's top floor, with a single window at one end looking out onto a rain-damp roof. A door in the curved wall clearly led up a spiral stair to one of the turrets, and this is where Cassia assumed they were heading, so hidden was the second doorway. It blended in with the panelling; even if one spotted it, it looked like a cupboard of some sort, nothing but a void under the stairs. Yet Jasper produced a small iron key and fitted it into the lock.

"Do they know you have that?" Cassia asked, nodding to the key.

Jasper grinned. "Of course not. I used to sneak it in and out of the key safe, then I realised no one ever questioned why it was missing. Now, it's mine."

Cassia wondered again how well she knew Jasper, the studious, well-mannered tutor her grandfather liked so well.

As he jostled the key in the ancient lock, Cassia turned the other way to keep a lookout, and felt the hairs on the back of her neck stand on end. She hadn't immediately objected to the idea of sneaking into the Wending Place. Jasper had been so energised by the idea that she mainly didn't want to let him down. But for the first time, she was afraid. She put it down to breaking the rules, until the door creaked behind her and the feeling intensified. She turned around as Jasper opened it, her apprehension telling her not to put her back to the growing chasm of darkness that appeared as the door opened wider.

"Is this a trick?" she blurted.

Jasper froze with his hand on the latch. "A trick?" he said, failing to mask a confusion that bordered on hurt.

"There's a glamour or spell or something," Cassia persisted, though she regretted opening her mouth at all. She gestured at the room with her chin. "Can't you feel it?"

Jasper looked into the darkness and back at her, his earlier expression melting into delight. "Oh, it's not a glamour." Though his face was full of light, darkness limned his voice. "There's a lot of magic in here. Look."

But this magic felt strange. Fetid, souring, like wine turned to vinegar, food turned to poison. Perhaps she was on edge, the intense atmosphere of the Wending Place and the junk room, and her anxiety about sneaking in combining to play tricks on her. Jasper was holding the door patiently for her, so Cassia pushed the feeling down and stepped inside.

The room was a lot bigger than she'd expected. It might have been that her sense of the building was muddled, but she had a feeling it was a trick of the Wending Place; that the room existed in the enchanted space within the walls and between the floorboards. A large window in the slanting roof revealed grey slate tiles and a grey sky beyond, but darkness still clung to the corners. Jasper found a lamp, and turned the mechanism to activate the lump of clara stone within – a quartz-like mineral that could be enchanted to glow.

On one side of the room, rows of shelving stretched away into shadow, but on the other, a space had been cleared, an array of random objects pushed up against the wall or into piles. A spinning wheel. A miniature shadow puppet theatre. A collection of rocks and uncut gems in a wooden display case. An entire barrel of marbles.

"Sorry about the mess," said Jasper, brushing his handkerchief along the windowsill and coughing when he stirred up a cloud.

"What is all this stuff?"

"Things I've found." Jasper shrugged. "Things I've made."

"Things you've…" Then Cassia understood what he meant when he said there was a lot of magic in this place. "These things are enchanted?"

His wicked grin was back. "Of course. What did you think I use the space for? It's a laboratory. These are my experiments."

Cassia wandered among the stacks of artefacts and bric-a-brac. There was a table crammed with glassware – beakers and boilers, some of them burned from use – shelves of bottles on the walls.

In one corner was a tailor's dummy. It wore the uniform of the stewards, the Whisperers' militia force. Except that the stewards' uniforms were midnight blue. This uniform was only that shade when she looked at it straight on. In the corner of her eye, it flashed teal and purple. At certain angles it became a shadow that reached for her until her eyes flickered back to it. Turning her back on it and walking away felt like running to the safety of her bed in the middle of the night when she was six years old.

Sorcerers considered their magic to be a sacred gift from the stars, and so nothing was forbidden. Experimental magic was an essential cornerstone of Sorcerer academia. New spells were invented and recorded continuously, in the same way that technical, medical, and engineering advancements progressed too. But magic was not technology, nor medicine, nor engineering; it was infinitely more dangerous and volatile than any, and experimentation in the realms of spellwork, potion making, the enchantment of objects – there were unspoken lines dictating what was considered fair play, and what was spoken of in wary tones. Judging by the contents of the junk room – and the fact he kept it all a secret – what Jasper was doing was, by silent agreement, usually the purview of the most learned scholars at the most prestigious institutions. Cassia wasn't even sure he was *allowed* to be testing his spells in secret.

He must have read some of these thoughts on her face. "This stuff isn't regulated," he said, a little defensively.

"That's the problem, isn't it? Who's going to correct you if you misstep?"

"I don't need correcting," he said, smiling.

"People *die* meddling in magic, Jasper—"

"Are you worried about me?"

Cassia understood his smile then. She understood the way he was moving closer. Perhaps this had been a bad idea after all.

"You're right. It's none of my business."

The attempt to brush his comment off didn't work. Jasper took her hand. Her instinct was to pull it free; her loneliness told her she didn't want to. But Jasper only pushed the key into her palm and retreated.

"Stay as long as you want," he said. "But, ah, try not to touch anything."

And then Cassia was alone. She locked the door and stood in the centre of the room, listening. But the silence was absolute; the Wending Place had swallowed up the shrieks and cheers of the Successors downstairs like it had Juniper Henry. She couldn't even hear the pigeons on the roof, though their wings cast the occasional shadow, and she wondered if there was an enchantment on the room to make it so. Either way, she could mess up a dozen spells and no one would come to investigate; her mother couldn't knock on the door or look down on the rose garden from the window. Jasper was right; it was exactly what she needed.

There was nowhere clean to place her bag, so Cassia spread her handkerchief on the floor and set it down on top, then retrieved the jar from inside and put it in the space at the centre of the room. It was filled halfway with soil, and she had punched holes in the lid. Wedged into the soil was a small cutting from the rose garden. It was her prop for the spell she had been developing for her initiation; the one she was yet to successfully complete.

Cassia took several slow breaths to chase away the sick anxiety that filled her whenever she confronted the spell, or the initiation. It wouldn't help her to grow frustrated before she even began. She took the lid off the jar and moved away.

A crowd-pleaser. Simple but visually impressive. That had been everyone's advice, asked for or not, when it came to the initiation. There was a formula for success, that was the implication; to succeed, one simply needed to know it. And who knew it better than a dynasty heir like Cassia Sims?

She took out the slip of paper on which she'd written down the intention – *bloom and grow* – and some notes to help her visualise it. More complex spells could be written out on hazel

42

wood paper, which had binding properties. The Sorcerer would enchant the paper to burn as they cast their spell, splitting the focus of their magic in a way that required a great amount of power, but purifying their intention into a single command.

Cassia had never performed such a spell; few Sorcerers her age were advanced enough in their talents. Cassia was merely using the notes as an aid, for the intention behind her spell was not as straightforward as some might assume. *Grow* was not all that descriptive, and that part had been the downfall of her first dozen attempts. She had once succeeded in swelling the cutting to the size of a small tree stump, shattering the jar before the thing withered without sprouting a single leaf.

So to help her clarify the command, Cassia had read half a dozen biology tomes, until she was confident she knew, scientifically, what she was asking for when she commanded the cutting to *grow*.

Then there was the trick of getting the resulting plant to *bloom*. Intense visualisation of the rosebush bursting into flower had caused more than one explosion. So Cassia had researched the way a rose plant moves through its annual cycle, to better understand how she was manipulating it. After eight weeks of practice and study, Cassia could name and identify eighteen species of rose, plus explain the mechanism of photosynthesis and the mathematics behind the arrangement of petals in a rose head, but still she had not enchanted a single starsforsaken cutting to grow into a rosebush and burst into flower.

And now she had two days left.

Jasper said she was overthinking it, that clear and visual intention was more powerful than knowing the specifics of what you were trying to achieve. But clear and visual intention was failing her, and she would try anything.

She fixed her eyes on the jar in the middle of the floor and summoned her magic, which rose within her as always. *It's there*, she told herself. *It's strong enough.* You're *strong enough*.

Bloom and grow, she commanded the cutting. She didn't need to say the words aloud, even under her breath. She was channelling her magic through her fingers and into the frail little twig in its jar of soil, where it would, hopefully, bind and stay.

The magic rose like smoke curling from a candle as Cassia directed it to her fingers. She knew the spell so well that the intention felt easy and clean. *Bloom, grow, become a rosebush and flower.* Muscle memory curled her hands into fists, turned them towards the sky, and unfurled her fingers like petals unfurling from a bud. Her hands couldn't command the jar and its contents, only her magic could do that, but it helped her visualise what she wanted to achieve and that was vitally important.

A rosebush. A beautiful, blooming rosebush covered in vibrant red flowers.

The magic streamed from her fingers and enveloped the jar, the little cutting shivered, and Cassia's breath hitched. Was this it? She banished her excitement and firmed up her intention. *Bloom and grow. Bloom and grow.*

A leaf. Then another. The cutting stretched for the opening of the jar, for freedom. White roots appeared in the soil, pressing up against the glass.

"Yes," Cassia heard herself say. Her hands shook. But she had got this far before. She needed to maintain it.

It was as the first bud formed that Cassia realised she wasn't alone.

"Are you doing magic?"

She screamed. Her magic spiked. The jar shattered, spilling dirt and rosebush everywhere. Her intention skittered away like a dream upon waking.

"Who's there?"

She had locked the door. Was this magic? Trick walls and false silence? Her frightened gaze went to the unnerving stewards' uniform in the corner. It hadn't moved.

"I am," replied a voice, childlike and lilting.

A shiver ran up Cassia's spine. The voice was coming from the shadows between the shelves.

"Show yourself," said Cassia. She backed towards her bag in the corner. The door key was inside.

The little voice laughed. "I can't," it said. "I'm a doll."

"A doll." Just a doll. It was an enchanted children's toy. Cassia approached the voice, her mind soothed – embarrassed, even – but her heart still catching up. It beat so hard she was shaking.

"Where are you?" she said, looking up and down the domino rows of shelves.

"Here."

The reply was inconclusive. Cassia picked an aisle and, turning sideways to fit, slipped between the shelves.

"I'm here," the doll said again.

There. She turned towards the voice and jumped. A face was looking down at her from behind a jar of viscous red liquid, stretched and warped by the shape of the glass into something monstrous. But a protruding foot – small and booted, on a stubby, jointless leg – gave the doll away. Cassia pushed the jar aside and lifted the doll down.

Enchanted dolls, spelled to hold simple conversations – usually to encourage young Sorcerers to practise their magic – were enduringly popular. This one looked old. The huge skirt of her purple dress was two decades out of fashion, as was the severe centre part in her black hair and the ringlets framing her face. A crack ran down one side of her white porcelain face from her forehead to her jaw. She had vivid green eyes, like Cassia, to match her black hair. In fact, she was just the type of doll one of her relatives might pick out because it looked like her. She could have been Cassia's when she was a child, had she been born twenty years earlier.

She had never had an enchanted doll herself. Had she grown up in the Heart, perhaps someone would have thought to gift her one, but Changeling children played with wooden animals that would help them learn new forms. Cassia's most beloved childhood toy had been a model lion.

"And how did *you* get here?" she murmured as she smoothed the doll's skirts.

"I think I was stolen," the doll replied cheerfully.

"Stolen?"

No reply. Cassia assumed the magic had exhausted its conversational capabilities – she doubted the enchantment stored any meaningful memories – but then: "I had a little girl, but she looked the other way, and I was stolen."

Things I've found. Things I've made.

"By a young man?" said Cassia, uncertain. "Red-brown hair, blue eyes?"

"Yes. Him."

46

So on top of meddling in experimental magic – magic that raised the hairs on Cassia's neck – Jasper stole from children.

"Why?" she said aloud. To make a test subject of an enchanted doll was vaguely macabre, but perhaps it was fitting of someone who would steal one from a little girl rather than walk into a shop.

"That doesn't matter," said the doll in her blandly happy voice. "It's brought us together. Let's practise magic. I'll help you."

Cassia let out a snort. "There's no helping me, I'm afraid."

"Everyone can learn," said the doll, predictably.

"Yes, I'm sure. And what help are you supposed to be?"

"You can practise your spells on me."

Cassia turned her so her dead glass eyes pointed to the scattering of glass and dirt in the centre of the floor. "Do you want to end up like that?"

"Do you want to keep failing?"

Cassia laughed in surprise. She had been expecting something like *you can do it* or *just keep trying*. And had she imagined it, or had there been a note of challenge in the doll's otherwise amiable tone?

"Ouch."

"Don't worry. I'm here to help you."

"Alright. Do your best, then."

"Can you glamour my hair blonde?"

Cassia deflated. It was all good fun to play along with the doll – until she was reminded that the spells it suggested were for eight-year-olds, and she couldn't do them. "Unlikely," she admitted.

"Have a go."

With a sigh, Cassia slipped out from between the shelves. There was a stepladder at the end of one stack, and she put it in the centre of the floor and sat the doll upon it. "This was your idea," she told it. "I take no responsibility for the outcome."

She took several steps back and summoned her magic.

"Think of your magic, and you'll feel it between your chest and your stomach," said the doll helpfully.

"Earth and stars," muttered Cassia, already raising her arms to cast the glamour. "I know how to cast a glamour."

The doll's response was quiet. "Could have fooled me."

Again, Cassia laughed in shock, then in delight, and something wonderful happened. She forgot to think of all the ways she could get the enchantment wrong, and before she could command it, her magic had risen to her throat and was waiting eagerly for her words.

"Blonde," she murmured hastily, visualising the doll's outdated ringlets growing lighter. "Blonde, blonde, blonde."

The spell flowed smoothly from her tongue and shimmered over the doll as the glamour began to take hold. Beginning at the tips, the doll's hair changed colour, until her ringlets and the intricate bun at the nape of her neck were golden yellow.

Cassia's breath rushed out of her.

Then the glamour failed, like a changing trick of the light.

"*No.*" The last shimmer of magic brushed her senses as the illusion fell apart. The light reflecting off blonde locks hung in the doll's eyes for a moment longer, shining gold then vanishing.

Cassia sighed. "I'm afraid the novelty of this has worn off," she said, moving to collect the doll and put her away.

"But we've only just begun!"

Cassia halted. She thought she'd seen the doll's eyes following her. They were looking right at one another. She stepped

48

experimentally to the side, and the illusion was broken; the glass eyes stared inanimately past her.

"One more spell, and then we can play," said the doll. "Can you cast one to mend my face?"

Mend was the most elementary bit of magic, so commonly used a Changeling in Camden had been able to explain it to her when she was a child. As foolish as it made her feel, Cassia didn't want the doll to see her fail at it.

"Your face is lovely just as it is," she said, turning away.

Again the doll was silent a while. "But I want to be beautiful like *you*."

Cassia looked warily over her shoulder and let out a sigh of relief to see the doll's eyes weren't on her. It was empty, pleasant chatter, that was all. Uncannily sophisticated, but nothing to be afraid of.

"Well. In that case…"

Cassia crouched down in front of the stepladder so they were eye to eye.

"Do you have any final words?" she said as she traced the crack in the porcelain with one finger and thought again of the exploding jar. "Just in case."

"My final words are… I like your hair."

"Oh." Cassia was *definitely* imagining things now; a toy could not possibly sound wistful about Cassia's more stylish hair. "Well, if we both make it through this, I promise I'll do yours just like it."

She stepped back and called her magic, picturing the crack in the porcelain healing as she channelled it to her fingertips. *Mend*, she nudged, and the crack down the doll's face vanished from the jaw upwards, like a seamstress was pulling her stitches

49

tight. Cassia waited. The doll's green eyes flashed gold; an echo of magic? Whatever it was, the spell held. Cassia let out a breath.

"Marvellously done," said the doll.

Cassia couldn't agree. She made a non-committal noise.

"Is something the matter?"

"Sometimes I get lucky," Cassia said with a shrug. "But that's no use if I can't reproduce the results, or diagnose the problem."

"Don't worry. Practice makes perfect!"

Cassia found a neglected broom, and started sweeping the glass and earth into a pile in the corner. It wasn't like Jasper could complain about the mess. "I suppose I'm the exception that proves that particular rule."

"Do you feel your magic when you call it? Between your chest and your stomach?"

"I already told you yes," said Cassia, pushing the broom too hard and sending shards of glass skittering across the floorboards.

"And you hold your intention clearly in your mind when—"

"Please don't. We were off to such a good start."

The doll did as she asked and went silent. Cassia finished her half-attempt at cleaning and had almost forgotten the doll when she spoke again.

"Some people have less magic than others. That's—"

"Let me guess. Nothing to be ashamed of?"

She knew what the children's spell books said about power. You were born with a certain amount of it. Training could make up some of the difference, but you couldn't increase the raw amount that was yours to control. But you had other talents, children were promised.

No one ever warned you those other talents mattered less.

"Actually, I was going to say that it's unfair."

Cassia glanced over at the doll. She had definitely heard a sharpness cut through the sugar of her voice this time.

"I want to help you."

"Well." Cassia collected her bag and prepared to sneak back out of the Wending Place. "I appreciate that."

"You're not going to leave me here, are you?" came the voice as Cassia fished for the key.

She had been thinking about it. She was too old to play with an enchanted doll; Jasper said the junk room was completely private, but if someone *had* caught her promising to fix a doll's hair she would have died of mortification on the spot. Besides, the doll didn't really care if she left her behind or reneged on a promise. She was an inanimate object, merely spelled to give the vague appearance of life.

And yet, whoever had enchanted her had done so incredibly skilfully. Cassia had little cousins who had such dolls, and theirs didn't have a sense of humour or a trace of sarcasm to them. How did one even spell an object that didn't have real eyes to recognise a person's hair? It was rather ingenious.

For this reason and this reason alone – and absolutely not because she didn't have a friend in the world, nor anyone to talk to – Cassia swept the doll off the stepladder.

"Do you have a name?" she asked it.

"My name is whatever you want it to be."

"I was afraid you'd say that," she muttered as she settled the doll into her bag. She was too big to fit comfortably, and her little porcelain head protruded from the top. "Alright. I suppose I'll call you… Violet."

5

It was still early in both the morning and the evening when Ollivan arrived at the library on Brompton Road in the get-up of a gentleman.

The librarian was at his work when he stepped inside, but he glanced up and did a double take. Ollivan had taken no more than three steps into the building before he rounded the desk and hastened towards him.

"What are you doing here?"

"Don't fret, Frederick. I'm only awaiting a message."

Frederick looked him up and down, arms folded across his chest. The attempt at intimidation didn't suit him. He was a slender man, mousy haired and moustached, with wire-rimmed glasses perched on his nose. A librarian, through and through. No one would ever suspect him of anything more.

"I'll deliver it to you," he said.

"Oh." Ollivan smiled. "Not this message."

Frederick shook his head. "I won't have any more trouble from you, Ollivan—",

"And I'll be none, on my honour." He put a hand on his heart. "Come now, Frederick. We both know you're not going to manhandle me out of here, at least not successfully." Frederick raised a hand and Ollivan sensed magic. "And you're having far too busy a morning to try anything like *that*," he added, looking around the library meaningfully. There were a dozen people in the main room, some barely out of earshot.

Frederick was turning red, but he lowered his hand. He was a proud man who valued his position and was loath to appear incompetent. And Ollivan specialised in making people look incompetent.

Throwing a final glare over his shoulder, Frederick retreated to his desk. Ollivan felt the librarian's wary eye on him as he meandered to the back of the library. In a gap between two shelves, in the much-ignored politics section – much ignored because it was poorly stocked; poorly stocked for this very reason – hung a large and unusually extravagant mirror. It filled the space from floor to ceiling, arching at the top under a gold-embossed medallion in the centre of the frame, and was wide enough for four people to stand side by side and see themselves.

Ollivan pulled a chair up in front of it and sat, anticipation fizzing beneath his skin. He admired the surface of the glass, entirely ordinary and yet perfectly peculiar; the way it threw the light in the library back at unexpected angles, the faint blue hue to its surface. Someone cleared their throat. Ollivan turned. Through a series of gaps between shelves, Frederick was watching him from the desk. This particular mirror was always in Frederick's line of sight. Managing the library was a secondary responsibility. Watching this mirror was the first. Ollivan raised two fingers to him in greeting, then checked the time.

It wouldn't be long now. He straightened his tie and made himself comfortable. Frederick's busy eyes continued to bore into him. Ollivan's mind wandered once again to roast duck. To daffodils.

Minutes passed, each one longer than the next, before movement in the mirror caught his eye. Someone was approaching. Ollivan got to his feet.

The young man appeared to float through the shelves behind Ollivan, stepping through one row after another as if they were a mirage, until he was framed in the middle of the glass. Then he raised a leg over the mirror frame and stepped out into the library.

A half second later, Frederick bounded into the aisle. "And who are you?" he snapped at the man from the mirror, gulping down air from his quick sprint. There was probably not much vigorous exercise involved in being a librarian or watching a mirror.

"Virgil Pike," said the young man dispassionately, then he held out a letter between long fingers. "You can show this to the enforcers when they question you."

Frederick paled. He snatched the letter out of his hand and tore it open. "Why will they question me?" he said, his voice rising in pitch and volume.

Virgil levelled a glare at Ollivan. It was so morose that Ollivan convinced himself it was bad news. The relief that washed over him at his answer set him trembling.

"Because Ollivan Sims is going back to the Witherward."

The tutor lets you break the teacup yourself.

"Good. Now, mend.*"*

You've cast this spell before. It's easy. But today Aelius and Hester are watching from the drawing-room window. No wonder they're curious; everyone here is a Changeling.

Everyone but you.

Your magic blossoms in your abdomen and your cheeks heat. Can they see it? Does it look strange to them when you work your magic? You don't want to know, so you nudge it back down.

"What happened?" the tutor asks you gently.

"It's too difficult," you mumble.

It's not a lie.

6

TWO HOURS EARLIER

"How do I look?"

Cassia twirled dramatically, the skirt of her dress fanning around her. It was pale pink satin, with fuchsia ruched ribbons at the neckline and along the edges of each layer of the skirt. She thoroughly hated it.

"You look divine," said Violet in a dreamy cadence.

The doll was propped against Cassia's lace-trimmed pillows, atop a pink brocade bedspread she also loathed. Her mother had welcomed her home two years ago with a lavish abundance of clothes, trinkets, and a newly decorated bedroom, and had continued to show her affection mainly through gift-giving. The dress for her initiation was the latest instalment. If there had ever been an opportunity to let her know she favoured dark colours and unfussy fabrics, Cassia had missed it.

"I would give it to you gladly," Cassia told the doll, "but I don't think it's your size."

"Nor would it look as lovely on me."

Tilting her head in curiosity, Cassia stood directly in front of Violet's immobile glass eyes.

"How is it that you can see me?"

Violet laughed melodically. "I have eyes."

"Yes, but…" Cassia didn't want to offend her, as silly as that might be. "I suppose it's part of your enchantment, isn't it?" She sidestepped out of Violet's line of sight and waved a hand around in what should have been her blind spot. "How much can you see?"

"I can see you wiggling your fingers at me like you're trying to get my attention. And I can see that those bouquets of flowers are upside down."

Cassia looked over her shoulder and laughed. "Well, yes, they are. They're drying."

Cassia's favourite occupation might be why her mother had mistaken her for the feminine sort. On her workbench, dried flowers were arranged by type in jars along the back. More hung in bunches from a string pinned to the wall, and yet more were hidden between the pages of the book stacks underneath the bench, weighted down with whatever she could find to efficiently press them.

In the main space of the desk were several unfinished projects; preserved blossoms artistically arranged between sheets of glass, or glued into journals alongside notes and musings. Still more bouquets sat in vases about the room, and in the rooms of her friends and loved ones who had received them – a little baffled – as gifts.

Among the flowers and sprigs of foliage were other natural artefacts that brought her just as much joy. A bird's nest. An antler. Snakeskin resting in a box of shredded newspaper. Animal bones that she had arranged against squares of black velvet, their skeletons incomplete while Cassia waited for other specimens to reveal themselves in gardens and parks, and on trips to the country.

She plucked a sprig of lavender from one of the jars. "What about the other senses? You can hear, of course." She held the lavender close to Violet's face. "Can you smell?"

"I *know* what lavender smells like," said Violet. "There's a difference."

"But you're aware of the difference? You understand your own impression of the world? The way your mind works?"

"Actually, it's that I don't have nostrils."

Cassia laughed so suddenly she snorted. "Yes. I suppose that's the giveaway."

She twirled the lavender between her fingers, considering how to test the boundaries of Violet's spell further. It intrigued and intimidated her, the complexity and ingenuity of such an enchantment. Would she ever be able to perform magic like this?

"Memories," she said. "Do you have memories?"

There was a silence that was somehow ponderous. "*Some* memories, from before. There was a woman who made me, in a shop, and a lot of other dolls, all different from me. I belonged to a little girl who grew older, then to her son, I think, then another little girl. And then I was stolen."

"Are you sad that you were stolen?" It seemed the thing to ask, though Violet delivered the fact with flawless cheer.

"Stealing is wrong," the doll announced. "I didn't belong to that young man."

"Yes, but did it make you *sad*?"

"I don't remember."

She made her indifference plain, the joy in her voice flattening slightly.

"How long were you in that junk room before I found you?"

58

"I couldn't guess," said Violet. "A while before, and a while after."

Cassia frowned. She was missing something. "You said you had memories from *before*. Before what?"

"Before I was enchanted, of course. The second time."

"The second time." Cassia looked hard at the doll, like her history might reveal itself in the set of her curls or the peculiar flash she'd seen in her eyes. Had Jasper unravelled and then spelled the doll again as some kind of magical exercise? Was that why the enchantment was so good?

But Cassia had no time to find out. Her mother called her downstairs.

"Wish me luck."

"You don't need luck," said Violet. "You can do anything you wish."

*

"How do you like the dress?"

Cassia's mother, Alana Sims, stood behind her in the hallway mirror and admired her daughter.

"It's beautiful," Cassia lied with a smile on her face.

It caused her a vague shame that the garments her mother chose for her were always girlish, as Alana herself had never worn a dress in her life. She wore trousers, which this evening she had paired rakishly with an open waistcoat and a man's shirt, oversized on her. Her hair – as black as Cassia's, but curly and wild – was loose about her shoulders. She must have believed her daughter so different from herself, so strange and unknowable. It hurt that, when faced with the challenge of getting to know her, Cassia's mother had opted instead for spoiling her with pretty gifts.

"Just think," said Alana, "in two years you could be running for Society President."

At another time, Cassia might have laughed, but between her nerves and the pink monstrosity, Alana's words felt like another blow. She had to be in denial to believe such a thing was possible, and that meant the truth – that her daughter wielded no influence in the Heart – was anathema to her.

"I'm not exactly president material," said Cassia.

"Nonsense. Three generations of this family have been President of the Society of Young Gifted Sorcerers at one time or another."

This included Alana, and Cassia's grandfather, Jupitus, who had been President *and* High Sorcerer of the Heart for the last year of his tenure. It was the legacy Cassia either belonged to, or didn't.

And you will have to content yourself with the fact your children never will be, she didn't say as she went outside to meet her carriage.

*

The grand parlour at the Wending Place had been decorated befitting the most important night in its calendar. Wall hangings depicting the Society's crest – a doorway, representing opportunity, surrounded by fanned keys, representing possibilities – hung along one side of the room, behind the dais on which the new President would be named. Silk garlands were wound around the carved pillars and along the length of the banquet table. The room was full to bursting with Successors and special guests who had been invited to witness the evening.

Over a hundred people would watch Cassia's initiation.

She checked her appearance in a mirror in the hallway. The pink of her dress clashed with the green of her eyes and did nothing for her pale complexion. Not that any gown would disguise her queasy pallor, let alone the pathetic jar of soil tucked in the crook of her elbow.

There was nothing for it. Cassia entered the hall and stood on tiptoes to look for Jasper. She spotted him filling in his ballot on hazel wood paper, and slotting it into the chest that would announce the winner of the Presidential election also happening that night. The chest was a relic of the Society older than her grandfather, but one forever associated with Jupitus Fisk. It was due to her grandfather's devoted patronage that the Society held such prestige. Membership had dwindled since the glory days, but throughout his reign, Jupitus had encouraged young elites to reap the benefits of membership, as he had done over fifty years ago. He was the one who would reveal the winning candidate, with the famed enchantment he had long ago placed on the chest and the hazel wood ballots inside it.

As Jasper turned to the room, Cassia implored him to notice her. But another already had. Every conversation to her left reached a lull as that familiar miasma of unspoken fear swept through them, moving closer. It accompanied a retinue of bodyguards – marked as members of the Sorcerer militia by the large gold pins on their lapels – and at their centre, the cause of it all.

"Grandfather," said Cassia as he stopped before her.

She had once been told that one wears their reputation as either armour or chains. Jupitus Fisk had crafted his into the strongest battle wear, buffed to a brilliant shine. He was not a physically imposing man; tall, but not conspicuously so; straight-backed and broad shouldered. He wore his silver hair meticulously parted on one side and oiled into place, with a moustache to match. Thick, groomed eyebrows that never seemed to move or offer any expression sat above light grey eyes, almost silver to match the polished air of the rest of him.

He cast his eye over her. "I trust you're feeling confident about the initiation."

Not a question; more like a threat.

Cassia pushed the sick feeling in her stomach further down and smiled. "Very confident, Grandfather."

A slight motion of his head conveyed his surprise. Cassia didn't know which was worse, the pressure to succeed or the underlying resignation that she probably wouldn't.

Before she had to cobble together anything else to say, one of the enforcers leaned over and whispered in Jupitus's ear. "Lord Voss has arrived, sir," he said.

And then her grandfather was gone again. It was about as much attention as he had ever paid her, and like their every interaction, left Cassia feeling as if she'd been found lacking. She watched him greet the newcomer; Jericho Voss, ruler of the Whisperer faction. The Whisperers were mind readers; they could also manipulate thoughts. It was an isolating magic that made the other factions wary of them. Even though the Principles said that no one could use their magic beyond their own people's territory – including their ruler – most of the other guests gave the Whisperer delegation a wide berth. But the High Sorcerer never missed an opportunity to do business if he could press an advantage. Cassia wondered what advantage her grandfather sought from this particular invitation. A chance to show off the best of his faction, perhaps.

"Second time's a charm."

Cassia turned to find one of the members, Lev Mallory, before her. Among her peers were those too polite to whisper in earshot. Rarer were those who attempted stilted conversation, even as their friends went quiet and the atmosphere turned awkward.

The rarest was Lev, who had probably never neglected to smile at someone or had an awkward conversation in his life. He had a voice and a laugh that sounded endlessly and carried a mile, and was out of place on the boy himself, who was short and slight. He had a mildly pleasant face if one ever caught him in repose, with narrow, black eyes and a wide mouth, and a catching smile at all other times, including now.

"What's the jar for?"

"It's a surprise," deflected Cassia, who would feel worse about her spell failing if she got anyone's hopes up. She clutched the latest jar closer to hide the cutting inside.

"Champion! I love surprises." He glanced around and leaned closer, but failed to lower his booming voice that much. "But if you want to know what the other initiates are doing, I've gathered all the details. I talked to them all."

Cassia smiled, perplexed. "If you like surprises, why did you ask them?"

"To be friendly," said Lev. "That Clement fellow was looking at us all like we were rabid tigers, bless his stars. So, do you want to know?"

She almost said yes, but thought better of it. She wasn't in competition with the other initiates, but if their spells were too impressive, she would lose the last of her confidence. "Thank you, but I'm better off in the dark, I think."

Lev nodded, his smile turning knowing. "You're nervous, aren't you?"

"Weren't *you*? Put on the spot like that in front of the whole Society?"

"You have to lean into it. Enjoy yourself." Cassia nodded, but the advice of anyone who could enjoy themselves while being judged by an audience of their peers probably wasn't for her. "The initiation is all about performance, not magic. You know I'm of mixed magic?"

She nodded. She knew this about Lev the way everybody knew she had grown up at the Zoo, the ruling seat of Camden. It was essential gossip; that only his father was a Sorcerer, but his mother a Whisperer. A person could only inherit one magic, but it was often diluted, or sometimes absent altogether.

"I get by, magic-wise, but I passed my initiation by putting on a show. All I did was enchant my second-best suit to dance and clown around. We waltzed. And we did a mirror bit." Lev mimed waving to his own reflection and being alarmed when it waved back.

"And that was enough for the Successors?" said Cassia.

"It was enough for enough of them! I scraped in."

This conjured a scenario that set Cassia's stomach to attempting an escape through her mouth. "But then you're surrounded by peers who voted to exclude you. That's no better than being turned down."

"Oh stars, the initiation isn't as serious as all that!" said Lev. He pointed to a nearby Successor and called out to him. "Riddenhour didn't vote me in, did you Riddenhour?"

Riddenhour, his mouth full of finger food, shrugged good-naturedly and spewed some crumbs as he mumbled an excuse.

"See? There's nothing personal about the initiation. It's just a lark."

Cassia clutched her jar tighter. "I'm afraid it doesn't feel that way once you've already failed once."

Lev's smile calmed down, and he nodded. "They're a tough crowd, aren't they? I know how you feel."

He did? Lev Mallory, the life of every party, knew what it was like to crave his peers' acceptance? It was hard to understand, and yet Cassia thought she did. The young Sorcerers of the Heart ostracised her because they saw her as part-Changeling, but Lev literally belonged to another faction as much as he did theirs. He seemed to read these thoughts as they crossed her face, and he laughed.

"You just need to find your angle, Cassia."

"My angle?"

"The thing that makes up for what they don't see in you. The thing they can talk about instead. And don't worry about the initiation. If it doesn't go to plan, there's always next year. It's with the stars."

It's with the stars. Cassia didn't put much stock in astrology, but it was the type of thing she heard from the faithful all the time. She gave a shaky smile, but it was different for Lev. For him, the Society of Young Gifted Sorcerers was a lark. For Cassia, it was an expectation.

"And what's your angle, Lev?"

"Isn't it obvious?" He pointed to his face, and broke into that grin; the one that ate his cheeks and eyes. Then he turned away and pointed to another Successor across the room. "Buxton!" he bellowed. "Champion game last night!"

And he was gone, weaving through a crowd who smiled back at him as he passed. If Lev could belong here, then Cassia could too, but she would have to do it without the help of a gregarious and lovable persona. That would never be who she was.

A glass chimed as someone called the grand parlour to attention. Helia Radlin, the outgoing President of the Society, had taken to the dais.

"Successors, initiates, and honoured guests," began Helia with easy poise. The last of the chatter died away as the room turned its attention to her. "Tonight is a doubly special occasion for the Society, as the business of replacing me coincides with our spring initiation. I hope you can bear me as your President a few moments more as we start with the latter."

Cheers of support punctuated the laughter. Helia waved them away and adopted a sombre air. "It is my duty, first, to tell our initiates of the legacy they are becoming a part of tonight. On this very spot, over five centuries ago, our six founders gathered with the intention of starting an institution to promote the talents and enrich the lives of each generation of London's Sorcerers as they came of age. They based our hallowed Society here, in a house they called the Wending Place; a house with four important rooms." She held up a hand and counted the rooms off on her fingers. "A library, to feed the mind of every member who passes through; a common room, so they may share ideas and forge friendships; a parlour, to host the greatest leaders, thinkers, and innovators of the moment; and a dining room" – a cheer went up for the fourth room, and the Successors joined in as Helia finished – "*because a full stomach strengthens magic and mind.*

"Legend tells that the founders built the Wending Place as an ordinary, two-storey house, and enchanted it to foster the words of the Society in the minds of everyone who stepped inside: *From Sorcery, eminence.* But the enchantment took on a mind of its own, and as the Society evolved, so did our headquarters. Just as every generation of Successors adds new branches, so the Wending Place sprawled up and out, a mirror of the growing legacy of the Society of Young Gifted Sorcerers. Tonight, we add to that legacy once again. Five young Sorcerers declare their wish to join our number. But, Successors, will we let them without proving their mettle?"

"No!" chorused the Society members, and stamped their feet. The whole room seemed to lurch, and Cassia wondered if she had time to heave up her dinner before she was called upon.

"No, we shan't. Each must demonstrate their skill with our magic and be deemed worthy of our prestigious membership. And who shall decide if they pass the test?"

"We will!"

More stamping. Cassia wrapped a second hand around her jar of soil, as the first had grown slick with nervous sweat. She locked her knees, fearing her legs would give way as the strength drained from them.

"Members, please congregate before the dais. If our distinguished guests would be so kind, would you please arrange yourselves opposite, before the windows."

But what about the initiates? As the crowd split in two and the centre of the room cleared, Cassia dithered, turning this way and that until her sights landed on another lost individual, one with a random glass jug dangling from his fingers. A prop for a spell. When the boy chose the 'guests' half of the room, Cassia followed.

"Our would-be new members will be called one by one to demonstrate their spell for all of us," said Helia from the dais, "but our guests are asked to remain quiet as we make our judgement. First, Aubrey Cai."

Aubrey looked just fifteen, newly eligible to join. He split away from the crowd by the windows, two or three guests attempted to clap. Cassia wasn't one of them. She had been first of the cohort to take her test a year ago, and she remembered all too well the vulnerable, stark quiet as she stepped into the middle of the room, the only sound her own heels striking the floor as if marching blindly to her doom. Those who had wished to clap quickly disguised the movements, and Cassia felt them feel it too; the change in the air. All the jovial spirit of Helia's speech was gone. What happened next was sacred.

Sacred, and terrifying.

Aubrey's prop was an ordinary-looking candle. Inductees were not permitted to speak during their initiation, not to explain their spell nor to excuse why it went wrong, so no one could know what Aubrey was about to do.

He placed the candle in the centre of the floor, removed a book of matches from his pocket, and lit the wick. It burned with a hiss, and released a thick plume of indigo smoke into the air. Aubrey crouched by the candle and his face went blank with concentration. He stared into the smoke, one hand outstretched, his fingers dancing slowly as if he were plucking the strings of a harp.

"Oh," gasped the man next to Cassia.

She followed his gaze upwards, as everyone began to realise the magic was not happening before Aubrey, but above.

Instead of dispersing as it cooled, the smoke was forming shapes. Wispy, midnight creatures were coming to life above the candle. Rabbits hopped through the air, streams of smoke curling in their wake as they descended, until they were among the legs of the audience, who laughed and shuffled aside as they bounded about the hall. Foxes prowled, tails swishing; cats pounced at one another. There were birds too, sweeping in magnificent arcs above their heads. A snake curled itself around a man's leg as he watched it warily and tried to laugh along with his friends.

Aubrey's smoke menagerie only lasted a couple of minutes, after which the boy blew the candle out, crossed the room, and opened a window. With a gesture of his hand, his creations obediently flocked to him, and as they slipped through the window, they turned once more into smoke, and vanished in the air.

Cassia could feel the observers around her resisting the urge to clap again, but she couldn't share in their delight. None of them had to follow Aubrey's act.

"Members," said Helia from the dais. "Aye or nay?"

"Aye!" they chorused unanimously, and only then did the room erupt into cheers. The brief moment of normality and congratulations cut blessedly through the tension, but Cassia's heart was beating hard. If she had to do *that* well in order to be cheered herself, she was doomed.

The next inductee had no prop. She stepped into the centre of the room alone, and gave a twirl, the skirts of her blood-red dress fluttering elegantly. Once again, there was a silent, dread-filled tension as nothing happened and no one made a sound. But then she twirled again, and as the light caught the satin of her gown, it flickered yellow. With each twirl, her dress flashed another colour of the rainbow; orange, purple, green. Fuchsia, jade, cerulean. She ended the display with making her dress ripple in every colour at once, like a rainbow hitting the ripples of the ocean. When her dress was red again, she turned to the dais, and the assembled members before it.

"Members, aye or nay?"

"Aye!"

And so the next two inductees were called. Every time, Cassia's heart galloped at the possibility of hearing her name, and every time, she was left to slowly deflate, hands shaking as the rush of terror temporarily subsided.

Only the penultimate hopeful, Clement, failed to impress. He was the boy Cassia had spotted toting a random jug, which he attempted to transform from glass into ice, breaking the unspoken rule about making one's initiation a spectacle. Perhaps no one had told him. Clement's jug frosted over, and his breath misted the air, but no one could be sure the spell had succeeded until one half of the jug disintegrated and sluiced onto the floor. Those nearest stepped back or lifted their skirts. A second later, the rest of the jug also melted into water, and Helia put him out of his misery with a hand raised. If Clement could be thankful for one thing, it was that he did not miss out on membership by only a few votes.

"Nay!" came the resounding shout, almost before Helia had asked the question. The guests averted their eyes as Clement accepted his children's spell book and returned to their side of the room with downcast eyes. Cassia estimated he was no older than sixteen; he would have other chances.

"And on to our last inductee – Cassia Sims, if you would step forward."

The crowd parted to let Cassia into the centre of the room, where a junior member was magicking away Clement's mess. To Cassia it was as if the hundreds of watchful eyes had reduced Clement to a puddle on the floor, and were about to do the same to her. The only way she could put one foot in front of the other was by looking at nothing but the spot where she would place her jar of soil.

The silence became absolute as she did; a silence louder than the other hopefuls had suffered, she was sure of it. She was light-headed, her throat dry. She wondered if the nearest Successors heard her when she swallowed.

One spell. Just one spell and everything would be different.

A movement among the members dragged her attention. Jasper stood a little way from the others, at the edge of the room. He had moved into her line of sight to catch her eye and shoot her a smile. He wasn't nervous for her, she realised. He thought she would succeed. She involuntarily picked out her grandfather in the corner of her vision.

Well, at least that made *someone* here who believed in her.

Cassia focused on the jar on the floor and nothing else. Her magic rose within her at a moment's thought as the intention rang clear and firm in her mind. She was prepared. She had prepared for weeks.

She reached a hand towards the jar, trying to ignore the way it trembled – just performance nerves; ordinary and expected – and called on her magic to flow to her as she thought: *bloom and grow*.

71

She saw the roots first; little white shoots emerging from the soil and plastering the inside of the glass. *Yes*, she thought, as her relief manifested in a shaky exhale. *Keep going.*

The rose cutting shivered momentarily, and then went still. This had happened during practice, she would remember later. Little pauses before another burst of growth, if only she kept her focus. Her breath stuck in her chest as she tried to picture one thing and her treacherous brain conjured another; smashed glass, spilled soil, ambivalent shaking heads. A realisation hit her, so obvious she wondered if she'd known it all along: a young Sorcerer needn't be all that good at magic if only they had friends in the Society to vote them in.

Focus, screamed a desperate voice in her head, and Cassia dragged the full force of her will back to the jar, pushing fiercely on her magic to make up for the lapse. As the thinnest, smallest shoot of the cutting sprouted its first delicate leaf, several things happened at once.

Someone moved behind her. Helia, bored, summoning the members' attention to call for the vote? But no, the members were on the other side of the room; it was just a guest shifting to get a better look. But in that second, Cassia became aware that she wasn't – as she had told her magic – alone. She was in a room full of people who would momentarily judge everything she had or had not accomplished by coming back to the Heart. She tried to resist the urge to glance up at their faces arrayed before her, and failed. Her eye was drawn helplessly to the movement of a member's hand as he raised it to cup his mouth and whisper into his friend's ear.

Don't fail me, she pleaded with her magic as a cage descended around her, curious faces peering through. *Please don't fail me again.*

But it was already happening. There was no dramatic smashing of glass. No spraying soil or tangle of out-of-control branches. The pathetic handful of leaves on her sapling wilted. The roots shrivelled and went brown. Cassia did not choose to lower her hands. They simply fell in defeat.

The sound of Helia's question was a dull murmur against the pounding in her ears. Look down, and she would see her defeat sitting pathetically in the centre of the floor. Look out at the room, and she would see the eyes avoiding hers as they voted to exclude her. The only place she could look was at Jasper, which is how she knew he did not vote her in. His downturned mouth opened on a breath as the 'nays' resounded, but at the last moment, no sound came out. Perhaps that was for the best. Perhaps the vote he stopped himself making was the wrong one.

As someone handed her the children's spell book, Cassia realised, stomach swooping, that her eyes were wet. Blink, and she would be crying, in the middle of the gathering with everyone looking at her. But she might have time to make it to the door, so she turned on her heel and with nothing left to lose, she ran.

Someone nearby barked her name as she reached the threshold. She tried to ignore them – her tears no longer cared if she blinked or not; the first were falling freely onto her cheeks, as insubordinate and wilful as her starsforsaken magic – but a firm hand snagged her by the elbow and she was swung around, right into the face of the High Sorcerer.

"You would do better to stay and not disrupt the evening further," he said in a low voice. He could be a hard man to read,

73

and he had better sense than to draw even more attention to her failure by making a big deal out of it. But Cassia was very familiar with his disappointment, and she saw it in the way he looked through her, and not at her. She had had an opportunity to elevate herself in his opinion, and now that she had failed, her grandfather had gone back to greater concerns, even as she stood before him in tears.

"Network," he commanded. "Not everything is magic."

Somehow, his complete refusal to acknowledge her tears pulled her above the tide of her self-pity. "Grandfather," she began shakily, "I really would rather go home."

He leaned in close, lowering his voice even further. "You are at the Wending Place, Cassia." He rarely used her name, and when he did, he made it sound like a reprimand. "For stars' sake, socialise with your peers and have the decency to salvage what you can of this evening for yourself."

He didn't mean *for herself*, and he knew exactly how much effort Cassia had already put into socialising with her peers; Cassia had overheard Jupitus and her mother discussing how unpopular she was on four occasions and counting. But Cassia was of his blood, and as far as her grandfather was concerned, that meant she had a duty to him and his reputation, and she had been given her orders.

She was staying.

As he saw her relent, he turned away, and she hastily brushed the moisture from her cheeks and lifted her chin.

When all else fails, spite.

The words belonged to another faction ruler in another life. Spite was what Hester Ravenswood, ruler of the Changelings, prescribed when there was nothing else left to draw from. Cassia had been seven years old, and the son of one of the Camden militia had pushed her over. She had run to her nanny with her grazed palms, and the woman had said that was how boys behaved when they liked you. This had made Cassia cry even harder; all she'd wanted was a pair of arms to wrap tightly around her and tell her they would protect her, and her nanny had not.

Neither had Hester. Cassia doubted the alpha of Camden Town had it in her to comfort a crying child. When she'd seen her in the doorway, listening in on her nanny's advice, she had expected Hester to shrink away from her tears with disgust. It would be about as much kindness as she had ever shown the little girl who was technically her ward.

But Hester marched into the nursery and took Cassia by the wrist, so as not to hurt her injured palms. It was the first time she had touched her. Then she marched through the house with Cassia jogging beside her. They were headed for the garden, Cassia realised, back towards the vicious boy who had pushed her down.

"No! I won't play with him."

"No, you absolutely will not," said Hester, command in her tone even as they agreed. "But you will play. You will play because that whelp can't stop you. He's pathetic, and beneath your notice, do you understand?" She knelt then, so that they were face to face. "Play to *spite* him, because he doesn't have the power to stop you." She had touched her again then, for the second time, placing two fingers under Cassia's lowered chin and tilting it up. "When all else fails, spite," she said with a wicked smile. "Understand?"

And Cassia *had* understood. The thought of relenting to her grandfather's wish that she stay and simmer in her humiliation made her throat close and her self-pity threaten to engulf her. She did not belong in this room, but she could lift her chin out of spite. She could manage that.

The evening was moving forward; the space in the middle of the room had been closed over by bodies as the guests and members mingled near the dais. Jupitus was talking to the Secretary of the Society, whose job it was to unpin the gold President's badge from Helia's collar and pin it to its new owner.

Jasper was speaking with another member on the far side of the room. His eyes no longer searched for hers, and Cassia found herself feeling equal parts betrayed and relieved. She didn't know how she would face him again after he had failed to stand up for her.

Lev caught her eye, then weaved through the guests to stand before her. He held her jar of soil.

"I wasn't sure if you wanted this back," he said.

Cassia mumbled her thanks and took the jar. "Next time, I'm sure," she said automatically. She had heard the empty sentiment two dozen times after her last failure, and wanted to beat Lev to it. But she didn't put enough false feeling into the words, and they came out too sharp.

Lev smiled. "Oh, next time for certain."

She was spared more of his kindnesses when Jupitus stepped onto the dais and the grand parlour fell silent. The High Sorcerer's reason for being here had arrived. He positioned himself behind the ballot box, which had been moved to the front of the dais.

"Successors, old and new," he said, nodding amicably to the new inductees he could pick out in the crowd. "Guests. The Society of Young Gifted Sorcerers has existed for five centuries

76

to celebrate our place within this city and herald new magic, new talent, and the coming of age of our future minds and leaders. It is time now for the hallowed tradition of seeing in the new, as the Society elevates one of its members to the position of President. For the next two years, this individual will forge the path forward for you young members, and lead you towards the future. Who knows, they may even be High Sorcerer someday."

There was a generous swell of knowing laughter at this. Everyone knew Alana Sims was intended to be the next High Sorcerer. And after her? Cassia looked down at her jar of soil. If her grandfather found her face in the crowd at that moment, she didn't wish to see what his glance held. Whoever took over the role from Alana, whether they were in this room or not, everyone listening knew that it would be a person of Cassia's family's choosing. That was the power they held in the Heart.

"Could the candidates please join me on the dais."

Three Successors climbed the dais to a smatter of applause. They were joined by Helia and her second in command, Society Secretary Jan Lenniker, whose term also ended this evening. Cassia leaned close Lev.

"Who's expected to win?" she said, realising that, in focusing so hard on her initiation, the rest of Society business had escaped her notice.

"Uh." Lev hesitated, the smile dropping off his face momentarily. "I believe it's all still to play for."

Cassia didn't miss the way his eyes went to the door, where Virgil Pike leaned against the wall, his head low, his solemn eyes tracking the crowd. The Successors were always tumbling one another, coupling or uncoupling, everyone trying their hardest to be the biggest scandal of the season. Lev and Virgil were one of its few love stories. She wondered why they weren't watching the election together.

Cassia's eyes followed Virgil's through the crowd as they landed on a series of people. Lev was not the only one who looked nervous. Harland Wise was chewing his nails. Tan Medhurst was shifting his weight. Cassia was suddenly cognisant of a tension in the air that wasn't quite excitement. The three hopefuls on the dais, plus Helia and Jupitus, were oblivious to it, but the intensity with which Jan stared at the floor threatened to burn straight through it.

"Let us find out who your new President will be," said Jupitus to the room.

Traditionally, the High Sorcerer performed the famed spell to reveal the election winner, but Jupitus stepped to the side and waved Helia forward, triggering a silence so absolute Cassia swore she could hear the gulls over the river. No one would whisper that the High Sorcerer was getting old, that his strength was not what it once was. Not now, not later.

Helia produced an enchantment of hazel wood paper and held it aloft, her other hand extending towards the ballot box. Cassia found herself pressing closer. She had never seen the spell performed, but she had heard it spoken of many times.

As the hazel-wood enchantment burned, the ballot box unfolded like a mechanical flower, spilling its contents down a narrow trough; contents that had transformed from slips of paper into brightly coloured glass balls. As they cascaded down the trough, the ballot balls separated by colour and dropped into bowls that materialised below them; blue, orange, yellow—

There were purple balls as well. A fourth bowl materialised alongside the others.

"A write-in candidate!" someone nearby exclaimed. A murmur of excitement rippled through the room. Cassia cast an eye over the members again – some wore expressions of unease, others of delight – then at Lev, whose smile was hard to read. Virgil looked as serious as ever, and had not moved closer as the count progressed.

"Green!" someone cried, as balls of a *fifth* colour intermingled with the others.

Write-in candidates were not unheard of. Society Presidents often went on to have illustrious careers in a variety of fields, and opportunities abounded. It was no mystery some members campaigned hard even after they failed to make the ballot.

But a significant number of balls were in at least four of the colours. Jupitus spoke over the chatter; something jovial about ambitious members. The watching Successors were splitting ever more into two groups: those shocked and curious at the turn of events, and those watching quietly. Some of the latter were buzzing with excitement themselves; others threw looks of outrage at Lev and Virgil, which grew in number as they whispered to one another.

When the cascade of balls ended, Jan and Helia removed the box and placed the five jars of balls before Fisk, in order. This took longer than the crowd had patience for, and involved some counting and discussion between Helia and Jan. As they eventually arranged the bowls, whispers of the problem trickled through the onlookers to Cassia and Lev: three of the candidates had scored the exact same number of votes, and the winner had scraped a victory by one. Cassia shot a questioning glance at Lev, but he missed it; he was looking at Virgil, who was rubbing his eyes in a defeated gesture. A ridiculous fear popped into Cassia's head. She banished it immediately.

The spectacle of magic was not at an end. Starting with the clear loser, the bowl of green balls, Jupitus wrapped his fingers around the rim and cast the simpler enchantment that would carve the name of the nominee into the bowl. His face betrayed mild surprise as he turned it to face the crowd.

Cassia's betrayed *significant* surprise when the bowl read *Lev Mallory*. Any eyes that weren't already on him swung round. Lev grinned broadly and shrugged.

As a spatter of applause filled the room, he leaned close to Cassia and said, "Next time, I'm sure."

Humour lit his dark eyes as he winked at her.

Jupitus moved on to the next bowl. Elric Verda was not nearly as gracious. He muttered something through gritted teeth and stalked off the dais. Cassia heard a nearby Successor whisper that he would age out of the Society before the next election.

The candidate to place third was August Ledford. He struggled to mask his disappointment, but shook the remaining candidate's hand and Jupitus's before he joined his friends in the crowd, who clapped him on the back and threw their arms around his shoulders. Cassia looked again for Jasper, who should have been that support after her initiation. He was on the far side of the room, looking bored.

Pella Olin and a write-in remained in the running. The members had fallen into silence. Cassia's pulse skipped pleasantly. Drama in this city often meant death; the chance to indulge in something so frivolous as a coup for the presidency of the Society of Young Gifted Sorcerers – a bloodless coup, conducted among youths – was impossible to resist. She was sure Pella was nice enough, but she hoped she would lose.

And she did.

When Jupitus turned the second-to-last bowl around, the room erupted. Elric grumbled loudly about the race being rigged, and got some support from those in the room who were the most surprised. They were quieted by a vehement dismissal from Jupitus.

"The right to run if one is not on the ballot is enshrined in Society law and has been for hundreds of years," he said. Quiet descended. "This is a hallowed democratic process and all members will honour the result."

As Pella was clapped off the stage, Jupitus put a hand on the rim of the final bowl and conducted the spell again. He had been composed and unperturbed about the success of the write-in, projecting dutiful indifference even as the excitement in the room grew and grew. But his efforts jolted to a sudden end when the name appeared on his side of the bowl. His lips thinned to a tight line, the silver in his eyes turned to ice. The hairs on Cassia's neck stood on end, and she took an involuntary step back. Jupitus's expression alarmed a lot of the audience, but only Cassia knew how truly furious he was.

The last time she had seen his face so marred was when...

Wordlessly, Jupitus turned the bowl around, and the impossible suspicion that had burst into Cassia's mind earlier was confirmed.

The new President of the Society of Young Gifted Sorcerers was Ollivan Sims.

Cassia looked at Lev. Lev looked at Virgil. Virgil sighed and vanished in place, transporting himself to stars knew where.

Jupitus's white-knuckled grip tightened on the edge of the bowl before he sent it crashing to the floor, where it shattered into a thousand pieces.

7

When Ollivan and Virgil transported into the entrance hall of the Wending Place, the first thing Ollivan heard was the smash of glass.

So his grandfather *was* here. Excellent.

"What is the meaning of this?" the old man bellowed.

Ollivan briefly checked his hair in the mirror and stepped into the doorway of the grand parlour. "I believe I can answer that, Grandfather."

He couldn't help the joy that rose in him as the members of the Society of Young Gifted Sorcerers turned as one to look at him, parting in the centre to reveal the shattered ballot bowl at the foot of the dais.

And above it, pale as snow and angry as a dragon, was High Sorcerer Jupitus Fisk. His grandfather.

Ollivan broke into a smile. He hadn't seen him in a year, after all.

"Ollivan." Jupitus's voice was deceptively level. Now that he knew Ollivan himself was to blame for the election coup, the worst thing he could do was lose his temper further. "This is a surprise. An unfortunate one, I'm afraid, as you have no business here."

He made a gesture, and his enforcers advanced towards Ollivan. Jupitus never went anywhere without a handful of his most trusted militia. It increased his ability to intimidate. Few would dare to acknowledge that the High Sorcerer was also losing his edge, and relied on the enforcers for protection. Among those who did was Ollivan, who did not flinch like those around him as the militia came forward.

"I have more business here than anyone," he said, gesturing to the purple glass balls on the floor. "In fact, the charter for the Society of Young Gifted Sorcerers would find me essential. Isn't that right, Jan?"

Jan Lenniker had taken several slow steps back and off the dais when Ollivan made his entrance, and Ollivan didn't blame him. He'd voted for him. If Ollivan were Jan, he'd be keeping his distance from the High Sorcerer too.

Jan sighed defeatedly and addressed Jupitus, but loud enough for everyone to hear. "As you're no doubt aware, High Sorcerer, our charter is magically binding. If the winning nominee isn't inaugurated and awarded the pin at the election ceremony, the Wending Place will eject all Successors from within and seal the doors. The, uh, manner of the ejection is unclear, but the charter hints that it could be... painful."

The Successors stirred. The enforcers encroaching on Ollivan halted; one even rerouted to be closer to the door.

"I'm familiar with the charter, Mr Lenniker, but be that as it may, my grandson is not a *legal* nominee." He set his coldest glare on Ollivan, for only him to see. "He is banished."

Ollivan winced sympathetically. "Jan."

Jan looked skywards and muttered a curse. "I'm *afraid*, High Sorcerer, that banishment, or in fact any wrongdoing which leads to banishment, does not automatically revoke Society membership or otherwise make one ineligible to run for President."

"Get me the stars-damned charter," snapped Jupitus before Jan had even finished speaking.

"That's funny, I thought you were *familiar with the charter*," said Ollivan as Jan dashed off to fetch it. "Never mind, why don't I tell you what it says?" He gripped his hands behind his back and paced slowly before the dais. "The charter of the Society of Young Gifted Sorcerers – a document written by six of our first and perhaps most pretentious members and enshrined in magic over five hundred years ago – requires only two things of a presidential nominee. That they have been a member for more than a year, and that they are younger than twenty, and so won't age out of the Society before their two-year term has ended. What the charter requires of the *President*, though, is where it gets interesting.

"The things required of the President are as follows: that they are present at the inauguration ceremony, which I am; that they accept the post willingly and knowingly, which I do; that they attend a minimum of four in five Society meetings for the duration of their term, which I will; and" – he paused in his pacing and faced the dais – "that they live in the Heart."

A smile relaxed Jupitus's face. "Which you do not," he said. "And therefore you are ineligible."

"Yes, one would think so. It probably would have been the sensible thing to do, but I suppose that's the type of oversight that happens when you uphold a document written several centuries ago by self-important fifteen-year-olds who we can reasonably assume were drinking large quantities of mead at the time, since they spilled a great deal of it across pages six to eleven. One does not have to live in the Heart to be *granted* the presidency, but one does have to live here while they hold the post."

Jan returned with the charter and handed it to Jupitus.

"Page eight," said Ollivan helpfully. "Careful of the sticky parts."

"But you're banished!" bellowed someone on his right. It was Elric Verda. The boy had turned the exact same shade of purple as the glass balls scattered across the floor. "You can't live in the Heart."

"I'm afraid I must. If I am the President I must live here, and if I am not the President, according to the people in this room, then I suggest we all make a swift exit before forces unknown drag us from these halls, because I can assure you, the Wending Place feels very strongly that I am."

Ollivan might have cast some magic to make the frame of the building groan at that moment, but there was no need. The delay in presenting him the pin already seemed to irk the old, spelled house, and an unnatural draft could be heard whistling through the nooks and crannies of the upstairs rooms before sweeping into the grand parlour and setting everyone's evening attire fluttering. Several guests elected to leave. More than one Successor shouted to give Ollivan the stars-damned pin already.

By his stars, Ollivan loved magic.

Jupitus ignored the agitation of the house and levelled his gaze across the top of the charter at his grandson. "Miss Radlin," he said. "When my grandson was banished from the Witherward and into the Otherworld, did you not think it fitting to also revoke his membership of the Society?"

It was a credit to Helia Radlin, the outgoing President, that she answered honestly, and kept her head held high. "No, High Sorcerer, I didn't. I'm sure you can understand that... *this* never occurred to me. Besides" – she shot a glance at Jan – "upholding Society bylaws is the Secretary's job."

"Stars damn you, Helia," snapped Jan. "Since we're so concerned with the specifics of the charter, let me just find the line where it says to make sure I revoke the membership of all murderers."

"I'm not a murderer," snapped Ollivan before the word had fully left Jan's lips. The room quieted. So the rumour was out. Pity; Ollivan had been enjoying having all eyes on him until that moment. He forced a smile that felt painful on his face and pressed on.

"Miss Radlin," Jupitus said, speaking with an authority that told Ollivan what he was going to say next. "Would you be so good as to perform your moral duty and revoke Ollivan Sims' membership at once?"

Helia hesitated. Ollivan laughed. "She can do what she pleases – or should I say what *you* please – but I'm afraid, High Sorcerer" – he gestured to the ceiling, heart soaring as an even stronger draft rattled the windows and slammed the door closed – "that Helia is no longer the President of the Society of Young Gifted Sorcerers." He spread his arms, as if anyone could have missed him. "I am."

8

That would teach Cassia for thinking an evening couldn't possibly get any worse.

The tiny upside, if Cassia chose to see it, was that her grandfather was far too distracted to notice her slip out around the time they were pinning the President's pin to her banished brother's lapel.

She alighted from the carriage in front of the Sims' red-brick townhouse and climbed the steps, wearily acknowledging the militia guards on duty. Silently, so as not to rouse attention, Cassia went up to her room, where she clicked the door shut behind her with the utmost delicacy. Then she threw off her coat and shoes, and sank face first onto her bed. With her head pressed into the pillow, Cassia bellowed a scream.

There was a knock at the door.

She hadn't managed to sneak in after all. Alana entered and hovered in the doorway, looking at her daughter like any sudden movements would scare her away.

They both knew what Alana wished to ask.

"I failed."

"You'll have other chances," came the reply far too quickly, and Cassia realised: all her talk of becoming President, and her mother had not believed Cassia would be initiated. She had not expected of her daughter what had been expected of her, of

Ollivan, of everyone they knew. Because Cassia wasn't one of them.

"Not many," Cassia mumbled.

"Enough. And a whole other year to work on it. You're descended from strong magic, Cassia, you should be able to cobble together a flashy spell to make the members cheer, for stars' sake." She finished with a laugh, but it was tainted with frustration.

"Well." Cassia went to her dressing table, unpinned her hair and removed her earrings, and tried to take her mother's words the way Alana had hoped she would hear them, and not the way they came out. "Perhaps I should be able to. But I can't."

"Is Jasper not a good tutor?"

"It's not Jasper."

"Perhaps if we hired back the older fellow."

"It's not Jasper, Mother." Cassia threw her earrings down in the rough vicinity of the trinket bowl in which she kept them. "It's *me*."

Alana didn't respond right away, which was all the response that was necessary. She perched on the edge of Cassia's bed; a sure sign this conversation wouldn't be over in a hurry.

"I think, perhaps," Alana said carefully, "that focusing all your energy onto the Society isn't the best use of your time here. It's not the most important thing in the world, after all."

"Perhaps that's true, but even if it were, how would you know?" She turned to face her in challenge. "You passed the initiation first time. So did Father, so did Grandfather, and so did—"

Ollivan. Her mother didn't know. Alana noticed the hesitation, her posture stiffening the way it always did at the risk of mentioning her firstborn. They didn't speak of him; they hadn't in a year.

Cassia didn't want to be the one to tell her mother that Ollivan was back. She didn't want to see whatever emotions crossed her face.

"The point is," she went on, scrabbling for her train of thought, "that it's different for you. You're the next High Sorcerer. You earned your place here. You're... respected."

"And you're my daughter. There's respect attached to that too."

Cassia studied her. "Is that what you think? Is that how you imagine my life is?"

"All I can do is imagine, Cassia," said Alana blandly. "I hardly know you."

"And whose fault is that?"

The words were out before she could consider them, but in the aftermath, Cassia knew she was trying to hurt her. Perhaps it was a blessing that it didn't appear to work.

"My own, probably," said her mother. "The stars know I was stretched too thin even before Hester dropped you back on our doorstep."

"I brought *myself* back. I wanted to be here. And I'm sorry it's such an inconvenience to you."

"Cassia. Don't put words in my mouth."

It wasn't a denial. Cassia waited for her to go on, but Alana was massaging her temples like one of her headaches was coming on. She was about to lose interest in the conversation altogether.

"Let's not fight," she said, right on cue. "I was simply suggesting that you waste less energy obsessing over joining the Society. All too soon you'll be on your way back to Camden and I—"

"I haven't decided that, yet," Cassia cut in.

She had said it enough times. Still, something in her reached out for the idea of going back and wrapped its jaws around it. It wasn't what she really wanted, she reminded herself. There had been people at the Zoo – Hester, Gedeon, Fyfe – who treated her like family, so of course she missed them. Of course, in her loneliness, those memories were the strongest.

But she had had only half a happy life in Camden, marred by an inescapable distance, as if she lived behind glass. She'd felt it every morning she practised her magic in a different room than her friends; every time someone whispered "that's the Sorcerer child" as she passed; every time they talked about the centuries of fraught history that separated *them*, the Changelings, from the Psi, and the Wraiths, and the *Sorcerers*. If she had less happiness here in the Heart, it was only because she hadn't proved herself yet. She hadn't shown them that she wasn't a Changeling. But these were her people. If Cassia couldn't belong here, then she couldn't belong anywhere.

Alana looked at her pityingly. "And what if your grandfather decides returning to the Zoo is the best thing for you?"

For you. There it was again. Neither of them was under the illusion that the decision would be made in Cassia's best interests. The only reason she kept insisting that she hadn't made up her mind about her future yet was the childish hope that if she said it enough times it would be true; the choice would miraculously be hers.

Maybe it would be. Maybe there was a way Cassia could take her life into her own hands, but if there was, she hadn't found it yet. Her request to come back to the Heart had only been granted on Hester Ravenswood's insistence that it would benefit everybody, and the promise that the Zoo would welcome her back should Jupitus see fit. She wasn't sure Hester could help her if that was the case.

She couldn't talk about this any more; not the initiation, not Camden. She was suddenly very tired, and tears were building again alongside the lump in her throat. She wanted to bury her head back in her pillow and be alone. So she said the one thing she knew would send her mother rushing from the room. But she turned away as she did, so that she wouldn't have to see Alana's face.

"He's back. He pulled some… trick to be elected President of the Society. The bylaws mean he has to be allowed to live in the Witherward again. Grandfather was forced to approve it. I expect he'll want his room back."

The door clicked shut before she had finished speaking. The silence was the loneliest Cassia had ever heard. And then she remembered.

"Who's back?" came the voice.

Violet had fallen onto her side and was half-hidden beneath the pillow Cassia had used to scream into. Her little voice soothed the wound Alana had opened up. As foolish as it made Cassia feel, this was a face that hadn't witnessed her humiliation this evening, that wouldn't have averted its eyes even if it had. This was the face of a person – or thing – that did not even know that Ollivan Sims existed.

"My brother," Cassia told the doll. She picked her up and stood her on her lap. "My brother's back."

There was a pause, and Cassia had almost put the doll back down when it replied, "And that makes you sad."

Was that what Cassia felt? She hardly knew her elder brother. Perhaps they had been close before she had been fostered with the Changelings, but Cassia had been too young to remember. Since then, Ollivan had never shown interest in her, though Cassia was sure that at some point in the distant past she had wanted him to. As they got older, and Ollivan's interests narrowed to strictly things he should not have been doing, her visits home had mostly been in his absence, precisely because of the expectation that he be there.

And then a year ago, he had shown everyone exactly who he was.

"No. Not sad," Cassia told the doll. "Angry."

"Angry?"

"He's... he's the stars-damned President of the Society of Young Gifted Sorcerers! The *President*."

"And you wish it was you."

"No!" Cassia placed the doll back against the mountain of pillows, out of reach of her shaking, apoplectic hands. "That's absurd. I would never be President. Even if I *could* get in in the first place. But you didn't see his face. His arrogant, smirking, *hateful* face. He doesn't even want to be President, he just wanted to show Grandfather up. He probably had a dozen other devious plans to get himself unbanished and he picked the one where he would get to make the biggest spectacle of himself."

In between her words of her tirade, Cassia wasn't getting enough air. As she pulled in a lungful, the doll finally had a chance to get a word in.

"Banished."

"Precisely. Three hours ago, the blackguard was a pariah, and now... it just goes to show. It doesn't matter what he does.

Because he's *Ollivan*." She snorted derisively. "Maybe I should get banished. Maybe then they'll let me in too."

"You wish to belong to this... Society of Young Gifted Sorcerers?"

"No. Maybe." Cassia rubbed her eyes and sighed in defeat. "Yes. I want to belong."

"How does one accomplish that?"

"You're asking the wrong girl."

"Then let me help you."

She looked over at the doll, who had slipped slightly down the pillow and listed to the right. Her empty glass eyes looked straight ahead, not quite at Cassia, but rather past her shoulder to the end of the bed. She wasn't really talking to a doll, she knew that. The doll was a vessel for a bit of magic. Granted, a particularly impressive bit. Her previous impression of enchanted dolls was that their conversational skills were limited to a few phrases and no real impression of sentience. This was the same thing, she reminded herself. This spell wasn't offering to help her because it cared; it was offering because that was what it was designed to do.

"I appreciate the offer," she said anyway, "but I'm afraid I'm on my own. I'm never going to be like Ollivan. And thank the stars."

"Yes, thank the stars. You must be yourself, in all things."

Cassia laughed wryly. It was a solid sentiment to teach children. At the age of seventeen, the shine had worn off the simplicity of such words. "I would rather be brilliant, I think, than be myself."

"And Ollivan is brilliant?"

"Oh, yes. I once overheard my father calling him the most gifted Sorcerer he had ever known." It was impossible to keep the bite out of her words. Her father had been distant when she

94

was a child, increasingly absent as she'd grown, and had quietly resigned his role as a member of their family altogether around Cassia's thirteenth year. When she had asked his whereabouts on a visit, Alana had told her quite calmly that Cassia wouldn't see him again. She didn't recall feeling much about it. That was their relationship, and still the man had paid enough attention to be impressed with Ollivan. "It's easy for Ollivan. It always has been. We couldn't be more different."

"No, you could not," said Violet. "You are hard-working! You strive to do better. That is much more valuable, Cassia."

The doll had said her name. Cassia hadn't been aware she knew it. But she was still wrong. "But being hard-working is worthless if nothing comes of it. No one will even know how hard you've worked if they don't see results."

"And that matters to you?" The question was ponderous and earnest.

"It matters to *everyone*. Anyone who tells you differently is lying. Lying while you disappoint them for not being as brilliant as your brother."

The doll was quiet a very long time.

"You are talking about your mother."

"My mother. My father. My grandfather." She let herself sink backwards onto the bed and stared at the underside of the canopy Alana had chosen: more pink. "The only parts of me they see are the ones that don't measure up to Ollivan. I'm not charming. I'm not bold. I'm not a leader. And I'm not a gifted Sorcerer. There are some exceptional Sorcerers in our lineage, and some adequate ones. There are no failed ones. Except for me. Perhaps that's why they sent me to Camden."

95

She added the last as a throwaway remark, and was disturbed to feel it tighten around her heart.

"Your family sent you away?"

"When I was five."

"Five?" Cassia startled at the tone in the doll's voice; sharp, and louder than usual. "Your family expected an exceptional Sorcerer at five years old?"

"Ollivan was three when he enchanted the music room to write and play symphonies all by itself," Cassia said flatly, staring into the mess of lace above her head. "A theatre director bought the rights to the music from him for a play. *The Pedlar of Dorberg.* It's still running."

"Earth and stars," muttered the doll.

"Precisely."

"It's unfair."

"It was a generous sum for a three-year-old, actually."

"It's unfair what they expected of you. You must be *yourself*, in all things."

It seemed she had extended the doll's enchantment to its limits. "Yes, you mentioned," she muttered, more to herself than the doll. She was surprised how sad she felt that the conversation was over; that the illusion of having someone to talk to had shattered.

"You must be yourself, yet everyone wants you to be Ollivan."

Cassia pushed herself up onto her elbows. The doll had not moved, and yet she appeared to be looking at her. Perhaps Cassia had jostled the bed when she lay down. She sat up further, and though the doll's eyes did not appear to move, she was still looking at her, like a portrait whose subject tracks you across a room.

"I assume this *Ollivan*, this brother of yours, was banished for wrongdoing?"

"For murder," said Cassia tightly. "He killed a man in a fight."

"Then why should you be like him? He doesn't deserve their respect. *You* deserve it instead."

Cassia couldn't disagree. Somewhere in the Sims children's stars had been an outrageous miscalculation. It had made Ollivan the President of the Society of Young Gifted Sorcerers the same night it refused Cassia initiation for a second time. It was a miscalculation that had been made again and again since the day her family had decided to train Ollivan up for the position of High Sorcerer and send her off to be some child ambassador for her faction. Out of the way. Dealt with, the way everyone had failed to deal with Ollivan. Even banishment hadn't stopped him getting his way.

Cassia knew all of this; it had been her lived reality for seventeen years. But never, in all that time, had someone else voiced the same thing.

"Let me help you," said Violet.

She had said this many times. It was the core tenet of what an enchanted doll was made for; so that young Sorcerers could practise wielding their magic. But *this* doll. It was a brilliant piece of magic. She almost had Cassia believing she could help.

"And why is it you want to help me?"

She saw it this time. Not a trick of the light or expert craftsmanship. The doll's eyes slid to face her, her green irises flashing in the lamplight, as if there were mechanical parts – or stronger magic – hidden inside. A thrill shot through her. She wasn't sure if it was unease or delight.

"Because you gave me magic," said the doll. "You brought me to life in that cold, dusty room, remember?"

Cassia shook her head. "It wasn't me. I only found you."

"You found me, and you made me what I am," said the doll more insistently. "Everything before was dull and undefined. And then we became friends, and I feel as if we could do anything together."

Cassia gave in. What was the harm of having a doll to pour her heart out to if it made her feel better? It was like having a journal, or screaming into a pillow, or composing letters to Gedeon or Hester or Fyfe before feeding them into the fire.

She smiled at Violet, knowing that by whatever magic she possessed, the doll could see her.

"Friends, then."

9

The celebration was inconveniently long.

To Ollivan's recollection, there was a Society soiree for every week of the year, so why the Successors felt the need to drink and dance and chatter well into the morning over an arbitrary election was beyond him. He needed to slip away, and he couldn't manage it while being expected to chat with every single member who approached him.

And that was all of them – all who were present, at least. He answered seventy-something questions about how in the heavens he had pulled off such a coup with some variant on "wouldn't you like to know" and a coy wink. He couldn't really blame any of them. The whole plan had been sheer genius.

It was several hours before he managed to slip from the grand parlour up to the President's Sanctuary on the floor above. The Sanctuary was a privilege of his new title, protected by a door that would only open to him and his chosen Secretary. Ollivan could feel the deep magic of the ward as he touched the doorhandle, the spell shivering in acquiescence as he stepped inside.

The Sanctuary was not much smaller than the grand parlour below. It was a long space with a desk at either end; the one near the door bore a wooden plaque reading *Jan Lenniker, Society Secretary*, which Ollivan tossed into the fire. Between the office spaces was a large sitting area, exquisitely finished in colourful silks and dotted with exotic plants. A potted orange tree was in bloom, filling the Sanctuary with its sweet aroma. Ollivan held one of the blossoms to his nose and breathed in perfume and magic. He could sink into a chair and linger here, soaking in his glory and relief – in everything he had worked for in the last year – but it wasn't time for that yet. He had come looking for a key.

The key cabinet was behind the Secretary's desk, but the hook with the key he needed was empty.

"Stars damn him," he muttered to himself as he rifled around, in case it was on another hook. But of course it wasn't. It could have been slipped from its hook permanently months ago and no one would ever have noticed it was missing. It was just like the deeply unwitting Jan Lenniker to forego warding the cabinet; or even, stars forbid, locking it.

But it was no great matter. He would simply have to try the unravelling spell scrawled on Mr Holt's sales ledger and tucked inside his jacket pocket. The chances were, he had remembered the ward correctly and would not be sucked into an unknown dimension...

He turned on his heel to leave the Sanctuary and his good ear finally picked up the sound of footsteps just as they reached the door.

"Ollivan?" came the call, accompanied by a knock.

With a sweeping flourish, Ollivan opened the door and welcomed Lev Mallory inside. Lev smiled, and Ollivan smiled back. For once, he thought his grin might be the wider of the two.

"Congratulations," said Lev. His eyes disappeared when he was smiling, which was always. "How are you?"

"*Astonished.* I can't believe you pulled this off."

"*We* pulled it off," said Lev, striding to Ollivan and throwing his arms around him. "Welcome home."

Home. Even as Ollivan warmed at the word, it reminded him of the obstacles he still needed to clear before everything was made right again.

"Do you want to know what you've promised your voters?" said Lev as he stepped away, freeing Ollivan's face from his fluffy black hair. Ollivan was not tall, but Lev was still half a head shorter than him.

"Fair warning," said a deep voice from behind Lev. "The list is long."

Hesitation clawed at Ollivan as he looked up. Virgil Pike's smile was as absent as Lev's was out of control. It was a sight so bittersweet it threw Ollivan helplessly back to the first time they met, eight years old and brought together by parents who hoped their precocious sons would be good for one another. But Virgil had not wanted his influence at all.

"I know who you are," he had hissed when Ollivan had dared interrupt his reading to introduce himself. The scowl he would grow so familiar with tugged the other boy's brows low over his eyes. "You'll be the High Sorcerer someday."

Ollivan had wanted to bat the book out of his hands, but his nanny was watching from a corner of the room. "Says who?"

"Everyone," said Virgil. "But my grandmother says leaders should be elected by *everyone*, not just the people with the most power."

Ollivan shot a glance at the nanny, stirred by the vague feeling that it wasn't the type of thing one was supposed to say, though he didn't yet fully understand why.

"Well I don't *want* to be High Sorcerer," he replied in a whisper, "so they can have an election for all I care."

That had been enough to convince Virgil's young mind they could be friends, and their bond had developed along much the same lines; Virgil railing against the ways of the world and Ollivan offering increasingly creative modes of protest. Virgil's parents' parties ran too late and too loud? Enchant their house to broadcast their gossiping to the entire neighbourhood. Too many of his sisters' ribbons and baubles scattered throughout the playroom? Turn the rings and earrings into beetles, the handkerchiefs and bonnets into bats.

Virgil had made Ollivan a radical, and Ollivan had made him a terror. Disrupting the farcical, self-satisfied traditions of the Society they had both been pressed to join by their families should have been the perfect reunion.

But a year ago, Ollivan had taken disobedience too far, and left Virgil behind. He seemed intent on reminding him of that, as he did so now; leaned in the doorway, his arms folded across his chest and that achingly familiar sullen expression marring his brow.

Ollivan did not want reminders. He wanted celebration, and he wanted his victory to be complete. The junk room called on him to make an excuse and duck out, but he owed his childhood friends everything, including his attention. The junk room would have to wait.

He leaned against the edge of Jan's former desk, which he was now relinquishing to a candidate of Ollivan's choosing. "Wait. Start from the beginning. I want to hear every glorious detail so I can tell you how brilliant you both are. I'm amazed that you even managed to split the vote evenly between Pella, Elric, and August."

Ollivan's coup had been an exercise in politicking that Jupitus Fisk himself could not snort at. There were seventy-seven members of the Society of Young Gifted Sorcerers, not including himself, and three candidates on the ballot. Splitting the vote between them meant Ollivan could scrape a victory with only twenty votes. With Lev and Virgil as a given, that meant persuading eighteen Successors to vote for him.

"Stars, that was the easy part," said Lev through his laughter. "We were lucky they were equally good candidates or it never would have worked."

"You're underselling us," Virgil said to Lev, though his disgruntled stare remained on Ollivan. "We've worked at this for months. Do you know how difficult it is to quietly campaign for three different candidates and make sure no one knows?"

"I can only imagine," Ollivan said, meeting Virgil's eyes straight on so he could see his gratitude. "How many did you have to sway?"

"When we canvassed everyone, it looked like August had a strong lead," said Lev. "Elric was the straggler. But a dozen members were undecided, and most weren't that much trouble to lead to one candidate or another. Then we targeted the least resolute handful of those who had picked a candidate and changed their minds. We had to persuade two of Pella's voters and seven of August's over to Elric. Then another eight for me." His smile widened. "But that was easy."

"Stars bless your natural charm, Lev," said Ollivan with a hand on his heart.

When Ollivan had done the arithmetic, he had quickly realised accumulating twenty votes would be impossible. He didn't have the leverage, and too many of the 'maybes' were a gossiping risk; he couldn't have anyone who would move to block him finding out Lev and Virgil were campaigning on his behalf. One quick amendment to the charter and Ollivan would be working the rest of his life in Pendergast's Occult Emporium.

So he had come up with a plan to shave a couple of votes from each candidate and earn himself an easier victory: add another write-in 'hopeful' to the race. Only eighteen to win.

"And my voters?"

"It was all just as you said it would be," said Lev. "You won your first three votes by just existing. Orson Halonen was the easiest – he barely needed reminding how bad you were for your grandfather's image before he agreed." Orson's father had been Jupitus's biggest political rival until he suffered a gruesome accident and untimely death. And they had comfortably banked on a couple of other members willing to quietly – *very* quietly – enable Ollivan in making Fisk's judgement look ineffectual. "Iwan Goff does indeed have an ideological issue with banishment as a form of punishment." Lev's eyes took on a haunted look. "Along with militia in the streets, centralised power, capitalism, the entire faith of the Oracle people…"

Virgil was nodding along empathically. "I can't say I agree with most of what he had to say, but he has a lot of fascinating ideas."

"What Virgil's saying is our conversation with him cost me three hours of my life, Ollivan. *Three hours.*"

Ollivan suppressed a smile imagining it. Lev was never interested in anything more serious than a billiards tournament. It was a miracle that he and Virgil were so in love.

"I'm sorry you were made to suffer so," he said, ignoring Virgil's indignant double take. "And Alden and Braswell?"

"Were bought with a promise of stocking snake-venom whiskey in the bar again. They're greatly looking forward to it. You better make it the first item in your budget."

Ten votes to win. "I have to write a budget?"

Lev laughed. "You have to do a lot of things. Including two lots of extra charitable duties every month for the entire duration of your term."

Ollivan's head fell back as the will to live deserted him. "I agreed to one additional monthly charitable task maximum."

"Well, Kiva moved on from her infatuation with you so we needed to improvise," said Virgil. He tilted his head thoughtfully. "It says a lot about you that you never questioned the limits of your charms."

"Kiva," said Ollivan wistfully. He had never entertained her advances, and yet he felt bereft. "But has she seen my rakish new scar?"

"Lenniker is very grateful for... whatever it is you did for him." Lev shrugged. "I mentioned the favour he owes you and he was agreeing before I could finish speaking. Then he vanished. Just transported himself right out of there."

"Perhaps he feared I'd told you all about the incident with the eighty-year-old Whisperer charlatan who compelled him to ask her hand in marriage one drunken evening when we were seventeen, and how I extricated him from the chapel just in time. But of course, I would never do such a thing."

Seven votes to win.

"And the, ah, *greyer* tactics I suggested..."

"The blackmail?" deadpanned Virgil.

"Now, that tone is unnecessary. The charter very clearly fails to mention that blackmailing voters is against the rules."

"Yes, I remember you assuring us of that fact. What I still wonder is when and how you had so much dirt on your fellow members."

Ollivan grinned. "Please. Did the name *Society of Young Gifted Sorcerers* fool you? It should have been called the Society for the Over-Privileged, Morally Corrupt Progeny of the Sorcerer Elite. The *dirt*, as you say, was just lying around. This place is filthy."

And Ollivan was smart enough to know in a city such as this, knowing *anyone's* weakness was a valuable use of his attention.

Not that every vote had cost him much attention. *He* had known at a glance that the mirror Tan Medhurst used in his initiation – which was spelled to reveal Drusella Square outside – had been enchanted ahead of time, which was obviously disallowed as anyone could have performed the enchantment. In the case of Tan's mirror, it had been spelled by Ollivan.

Harland Wise had been dosing the Wraiths with whom he played cards with a beautifully clever potion that mildly dulled one's reasoning skills. Ollivan knew because he had supplied him with it.

And Patience Cleverly interned with his grandfather's treasury. He knew she had found a way to siphon a little of the Heart's money into her own pocket because he himself had casually pointed out to her the flaw in the way they accounted the protection fees the people paid to Jupitus. For that matter, he had suggested she take the internship in the first place.

Four to win.

Ollivan hadn't had blackmail in mind when he aided his peers in their creative wrongdoing. He had simply enjoyed a little disobedience, especially of the kind that caused problems for his grandfather.

But he was past that now. The newly repatriated Ollivan Sims had his priorities in order. Or rather, a single priority: stay in the Witherward. Live a life of magic.

"Well, you're not the only one who can gather dirt," said Lev, smugly straightening his shirt-cuffs. "Lucas Viotto has a secret too. He's romancing the daughter of Madam Arcana, dressmaker to the elite."

Ollivan frowned. "That's not a secret. They've been involved since before I was banished."

"He's romancing the dressmaker too."

Ollivan let out an involuntary sound akin to a bark. "Stars! I'm not sure I can blame him, she's far more charming than her daughter."

"We were lucky with the timing of the election. He ages out of the Society in a *month*."

"Gale Garner was too smart for us," continued Virgil.

"He's a smart fellow."

"He could smell the potential for bribery a mile away."

"What do I owe him?"

"Dinner."

Ollivan cocked his head to one side. "I thought he liked girls."

"He does. One girl in particular. He wants dinner with your family. Three evenings. Cassia has to be there."

Ollivan winced. "That's all I can promise him. I don't have any sway with her."

"I told him that." Lev nodded at Virgil. "But we think they're a good match. He's too good-looking for anyone else. And he won't care that her mother's the next High Sorcerer."

"*You* think they're a good match," corrected Virgil. "That much cynicism in one room can't be good."

"So that just leaves…" Ollivan made a gesture that he hoped they could interpret.

He had worked very hard at pulling off a legitimate win. He needed a victory so watertight that reversing it and sending him back to the Otherworld would mean all but dismantling the Society – a defeat he knew Jupitus would refuse to be forced into, as a matter of pride. And he had got so very close to everything being – at least by the standards and oversights of the Society charter – above board. So close, in fact, that he would allow himself to be proud of the accomplishment.

But after accounting for every vote he could squeeze from the members by all the usual means, he still couldn't reach the minimum threshold they were wildly hoping would get him through.

That is, if everyone voted.

So they had formulated a last-ditch plan to shave off another vote. Ollivan listened for sounds from the corridor, then lowered his voice anyway. "Did everything go smoothly?"

"Easy peasy," said Lev, shuffling from foot to foot. "I invited the four of them for lunch this afternoon, just as you said. And you were right, yet again" – Ollivan allowed himself to preen, then stopped when he caught yet another of Virgil's glares – "lunch on me was enough to get them to pretend to entertain the idea. And who can resist the beef bourguignon at The Beringer?"

"*You* can," said Virgil seriously. "Because you're experimenting with vegetarianism."

"Precisely. One of them mentioned that the stew tasted a little funny but he clearly ate enough of it, and no one else seemed to mind. They'll all be right as rain by tomorrow, won't they?"

"Absolutely," said Ollivan with a hand on his heart. "The tonic is designed to mimic food poisoning, and will pass through their systems by morning. In the meantime... well, stars watch over them for a night of clinging to their chamber pots."

Virgil made a noise that sounded like a huff.

"What's wrong?" said Ollivan.

"What's wrong is that you're back, you're unbanished, and you've been behaving like a renegade even before it was official. Only this time you have Lev and me in it as well. Neck deep in it, Ollivan, while you were twiddling your thumbs in the Otherworld and selling healing crystals to people who didn't know any better."

"I can assure you, Virgil, they knew better by the time I saw them out."

"Blazing stars, *that's* what you heard?"

"It's not everything I heard, just the most unfair of several spurious accusations."

"And what were the others? That you were somehow able to blackmail half the members into voting for you—"

"*Four.*"

"—that you resorted to poisoning them when that wasn't enough?"

"*Lev* poisoned them."

Virgil's hands balled into fists. "I swear to all heaven and earth—"

"Virgil." Lev's usually booming voice was soft and carried the weight of conversations Ollivan hadn't been privy to; fights

109

they'd already had as they worked and scraped and fought tooth and nail to bring him back. "You said you'd give him a chance."

Ollivan's irritation had been rising, but it collapsed, and his throat closed. Because Lev still believed in him, and because Virgil didn't.

When they had found him at Pendergast's, Ollivan had told them the truth of what had happened. Not all of it, for reasons he maintained, but that he was innocent of the murder of the Wraith Jonas Benn, the crime that had been the final nail in the coffin for Jupitus, Jupitus's advisors, and his own mother. And they had believed him. Or, at least, they had said they did. As he looked at them now – Lev imploring Virgil with a look, Virgil slowly relenting, as he always did for the boy he loved – Ollivan had an uncomfortable awareness of things not being as right and hale as he had hoped.

"Believe me, Virgil, I will spend the rest of my life repaying you for this," he said. "It's the single greatest thing anyone has ever done for me. As a start, I'm making you joint Secretaries."

Virgil swallowed. Lev laughed nervously. "Actually, that's not possible," he said.

"Against the rules? That's a shame. We'll have to flip a coin."

"No, I meant the position's already been filled."

Ollivan gaped. "But the President gets to name a Secretary. I'm the President."

Virgil snorted. "How's your arithmetic, Sims?"

"Beg pardon?"

"That's only seventeen votes. Don't you want to know who cinched you the presidency?"

"You… you bribed someone with the Secretary role?"

"It's not that simple," said Lev, shaking his head. "All the cross-campaigning got too risky. Some of the people we would have needed to vote different ways are good friends; they would talk, and they would realise that we had persuaded them to vote for different people." He scratched the back of his head self-consciously. "After everything, we simply needed another body."

In planning the coup, Virgil had raised the idea of getting one or two of their blackmailed voters to persuade a second, or even third person, as part of the deal.

Ollivan shook his head vigorously. "I rejected that plan. You said you agreed that coercion was too nebulous a way of getting someone to behave as one wishes. The chance they would rebel, or muck it up, *especially* in a task as delicate as covert persuasion. This whole plan was already balancing on a knife's edge."

A female sigh sounded from the open door. "Earth and stars, do you always have to be so dramatic?"

Ollivan went cold and hot all at once. His eyes locked with Lev's, who mouthed *sorry* even as an entertained grin crept unbidden across his face. Ollivan shot him his best death stare as he turned around and, for the first time in over a year, came face to face with Sybella Dentley.

He was devastated to find she was just as lovely as he remembered her. Wide-set, light brown eyes looked out at him from a freckled, brown face. Her curls were pinned back and falling over one bare shoulder. It was whispered that she glamoured those curls to shine as they did; Ollivan had never learned if it was true. With the added width of her ruched taffeta skirt, her frame filled the doorway. Her mama said she was too fat, whatever such a thing meant. Ollivan thought she was perfect.

He could tell from the way her chin was dimpled that the air of cool nonchalance hid a thousand barbs, no doubt for him. It made him wonder if she'd been drafting them in his absence; if she'd been thinking of him.

"Ellie."

"*Miss Dentley*," she corrected.

Ollivan cursed the heavens. Were they all determined to take him to task?

He turned to Lev. "You needed a body," he said slowly, "and the best person you could think to ask for help was... *Miss Dentley*?"

He aimed the last two words at Sybella, and she widened her eyes in challenge.

"*Actually*, I found them out," she said with a sing song lilt to her voice and a toss of her hair. Earth and stars, Ollivan hated her. "Jan Lenniker cornered me all a-fluster about a month ago, and asked who I told about that night with the Whisperer woman, do you remember?"

Ollivan cursed himself. Of course he had remembered Sybella had been there, he just hadn't considered that Lenniker would double-check whether he was really being blackmailed by a boy in another dimension.

"Sybella came to us and said she knew what we were up to," said Lev shame-facedly. "Only—"

"Only she didn't know," finished Ollivan, already seeing where this was going. There was a reason they had once been joined at the hip. Ollivan and Sybella's poison had been trouble, but in the end, her taste for it had only been a phase, while Ollivan's had been a calling.

"I did, once Lev and Virgil were kind enough to confirm my suspicions." She pouted. "What's the problem, Mr Sims? You seem so fond of a little blackmail."

Ollivan folded his arms, so that she wouldn't see him clenching his fists. If Sybella Dentley got the slightest hint that she was getting under his skin, the humiliation would be so acute he may as well walk himself straight back to the portal. "And now you're Society Secretary."

She beamed. "Aren't you going to congratulate me?"

"Congratulations. I hope you know you're about to have your work cut out for you. Being President of the Society of Young Gifted Sorcerers is an irritating means to an end for me, and I plan to treat it as such."

"Oh," she said softly. She had come very close; so close Ollivan could see the flecks of green in her caramel eyes, and smell the lily scent of her perfume. "I'm afraid that's not how this is going to go. You see, at the end of your term, I'll be eligible to run for the presidency. The more successful my tenure as Secretary, the more likely I am to win. And I will win, Ollivan. Anything you do to get in the way will see you whisked back to the Otherworld before you can say 'food poisoning'. Probably with Lev and Virgil too. The charter may neglect to say anything about blackmail, but it's perfectly clear about voter suppression. So I suggest you strive to be the most perfectly adequate president this society has ever seen, and do exactly as your Secretary asks of you. Now, do you mind? You're leaning on my desk."

Few things could have truly dampened Ollivan's spirits this evening. The reality of working with Sybella Dentley – and working *well*, on threat of exposure – was one of them. All the magic and peace of the President's Sanctuary leached away; it was a cage that he would share with her. He could not get out of there quickly enough.

Sybella spoke again as the three of them were leaving.

"Close the door behind you."

His friends didn't catch the tone, but Ollivan spun, horrified. Sybella was smiling sweetly at him, venom in her eyes.

She knew exactly what she had said. They were the starsforsaken words she had spoken on the night she broke his heart.

"Where's my book?"

Hester might be talking to you, but your eyes bore a hole in the chessboard, your whole body tight with anticipation.

"On the table by the window," says Fyfe breathlessly.

The table beyond the sofa, where Gedeon is hiding.

You dare to look up as she crosses the drawing room, unawares. Gedeon's timing is perfect as he springs, lion-shaped and roaring. It scares you and terrifies Hester, whose fright transforms her into a tiger.

A second later they're both human, and a lamp lies decimated on the rug.

No one breathes. The prank is ruined. Then from across the chessboard, Aelius gasps. No, laughs. Fyfe falls next. When Hester joins in, you know it's safe.

"And you, Cassia! You were in on this?"

You were. The newcomer; the quiet, unsure Sorcerer, a co-conspirator. Hester scolds you with a smile and a swat on the arm, and you swell to the size of a tiger.

It was the sort of family dinner that made Cassia wonder why she had ever wanted to come home.

The five of them picked awkwardly at their food; Cassia, her mother, her grandfather, Ollivan, and – for reasons unknown – Gale Garner. More perplexing than his presence was how pleased he appeared to be there. He kept catching Cassia's eye and shooting her smiles from across the centrepiece.

It was not as disconcerting as the seething rage burning her from her grandfather's end of the table. If she were Ollivan she wouldn't be able to withstand it. But her brother had never cared what anyone thought.

"But how did you campaign without access to the members?" said Alana, obviously rapt and not trying to hide it. If Cassia clenched her jaw any tighter it was going to pop. It had been a day since the election, which in her book was ample time to have stopped talking about it.

Ollivan took a bite of his meal and answered with his mouth full. "Lev and Virgil handled the communications for me. They did an absolutely stellar job, I couldn't be prouder. Grandfather, you ought to consider hiring them in your propaganda office."

Jupitus looked up like he hadn't been entirely present. Cassia, too, tried to tune Ollivan out when he spoke, but she couldn't manage it this evening. His presence was still too jarring. Yesterday she only ever thought of her brother as a relic of her family's past. Now, here he was, holding court at the High Sorcerer's dining table.

"And your policies?" said Alana. "They must be extraordinarily compelling. I don't remember a write-in candidate ever winning the presidency, do you, Father?"

Jupitus gave no reply.

"The policies," repeated Ollivan, chewing pensively. It pulled at the ragged scar that razored down one cheek from his eye socket to his jaw. He had got it in a brawl; the one that had supposedly made him a murderer. As Cassia was leaving the Wending Place the night before, she had heard Kiva Mediova say, with a giggle, that it made him look *dangerous*. "Oh, you know, the usual. Parties and salons and a well-stocked bar. Opportunities to meet important people. The stuff that *truly* matters to the members of the Society of Young Gifted Sorcerers."

Cassia slammed her wine glass down a little too forcefully, and everyone turned to look at her. Gale reached for the carafe between them.

"Allow me," he said, as he topped up her glass.

"Don't drink too much, Cassia," said Alana distractedly, turning back to Ollivan. "And your campaign managers disseminated all this without the whole Society finding out? How? Why?"

"Isn't that obvious?" said Jupitus, his voice a snarl. "So that we would have no chance to stop him."

Alana appeared to catch herself and nodded, tight-lipped. Still, she did not take her eyes off her son.

Cassia spoke without meaning to. "You're happy he's home," she said, stunned. She looked from her mother to Ollivan and back again. "Aren't you?"

Ollivan tried to glower at her, but Cassia was watching her mother, who spared her a glance before going back to her meal.

Cassia had witnessed the year leading up to Ollivan's banishment and seen just how much he had put their mother through. Screaming matches at four in the morning, when he had wandered in with his lip bleeding and his pupils blown. Accusations from her friends and colleagues – the people she would need to support her claim to the office of High Sorcerer – that her son had broken into their home, or caused a scene at their party.

Now he had conned his way out of a punishment he'd well and truly earned – one their mother had agreed to – and Alana was not only *impressed*, she was also glad of it. They could fight, he could hurt her, shame her, threaten their family's legacy, *kill someone* – and there was nothing he could do to lose her love. And perhaps that's how a mother's love should be, but Cassia didn't recognise it.

"Cassia, none of us *wanted* Ollivan sent to the Otherworld."

"Say banished," snapped Cassia. "He wasn't sent to the Otherworld like I was sent to Camden. He was *banished* for—"

"And it was upsetting for all of us." Alana raised her voice to cut her daughter off. Gale suddenly had no smiling looks for her; he was concentrating on his braised carrots like they might all forget he was there if he was quiet enough. "But your brother is back now. This is another chance, and I for one am willing to give it to him. I would like to see you do the same."

"Hear, hear," said Ollivan, raising his glass in her direction.

Cassia tried to catch her grandfather's eye. *He* would be an ally in this, surely. But Jupitus, while still as surly as he'd been all evening, offered nothing to the discussion. He sat in silence and brooded. Perhaps he felt he had already lost, and letting anything Ollivan did rile him further would only prove who held the power, at least at this moment, in this room. If nothing else, Cassia had to admire her brother's nerve for walking this line with him.

She became aware that the table had gone quiet, and someone had said her name. "I beg your pardon?"

"I said, how was your lesson today?" said Alana.

"Oh." Brilliant. Another topic Cassia hated. "Jasper didn't turn up."

"He didn't? Did he send word?"

Cassia shook her head, and opened her mouth to say she'd sent a message checking on him, but Ollivan was quicker. Choking on a mouthful of wine, he spat out, "Jasper Hawkes?"

Cassia raised an eyebrow. "Yes?"

"Jasper Hawkes is tutoring you?"

"Ollivan, what's the matter?" said Alana.

Ollivan had downed his knife and fork, and a peculiar confusion had come over his features. His eyes were hard. After a moment, he shook his head. "You should stay away from him," he said steadily.

"Ollivan, Jasper was a friend to you," Alana said gently. Jupitus, suddenly attuned to the conversation, made a noise of agreement. "At a time when your other friends felt you didn't deserve any."

"Because he didn't," Cassia muttered.

"Yes, Mother, in my year or so of pushing boundaries and bending rules until my own grandfather saw fit to expel me from this universe, my only friend was Jasper Hawkes," Ollivan said slowly. "What isn't adding up for you?"

"I won't hear this nonsense," cut in Jupitus. His steel-grey eyes met Ollivan's identical ones. "Mr Hawkes tried hard to curb your tendencies, and this is the thanks you give him?"

"He gave testimony to your grandfather after... what happened," Alana said, her eyes on her plate.

Ollivan's lips had paled. When he lifted his wine glass to his mouth, his hand trembled. "I'm sure that he did."

Cassia laughed. Not a snort, a full-on laugh. It was too funny. "Oh, I understand now. It's *Jasper's* fault that you're a lying, thieving, brawling, lying, drinking, heartless, violent narcissist."

"You said lying twice."

"The chicken is exquisite, how is it cooked?" said Gale in a voice several octaves higher than usual.

"Cassia—" began Alana.

"Alright." Jupitus raised a hand, and the table quietened. He fixed his eyes on Ollivan. "You will not bring this *circus* to my dinner table."

"*Me?*" spat Ollivan. He was halfway to gesturing at Cassia when Jupitus cut him off.

"There are to be rules if you are to live in my quarter, and if you break them, stars help me, should it take every drop of magic in the city, I will find a way to dissolve the magic of the Society charter, release you from your position as President and throw you back through the portal permanently, understand?"

Cassia couldn't believe the effect this had on Ollivan. At first, he cut in every other syllable to raise a remark or grievance, but by the time Jupitus was threatening to reverse everything his silly coup had achieved, he had gone still in his seat. His face cycled through several expressions as he beat back outrage, indignation, and pride. When he spoke, it was through a clenched jaw. His words were the last words she had expected from him.

"Yes, Grandfather."

Jupitus narrowed his eyes in suspicion. Alana took her son's hand briefly and squeezed. It was a gesture of thanks, or pride, and it was exactly the wrong thing to do; Ollivan's strained expression tightened further, and he closed his eyes.

Jupitus cut to the chase. "First, you will pass every night in your own bed in your mother's home, and you will be there by midnight."

"One o'clock," chanced Ollivan.

"This is not a negotiation. You will not leave the house without telling your mother where you are going, what you are doing and with whom. Not a servant, not an enforcer. Your mother. Then, every day, you will report in detail on everything you have done. I advise that you are not caught in a lie. My enforcers will be watching closely."

"Alright."

"If you can abide by these rules, without fail, then you will be allowed to stay until the end of your term as President."

Ollivan's eyes widened. "And what happens then?"

"*Then* you will return to the Otherworld and serve the rest of your life in banishment, as your punishment intended."

"What?" Ollivan was out of his seat. Cassia had thought she would enjoy this, and in principle she did, but the reality of hearing her grandfather lay down the law, and watching her mother do nothing, stirred a familiar helplessness inside her. "You're telling me that I could be a model citizen for the next two years – one in a very prestigious role, might I add – and still you'll be waiting to cast me out?"

Jupitus stood too. He didn't accomplish it with the explosive movement Ollivan had, but something about his calm slowness was equally powerful. "Would you prefer that I hand over the execution of your punishment to the Wraiths?"

"Father—" said Alana, lifting a hand to grip Jupitus's arm.

He shook her off. "You may have coasted on the ambiguity of this… duelling evening, at which you killed one of their people. But do not believe that because Lady Wrike and the North were merciful enough to leave your punishment in my hands that it must stay that way. It would have been a much cleaner application of the Principles – rules I helped write and swore to uphold – if I had let them have your life. I did not, to save your mother from being forced to stand back and let them kill you. To save *you*, from breaking her heart worse than you already had. But understand this: one word from me, and I promise you the Wraiths will not find the death of the man you murdered so ambiguous after all."

Ollivan stared at the table. A muscle fluttered in his jaw as he still continued to hold back his words. Cassia wished she were a Whisperer. She wished she could tell her idiot brother to back down.

"You gave your grandfather no choice, Ollivan," said Alana.

"I gave him a very simple one," said Ollivan with deathly quiet, "and I'll spell it out again now. Banish me or believe me."

"It's done," said Jupitus firmly, sitting back down and cutting into his chicken breast, like Ollivan was one of his enforcers come to relay a message and then leave. "Be grateful for my leniency. It is not in my nature to offer it, especially to those who threaten the peace."

122

"Understood." Ollivan's voice was toneless. "Am I excused?"

Jupitus waved a dismissive hand.

"I'm going home," he said, and then Ollivan transported himself away.

Ollivan landed in his bedroom, snatched a book from his desk, and threw it at the wall.

A curfew. Reports on all his comings and goings. And all to be shooed back to the Otherworld at the end of two years. His grandfather had to be going senile if he thought Ollivan would abide it.

It was not that the threat of being sent back had surprised him. Winning the election had been a first step, a temporary solution, one that would buy Ollivan time to come up with a way to have his banishment revoked entirely.

Phase two had involved his best behaviour and a hope that, if he could keep in line just enough to rehabilitate his grandfather's opinion of him, he could make the man listen. He could make the High Sorcerer realise he never should have banished him in the first place.

But no. Jupitus had made clear tonight that his obedience would earn him nothing, and yet he demanded it anyway. He expected Ollivan to jump through his hoops to keep his life, just to take it away when he was done bending over backwards for the old man's rules.

He picked up another missile; a paperweight. This one he aimed at the mirror.

It shattered with a soothing crescendo of angry noises,

fragments of glass raining down on the carpet. The silence that followed rang even louder, and with a lungful of air, Ollivan cleared his head.

So his grandfather was not yet sold on the idea of revoking his banishment. That was to be expected. Jupitus was proud. Being shown up by his nineteen-year-old grandson – who was a better Sorcerer at nineteen than Jupitus had been at his very prime – was a terrible insult, second only to exploiting an institution he revered in order to do it. But Ollivan couldn't help it. Jupitus made it so easy. And anyway, undermining the election had been necessary, whether he got a kick out of the look on his grandfather's face or not.

And keeping up appearances was necessary too. He could still change the High Sorcerer's mind. He had two whole years in which to do it. And if no other strokes of brilliance like the one that had got him home presented themselves, his good behaviour would be all the more important. It might be the deciding factor.

Which was inconvenient, since Ollivan needed to sneak out *tonight.*

He had wasted enough time. He had reunited with his friends, and caught up with his family. He had put his room back together the way he wanted it, with what belongings his family hadn't disposed of – thankfully, his books had been boxed up and put away safety in the attic; several years' worth of notebooks had vanished entirely, but he had already prepared himself for that. He had even made a decent start at squaring things with his voters, though he doubted Gale Garner was getting what he'd hoped for out of his first dinner invitation.

But Ollivan had more immediate problems, and to fix them, he would have to bend Jupitus's rules. *Today I disarmed a trap I set a year ago that might have caused untold destruction had the spell been woken* was not something he wanted to report in his evening run-downs of his activities.

Jupitus knew he couldn't keep track of Ollivan. Like Wraith magic – which allowed one to move faster than a bullet and pass through walls – and Changeling magic – with which a person could become a bird and fly away, or a mouse and slip in and out unseen – a Sorcerer's talents lent themselves to losing a tail and flitting about unnoticed. It was bad etiquette to use a transporting spell to do so, and some places were warded against incoming bodies, even if they could not be warded to *keep* them in. But Jupitus could have no such ward placed on Ollivan's room; his own enchantments made sure of that. Nor could he truly have Ollivan watched as he had threatened to, though he was sure every enforcer in the Heart would be instructed to be on the lookout for him. It had also not escaped Ollivan's notice that his grandfather might have forbidden him from leaving the quarter, but had not. He might think of it later, and undoubtedly would if Ollivan gave him reason to, but for now he would go where he wished.

No, Ollivan could not be stopped, but he could be caught. He paced the room as he weighed the risks. A headache started pounding at his temples as he pictured all the obstacles pressing down on him like shovels full of earth on a coffin.

But Ollivan was a problem-solver, and problems were solved one at a time. Just tonight, for just this task, and then he would give his grandfather's rules a try. At least until he came up with something better.

To keep anyone from entering his room was too suspicious; a fact he had learned by the age of twelve. But he could appear to be sleeping should anyone check on him. He began to cast a glamour over the bed, then stopped; he could do better.

Glass was still scattered across the floor from the mirror, and the book he'd been using to make notes on the applications of Tumanese silkworm venom lay face down in a corner, the pages crumpled against the floor. He left them. He set a chair facing the window and lit a single clara stone lamp, which he placed nearby. Then he glamoured his brooding façade into the chair; a version of himself looking out at the city. From the door, one would see only his shoulder, and his hunched shadow looming on the wall. If they got closer, and spoke to him, the glamour would only continue to glower out into the night as if they weren't there at all. It painted a scene of a young man with a temper, who had stormed from his grandfather's dinner party and now refused to talk to anyone. It was who they all thought he was, and it was infinitely less likely to raise suspicion than if they found him slumbering.

And then he was gone.

Not all Sorcerers could transport, and not all those who could, did. Ollivan blamed the way it was taught, which focused excessively on the mechanical details; how transporting was like being pulled into the earth by a thread tied to your destination; that you must be on or over land. What many who were new to the spell weren't taught was that it took a relationship with one's magic that was free of doubt, fully trusting, and perfectly humble. A Sorcerer did not transport themselves, magic did it for them, and if they forgot that for one moment and tried to take control, the consequences could be deadly.

He transported straight into the President's Sanctuary at the Wending Place. Only Successors could transport into the Wending

Place, and only the President could transport into the Sanctuary. The details of the specific ward or spell that made it so had been lost to history, and it hurt his heart that so few members would ever care, so long as the bar kept admitting them and the corridors kept sprouting dark corners in which to steal heated moments with one another.

There had been a night a year ago when Ollivan had risked the magic of the Wending Place. Looking back, it was a testament to the strength of his fury that his revenge had taken precedent over the safety of a piece of magic he revered and treasured. But tonight he would make it right.

He lit the lamp on his desk and noticed for the first time the pair of chairs before it, no doubt so the President could conduct their tedious meetings with the heads of this and that committee who required something of them at all hours of the day. Ollivan wondered about what Sybella's idea of an 'adequate' president looked like, and prayed to every constellation that it was one who let her take charge.

In the Otherworld they had a superstition about the *devil*, a servant turned antagonist of their god; about how speaking his name caused him to appear. Ollivan couldn't help but question his faith a touch when the silhouette of Sybella Dentley manifested suddenly across the room.

Ollivan took back every pleasant thing he had thought about the Wending Place and glared at the ceiling. "If it means anything to you," he said to the building, "my idea of a *sanctuary* does not admit Miss Dentley."

"That's too bad," said Sybella lightly. "The Wending Place may be kind to the President, but it's kind to the Secretary too.

This morning, the portraits in the entrance hall all curtsied to me as I passed. I must say I'm enjoying this job immensely."

"That makes one of us," muttered Ollivan. "How long have you been here, Ell—Miss Dentley? It's late."

"There's a lot to do," she replied. "Which you would know if you'd come when I messaged."

"You messaged?" Even as he asked the question, Ollivan vaguely recalled tossing a note in her handwriting onto the fire earlier that day. It had arrived at a sullen moment, before he had had his morning coffee, and Ollivan had a strict policy of not thinking of her at low moments. It only ever made matters worse.

"You need to approve the menu for the militia luncheon on Saturday, and arrange a date to draw teams for the spring croquet tournament. You know if we don't announce it with plenty of notice no one will come and then they'll all cry cheat when they don't like the teams. Also, I should remind you that you're expected to give a speech before the annual spring scavenger hunt tomorrow night, so write one. And Edward Dvorak was stuck in the broom cupboard all of last night after someone charmed the door out of existence. He says it was that new initiate, Aubrey Cai. You'll need to mediate a grievance hearing. Preferably tomorrow."

There was a pause as Ollivan waited for a punchline that never came. "None of that sounds interesting." Sybella's eyes hardened. "Ellie—"

"It's *Miss Dentley*," she bit out, startling Ollivan with the bite in her tone.

"Miss Dentley," Ollivan corrected calmly, though every stars-damned utterance of the formal address twisted the knife she had buried in his chest. "I don't believe for one moment that you truly care about any of this stuff, so why don't we agree not to care together and end this mind-numbing charade? Arranging grievance hearings for what sounds like a perfectly entertaining prank isn't you."

Sybella cocked her head to one side. The frown brewing across her brow had only deepened as Ollivan went on. "You know this *does* matter to me," she said quietly, as if she feared invoking days gone by. "I've talked of politics for years."

Ollivan made a non-committal sound. "I know you *talked* of it." Sybella's parents had pushed her in similar ways to Ollivan's. Venting their frustrations about the paths they were expected to follow was how they had first grown close, aged just fourteen. But somewhere along the way, Sybella had started echoing the things her mother and mama wanted for her. "I never imagined that you were serious. I suppose that was my fault."

"Of course it was your fault," she said irritably. "I expect the courtesy of being taken at my word, Ollivan. You just never wished to believe I wanted something so beneath you."

Ollivan drew breath to argue, but he was overwhelmed by the unfairness of the accusation. Being angry with Sybella was uniquely torturous. When he directed it at others, anger was its own reward, its own release; with her, he was fighting through it to be understood. It was like being pulled under by the current; like he could clear all the obstacles of their own frustrations if only he kept kicking.

It galled him to know that nothing had changed.

"Politics is not *beneath* me," he said with all the calm he could muster. He had to close his eyes. His headache was returning. "It's just not *for* me. You know that."

He readied himself to be rebuked for presuming what she knew, but Sybella's reply was worse.

"Did you do it?"

Ollivan's eyes shot open. She met them with a defiant stare, but the fragile whisper of her question belied her steel.

Ollivan's voice was just as quiet, and laced with fury. "Why would you ask me that?"

"Because I need to know."

"Why are you here, Ellie?"

"It's Miss—"

"*Why are you here?* Is it to torture me? Because it certainly isn't that you enjoy my company any more, you made that perfectly clear."

Sybella sucked in a breath. The hurt on her face seared his soul, and yet he was glad. He didn't wear his hurt as openly as Sybella did, but she should know how he felt. That she of all people would suspect him of having done what the rumours said he had; it made him wonder, for a fleeting moment, if he had ever belonged here at all, if even she did not know him.

"I tried—" She cut off, swallowed, and started again. "I tried to tell you, back then, but you wouldn't listen."

"I remember," said Ollivan softly. He stood and rounded the desk, stopping when she took a step away from him. "I was in your house for all of sixty seconds when you swept the rug right out from under me, and then you kept talking, like you expected me to stand and attend to you any longer. Well, I couldn't."

Ollivan tried to never think of that day, but stood in front of her as she wore the same look on her face, it was impossible. He had been late, and she hadn't commented on it, which was how he knew something was wrong. She hadn't come to him when he crossed the room to meet her, hadn't slipped her arms around his waist and smiled up at him like she always did. He'd thought she had had bad news; that her mother or her mama was ill, that the adoption of her little sister had fallen through. Still, he had no clue. He was entirely unprepared when she told him he wasn't hers any more.

"In fact, I take back what I said," he went on. "This busy-body, bureaucratic tedium might be *exactly* who you are. Who am I to say, when I only ever thought I knew you?"

Sybella's face crumpled, and Ollivan staged a dramatic exit, sweeping around her and storming from the Sanctuary so that he wouldn't have to watch her cry.

*

The Wending Place was quiet, as Ollivan had hoped, and the only other members he saw were those in the bar as he crept past. When he reached the corridor where the door to the junk room waited, he knew he was alone. No one ever came this way.

Sybella would not leave his mind. The whole thing was so wrong; so uncanny. The same perfume, longer hair; the space between them that never used to exist when they were alone. Ollivan hadn't considered himself a tactile person before they fell in love, but they had always been touching.

Before *he* fell in love, he reminded himself for the millionth time. It had never been what he thought it was.

He shook the handle of the junk room door but, obviously, it was locked. He could also sense that the ward was still in place. A Sorcerer needed to understand the mechanisms of a piece of magic to *unravel* it. It was like untangling a knot, except instead of using one's eyes and fingers to navigate the loops and snags, one used precise intention. The more specific a request, the more successfully magic obliged it.

And very few knew the specifics of this ward. Ollivan had found it among some little-known records of magic; a series of ledgers recording the discoveries and missteps of Sorcerers whose lives and existences had otherwise been lost to history.

No, lost was not the word: they had been erased. Sorcerers whose appetite for discovery – and sometimes for violence, and destruction, and the purely macabre – had been so inconvenient to society that they had to be disposed of.

Sorcerers like Ollivan.

Yet someone had seen fit to preserve the work of these Sorcerers for posterity, and Ollivan and Jasper had pilfered them. This particular ward was insidious for its apparent lack of violence. It sounded mundane, even, on paper. Should someone attempt an unlocking spell on the door, it would swing open obediently and reveal the junk room beyond. But should the spellcaster step over the threshold, they would find themselves somewhere else entirely. Where, Ollivan did not know, but he had conducted some experiments on the door and he didn't believe the destination existed in this reality. No one cared to visit the junk room but him and Jasper, and so the only victim of the spell had been an unfortunate rat who had nobly tested the mechanism for him. As Ollivan knelt by the lock and unravelled the spell with the notes he had made on his last morning at Pendergast's, he sent up a quick prayer for the intrepid rodent.

The ward came down, and Ollivan cast his senses about for any other magic on the door, but it seemed it was safe to force entry. He wrapped his fingers around the latch and his magic popped the lock. He pushed the door open – then leapt back as a high-pitched, tormented squeal came from within.

A rat burst from the room, skinny, red-eyed and shedding patches of its fur. The end of its tail was dyed blue. Ollivan had dyed it, so he could identify him later. The rat cowered, trembling, against the skirting board and would not cease shrieking. Alarm coursing through him, Ollivan enchanted him with a wave of calm; a spell useless on other human beings, but employed by stable workers, shepherds and the like on their charges.

The rat quieted. Ollivan released a shaking breath.

He enjoyed the ward for its myriad mysteries; for the theoretical possibilities it posed. Now, he wanted to fall to his knees and thank every last constellation that no one had been reported missing from the Wending Place since he cast the spell, for this was what would have become of them.

He stepped warily over the threshold, and when nothing launched out of the gloom to decapitate him, he ventured inside, treading lightly and ensuring he didn't touch anything. He didn't know what dangerous magic had been developed and tested in this room since he was last here.

The same familiar smell – chemical, but also botanic, like sulphur mixed with thyme – permeated the room, and as Ollivan inhaled it, he was taken back to all the wonderful things that had happened in here. The discoveries, the euphoric feeling of unstoppable power. He must have been younger than he knew. None of the spells he had cast in here seemed so appealing now.

He found and lit a lamp, and raised it above his head to cast its glow over the junk room. The first thing the light caught was something sparkling in the centre of the floor. Several somethings, Ollivan found as he bent to inspect them. Shards of glass. There was something that looked like soil too, faint lines of it, as if someone had tried to sweep it away.

Most of the objects he had enchanted in the year before his banishment were where he had left them. There was the spinning wheel that, when turning, emitted an enchantment that would put everyone in a quarter-mile radius to sleep, save the spinner. They had only tested it once, giddily nervous and snickering like schoolboys, and only for ten seconds or so; just long enough for one of them to collapse and the other to confirm it worked. No one had died when they fell asleep on the spot in the middle of a normal working Tuesday, thank the stars, though a Changeling in flight on the other side of the river had plummeted to the earth and broken all their limbs. Jupitus and his enforcers had tried to investigate the spell, to no avail.

There were the seemingly empty glass vials that drew sounds of violence from the air when they were unstoppered. Ollivan could only assume their purpose was hurting people without anyone hearing them scream. He hadn't enchanted the vials with that intent, he just wanted to know if they worked. They did, as his sister could attest when he shot her in the neck with a pea shooter and her shriek was sucked from the air.

There was no sign of the ledgers. That was to be expected. If Jasper had any sense, he would have destroyed them the second Ollivan stepped back through the portal.

But to Ollivan's horror, the most dangerous thing that had ever been in this room wasn't there either. The Guysman enchantment was gone.

135

"Heaven, earth, and all the damned constellations," muttered Ollivan, trying to think. Could the trap have been set off? Maybe Jasper had disarmed it somehow. Maybe it had done nothing, and all his months of fear and second-guessing had been in vain; the danger he was trying to get ahead of had been a phantom conjured by his paranoia. Surely, if it had been triggered and gone as wrong as he dreaded, he would know by now. Unless…

Ollivan set the lamp down so that his shaking hands wouldn't drop it. Jasper had not turned up for his tutoring session with Cassia today. What else had his sister said? Had she spoken to him since? Ollivan couldn't remember. He had assumed that Jasper was absent because he hadn't wanted to run into Ollivan at the house, but what if, by another stroke of Ollivan's incredible misfortune, Jasper had woken the Guysman the very week Ollivan had returned to the Witherward? If the spell was nascent, perhaps they hadn't seen the full effect yet.

Whatever that effect turned out to be. If it was as Ollivan intended, and the spell was out there, it wouldn't be long before the whole quarter knew that something was happening. But if it wasn't, as he feared…

He found he was feeling something about Jasper he would never have imagined when he placed a trap to destroy the other boy's life:

He did not want to have killed him.

Ollivan had done a lot of bad things, and cast a lot of dangerous and unsavoury spells. The *limits* of magic were what truly fascinated him, but the fact was the limits were frequently horrifying. Spells that forged weapons from things one would never have imagined as a weapon before. Spells that were done to bodies and minds; things that required stolen cadavers to test in practice. In fact, for a period of six months or so, his primary fascination had been with the intricate magic of spells used for stealing itself; variants on transporting magic and elaborate glamours that could conceal – at Ollivan's most extravagant theft – a grand piano.

And he would freely admit, with very little shame, that the death of Jasper Hawkes had once been his heart's desire. But he had never acted on that wish, though several of the artefacts in this room would have made it easy. Because Ollivan had never intended to be a killer.

It might be too late for that, but there was only one way to find out.

I 2

Cassia snapped her shears and the flower heads tumbled to the ground.

"If you like flowers, why do you wish to kill them?"

Violet was propped on the bench that lined the edge of the small pavilion at the bottom of the Sims' garden. It was late to be collecting cuttings for drying, but Cassia had left her grandfather's dinner party wound tight with frustration, and this corner of the garden was her bit of calm.

It also helped to have something sharp in her hand. With each snip of her shears, she cut away thoughts of Ollivan's smug face and entitled words; of her mother's enraptured gazes at her firstborn, the way she danced around the truth of his banishment. Even her grandfather, who would let the rules of his revered society win out without even *attempting* to magically alter the charter. Perhaps Jupitus thought he was winning by not letting Ollivan destroy the Society as they all knew it, but he was playing right into his hands.

"I wish to kill a lot of things right now," she replied, dealing a series of lethal blows to the climbing blossoms spilling into the pavilion. "Be thankful I'm restricting myself to plants."

"So you do this to get the violence out?"

The thinly disguised note of alarm in her voice made Cassia smile. "It's not the *main* appeal."

"Then why?"

She collected the stems from the ground and held one to her nose. "After the bees and perfume, flowers will die, whether I cut them or not. But I can let a flower drop its petals, and the petals can rot on the ground, or I can protect them as they decay, so that they transform into something else. Something with a different kind of beauty."

"But they won't be as beautiful as a fresh flower."

Cassia smiled. Violet wasn't the first to find her predilection strange, but she didn't mind. If it was only for her, that made it all the more precious. "They will be to me. Sometimes a thing is beautiful because it has endured. Like a sparrow's skull, or a pale blue eggshell. Just because something is dead, it doesn't make it worthless."

She gathered the cut flowers into a neat pile on the bench. All the while, she sensed the doll taking her measure.

"These dead things are a comfort to you," Violet said at last.

"Yes."

"They're sort of like... treasured toys."

Cassia considered the pile of cuttings and shrugged. "I suppose, in a way. Though I don't think people my age attach themselves to their toys the way children do."

A noise sounded from near the garden gate, and Cassia turned towards it. Sat as she was under the clara stone lamp of the pavilion, everything beyond was dim, but she could just make out the shape of a bird rustling the branches of a pear tree as it took flight.

Cassia sank against the bench. What had she expected? That Jasper would let himself in, place his books on the bench, ask her how she'd slept? That was how their lessons always began, but today, he had never showed up.

She had sent a messenger checking on him, knowing it was both the polite thing to do and a burden on Jasper, who had already made clear he was distancing himself from her on initiation night. She had looked for him one final time as Ollivan made his dramatic entrance, and seen him stalk from the room with a cold sneer. Cassia would probably have distanced herself too after her embarrassing display.

Still, it had left her feeling confused and hollow to lose him. He had never seemed to care that she wasn't skilled with her magic. He had been patient and reassuring through their lessons, determined that she would succeed but not irate when she did not. And now, out of nowhere, the only friendship Cassia had made since coming to the Heart was over.

"*I* would like to be a comfort to you," said Violet, and Cassia started. She was slow to remember what they had been talking about, and Violet's wistfulness had caught her off guard.

"You are a comfort to me. Dead flowers and animal bones don't talk. It's a different kind of comfort."

"And you have no other toys to talk to?"

"Well. No, I don't." *Or people.*

"So you're attached to me?"

Cassia reminded herself for the thousandth time that Violet was just a doll. She was asking for her affection because that's what enchanted dolls were *for*. Her voice was full of hope because it had been designed into the magic, and not because it mattered what she said next.

"In a sense, yes," she said lightly, judging it to be a good

140

balance between her sentimentality and her pride. Then for good measure she changed the subject. "You have a petal in your hair. Hold still a moment."

"Very funny."

Cassia brushed the petal away and rearranged Violet's ringlets. "There. As lovely as ever."

For a moment, Violet made no reply. Cassia wondered if she was upset that she had deflected away from the question of caring about her. Was that even possible?

"You promised you would fix it like yours," she said eventually.

"Oh." Cassia drew up, surprised. She *had* told Violet she would restyle her hair, back in the junk room, but something about the doll bringing it up unsettled her. "Alright. Let's see."

She pulled the doll closer and looked at her hair under the light. "Ah. The style has been glued down."

Violet gave a tinkling laugh. "Then use magic, silly."

"Magic. Right."

Cassia raised a hand to hover over the doll. If she cast a spell to unglue the hair, that would be simpler. Then she could style it by hand. That was a very straightforward intention. It was best not to overthink it. She summoned her magic and, with a push, channelled it through the intention: *unstick*.

There was a calming, warm feeling, when magic left one's body to set to its work. Or perhaps it was just Cassia. Perhaps it was relief that the block she suffered so often had let her be this time.

Was this how Ollivan felt when he enchanted the music room all those years ago? Or when he had summoned every robin in a five-mile radius to the garden as a solstice gift for Alana? Or when he had thrown the voices of everyone in the house, as if they were all ventriloquists, so that a simple conversation became impossible, and any moment alone came with the risk of an unembodied voice in your ear that actually belonged to someone several rooms away—

"Cassia, concentrate!"

Cassia jolted back to the moment, and cut off the spell. Thoughts of Ollivan had tempered her intention with bitterness. Bitterness that had manifested as decay. Violet's hair was unaltered, but her dress was moulded and moth-eaten, and tattered at the hem as if she had been walking through underbrush in it. The purple had faded like it had been washed too many times.

"Well. At least your hair is the same," said Cassia dryly.

"Do you want to try and fix it?" chimed the doll in her blandly encouraging voice.

"Alright. But just—"

"Don't move?"

"Precisely."

But Cassia couldn't get her concentration back. When she looked at Violet in her tattered dress, she couldn't see a canvas for a magic. She only saw the way she had failed. She let her magic rise, but her intention was caught somewhere between desperation, and the fear that desperation would ruin everything again.

She sighed and rubbed her tired eyes. "I'm sorry, Violet. I think your dress is stuck like that."

When Cassia lowered her hands and looked up, she couldn't contain a gasp. Violet's gaze had slid to the side, and she was looking past Cassia's shoulder to the garden gate behind her.

Cassia turned to face the gate just as a hand emerged from the darkness on the other side to clutch the bars. She leapt up in fright, knocking Violet under the bench.

A heartbeat later, the hand's owner materialised in the moonlight.

"Jasper."

He unlatched the gate, which gave a metallic squeal as he pushed it open, and stepped through as he did every day. Only this time, he was hours and hours late.

"Jasper – it's the middle of the night," she said. Her voice was pitchy and high, but she fought to calm herself.

Not that Jasper noticed. He had crossed to the pavilion in an instant, and when the light of the lamp hit him, his features came into even clearer relief. He looked terrible, his skin tinged grey and his eyes bloodshot.

"I wanted to see you," he said. But it wasn't true. Or if it was, there was more to it. Even as he smiled at her, he kept darting glances at the house. That was a first; she had never suspected lies from him before.

Cassia folded her arms and tried not to let the sudden rush of hurt she felt at seeing him show on her face. "You could have seen me this morning. At our lesson?"

"I couldn't come this morning."

"Clearly."

"Cassia, I'm sorry, but—"

"And my initiation?" That got his attention. His frown deepened with confusion, but there was wariness there too. Cassia wondered if he really didn't know what he'd done, or if the confusion was a lie. Another one. Unbidden, something that had meant nothing to her at the time resurfaced: Ollivan had told her to stay away from him.

"What about your initiation?"

Cassia forced herself to meet his eye as she confronted him. "You didn't have to vote me in," she said. "I would have understood. I didn't deserve it. And you didn't vote me *out*, which I suppose I should appreciate given my performance. But... but you ought to have at least *spoken* to me afterwards. Instead you acted like we'd never met, just as everyone else here does. So excuse me for being a little surprised that we're friends again, and that you're here."

"Friends, again?" Jasper shook his head. He reached for her hands and Cassia gave them to him, as much out of surprise as anything. "Cassia, we've always been friends. It wasn't what you thought. I was sad for you, after you worked so hard. I couldn't bear to see the hurt on your face and know I couldn't do a thing to fix it. It was selfish of me. I'm sorry."

"Oh." But the look on his face had been so clear. Had she misinterpreted what she'd seen? She had been so ready to assume that even Jasper would want nothing to do with her, and maybe she was being unfair. His thumb brushed in circles across her knuckles. It felt nice. "I suppose I thought that—"

"Is he here?"

"Hmm?"

"Your brother," said Jasper venomously. "Is he home?"

Cassia pulled her hands away. Jasper didn't notice; he was looking over her shoulder at the house again. "This is about Ollivan."

"I knew he was going to do something like this." He started pacing. "I *knew* it. I even prepared... I need to know where he is."

Cassia started collecting up her cuttings from the bench and rubbed her eyes tiredly, hoping he would get the hint. "Grandfather's given him a curfew."

Jasper laughed bitterly. "But is he *here*?"

It was a fair question, but Ollivan seemed to have finally been cowed by Jupitus's threats over dinner. "He said he was going home. I think he took Grandfather seriously. And his light was on when I got home." She considered Jasper's nervous energy. There was a glint in his eye like the edge of a knife. "Why do you want to know?"

"Because I don't trust him."

"Nobody does, Jasper. He's a murderer."

"He's going to try something."

He was barely making sense, but Jasper's bloodshot eyes and ragged appearance were a piece of the puzzle. He hadn't been sleeping.

"You mean... to *you*," she said. Jasper's head whipped round.

"What has he said to you?"

"He hasn't said anything," said Cassia, then realised that wasn't true. "Actually, he... said something about you giving a testimony to Grandfather. He called you a liar. What did you say?"

He raised an eyebrow, his expression darkening. "Why? Don't you trust me over him?"

It was such an absurd question that Cassia almost laughed. "Stars, of course I do. We all know you tried so hard with him. I'm just sorry that Ollivan doesn't appreciate it."

Jasper grinned, and with a flash, he gripped her by the shoulders, fingers firm against her flesh. "Come to the Wending Place with me."

Jarred by the sudden change and the strength of his hold on her, Cassia tried to lean away. "*Now?* It's gone midnight. Besides, I—"

"I know it's late, but I want to share something with you. A secret."

With a twist of her elbow, Cassia managed to extricate herself from his overenthusiastic embrace. She feared what Jasper's secret might be, but in that moment, for reasons her mind resisted, she also feared disappointing him.

"Can't you tell me here?" she said.

Jasper's smile grew. "It's not that kind of secret. This one, you have to see. Come on, we can sneak out through the gate." He took her hand and tugged her closer. "I wouldn't want to scandalise your mother."

His eyes met hers with a look that unequivocally invited her to scandalise her mother with him, and despite herself, Cassia entertained the idea. Maybe behaving like Ollivan was what it took to be valued like him. But not like this. She wasn't about to use Jasper in a rebellion experiment.

"Another time," she said, and forced a smile.

She regretted it instantly. The smile convinced Jasper that she could be persuaded.

"Not another time. *Now*," he said, laughing and pulling harder on her hand. "This is too good to wait."

Cassia stumbled, pulled off balance as she struggled against him. Some of her cuttings tumbled to the ground. That was the end of her polite smile.

146

"Stars, Jasper, I'm not going with you." She yanked her hand free and stared him down to let him know she was serious. "I said no."

Jasper's humour vanished. He was stock-still a moment, his expression as cold as ice. Unwillingly, Cassia took a step back. She didn't want to show her fear, but something was wrong.

"I chose you," he said quietly. "Of all the people I could share this with, I wanted it to be you. I thought we'd grown close these last few months." Cassia only hesitated for a second, but it was enough for Jasper. He laughed, but his usual smile was replaced with something like a sneer. "Was it all in my head? What's been happening between us? Just tell me if it was."

This was what she had dreaded; Jasper telling her how she feared he truly felt. A line crossed that left their friendship behind forever. Was honesty the right thing, when it would cost the both of them so much?

"I just need time," she said without meeting his eyes. Stars, she was a coward.

"Cassia, just—" He rubbed a hand over his face and groaned in frustration. "Just come to the Wending Place with me. Please."

"Why?"

His reply was slow, teasing, as his wild smile crept back onto his face. She had given him hope again. "Because magic goes so far beyond what they teach us as children, Cassia. Things you couldn't even imagine. Things I can't describe. But if you saw it – *felt* it – I can't explain why, but I *know* you're struggling because you have the wrong material. You'll take to what I want to show you, I promise. You just have to trust—"

He cut off as his gaze caught on something behind Cassia; something low to the ground. "What's that?" he said mildly.

Cassia turned and followed his line of sight. She thought Violet had fallen under the bench, but she was right there in front of it, sat upright on the ground by Cassia's legs.

"Oh." She dug around for an explanation that didn't make her sound pathetic, and was slow to realise there was more at stake than looking like a child with a doll. Jasper got there at the same time.

"Did you *steal* that?"

The undisguised tone of derision in the question made Cassia wince. She opened her mouth but her mind was empty, and she could feel the flush creeping up her neck and into her cheeks with every burning moment that she continued to draw a blank. Jasper's eyes flashed as he turned, part mockery and part rage, as his lips curled into a sneer. He took a step towards her and she felt her magic flare in response. Jasper froze, and the expression transformed through confusion into horror. His every muscle tensed, the tendons in his neck pulling taut and his breath coming out in glugs, as if he was choking.

"Jasper?"

One shaking hand reached for her, his fingers curling stiffly into a claw. "*You—*"

Cassia's blood pounded in her ears. He had alarmed her, and her magic had responded. Had she done this, whatever it was? She didn't know a person could perform magic without intention, but Jasper's index finger was slowly, painfully reaching towards her in accusation. Maybe she *had* given her magic an intention. Her mind had been scrambling around so desperately that she couldn't be sure.

"Jasper." She reached for him, then lowered her hands, helpless to do anything. "I don't know how to make it stop!"

Pain was etched across his face as the blood drained from it. Less than ten seconds had passed before he dropped, empty-eyed, to the ground, where he lay as motionless as the doll by his side.

13

Jasper lived above an abattoir in an alley on the north bank of the river. The surrounding buildings were warehouses and wholesalers, all of which were closed up at this time of night. The street was packed earth, not cobbled or paved, and no lamps illuminated the way. The moon caught the ripples of the river at the end of the street and picked out roof tiles still damp from rain, but the west side of the alley was in shadow, and there Ollivan stood, watching the flat.

The life he was trying to win back was the one he'd had before Jasper was ever in it, and he had hoped never to return here. A patch of street in front of the abattoir was stained dark; maybe from an upended bucket of soiled water, but more likely with blood. It wasn't the type of place one expected to find the educated son of wealthy parents, but that was why Jasper had chosen it, and why Ollivan had loved it too. It was a rejection of everything they'd been brought up to be. Now, every memory of being here, and of that year leading up to the murder, rang like a warning bell he'd been too consumed to hear.

*

It had begun three winters before at the Wending Place.

Ollivan had been pressed into becoming a Successor by Jupitus and Alana, so could never admit freely that their games and parties were usually riotous fun. That evening was an exception.

He arrived alone, morose and missing Sybella, who was out of town with her parents. The common room was airless and overfull. The condensation pressing against the windows was thick enough to hide the flecks of fluffy snow collecting on the other side. There was so little else to do in July, in the deepest ebb of winter, other than attend Society events, and everyone had turned out for this one.

He was not in the mood to socialise with most of his peers and had expected Lev, who lived nearby, to be there before him. But he wasn't. Instead, Ollivan had to listen to Tomas Otueome soliloquise on the virtues of one of his favourite tailors versus another for thirty minutes, while scanning the room for the only people he really cared to spend time with.

The evening's game was moments from starting when Lev and Virgil appeared in the doorway of the common room together. They had confessed to him that they were in love some weeks previously, and though their cheeks were flushed from the cold, the smiles they bore for one another said they didn't feel it. They did not look for him.

"Successors!"

Etta Flint, who would be President for two more months, had climbed onto a table to address the packed room. "Welcome to tonight's enchantournament!"

"It doesn't work, Etta!" called someone from near the bar.

"Well we decided that's what it was called," snapped Etta. She brandished a top hat at them and explained the rules of the game; competitors would be chosen, then she would draw a prompt for a spell from the hat and the best execution won. The crowd would choose the winner in every bout until they had two champions.

Because the game was played in pairs.

"You have sixty seconds to choose your partners. Begin!"

The Successors swarmed about the room like ants on a strawberry. As Ollivan pushed towards Lev and Virgil, he wasn't sure where he ended and his peers began. Perhaps that was why his friends didn't see him making his way over, but they had always had a tradition of rock, paper, scissors for games played in pairs; as a consolation prize, the loser chose a dare the others had to complete. They employed it less often since Sybella had entered the picture, but she had her own friends. Ollivan still needed his.

But as Ollivan got closer, he slowed. Virgil had slipped his hand into Lev's. Then they squeezed through the throng in the wrong direction, perhaps because they thought to look for him there, but perhaps because they meant not to. He didn't want to find out. It was better to let them form a pair and break tradition than to make them keep it out of politeness.

Suddenly, he knew that his dour mood, growing ever darker, could not be helped by being here. He would leave, go home and miss Sybella and try hard not to think of anyone else he loved and whether they still cared for him.

He had nearly escaped the common room when Jasper Hawkes drew his eye simply by being still when everything else was in motion. He stood against the wall and was staring at Ollivan, as he had done many times before. It was enough that Ollivan had begun to wonder if he was in love with him; a tendency of thought Virgil had since pointed out stemmed from arrogance. It was just that the Hawkes boy seemed disinterested in almost everything but him.

But as Jasper came over, it was clear the look in his eye was something else; a challenge.

"Partners?" he said.

Ollivan looked over his shoulder and caught a glimpse of his friends just as Virgil spotted him. He looked briefly guilty before seeing that Ollivan had found a partner in Jasper. But the damage was already done, and now Ollivan couldn't leave, or he would look petty and bitter. He *felt* petty and bitter, but he didn't need Lev and Virgil knowing that.

"Partners," he said to Jasper, and it was done.

They stood in awkward silence on the outskirts of the room as the enchantournament began. It was Jasper who spoke first.

"I admired your initiation spell. That you enchanted your phantoms to move as the High Sorcerer moved." A sharp-edged grin spread across his face. "And that you made him laugh at it."

That had been the real trick of the performance. It had been a year since Ollivan had finally been pressed into gaining admission to the Society, and he had taken his revenge with his chosen enchantment. He had conjured three dozen sparkling, pearlescent spectres of his grandfather; pretty, ethereal things each in a different hilarious garb; babies' overalls, nightclothes, frothy, hoop-skirted dresses. He had designed the spell to latch onto Jupitus; to raise the spectres' hands when he did, to promise death with their glares when he saw Ollivan was making a mockery of him.

But no one made a mockery of the High Sorcerer, especially someone he should have more control over, and so Jupitus had been forced to save face by laughing along. The Successors likewise had no choice but to laugh too, and Ollivan had been voted in unanimously.

Was that the reason Jasper Hawkes watched him from the corners of every room he entered at the Wending Place? No other member had ever dared make mention of the prank beyond that night. And it was not just Ollivan's magic Jasper was complimenting, it was his rebellion.

They played a couple of rounds of the competition in easy company with one another. Jasper was more proficient with his magic than Ollivan had known, and they shared an eye for spectacle. In their first bout, Ollivan caused the floor of the common room to ripple, lifting waves of onlookers towards the ceiling and back again, which they found so fun they asked him to do it again. In the second, Jasper opened a window and drew in a flurry of snow, which he turned rainbow-coloured and sweet-tasting as it fell on the Successors. Inevitably, they wanted more of that too. To call either round a competition was too generous to their rivals.

They were awaiting their third match when Jasper spoke quietly in his ear.

"If you'd rather a *real* challenge, I know of one not far from here."

Looking back, Ollivan realised that Jasper was lonely, in his own way. In the way an actor performing the role of a lifetime to an empty theatre is lonely. He craved a witness as much as a friend; someone to think him clever and daring, to reaffirm the man he was trying to be but was forced to be in private. And he had chosen Ollivan as the safest confidante because he believed them to be the same. In some ways, they were. Hadn't Ollivan been lured in that evening by a compliment no one else dared to pay him? Hadn't he been entirely helpless to refuse when

Jasper had told him with a look that where they were going was a dangerous secret?

No one noticed them leave. They followed the river west, collars pulled up to their ears, heads bowed against the snow. Jasper walked with long, loping strides and did not keep step with Ollivan, instead walking several paces ahead. But the frequency with which he looked over his shoulder – every few strides, as if he feared Ollivan would disappear – belied any nonchalance.

By the time they reached the shelter of the tunnel beneath the railway bridge, Ollivan was soaked through, and his face and fingers were numb with cold. The crunch of pebbles underfoot echoed off the arch above as he blew into his cupped hands. He almost stumbled into Jasper's back when the boy stopped before a metal door halfway through the tunnel. He rapped twice, and the hollow thud rang around them.

The door opened a crack and Jasper spoke to someone on the other side, then they were admitted into a dank, brick corridor that sloped gently down. Sounds like those of a raucous party or a heaving market grew louder as Jasper confidently led the way around several turns. A warmth Ollivan knew to be body heat burned his numb fingers but pulled him onwards. When the final turn ended in a crowded mezzanine and a set of rusting stairs, he knew in his whole body that whatever lay below was the thing he had been looking for.

Five hundred people, maybe more, were pressed together around an Oracle woman and a rangy, snarling dog. The woman wielded a long staff, and was using it to take hits at the beast as she danced to keep out of its reach. The dog had set itself to disarming her; every time the woman got close, it snatched at the staff with its jaws or tried to swat it from her grip with a paw.

A real animal would have no such sense. The woman was fighting a Changeling.

"Jana is one of the best duellers here," Jasper shouted over the crowd. "She's an acolyte, trained in combat."

Acolytes were the militia of the Docklands. In the fathomless mass of all space and time an Oracle was capable of Seeing, they sought only to know the very next moment; to See where their opponent would step and know how to strike them down. No wonder she was winning.

But even as Jasper spoke, Jana stumbled, exhaustion wrought on her sweat-soaked face. The Changeling saw their chance and lunged, but before they made contact, Jana ducked under their guard, and with a two-hand grip on her staff, forced the dog away from her and out of the ring.

The crowd roared. Money changed hands. The dog became a man who was pulled to his feet by onlookers. He spat blood in Jana's direction and limped away, cupping his jaw. New fighters were announced – a Sorcerer and a Wraith – and the next duel commenced.

"We meet under every full moon," said Jasper. "Dozens of different locations all over the city. Every faction."

Ollivan's blood was pumping. He felt like he had stumbled upon treasure; like a child waking up on his birthday. *Every faction*; all fighting with magic outside of their own territory, all of it against the Principles and right under Jupitus Fisk's nose. It was the perfect revenge for the old man's authoritarian hold on his life.

Ollivan started duelling at every evening. Every opponent was his grandfather, every broken rib and exquisite pain was a medal that said he had fought back. He introduced Jasper to his distributor, who sold the magical drugs he designed to customers all over the city. Jasper introduced Ollivan to the crook who auctioned his stolen wares and ferried them out of London. There was no trust required to fall in together, or so he'd thought; the risks their choices brought were all the insurance needed. If they went down, they were going together.

It was only in hindsight that Ollivan realised how little he had ever known of Jasper Hawkes. He was an only child who thought of his father the way Ollivan did Jupitus, though in private Ollivan sneered at the comparison; boys like Jasper would never appreciate how inconsequential their petty complaints with their families truly were. He was disinterested in girls, not because he was unattracted to them, but because he found their attraction to *him* unappealing. He kept a cat. In places with Changelings, pets made most people uncomfortable, including Ollivan. Even working animals were only relied upon when absolutely necessary. But Jasper was fond of the things that made people uncomfortable.

He was working on an enchantment to that effect the night Ollivan had let himself into the flat above the abattoir and collapsed onto the moth-eaten couch. Jasper ignored him. The cat sat on the arm and stared with round green eyes until Ollivan looked away. He didn't *think* those eyes were human, but it was hard to know for sure.

"Look," said Jasper after many long minutes of toiling at the table. He tossed the thing he had made to Ollivan, who caught it.

It was a locket removed from its chain. "It's my aunt. My mother wants a locket with her sister's portrait for her birthday."

He was holding back giddy laughter, so Ollivan opened the piece to see what Jasper had done. The animated woman in the frame was screaming silently at him, horror wrought on her tiny features. She slammed her fists against an invisible barrier, and cried and begged as if desperate to escape the painting. It was pointless and unsettling, and not even very clever. As Ollivan wordlessly threw the thing back at Jasper, he wondered if this wasn't all very boring.

Jasper's joy shattered. "What's the matter with you?" he sneered.

Ollivan let his head fall back against the couch and closed his eyes. He swallowed before speaking, but his voice still broke. "Sybella's left me."

He had not said the words out loud. They shocked him as acutely as they had coming from her.

Jasper made a disdainful sound. "You were tired of her anyway."

"No—" Ollivan began, but he couldn't find the calm to tell Jasper how he was wrong, or ask how a person grew *tired* of Sybella Dentley. If Jasper believed that, it was because Ollivan had allowed him to believe it. But the truth was Ollivan had seen the rest of his life with Sybella in it. He could not convince himself that only a month had passed since they'd been curled around each other in the chair in his bedroom, murmuring plans about a house in Chelsea, with windows that moved in a circle to look like the gondolas of the big wheel where they'd first kissed, and a gaggle of children with her freckles and his eyes.

Stars, he was drowning. Ollivan loathed nothing more than his own helplessness, and while he couldn't persuade Sybella back, he could take his mind off her. And he would do so in the most spectacular fashion.

He lifted his head off the couch. "Hey. Do you remember that door?"

Jasper looked up from packing the macabre locket in a gift box and grinned. Of course he remembered the door. For a time, it had been all they talked about. They had found it one night when they had broken into the Chambers of Alchemy to lay pranks to trip up enforcers; a wholly unremarkable door at the bottom of a staircase thick with dust and cold with disuse. Were it not for the sharp sting of magic they both felt when they touched the handle, they would never have thought on it again. It must have been storage of some kind, they had decided. Storage for valuables, Jasper had theorised. Storage for secrets, thought Ollivan.

"You mean the door with the ward we couldn't crack?"

Ollivan smiled. "I think it's time to try again."

*

Ollivan trod softly as he approached the apartment. If Jasper was dead, he didn't want to be caught at his home; if he wasn't, the risk was being seen by Jasper himself.

He thought again of this boy tutoring Cassia, and his stomach turned. What was his interest in her? Did he think she shared her brother's inclinations, and that he could welcome her into the fold of his misdeeds? Had he used her to get at Ollivan's notes?

He feared the answer was worse; that Jasper's interest in Cassia was sincere. His sister was beautiful, an outcast, a little odd. She had a standoffish, stone-faced way about her that might convince Jasper that she disdained all the same things he did. What was worse, Jasper could play a charming, mild-mannered young man

159

when it served him. He didn't doubt his nemesis's ability to cheat his way into Cassia's heart if he put his mind to it. Ollivan made a mental note to double his efforts to convince Cassia to stay away from him.

But there were no lights on in the rooms Jasper occupied. They ran above a narrow alley that led to the back of the abattoir, through which was an external staircase that led to the flat. Ollivan crept to the bottom and listened. There was a feeling he had in being here; a slimy prickling on the back of his neck. A tightening in his stomach. It put him on edge. He stood for several minutes in perfect stillness, not daring to look away from the window above the alley and miss any signs of movement in the flat.

Because if Jasper wasn't dead, perhaps he was inside, and perhaps he was waiting for him. Ollivan wasn't here for revenge, but if the opportunity presented itself, he would take it. He didn't want to kill Jasper; he would gleefully hurt him though. And Jasper would expect as much. It gave Ollivan a sick thrill to imagine that the boy had got little sleep since he had stepped back through the portal.

In some ways Ollivan's year in the Otherworld had been a period of cooling off; in others, it had festered resentments. The only reason revenge was not his first port of call was that it didn't serve his purpose. And his purpose was what mattered most; his life back. Magic. Unravel the Guysman before it incriminated him and made matters with Jupitus irreparable.

But silence reigned, and the curtain did not flutter, so with slow steps Ollivan climbed the stairs. The old wood creaked under his weight, sending a fresh wave of anxiety over him with each step.

He readied a spell at the tips of fingers he could not convince to stop shaking. Three steps from the top, he heard a soft click, and then a whirring, fizzing sound halfway between a grinding cog and steam escaping.

And Ollivan understood. The prickling on his neck. The tightness in his stomach.

It wasn't just tension. It was magic.

A flare of burning orange burst into life on his left. Ollivan didn't wait to see what the spell was. He leapt out of its path – backwards, air replacing wood as he missed the steps and went tumbling.

He was not fast enough to miss the flaming darts entirely, which caught him on one side and tore through layers of clothing to bury themselves in his flesh.

The world spun around him, fire consumed him, and all Ollivan could do was brace to hit the ground.

Jasper was dead.

He had fallen face first to the ground, arms at his sides, one leg askew, one cheek mashed against the bricks that lined the floor of the pavilion. He looked somewhat comical.

"Jasper?" It was just a whisper; her true voice stuck in her throat.

Cassia crossed the pavilion slowly – eking out the moments before she confirmed what she already knew – and knelt beside him. It wasn't so easy to find where his pulse should be with his head bent at such an angle. She poked clumsily at the flesh under his chin a couple of times, but found nothing.

Her next instinct, she was ashamed to find, was to turn off the lamp that hung above them and douse the scene in darkness, then retreat; out of the pavilion and into the shadow of the hedge where she was as good as invisible. There, she gulped in air to keep up with the galloping of her heart, and tried to think of what to do.

Cassia had never killed anybody before, which was unusual for one so close to the powers in London; so close to Jupitus Fisk especially, for whom violence was a core tenet of leadership. She had always reasoned that it would happen eventually, but she had imagined it differently. First, that it wouldn't be until after she'd mastered her magic. Second, that it would be in defence of something worthwhile, like her people, or her own life. And third, that it wouldn't be a fellow Sorcerer.

Was it better or worse that it wasn't a militia of a rival faction, or a would-be assassin come for her grandfather, or someone else of value in the Heart? It did not break the Principles to kill one of her own people; that was a matter dealt with by every faction in their own way. Jupitus's way was execution. If he favoured her for being his granddaughter, perhaps she would only be banished.

Would that be so bad?

The thought surprised her, the implication so dismal that it stung the backs of her eyes. Were things so awful, that she would shrug at being banished to another world? She could fit into the Otherworld London with a little effort. Forget magic altogether and find something she was actually good at. Growing things, perhaps. Cassia would like to grow things. Or perhaps the reason she was drawn to banishment was that she wanted to prove that she could do something Ollivan had failed at.

Ollivan.

Her brother would not turn her in. Not out of love, or loyalty, but out of a life-long disrespect for their grandfather's rule. Nor was he likely to care that it was Jasper she had ended, given the way he had spoken about him at dinner.

It was a risk; she would turn *him* in without a second thought, after all. But she doubted Ollivan thought of anything beyond himself enough for Cassia's animosity to be mutual. Her brother barely knew she existed.

That was about to change.

The servants had all turned in, so she slipped through the kitchen unnoticed and crept silently up the stairs. The light was

163

still on in Ollivan's room, and Cassia didn't knock. Being caught willingly interacting with him would be as damning as the body she had left in the garden.

The broken mirror was the first thing to catch her attention. He had probably smashed it in one of his rages when he transported home from their grandfather's dinner. That he hadn't mended it – a spell well within his capabilities – was the first piece of evidence that he had not let the matter go.

The second was that he didn't acknowledge her when she entered without knocking. He had moved a wing-backed chair to face the window, and he sat with an arm draped despondently over the side, and a foot propped against the windowsill.

"Ollivan," she whispered as she shut the door gently.

She only realised she was still breathing hard when she crossed the room to stand by the window and thought how she must look. Pale, probably, and wide-eyed. Not unlike Jasper when he had showed up in the garden. "Ollivan," she said again.

Still, he did not acknowledge her. The scowl he aimed out at the world did not even twitch. Typical. Nineteen, and still throwing tantrums like a five-year-old.

"Ollivan, Jasper is dead."

In her brother's defence, she couldn't fault his thinking. There weren't many things one could say to him in such a mood that he would listen to. How was he to know she would burst in here in the dead of night and announce a murder? It was the one misfortune that would catch him out.

For Ollivan had no response to the news at all, proving that this was not Ollivan, but a glamour designed to hide the fact he was not in his room despite his curfew.

A disrespect for their grandfather's rule indeed. And Cassia had truly believed him sufficiently warned this time.

"Stars forsake you, Ollivan."

She pressed her head against the window and tried to think. The body in the garden thrummed in her awareness in the same way as someone talking about her across the room, yet here, away from it, it seemed too impossible to be real. How had this happened? How had she lost so much control of her magic that it was capable of doing something like this against her will? She had never even read of a person's power going rogue that way, let alone how to fix it.

Cassia turned back to the room. Ollivan's books. He had thousands of them, on all kinds of magic. They lined most of the room across dozens of shelves; shelves that sagged under the haphazard piles of volumes he had crammed onto them. Ollivan wasn't here, but the answers to what had happened in the garden might be. She would start there.

There turned out to be some sense to Ollivan's chaos; *if only in how he organises his books*, Cassia thought. Volumes about potion-making were stacked onto adjacent shelves, those about glamours and corporeal magic also. There was also a section on spell theory that could hold the answers, but how could Cassia guess when she didn't know what she was looking for? She could only grab for the nearest book that looked like it might have some relevance and start skimming through.

She had a pile of discarded books beside her, and an ancient-looking, leatherbound tome in her shaking hands when she heard a creak of a floorboard and a flapping, like wings.

She spun. Ollivan was fighting his way out of his overcoat, which was on fire. He threw it to the floor and stamped on it, while

165

simultaneously pawing at one side of his torso. There were...
spikes impaled there, Cassia realised, as he tore each from his
flesh with a groan, still dancing on his blazing coat. Then his eyes
landed on the jug on his washstand, and in one motion he grabbed
it with both hands and tipped it over himself and the coat.

Dropping the jug unceremoniously onto his coat, Ollivan half
collapsed across one corner of his bed, an arm gripping the bedpost
like a sailor clinging for life to the mast of a ship in a storm. It was
then that he finally saw Cassia standing in the corner with a book
in her hand, and froze.

They stared at one another. Ollivan pushed himself upright,
one arm cradling the injured side of his torso. He glanced at the
glamour by the window and back at her, then sighed like the whole
thing was a grave injustice.

"Oh, earth and stars," he muttered. "Listen. Cassia—"

"I've killed Jasper Hawkes."

Ollivan's expression wiped blank, his mouth hanging open
on whatever excuse he had been about to give. Then he blinked
several times and regarded his sodden person with what appeared
to be scepticism.

"*Where?*"

Where wouldn't have been Cassia's first question, but it was
better than marching from the room to tell their mother.

"In the garden. Just now." Ollivan's eyes flicked around
the room, and Cassia intuited the next question. "I left him in
the pavilion."

"You killed Jasper Hawkes? *You?*" He shook a sleeve of his
dinner jacket, and more water splattered the floor. That Ollivan
wasn't all that perturbed by the news boded well for her. But then

she realised the arm he shook water from was a distraction. The other waved vaguely in the direction of the window and undid the glamour he had used to disguise his own wrongdoing that evening, and the relaxed levity in his manner made sense: Ollivan may have broken his curfew, but Cassia had killed someone. This time, he was off the hook. "Did you use a weapon? I don't mean to disparage you in any way, but I hear you and magic are struggling with some differences of opinion."

Cassia snapped the book shut and set it down. Was she really having this conversation with him? Had any of this really happened? "I'm not sure what I did, exactly. One moment we were talking and the next, he had keeled over."

"Could it have been poison?" Ollivan gestured to her fingers, which were stained green. "I assume you were handling a range of flora out there."

Cassia turned over each flower she had plucked in her mind, but she didn't know of any that could kill someone on contact. Besides, if it had been poison, wouldn't she be lying cold in the pavilion too?

"It wasn't poison." She pushed down her pride and did what she had come to his room to do; the only thing she could think of. "Will you help me?"

Ollivan was watching her sceptically, like he thought this was all some kind of ruse. She couldn't blame him; she wouldn't believe her either. But she needed his help, and if it meant saying please...

Cassia took a deep breath and prepared herself. "Pl—"

"Well, I can't pretend I'm not curious," said Ollivan, and he disappeared.

Stunned, she stood for a beat in the sudden solitude before racing back to where she had left the body. When she emerged from the hedge around the rose garden, she found the lamp in the pavilion illuminated again and Ollivan stood beneath it.

But the pavilion was otherwise empty.

"You didn't *eat* any of these plants, did you?" said Ollivan, whose mood appeared to have plummeted upon *not* discovering a dead body in the garden. "Those blue ones look like they could cause hallucinations."

"I left him here." Cassia stepped slowly into the pavilion, braced for whatever this night's hundred-and-tenth nasty surprise would be, but Jasper was truly, fully gone. She squinted across the garden. The gate was open. After his unexplained episode, it seemed Jasper had got up and walked away. At least, she could hope that's what had happened. "I thought he wasn't breathing. I couldn't find a pulse."

"Well, it seems he found it by himself. Next time could you please be *sure* he's dead? Something sharp in the jugular ought to do it."

Cassia rubbed her eyes. "And he took Violet, of course. I forgot about her."

"Who's Violet?"

"She's this... doll that I found."

Ollivan's head snapped up, his eyes wide. "What doll?"

When Cassia hesitated, caught off guard, he snapped the question at her a second time, the urgency even sharper. "I found an enchanted doll," she hastened to explain. "I know it's a children's toy but I just sort of—"

"Found it where?"

"At the Wending Place. Jasper snuck me into the—"

"—junk room."

Cassia felt cold. Was it looking at Ollivan, soaking wet, or the dawning sense that something she couldn't grasp was happening?

"Where did you leave it? Cassia!" When she was slow to reply again, Ollivan took hold of her shoulders and ducked so they were eye to eye.

But Cassia barely noticed him. She was gazing uneasily at something behind him, something that hadn't been there a moment before. "She's right there," she said quietly.

Violet was standing at the other end of the pavilion. She was supported by nothing but her own small legs, and in the light of the clara stone lamp above, her glass eyes appeared to glow, the way they had in the junk room.

"Violet." Cassia took a step towards the doll, reaching down to grasp her, but Ollivan pulled her back and put himself between them.

"Don't," he said, his voice soft. "Don't go near."

He shucked off his sodden dinner jacket; wincingly, but without making any sudden movements.

"Ollivan?"

"It's a Guysman spell," he said in answer to her unasked question.

"A what?"

"Everard Guysman. He was a fifteenth-century spellmaker. And a madman." He said all this in a quiet, flat voice that gave away his tension. He took two long, slow steps towards Violet, jacket raised before him, as the doll stood unthreatening and silent. When he was in range, he threw the waterlogged jacket over Violet, and immediately crouched to wrap it tight around her. Cassia sensed a flare of magic as he cast a spell on the jacket – a binding spell of some kind, she guessed – then the tension leached visibly from his shoulders, and he looked up at her.

"How long have you had this?" he asked.

Cassia still wasn't sure what a Guysman spell was, but the words *spellmaker* and *madman* told her all she needed to know. "It's yours, isn't it?"

"In a manner of speaking. How long has it been... moving on its own?"

"Moving?" Cassia thought of Violet's roaming eyes, but she didn't think that's what he meant. "She doesn't."

"*She?*"

She refused to flush in front of him, and opted for scowling instead. "*You're* the full-grown man who apparently owns an enchanted doll."

Ollivan climbed to his feet with a heavy sigh. The doll-jacket package dripped in his arms. "*She* is not an enchanted doll. Now if you'll excuse me—"

"Where are you going?"

"Bed."

"But—" Ollivan held the jacket at a distance, as if it carried refuse fished from the Thames and not something that mattered to her. "You can't just... *take* her. She's mine."

"You just said she was mine."

Cassia couldn't push any harder without making a fool of herself – it was a *doll*, for stars' sake. Ollivan raised an eyebrow in challenge, or maybe victory.

And then he was gone.

Cassia stared at the spot where Violet had been standing and shivered. *Not an enchanted doll.* Perhaps she should have known that; the spell had been far too sophisticated for a children's toy. And deny her senses all she liked, she had been unsettled to see Violet *standing* where she hadn't been a moment before.

But now she had even more questions than before. She was at Ollivan's bedroom door a minute later. She tried to let herself in, but after transporting back up here, Ollivan had clearly had the sense to lock the door, if not sense enough to know that wouldn't stop her. She crouched down and put her mouth near the keyhole.

"Ollivan," she hissed. "Do you forget I know you weren't in your room all night?"

For a moment, nothing. Then the key rattled in the lock in a decidedly irate fashion, and the door opened. Ollivan was halfway out of his waterlogged clothes. "Be so good as to fetch me a towel and you can come in," he said.

Cassia had no chance to tell him he wasn't in a position to negotiate before he closed the door again, so she swallowed her frustration and fetched one.

Ollivan had discarded his clothes in a heap when she returned, and he sat slumped on the edge of his bed with just a blanket across his lap. A blanket that he tried to use to hide the five or six ugly, bleeding burn marks on his chest and ribs. When he saw her looking at them, he gave up and finished applying ointment from the tin on the bed beside him.

"How in the heaven and earth did you get into trouble between dinner and now? And after Grandfather gave you a curfew."

"You should see the other fellow. At least I assume I fared better, since you mistook him for a corpse just now." He was

171

rubbing his hair with the towel, and when he emerged from under it, he attempted a smile. Cassia didn't return it. "It seems the bastard had the sense to booby-trap his flat to the nines. I did try to tell you to stay away from him."

"Forgive me if I don't consider you a fountain of sage advice."

"You should. I'm smarter than you."

Incensed, Cassia snatched at the towel she had brought him. He tried to grab onto it but she was faster, and yanked it from his reach. "Then what did you do, genius?" she demanded, holding the towel out of reach. "What in the heaven and earth is a Guysman spell?"

Ollivan sighed. He leaned back on his hands and stared at the ceiling. "Jasper snatched that enchanted doll off a child for sport. There was a spell he had in mind, I don't remember what, but he kept the doll because it would make a good test subject." He grinned, but it didn't reach his eyes. "I turned it into a trap. The Guysman spell is an enchantment we... found. Or rather, the workings of one. A draft. Everard Guysman never finished a working version of it, but I had some ideas on how to build upon what he'd started. How to make something that absorbs magic."

Cassia couldn't help but shudder. It was perverse, horrifying, that a thing could exist that was capable of sucking away magic like that. It threatened everything that mattered to the people of the Witherward. And Ollivan had made it.

"Guysman designed it as a way of neutralising the work of another Sorcerer. He had a rival he wished to sabotage at a showcase. He imagined the enchantment would be performed on some kind of object with a shutter or a stopper. One he could open and close at will."

"Is that why you put it in the junk room? Because Jasper does all of those experiments in there and you wanted them to fail?"

"I left the doll where I'd found it, so Jasper would enchant it as he'd intended to. My take on the Guysman was not so… controlled." He smiled cruelly. "If you ask me, the man's idea of sabotage was a little tame. There were some records in that junk room; Guysman's notes but a wealth of other spells too, things that would ruin Jasper's life if the wrong people found out he knew about them. Maybe even get him killed."

He gestured for the towel and Cassia let him have it back. "What are you talking about? Magic isn't regulated like that. It isn't regulated at all."

Ollivan laughed. "That's what we're supposed to think, yes. The records we found – a series of ledgers – were locked in an archive beneath the Chambers of Alchemy. They tell a different story. Officially, raw magic is this… sacred good, and a gift from the stars. Oh yes, if we manipulate it in certain ways, it can cause suffering – death, even – but that's the failing of human beings, not of magic. Sorcerers can never be persecuted for what we are because our magic is pure. Untainted. Don't you see how some might find that a lie worth protecting? Because it *is* a lie. Magic is capable of terrible things, with the right application. And the powers in the Heart have been making it their business to bury those things for centuries, along with everyone who ever knew them. And then Jasper and I stole them."

Cassia couldn't help but ask, even though she feared the answer. "Terrible things like what?"

Her brother gave a nonchalant shrug. "Oh, let's see. Animating a corpse? Turning an animal on a victim to ravage them until the beast's heart gives out? A thousand-and-one things to get addicted to, before they kill you. I've seen recipes for potions that make one crave the taste of human flesh—"

"Stop." She realised she had put her hands over her eyes, perhaps because she couldn't look at him any more. "I understand. Somebody had the sense to ban these things and that was enough for you, wasn't it? You were like a moth to a flame." Ollivan shot her a hurt look and she ignored it, because she knew she was right. But there was more. Rebellion had led Ollivan to plenty of places, but it had led him to magic for a reason. "Father made you like this, didn't he?"

He looked up, surprised by the rare mention of Grayson Sims, who had made the study and teaching of magic his life's work.

"It probably started like that," said Ollivan. "I used to visit him at the university when I was small. I even saw him give a lecture or two. Sometimes it felt like the only way to get his attention was with magic."

Cassia made a noise, half agreement and half surprise. It seemed a small thing, but that flame of something – something deeper than understanding – was so foreign when it came to her brother that for a second it flared inside her like an inferno. Repulsed, Cassia snuffed it out.

"But we're talking about magic, Cassia. *Magic*. The very nature of the world – what's possible – it's defined by the boundaries of what magic can do. And no one even knows where those boundaries truly lie, or *why*. Just think about that. Isn't it enough of a reason?"

It was enough of a reason, when he put it like that. But it didn't make her first instinct wrong. There were countless ways to explore and practise magic; Ollivan had picked the one that pitted him against Jupitus.

"And you... *practised* this banned magic?"

Ollivan was rueful. "Some of it. Those were only the worst examples. Besides, as I say, *my* interest was in the theory. The underlying mechanisms."

He did not say Jasper's name, but the implication was clear.

"I left the Guysman in the archive so that when spells started winking out like candles all over the Heart, it would eventually lead back to those ledgers; to that room. The effect would be fastest and most destructive at the Wending Place, so someone would trace it to there eventually. I even worked a safety into the spell so that I'd be long gone and above suspicion when the chaos started. A delay, so that the spell wouldn't wake until I was in the Otherworld."

Cassia felt her lungs release. "So this Guysman spell hasn't been woken yet," she said.

Ollivan shot a look at the bundle that was leaking onto his desk. Cassia didn't like the thought of Violet inside that mess. It caused her a pang of guilt to realise her hair would be ruined.

"That depends. I assume *Violet* encouraged you to practise an enchantment on her?"

"Well... yes."

"And did you? Has any magic touched her at all?"

As if playing with a doll wasn't embarrassing enough already. Cassia massaged the spot between her brows. "I woke the enchantment, didn't I?"

"Given Jasper's unexplained almost-death, I'm assuming so. I designed the delay so that the vessel needed a taste of magic before the spell would activate. I imagined that Jasper would trigger it unwittingly when he got round to experimenting with the thing, and the longer it took him, the cleaner I would look. I just didn't imagine I would be back in the Witherward before then."

Cassia narrowed her eyes at him. "You think it was Violet who did... whatever that was to Jasper."

Ollivan laughed. "Well it wasn't *you*, was it?"

She didn't think he was even trying to sound condescending; it was just so obvious that he couldn't help it. Of course Cassia hadn't magically attacked someone without even trying. What had she been thinking? That her magic had sensed her tension and leapt to her defence?

It was typical. Not only had it not been Cassia's magic; it had been Ollivan's. Only her brother could make her feel small for *not* killing someone.

"You said Violet was supposed to neutralise spells," she said, hearing the resentment in her own voice, "so what did she do to Jasper?"

Something I didn't mean her to, was the answer written across his face. It gave Cassia a pang of satisfaction to see him struggling with how to reply and keep his dignity.

"This is why I've been looking for that starsforsaken doll since I got back," he said. "I didn't have long to set the enchantment, five minutes at most when I was supposed to be saying goodbye to Mother and... I was emotional. But I was getting shunted through the portal at first light and I couldn't wait to be in a better frame of mind before performing the spell. There would *be* no other time."

"So your intention was poisoned," said Cassia.

"*May have been* poisoned."

176

"Earth and stars, that doll knocked someone out, Ollivan. And who knows what else it did to him."

"Well it seems he was well enough to get up and walk from the garden." He rubbed his eyes. He put a finger in his right ear and jiggled it around. Perhaps it was waterlogged. "But. Yes, the intention was not my finest work. When I was in the Otherworld, with nothing but a bleak, grey future staring me in the face, I started to consider the spell a bit more. Where its... weaknesses were."

"Where you got it wrong, you mean. That enchantment could do *anything*, and we have no way of knowing what, because you were too hot-headed to think."

"I am trying to be forthcoming with you, Cassia," he snapped. "I don't have to tell you any of this. And if you hadn't stolen it in the first place, that spell would still be sitting dormant in the junk room."

"If *I* hadn't—" He shot a look at the door and Cassia realised she was shouting. It occurred to her somewhere in the back of her mind that the only thing that ever made her raise her voice was her brother.

"What were you doing in the junk room in the first place? Or the Wending Place for that matter? Excepting occasions, only the President is allowed to have guests."

"It was so I could practise my magic in private. Jasper said no one ever went to the junk room. He'd stolen the key."

Ollivan smirked. "It seems Jasper wants a new me. He's certainly chosen the right family to try to ingratiate himself with."

"Why are you such a bastard?" Cassia whispered.

His head snapped up. His eyes flashed with that famous temper. "Excuse me?"

177

"Not everything is about you, Ollivan," said Cassia, her own temper flaring. "Jasper and I are friends."

Ollivan stifled a laugh and put on a serious face. "Where did you and Jasper conduct your lessons?"

"What's that got to do with—" Cassia huffed out a breath. "In the garden."

"And did you ever show him around the house? Did he ever *ask* you to show him around?"

"Well... yes."

"Was he curious about my belongings? Storage? What Mother had kept, and where?"

It had only been a month or so ago. Cassia had been losing patience with a spell, and Jasper had suggested a distraction. "I pointed out your room. He was just making conversation," she said slowly, though doubt was creeping in.

"I had notes. Books' worth of them, on spells from the ledgers. *Evidence* that would incriminate him as much as it would me, if I decided revenge was worth it. They're gone. So are the ledgers."

I knew he was going to do something like this, Jasper had said. *I even prepared.*

No. This was Ollivan she was talking to. He was just trying to make her feel a fool. "You're lying."

He was quiet a moment as he studied her with a scowl. Cassia readied herself to fire back with as much venom as he gave, but after a while he looked away. "I suppose it doesn't matter," he said quietly.

"Why, Ollivan? Why do all of this to set Jasper up in the first place?"

"Because he got me banished," he said fiercely, eyes flashing. "He tried to ruin my stars-damned life."

Cassia smiled. She modelled it after one of his smiles; the derisive half-smirk, half-grimace that he liked to level at people he thought were stupider than him. "Tell me, *please*, how you killing someone was Jasper's fault. I haven't had a good laugh in a long time."

There was the smile; the very one. She folded her arms to maintain her composure.

"Say I laid the whole thing out for you, exactly what happened." His voice was level, but there was self-pity behind it. "Say it was his word against mine. Would you believe me?"

Jasper had asked her something similar that same night, and she had not hesitated over the answer. But still, Cassia gave Ollivan her full consideration. She had seen a different side to Jasper tonight, one that threw the sensible, gentle version she knew into question. But Ollivan had it in for him, she knew now that it was true. Cassia would probably have as much nervous energy if a Sorcerer with Ollivan's skill and a fierce vendetta had just landed back in her universe. And then there was Ollivan's claim about Jasper becoming her tutor; a watery assertion that whatever his reasons – an interest in Ollivan's belongings or an interest in the High Sorcerer's family – Jasper was using her. As if Ollivan knew more of what had occurred these past few months from another dimension than she did living it.

She studied him. He had come home about as worse for wear two dozen times in the only year they'd lived together since she was five. He wore an angry, sullen glare as he waited for her response, the same starsforsaken expression he always wore when he challenged someone to call him out on whatever awful thing he'd done or blatant lie he'd told. Yes, she had seen shades of wrong in Jasper tonight, but she saw Ollivan in full colour.

"No," she told him. "Of course I wouldn't believe you."

His head dropped, but not before Cassia saw the hurt in his eyes. The flutter of guilt came before she could convince herself it was an act. No, not an act. Ollivan always truly believed himself the one wronged.

"So Jasper has you on a string, as he once did me."

She shook her head. "It's not about Jasper. It's about you. I suppose you think Jasper's also to blame for maybe nearly dying in our pavilion because he provoked you into this most recent stupid idea of yours." She gestured to the wet jacket in which Violet was still bound. "Just tell me you know how you plan to destroy it."

"Of course I do. I've been perfecting the unravelling spell for a year. If you would just pass me my notebook, the red one – ah."

"What's *ah*?"

"I left it in the President's Sanctuary." He yawned loudly and fell back onto his bed. "All the better. I'm too tired to deal with it now. I'll take it to the Wending Place with me in the morning."

He looked exhausted. She hadn't even got to the bottom of how he ended up on fire by some workings of Jasper's – ostensibly – but she was exhausted too, and being around him only made it worse.

She turned to the door, then back, the jacket on the desk tugging at her. If Ollivan was right about how dangerous the spell was – and he would never have exaggerated how stupid he'd been – then there was nothing for it; Violet needed to be destroyed. Cassia

180

wished she didn't regret that so much. She had the melancholy urge to say goodbye but did so silently, like a prayer to the stars, so her brother couldn't mock her.

"Make sure you do," she said as she left the room. "And hope that I don't see fit to tell Grandfather that you made it in the first place."

His humourless laugh came to her as she shut the door. "Right. If the first dozen threats don't sufficiently frighten me, I'll be sure to keep yours in mind."

"… and once the burn victims are pickling happily in their ointments, I'll be heading back to the Wending Place to deal with three dozen scintillating tasks Miss Dentley has earmarked for me. I plan to escape in record time, but I fear I'll be stumbling home just before midnight. So please don't set a place for dinner."

Alana rubbed her temples as Ollivan's ten-minute soliloquy came to a close. "What a life you're leading these days. Did your grandfather mention for how long I have to hear these morning sermons?"

Ollivan put a hand to his heart in mock offence. "But you always said we should spend more time together."

"I was imagining afternoon tea once in a while. Trust you to let it come to this."

"Then I'm dismissed?"

He was turning on his heel when he heard Alana rise from the couch. "Just a moment."

A man has a way of recognising his mother's tone. This one told Ollivan that he might as well put his case down. He had lined the inside with linens; it ought not to leak onto the rug.

"Ollivan, you know that your grandfather took no pleasure in banishing you, don't you?"

He narrowed his eyes. "Let's not be so sure about that."

"Well…" She shook her head in a long-suffering manner, and Ollivan offered a smile. She returned it gratefully.

They could be like this, when all was well. By the grace of the stars, his mother was not the thug her father was. Perhaps that was *because* of her father's thuggishness. Perhaps she had been the one tasked with tempering him after her mother, Ollivan's grandmother, had died when Alana was just a child. Whatever the reason, he was hopeful Alana would make a more even-handed ruler than Jupitus one day.

She ruined that illusion as soon as it entered Ollivan's mind.

"The fact is, your grandfather's first duty is to the Heart," she went on, sobering like the man himself had stepped into the room. "Not to us, his family. I forgot that last night. But he has no choice but to treat us – to lead us – the same way he would lead any other Sorcerer." Her eyes flickered away from his. "And it's the same way I must rule when I'm High Sorcerer. You know enough of how this works to understand that."

He knew enough, because she had trained him. *If you had turned out how we hoped, if you hadn't been made a pariah, if you had been High Sorcerer, it would be expected of you too.* If she was trying to engender some understanding of the way he had been treated by implying he would treat his children and grandchildren that way too, she was going the wrong way about it. It was precisely why Ollivan despised the very idea of power and everything it stood for. He did not wish to bow to his own office, as his mother had clearly already resigned herself to doing.

"If," Ollivan said.

"What?"

"*If* you are High Sorcerer, Mother." He spread his arms and gestured to himself, then reclaimed his case from the floor. "Clearly, things do not always go according to Grandfather's design."

Again, he attempted to leave, and again, Alana stopped him.

"You should spend some time with your sister, while you can," she clipped. He had clearly struck a nerve; her tone was full of accusation. They were back to swiping at one another. "Make *some* effort to get to know her."

Ollivan could not quite account for the quiet fury that set him alight, but this one accusation – *this*, of all things – he knew he could not endure. He let the case fall from his hands once more and hit the rug with a thud, only belatedly worrying for the binding spell on its contents.

"I've failed to make an effort to know my sister? My sister who you sent away when I was seven years old? Whom I was never allowed the chance to know after you made her a pawn of the Heart because your papa told you to? Tell me, will you groom *her* for politics now that I've outlasted my usefulness in that lane, or is there a nice place for her among Grandfather's foot soldiers perhaps? The ranks are a little thinner after this morning."

Alana had drawn so tense he could see the tendons in her neck and the whites of her eyes. "You know nothing," she hissed at him, spittle flying from her lips. "*Nothing* of what it takes to wake up and coax hundreds of thousands of people through survival every day. You were lucky to have been banished. You would never have lasted in this London."

Perhaps he got his temper from her. He only wished she would unleash it as freely on her father as she did on him. He had been entirely wrong, he thought, as he swept up his case and left.

Alana Sims had all the makings of the tyrant her father was.

*

The Whisperers had pushed into the Docklands – Oracle territory – in the early hours and won a stretch of road that was easier to defend than their previous border. It had probably helped the Whisperers that the Oracles had had problems near their southwest border too; the border they shared with the Heart. A distillery had exploded in Southwark, wreaking havoc and causing death and injury on both sides of the border. Eight Sorcerers and considerably more Oracles had lost their lives.

Five of the Sorcerers killed had been militia. They had realised the danger to their own people when the distillery caught fire, said their surviving comrades, and a band of them had flocked into the Docklands to try to stop the fire. The effort was unsuccessful, and the Oracles had suffered two crushing losses, their militia and their Sight weakened by the double misfortune of an attack at one border and a horrendous accident at another.

This Ollivan pieced together by talking to some of the sixty-something injured he was helping to tend at an overrun hospital on Blue Anchor Road. Sybella had offered the Successors' help and called upon a dozen of them to fulfil their charitable requirement. Given the extra shifts Ollivan had taken on, it was basic arithmetic that he was likely to be among them.

The rest of his understanding of the events he pieced together alone. His grandfather had long wanted that distillery, and he would wager that an Oracle questioned about how the enforcers came to be there would give a different version of events. It was just a little too inconvenient for the Docklands that at the same time Whitechapel attacked, a valuable asset elsewhere was in danger, less than a week after Lord Voss and the High Sorcerer parleyed at the Wending Place.

How the distillery came to be destroyed – well, Oracles were the ones blessed with Sight, but anyone paying attention could predict them as well. When they Saw they would lose the distillery to Jupitus, they had blown it up, the victims among their own people be damned. They had shown as much care for their own countless times before, and Jupitus had shown as much cunning. Ollivan was in no doubt the explosion wasn't an accident.

"Does Sybella dislike me?" said Lev, breaking Ollivan out of his dark thoughts; thoughts of how he would ever get the better of someone who would go to lengths he dared not.

They were at the makeshift medicine counter that had been set up in the middle of the hall, Lev soaking strips of gauze in the burn salve Ollivan was making. As well as the salve, they'd been making pain tonics of rudimentary formulas, a smell-inhibiting potion – for those who couldn't stomach the smell of burning flesh – and a powder that, when brushed over a person's eyelids, caused them short-term memory loss. Lev had wondered aloud about the need for the latter – until a man was brought in screaming in shock. He had seen the burned-up husk of a dear friend's body. Now, he had unseen it.

"Nobody dislikes you, Lev," Ollivan assured him.

"Then why couldn't she assign this duty to someone less passionately committed to having a good time?" he said, transferring the ointment-soaked gauze to another bowl at arm's length. "*This* is not a good time."

He could have fooled Ollivan. Between batches of medicines, Lev had been working the room like they were at a soiree, making patients laugh and flirting with healers.

"I'm sure you can offset the difference with the three party invitations you've collected."

"It's four now," said Lev, beaming.

Ollivan tried to share in his good spirits and failed. They had been brainstorming ideas to keep him in the Witherward, and no solution was presenting itself.

"Have you thought of adding an amendment to the charter?" Virgil had said when he came to collect more gauze. He had volunteered for the least pleasant job going; cleaning and dressing burns. Ollivan sometimes wondered if Virgil was only happy when he was miserable. "Something that says you can run for a second term, to give yourself more time."

Ollivan shook his head. "It's been tried, by multiple people. The Wending Place has not taken kindly to any one of them. The last fellow fell through a hole that spontaneously generated in the floor, into the cellar that doesn't exist, and hasn't been seen since. You know that stone hand that emerges at the bottom of the main staircase every once and while and trips people? They think it's his. Besides, I'm nineteen. I'd be too old to run in the next election even if I was eligible."

"What if you found somewhere to live in another territory?" Lev said now. "Like Whitechapel! You could room with my cousin Finlay, start going by a different name, get out of your grandfather's field of influence."

"Does your cousin Finlay like you enough to risk Jupitus Fisk's wrath?"

"Everyone likes me, remember?"

"All the same, if I'm to retreat to another quarter, I'll do it in secret. The more people involved, the more heads for Jupitus to make roll."

"Like mine?"

Ollivan stopped funnelling swiftberry juice into the salve and turned to his friend. He knew all too well the things his grandfather would threaten if he thought it would give him some leverage. He had made that fact very clear to his friends before he involved them in his coup. "Are you afraid of him?"

Lev grinned. "Of course not."

Perhaps you should be. He dumped the rest of the juice into the flask too quickly; it foamed threateningly and started turning blue. "I meant it when I said I'd do everything I could to protect you and Virgil, Lev," he said. "But I'm back now. You've done your part. Maybe you should leave the rest up to me and keep your distance. I've got two years. I'll think of something."

Ollivan added a pinch of ash to his concoction to undo the foaming and swirled the flask. It was several moments before he realised Lev had stopped his work. He was leaning against the workstation, worrying at a bit of dry skin on his palm that the salve had given him.

"It's not that scheming with you isn't the peak of good fun for me, Lev," he began, but Lev was shaking his head.

"You wouldn't be in this mess in the first place if it wasn't for me," he said.

Ollivan set the flask down gently to avoid a repeat of his last mistake. Then he turned to face his friend. "What in the heaven, the earth, and all the constellations could you *possibly* mean?"

"Come on, Ollivan. I swept in and snatched your best friend away." He scrubbed at his hair, gaze drifting across the hall to where Virgil was kneeling before a soot-coated man as he cleaned the burns on his legs. "And at first it was alright. When Virgil and I were just friends and it became the three of us, instead of the two of you. But when we started wanting to spend time together alone, when we realised we weren't just friends; that's when things changed for you as well. It's because we weren't there for you that you started spending your time with Jasper Hawkes."

Ollivan tried to keep his expression neutral. He had told his friends nothing of Jasper's role in his downfall. "What do you know of Jasper Hawkes?"

"Only that whenever anyone asks him about you, Hawkes always says he tried to temper you, to straighten you out."

"And they believe him, of course."

"They don't have the full history. They didn't see the correlation as Virgil and I did. We knew you well enough to know about the duelling evenings, the stealing, those narcotic compounds you got so popular making – that's not who you are. I don't care that he comes across as boring as supper at my grandmother's. Just try and tell me it wasn't Jasper's bad influence."

Ollivan longed to tell him everything, but a wary fear stopped him. He had shouted his innocence until he was hoarse; to his grandfather, his mother, half a dozen of his grandfather's advisors. They had agreed unanimously that he was lying. They took it as further proof that the only solution was to take from him everything he cared about. The whole truth would only have made things worse, so he hadn't told it; but surely he could confess to one of his dearest friends.

189

He kept stirring the ointment and didn't turn around, but Virgil's presence across the room was like a burning hearth at his back. Each glance from the other boy carried a hint of wary suspicion, as if he were waiting for Ollivan to slip up and confirm his shattered trust. Lev might believe him if he told them the truth. But Virgil would not.

So he flashed Lev a grin and replied smoothly, "If you know me so well, Lev, I will thank you to remember that *I* have always been the bad influence."

"There's playing pranks on the border guards, and then there's whatever you got caught up in." Ollivan opened his mouth to deflect again, but Lev wouldn't be dissuaded. "I'm trying to apologise. Just have the grace to accept it so I can go back to talking to that pretty healer."

"Impossible. For a start, one does not *snatch* another's best friend away," he said to the table. "People make their own choices."

"So you are resentful about it, just not towards me."

Ollivan felt a presence behind him. Virgil had come closer. He was replenishing his supply of gauze at the next workstation and pretending not to listen. Ollivan suddenly felt a pressing urge to say what he wished to; that they could each have fallen in love with anyone of their choosing, and they had chosen each other. That they had derailed their entire dynamic as a trio.

"It was you who brought me into the group," Lev pressed. "After that winter solstice party, do you remember? I stole a bottle of port and you found me sipping from it under one of the tables."

"Of course I remember," said Ollivan.

"You were the one who held the three of us together, and then you weren't."

It was so close to what Ollivan had been thinking that he wondered if Lev hadn't inherited some of his mother's magic after all. Still, he shook his head, his eyes firmly on the task in front of him. "We can't compare friends and lovers," he said. "You and Virgil had every right to want to spend time together without me."

"Just because you understand, it doesn't mean you enjoyed it."

Ollivan was spared from replying by a healer, who slumped heavily against their workstation and let out a sigh.

No, not a healer. The man was dressed in soot-covered street clothes, his cap pulled low on his brow. And it had not been a sigh, but a moan of pain.

"I'll get him to a bed, you fetch a healer," said Lev, but when he approached, the man shrank away from him.

"Please," he gasped. "Help me."

It was then that he looked up, glancing furtively around before his eyes met theirs, and Ollivan understood the problem. He had taken the pallid quality of the man's skin as a mark of his injuries, but his entire people were naturally so bloodless, with skin that perpetually appeared to be coated in a sheen of sweat. But his most damning characteristic was his eyes, which had no iris and no pupil, but were a pure milky white through and through.

He was an Oracle, here in a Sorcerer hospital, and gravely injured. One side of his shirt had grafted onto his burn wounds all along the arm and ribs. The Docklands were treating their wounded, but they didn't have the capability, nor the care, to tend to their people in the same manner as the Heart.

Ollivan swept closer, and stood between the man and the hospital floor to shield him from view, Lev blocking him from the other angle. He glanced about the room. The Oracle wouldn't be

"Oh, stars." He backed towards the wall and leaned around the edge of the curtain. "No chance you're ready to usher our friend out already?"

Lev and Virgil were working with impressive speed and coordination, Virgil applying salve and Lev following behind with the bandages. They had dosed the Oracle with enough painkillers that his white eyes were closed and he made only the faintest murmurs of disorientated protest.

"We've got trouble?" said Lev without looking up.

"I'll head her off," Ollivan replied, "but hurry."

Virgil frowned. "Ollivan."

"I'll handle it."

The healer was upon him. "Where's the gauze?" she said. The distraction spell kept her curiosity away from the curtain.

"Used it all," said Ollivan, turning her back towards the room. In doing so, he lost sight of the opposite corner of the cubicle. His first indication of the mistake was the shriek of the metal rings on the curtain rail.

"What is this?" said a second healer, a man.

Perhaps Ollivan should make himself scarce. Lev and Virgil would get a stern dressing down at best, an audience with the High Sorcerer if they deemed the wasting of Heart resources on Oracles to be an especially grave crime. No one would be so forgiving of Ollivan. It would be best if he took Virgil's advice.

Perhaps that's what I should do, he thought as he placed himself between the healers and his friends.

"Just another walk-in," said Ollivan, trying to sound casual. "We have it under control."

"You were informed of procedure," said the man. "New patients need to be signed in so the enforcers have a list of all the injured. He can't be compensated by the High Sorcerer if no one knows who he is."

"Thank you kindly! His name is Pendergast. P-E-N-D-E-R-G-A-S-T. I believe the sign-in sheet is back over there." Ollivan put a hand on the man's arm and pushed him gently in the direction of the door, and the sign-in sheet.

"Wait a minute."

It was the first healer. Once the second had pulled back the curtain, Ollivan's glamour had fallen away. Virgil was trying to block her line of sight, but the way she craned around him, and the alarm mounting across her face, said that she had seen his eyes flutter open for just a moment. "Is this man a Sorcerer?"

"What a preposterous question," protested Ollivan. "This is the Heart, is it not?"

The second healer tugged free of Ollivan's grip on his arm. "I'm fetching the enforcers."

"Sir!" Lev extricated himself from the business of wrapping the man in bandages and scrambled into the healer's path. He was much shorter than the other man, who was forced to step back to meet his eyes. "We're almost done, then we'll drop him at the guard point and the acolytes can see to him. It will take us barely ten minutes. We can make more ointment."

"We can make a *better* ointment, in fact," added Ollivan, "if only you'd let us. Opal root powder is a far superior binding agent when swiftberry is involved, which I *tried* to tell your splendid colleague here."

Drawing helpless rage out of others was one of Ollivan's finer skills, and without using a lick of magic the healers were frozen to the spot as they absorbed the slight. As they did, Ollivan threw up a second ward, this time around them all.

But the healer in front of him clocked the spell. His hand flexed like he was readying to stun him. In the man's defence, it was bad magical etiquette, and had been an escalation on Ollivan's part; he couldn't fault him for responding. He *could* fault a healer for refusing to heal, however, and everything he might do to avoid it, including stunning him.

"Listen," Ollivan said. "We're only doing what you cannot find the decency to do yourself. I don't want any trouble, but if you loose that spell on me, I'll do the same."

"He won't," said Lev, throwing a glare at Ollivan. Virgil continued to bandage the burned man at top speed.

"No, Lev, I will."

"Venda, fetch Sibley," clipped to healer to his colleague.

Venda did not tempt a confrontation; she transported on the spot, landing across the long ward next to Sibley, the enforcer in charge. Ollivan knew of Sibley, and knew that he wasn't furnished with the ability to transport; their only saving grace. They had thirty seconds at most.

"Virgil—"

"I can't go any quicker."

The healer spoke between clenched teeth. "I know who you are. The High Sorcerer will thank me for reporting this to him."

"And I'll thank you not to, so it seems you're at an impasse." Ollivan let a spell dance at his fingers. "If you know who I am, you know what they say I've done. Do you really want to get in my way?"

196

"Ollivan," hissed Lev in warning. He swung to face Virgil. "Are you going to let him fight this fellow?"

"That's his area of expertise, isn't it?"

"Virgil's busy, Lev. Let him be," said Ollivan without taking his eyes off the healer, but in his peripheral vision he saw Virgil help the patient to his feet. Lev dove to help them. They were almost clear. He just needed one final flourish to ensure this didn't spell the end of him.

But Sibley was upon them, Venda in tow. He was a heavy, square fellow with a nasty snarl that he levelled at Ollivan. "Sims. In trouble already."

"Oh, I wouldn't worry about it, Sibley, lad. I don't intend for anyone to find out about this." He glanced over his shoulder. Lev and Virgil had their patient propped between them and were gauging the distance to the side door halfway along the hall. It was time. "Go now," he told his friends, and then he transported.

He landed across the ward, back at the medicine counter. His friends were watching him wide-eyed, abandonment on their faces, and Sibley and the healers closed in on them. Two years ago, they would not have second-guessed him in such a bind, but Ollivan pushed the hurt down, grabbed two rough handfuls of what he was there for, and transported back into the fray.

Sibley, taken by surprise at his sudden reappearance, stepped back – to the perfect distance for Ollivan to dust him with the forgetting powder. He swept his arm in a broad arc, letting the blue dust gust into their faces, then tossed the second handful at them for good measure. Venda sneezed. The nearest patient glanced their way dully, but Ollivan's glamour held, and they found nothing of interest in the scene. If they remembered anything later, they wouldn't be able to describe it. All anyone would know was that Ollivan had been with Lev and Virgil as they bundled an unidentified man out of the hospital; suspicious enough for Jupitus to form opinions if he heard of it, but not enough evidence to send him back to the Otherworld.

It wasn't far to the border. They let Virgil approach the guard point with hands raised to explain the situation before they delivered the Oracle to the acolytes. Tensions were high, and the Oracles knew – even if the Sorcerer citizens did not – what had happened that morning at the distillery.

The acolytes took him without a thank you or a backward glance, and then the three of them walked in silence back towards the Wending Place. They were almost there when Lev stopped suddenly.

"Where – I thought that we – were we not just…" His mouth opened stupidly, and he looked about in confusion. A faint dusting of blue powder peppered his black hair.

Ollivan winced. "Stars. Sorry, Lev." He looked up at Virgil warily. "I didn't get you too, did I?"

Wordlessly, Virgil dusted the forgetting powder out of Lev's hair, and ran a handkerchief over his face for good measure.

"You, ah, missed a bit just—" Ollivan cut off as Virgil turned on him, his glower levelled like a weapon. A silence stretched between them until Ollivan was forced to break it. "What was I to do? Turn the man away? Trust me, Virgil, I'm not actively clamouring for ways to ruin my life. I would have been glad to—"

"You were right." Virgil folded his handkerchief neatly and put it back in his pocket. Behind him, Lev spun on the spot like he was lost. "There was nothing to be done. You didn't turn him away to save yourself. It was the right thing."

Ollivan chanced a grin. "Noble, one might say."

"Don't push it."

"Right." He gestured to Lev, who had ceased spinning but was frowning at the ground like he was trying to remember where he had lost something. "I'm sorry about…"

Virgil took Lev by the arms and lowered his face so they were eye to eye. "We were at the hospital, but you caught a little forgetting powder, so we left. You haven't missed much, Mallory. You'll be alright." He brushed Lev's floppy hair back from his face tenderly, and Lev calmed.

"Oh," he said, breaking into a grin. "Champion."

Virgil turned to look at Ollivan, and though he did not smile, his eyes softened, and Ollivan's heart leapt. "About what Lev was saying earlier. I'm sorry too."

Ollivan still wanted to protest. He knew who he blamed for ruining his life; he knew it with incessant keenness of a splinter throbbing in his thumb. He had held it in his blackened heart for a year, as if it was something precious. He would not have his friends thinking differently. But it soothed something older to hear them acknowledge the pain that had driven him away from them. Pain that wasn't truly anyone's fault.

"What was I saying earlier?" said Lev, still frowning.

Ollivan put a hand on his shoulder and turned him towards the Wending Place. "It doesn't matter," he said, his eyes meeting Virgil's. "It's in the past."

16

The evening was overcast, the dark gathering as Cassia looked up at the Sidus, the symbol of the faith, where it hung high above the temple door. It was a copper sun with flames licking around its edges, melded with a crescent moon. But cloud cover or burning sun, the Sidus would not shine in the light. No Sidus ever did, for the copper was a milky green; tarnished. All such symbols were laid out under the night sky to patina before being placed above temple doorways, as a way of blessing them.

If Cassia lay under the night sky for long enough, would it do the same as entering the temple and asking the astrologer for guidance? Because she liked stargazing. She did not like temples, or prophecy, or the superstitions of religion.

Her mother had asked her on one visit home if she went to the temple in Camden.

"I believe the only way of truly knowing the future is getting there," she had responded.

Alana had tutted. "Astrology is not about knowing the future, Cassia," she had said in the tone of one long accustomed to defending an inclination. Her husband had had no faith, nor did Jupitus. The only one of them she had gotten through to even a little was Ollivan. "Nor is it truly about making the best decisions in the now. We trust in the universe because it *made* us. It *is* us. When we honour the stars, we honour ourselves. And if they see fit to grant us guidance, it's because they acknowledge our devotion. That's gift enough in itself."

"Whatever the guidance?"

"Of course."

Cassia had nothing to say to that, but she suspected astrology was for those who feared being responsible for their own choices.

What had changed, that she stood before her mother's temple, weighing the decision to go in? Lev's comment about the power of the universe over her initiation would never have popped into her mind again if she'd passed. But things had been going from bad to worse since that night, and though she stubbornly held Ollivan in her mind as the architect of her misfortune, in secret, she also had to blame herself. She had failed to recognise that Violet was dangerous because she was lonely. She had let Jasper into her life and trusted him for the same reason. And she was growing sick of wondering where she was going wrong with her magic, but she knew that was down to her too.

Had she become like her mother, afraid of responsibility? Cassia coveted the freedom to make her own choices. No fear loomed larger in her mind than the way her future might be pulled this way and that by her grandfather's wishes and needs. Who would win in a battle of wills over her fate – Jupitus or the stars? Perhaps that was why she was here. To entertain the hope that it rested with the stars, she would need to trust in them.

"Your fortune, my sweet?"

Cassia looked over her shoulder, and jumped to find the Oracle woman so close.

The Oracles alone kept a different faith – what need had they of the stars when they Saw their own fates? – and their gods cautioned them against sharing the knowledge their Sight gave them with non-Oracles. But it was not a well-kept rule, particularly when there was money to be made.

The woman was brandishing a hand in the hopes Cassia would drop a coin into it. When the Oracle passed the guard point to leave the Heart, she would be taxed half of her takings. Reading fortunes in the Heart was a desperate solution to make very little coin, and any Oracle so poor was likely to be untrained in their magic to begin with. Whatever fortune she claimed to See would probably be a lie.

But Cassia took pity and paid the woman generously, then took her offered hand and let the woman grasp it in both of hers. Proximity allowed an Oracle to See the life of someone more clearly; touch was even more effective.

"Let me look," the woman muttered, closing her eyes. "Ah. I See you smiling, but I also See you in pain."

"Of course." Cassia sighed. She hadn't known she was holding out hope for a real glimpse of her future until the woman started uttering platitudes. "Thank you for your time."

She tugged her hand free, and was about to turn away when the woman snatched it back. Her eyes flew open. They rolled in their sockets as the Oracle squeezed her fingers painfully.

"Why is there such darkness?" she said in one breath.

"Pardon me?" Cassia's hand was trapped in the vice of the woman's grip.

"You stand before a mirror in candlelight. You're brushing your hair. Beautiful, black hair."

This was a real vision, she realised, but that didn't make it a meaningful one. Nor was anything the woman might say destined to happen. The future could change. Cassia continued to tug on the woman's grip, but she would not let her go.

"You wield immense power." The woman let out a distressed cry. Cassia stopped struggling. "Why do you use it to do such harm?"

Harm? Power? Cassia shook her head. "You're mistaken."

The Oracle pulled her closer, until their faces almost touched and her breath gusted on Cassia's cheeks. "You must confront yourself, girl, or you damn us all."

The Oracle pulled away suddenly, blinking as she came back to herself.

"Confront myself how?" Cassia said. "What is any of that supposed to mean?"

She stepped forward and the woman jerked back, fear on her face. Her hands hovered before her mouth, fingers trembling.

"Pray, my girl," she whispered, backing away. "Pray to whoever will listen."

Cassia huffed in irritation as the woman turned and scurried away. If there was truly a version of the future in which she caused terrible harm – one she was on a collision course with at this particular moment in time – she was no wiser as to how to stop it. *Confront herself.* Confront herself about what?

She didn't know, but since she was out this evening looking for answers, she would take a hint when it was handed to her. She started up the steps of the temple. Perhaps she could ask the astrologer to divine what the Oracle had meant about damning them all.

As she reached the door, a hand grasped her arm. She turned, expecting to find the woman back with another vision, but she was wrong.

"Jasper," Cassia breathed. "You're alright."

"Let's talk," he said tersely. He pulled her the rest of the way into the temple and to one side of the empty square hall, under the shadow of the arches that encircled the space. Their footsteps echoed off the stone as they swept over the depiction of the constellations, characteristically inlaid in gold into the polished floor. Only a couple of people stood in prayer and contemplation in the hall, while a couple more waited to speak to the astrologer in session. Like many larger temples, one wall of this one opened into an alcove-like observatory, where the astrologer went about their work upon an ornate brass platform. Tradition dictated that they could not speak or be spoken to when upon the platform, but they would come down periodically to tend to the faithful.

When they stopped, Cassia wrenched her arm away from Jasper and gave him a sour glare. "I'm quite tired of being grabbed at. The next person to try it is going to—"

"Have their magic drained by a possessed doll?" Jasper's jaw was tight.

"Your... your magic is gone?" Cassia gasped.

For an endless moment, he only glared at her. Then he sighed and let his gaze move away.

"No. But it *was*, for a few hours. That's a powerful artefact you're using on people, and it sounds like you don't even know the extent of its effects. Cassia, what in the heavens were you thinking?"

His words, though low, echoed around the hall, and more than one devotee turned to scowl at them. Cassia moved them behind a pillar and out of sight.

"It's not my enchantment."

Jasper laughed humourlessly. "I know that." Then he added, almost to himself, "You couldn't enchant a duck to quack."

Something inside her tightened, then went very still. She watched him react to her shame and hurt as if from somewhere above herself, and wondered distantly why he was looking at her like that; like she was the one who ought to thaw this cold, cold silence.

Finally, Jasper groaned and shook his head. "Look, I suppose it's as much my failing as your own. I am supposed to be tutoring you after all. But you understand why you can't keep the thing, don't you? Where is it?"

"Where—" Cassia was a step behind, still unpicking Jasper's words and realising they didn't contain an apology. But belatedly, she understood that he was asking for the doll. "You don't understand. I didn't *mean* for her to do that to you. She's not under my control."

"All the more reason for you to give it – *her* – to me. Cassia," he said, his voice softening. He stepped towards her, raising his hands like he would touch her, and Cassia stepped back, the memory of the previous night turning Jasper's gesture sharp and hostile. It pulled the overwrought thing inside her back into alignment, and she met his bemused gaze with her sure one.

"You misunderstand me," she said firmly. "The enchantment on Violet can't be turned off and on by a person. She's not controllable that way. And she's dangerous."

"Let me be the judge of if she's controllable," Jasper said, and Cassia clenched her jaw. "I've seen magic like this before. I can deal with it."

Ollivan had said he and Jasper had found the Guysman spell together. He had also implied Jasper had since expunged all record of it. Cassia's curiosity got the better of her.

"What happened between you and my brother?"

Jasper startled at the sudden turn in the conversation, and his eyes narrowed.

"You know what happened. He murdered someone. I don't keep company with people like that." His words grew slower as he spoke, like he was piecing together the implication of her asking. "Why? What did he say to you?"

Could Cassia repeat what Ollivan had said to her? More pressingly, could she *resist* repeating it, and hearing what Jasper had to say? She injected some lightness into her tone and shrugged dismissively.

"You must know what he can be like with his back to the wall. He said what happened was *your* doing."

Jasper grinned. "He tried to claim the same at the time."

"He did?" Cassia hadn't known that. The details of Ollivan's crime and banishment had been kept between as few people as possible, and Cassia hadn't asked. She didn't need persuading that her hot-headed brother had killed someone in a fight.

"Thankfully the High Sorcerer knew better than to put any stock in his story." Jasper's expression grew wry. "No doubt *you'll* be his scapegoat for this business with the doll."

Her brain scrambled to deny it, but one look at Jasper's smirk told her there was no use. Of course he knew Ollivan was behind the Guysman. And perhaps it was good that he did. Ollivan *would* try to put the blame on her if it would save him. Having

Jasper in her corner – as a contingency plan – couldn't hurt.

"It doesn't have to come to that," he said, as if he'd read her mind. "Listen, Cassia, if I'm not mistaken, you took that doll from among my things at the Wending Place, did you not?"

"Well I—"

"So regardless of what you think I should or shouldn't do with it, it belongs to me. And if you don't give it back, I'm going to be forced to tell your family you're dabbling in magic beyond your capabilities. I will have to tell them what you did to me, so that they understand just how in over your head you've become." His expression softened. "I just don't want to see you get hurt, Cassia. You know that, don't you?"

Cassia wasn't sure what she knew. She *had* gotten in over her head, and if Ollivan hadn't already taken Violet off her hands, she would be glad of someone assuming responsibility for her. And she would never believe she ought to stay away from Jasper just because her brother said so. Perhaps he did care for her, and this was all just a perverse way of showing it.

It didn't make it *not* blackmail.

But Jasper didn't have the full picture. She could be done with this unpleasantness while doing everything he asked and risking nothing. Ollivan was unravelling the Guysman; may have done so already. If Jasper wanted Violet back, he could have her.

"Alright," she said, adding a sigh to her voice for effect. "I'll get the doll and bring her to you tonight."

Jasper released a breath and smiled. "Thank you," he said. "Let's meet in an hour."

"In an *hour*?"

He cocked his head to one side. "That's not a problem, is it? If the thing is truly as dangerous as you say, the sooner it's with me, the better."

Cassia would simply have to hope Ollivan had dealt with the enchantment. She could get to the Wending Place, retrieve Violet, and get to Jasper's in an hour, as long as her brother didn't try to get in her way. He needn't know the doll was for Jasper.

"In an hour, then," said Cassia, and having lost her desire to pray, she swept from the temple out into the darkening night.

17

Ollivan had thought Sybella simply wanted nothing to do with him. It transpired that day that she wanted him dead.

Since the previous evening, she had devised a further dozen tasks that fell within his presidential remit. Letters announcing his appointment and intentions for his term to the Society's friends. Proposals and requests from the members, which he learned he could not simply refuse, but must give a reason for each, no matter the answer. There were obscure rules he had not read in the charter and was half-convinced she was making up. If, in one of the endless contests of magical skill between members, no victor could be firmly decided, the President was to declare a winner. If any enchantment was cast upon the walls, doors, or other fixtures of the house itself, the President must rule if the spell improved upon or damaged the room before it could be unravelled.

Avoiding it all was exhausting. Ollivan wished he could just go home, but he had placed the Guysman in the President's Sanctuary before he was summoned to the hospital, and there it still sat, next to the notebook containing the spell he had devised to undo it. And Sybella was watching the Sanctuary. He wasn't sure how, and had to admire whatever enchantment alerted her whenever he transported inside. All he knew was that whenever he found his way there, she appeared, rapping on the door with a stack of papers before he could scoop up the Guysman and the notebook and disappear again. To Ollivan's overwhelming chagrin, he found it no easier to refuse her now than he ever had before. He feared it was the sight of her brown eyes gathering tears when he had accused her of playing him for a fool, but he couldn't bring himself to shrug apologetically and transport away, as he would if she were anyone else.

But he had a way to lose her.

If any proof was needed that the Society of Gifted Young Sorcerers was an institute of mindless revelry, and not one of learning and magic, it was that the oldest event in its calendar was the spring scavenger hunt. For the truly irresistible prize of being called 'Your Majesty' by the whole Society until the summer solstice, Successors competed to be the first to find an ancient tin crown hidden by the Wending Place itself. Historically, more members went missing or were grievously injured during the scavenger hunt than on any other night of the year. In short, it was a riotously good time.

But Ollivan would be missing it. He began the game with a speech he improvised, having resisted Sybella's four reminders to write one; he would not waste time and energy on people who did not mind what he said so long as he implied everything they did was important; and who, in any case, were already too drunk to pay attention.

Then he fed the tin crown into the fire in the common room to activate the spell. He watched in awe with the rest of them as the mirror above the fire misted over, and the first clue scrawled itself onto the glass. Another fifteen or so clues, and the victor would find the crown where the Wending Place had hidden it.

With any luck, no one would fall three storeys through a hole that had once been a staircase, or get magically trapped in a suit of armour before the game was up.

When the Successors had clattered from the room, Sybella among them, Ollivan returned despondently to the Sanctuary. But it was his one chance to deal with the Guysman while Sybella was risking herself with the other members in the name of good fun.

In the Sanctuary, he sank gratefully into the oversized chair behind his desk, his spine loosening as he did so. Of everything he had unwittingly taken on, he truly had not minded helping at the hospital, but stars; just the thought of two more members' charitable hours, including his own, on top of what was transpiring to be a less escapable responsibility than he had hoped the presidency would be, was enough to wear him to his core.

He rubbed his face with both hands, trying to force some liveliness back into himself, and finally pulled the inanimate bundle comprised of his jacket and past transgressions towards him. It smelled of smoke and stale water.

The place in his notebook was bookmarked and waiting. He had been fine-tuning the spell for months, alongside his plans for the election, in case the latter worked. Yesterday he had written the final version out on hazel wood paper and tucked it inside. He took the spell in hand before unfolding the jacket and breaking the binding spell he'd placed on it. The doll had knocked Jasper unconscious, which had not been among the accidental outcomes he'd been fearing. It left him highly aware that there was no telling what else the artefact was capable of. He would take a moment to be grateful it hadn't created some kind of cataclysmic magical event, and then he would treat it like it might at any moment.

When he fully unwrapped the jacket, however, the results were unspectacular. The doll lay there, face down, her hair a damp, knotted clump. She had had ringlets, he believed, before he had thrown a boggy garment over her and left her in it for a day.

He hesitated, at first for just a flash, the way an animal freezes when it sights a predator; just long enough for the doll to spring at him if it was going to. Yet when it didn't, he found himself hesitating still.

So his Guysman had not worked as expected. But what had really happened to Jasper when he was attacked? If he hadn't been in mortal enmity with the other boy, he would have loved to ask him. It pained him that he would never know. Unless…

He had reached a hand towards the doll before snatching it back as he suffered a flicker of doubt. This was his vice; his *true* vice. Not chaos, or rebellion, or a taste for the edge of the knife. Ollivan's vice was discovery. Magic. Wanting to know it fully, intimately. Everything it could do, the wondrous and the ugly. If he unravelled this spell, could he recreate it? At another time, under controlled circumstances? Impossible. The spell was wrong, it didn't work, and he couldn't truly know why, because emotion led to unpredictable results.

He could perform a revealing spell. It was simple, tempting magic, but cautioned against in most circumstances. This particular circumstance was a textbook example of when *not* to invoke the simple intention of a revealing: *show me what you can do*. Such a warning ringing in his head would not normally dissuade him, but since he was likely to pass out, there wasn't much point.

So he mournfully placed a hand over the doll, held the paper aloft, and burned.

When it was done, he propped the doll upright, wiped the watery residue off his fingers with a handkerchief and allowed himself a deep and nourishing relief. By some magic he had yet to learn, all his other problems shrank. He held them in his mind and turned them this way and that, and couldn't fathom how he had ever thought them so insurmountable. He had two whole years to find another way to stay his banishment. And when he did, he would no longer be President. He would never have to mediate another grievance, or approve another proposal. He may never even have to see Sybella again, and the problem of his weak and aching heart – the problem he had carried to the Otherworld and back again – could begin to be dealt with.

It called for a drink. He left the doll on his desk, turned off the lamp and ventured out into the hall, his breath catching in his chest when he found he was not where he'd expected. The corridor he had emerged into was a dark and draughty passage he believed led to the library.

The scavenger hunt. He had forgotten. As the Successors navigated the house in search of clues, the Wending Place was laying a maze for them. The corridor was deserted, the lamps all doused. The sounds of revelry seemed very distant.

He had an hour until his curfew; enough time to join in the hunt, if not enough to win it. But with the unravelling of the Guysman, he found himself so content that he could not imagine wanting anything more than to bask. He followed his elongated shadow into the first-floor common room, where a single light above the bar called him to come closer; to pour a glass of the expensive snake-venom whiskey that had helped him win the election and raise it. How long had it been since a moment had delivered everything he wanted of it; solitude, satisfaction, relief? It was all the sweeter for how long he had waited, and how deeply he ached from the longest of days.

And then a sound ruined everything.

It was a series of thuds; organic, irregular, and ending abruptly. The glass was still a breath from his lips, and it paused there as he listened. The Wending Place made noises sometimes as it went about its mysterious business, and this night its business was especially enigmatic. But the noise had come from the direction of the Sanctuary, and the feeling that it was something he needed to attend to was instinctive.

Still holding his drink, Ollivan went back down the hall, listening all the while. He had pulled the door of the Sanctuary closed as he left, hadn't he? That it was open could only mean one thing.

"Miss Dentley?" he called into the shadows of the Sanctuary.

All the lights were out, as he had left them. He stood in the doorway and swept his gaze over the room. The Wending Place playing a trick on him, surely. Nothing was out of place, except—

A dark shadow lay near one of the couches. Ollivan reached for the lamp on Sybella's desk, and felt his heart fall out through his feet when he turned it on.

She was unmoving, a crumpled heap on the office floor, her brown curls in disarray about her face.

He didn't know if the glass fell from his fingers or if he tossed it aside, but it shattered on the floor at the same moment Ollivan slid to his knees by her head.

"Ellie," he barked at her. He took her head in both hands and held it firmly, but she made no response. "*Sybella!*"

He gripped her by the shoulders and shook her more roughly than he intended, which prompted him to sweep a gaze over her for injury. He found none, but still she didn't wake. Her skin was cool and pale. She couldn't be – she wasn't—

Her mouth opened, just a little, and she drew in a desperate breath.

"*Ellie,*" he breathed. How had he thought what he was feeling in the common room was relief? *This* was relief. He moved his hands to her face again, but resisted the absurd desire to force her eyes open; to see them, and see life, and make her come awake at once. "Wake up."

Sybella's eyelids fluttered, and she moaned softly – like she was in pain? As she struggled to come round, Ollivan's gaze skittered around the office for whatever had harmed her. There were no fallen objects, no misplaced furniture, no damage to the floor, the walls, the door. Everything was as he had left it five minutes before. Everything except—

"Earth and stars."

His coat lay across his desk, the notebook beside it.

And the doll gone.

"Ollivan."

Sybella opened unfocused eyes into his. There was some colour in her cheeks now. She was alright. She had only been knocked out by the same spell that had injured Jasper.

A spell of Ollivan's making.

He scooped an arm around her neck and helped her sit. "Are you alright? Are you hurt? Can you breathe? Are you faint?"

"I'm alright," she said blearily, before correcting herself. "Faint. Yes."

There was a pitcher of water on a console behind his desk. He couldn't reach it from here. "Can you stand?"

Sybella nodded her acquiescence and unprotestingly put her arms around his neck so he could lift her to her feet. She swayed, too weak to support herself, and he gripped her tighter and guided her to one of the chairs in the centre of the room. That she let him, without a flinch or a protest, was testament to how unwell she still felt.

He fetched some water – spelling it to icy cold as he poured – knelt before her, and folded both of her shaking hands around the glass to be sure she could hold it. All the while, the persisting danger assaulted his thoughts – the Guysman was still intact, and it was gone – but he would tackle one problem at a time. The most pressing was that Sybella was hurt.

"Sybella," he said, not softly. He needed her attention. "What happened? Where's the doll?"

"Doll," she muttered thickly, and took a drink. The cold water appeared to revitalise her, her eyes gaining focus as she drew several long gulps. When she lowered the glass, they had taken on an alarm and an urgency that he found perfectly fitting. "It was standing on the desk."

Standing. "Did it move? Did it speak?"

Sybella searched the desk, then his face, like she couldn't believe Ollivan hadn't removed it while she was unconscious. It hadn't moved, then. Not in front of her, at least.

"What did it do to you? Did it—" He stopped himself, all his earlier questions, desires, and dreadful fears coming back to him. He had got exactly what he wanted; a second victim of his creation he could use to understand the Guysman. But not like this.

"Ellie. I mean, Miss Dentley." She looked at him strangely, like the awful formality between them had been his idea. "How do you feel?"

Sybella's eyes unfocused. "Strange. Like there was something... wait." Her expression wiped clean in shock, and she gasped. "Ollivan. My magic. I can't reach my magic."

It was as if she had tipped the ice-cold glass over his head. He had designed the Guysman to absorb magic, but not like this. Not from a person. Had the same thing happened to Jasper? He had got up and walked away, they presumed, but had his magic come to him when he called it? Had the Guysman broken something in him?

Magic could be lost. The physical power or Wraiths and Changelings could suffer from injury. The psychokinetic Psi had been known to lose fine control of their skills if the markings on their brows – those that glowed silver when they used their power – were scarred or damaged. A head injury could silence the mind of the Whisperer forever. He had never heard of such a thing happening to a Sorcerer.

"What did that thing do to me?" Sybella said, her voice trembling.

"I don't know yet," Ollivan replied, and the words killed him.

Sybella made a sound like a sob. He could tell that she was mining for her power like it was drowning down there without her, despair and grief wrought across her features. Tears filled her eyes.

"It's alright," he said, squeezing her hand and praying to the stars it wasn't a lie. "You're still recovering, perhaps your magic will—"

"Ollivan," she cried again.

And Ollivan was helpless. He stood abruptly and turned away, for he couldn't think clearly in the face of her anguish. He knew panic might come, but not yet. Not until he had considered all the solutions. Now that he was reassured that Sybella was at least physically unharmed, he had come back to himself; he was once again the person who would not believe all was lost until he had proven it to himself.

And Ollivan had a solution.

A fool's hope, perhaps, and a dangerous one. They could wait. It was the scientific thing to do. If the Guysman drew a person's magic from them, against their will, there was no reason to believe it couldn't keep doing so after they lost consciousness. But the spell appeared to have stopped of its own accord both times. There had to be some type of disruption, some end to what it could draw from. It made sense that a recovery period existed. Perhaps they should wait and see.

Perhaps that's what I should do, his inner voice said wryly as he turned back to Sybella. Perhaps, but she was panicking, as he would if he called on his magic and nothing responded. He couldn't let her wait – and for how long? An hour? A day? – and suffer, when the potential solution had sprung straight to mind.

"Miss Dentley, I need you to do something very difficult."

Sybella halted her tears, perhaps sensing from his tone that he had a solution.

"I need you to trust me."

He knelt before her again, and took a moment, then two, to collect the best words. "I don't believe your magic is gone. We're Sorcerers. Conduits for raw power, nothing else. We have no organ or method of channelling power that can be lost or damaged. So it doesn't make sense to me that any spell could entirely turn our connection to magic off. But the connection might need to be woken up. And I think I can wake yours."

Sybella shook her head. "How?"

"I can channel my own magic into you. A spark, for your flame." She gave an involuntary laugh, that stymied swiftly when she saw he was serious. Ollivan went on, so as to avoid any questions. "I know it sounds unorthodox. I know it's not the way magic is supposed to work. But I'm not talking about performing magic *on* you, as in all those cautionary tales they taught us as children. I'm not going to try to enchant your mind or change anything about your body. I'm going to *give* you the magic, and I'm hoping your own will respond."

Sybella shook her head throughout his whole explanation. "Ollivan, I know you're brilliant. It's the thing I hate the most about you." She said the last softly, and it didn't sound like hate at all. "But it's not possible. Sorcerers would be combining their magic all the time if it were."

"Not if someone judged the cost of that knowledge to be too great."

She cocked her head to one side as she tried to puzzle out his response. Ollivan averted his eyes. They both knew if she pressed hard enough he would crumble. He could only hope she knew how cruel it would be to play on his sympathies that way.

"Just because you read a bit of bizarre theory in some little-known journal of some medieval eccentric, it doesn't make it practical magic," she said. Ollivan almost made a quip about how uncannily spot-on her assumption was, but she dropped her voice, fear creeping in as she added, "I don't want to join that list of cautionary tales."

"Do you want to be without magic?" He met her eyes, and hoped she saw in his the boy she had once trusted never to hurt her. The room was dim, but the lamplight still caught her tear-limned eyes and lit them on fire. They were brown and gold and green and orange. Ollivan could have forgotten the Guysman, her missing magic, the time ticking towards his curfew – towards risking everything, yet again – for this, he could forget that it existed. His hands rested either side of her, on the arms of the chair, and he gripped them hard to stop from reaching for her. When she sighed, he almost gave in.

Her voice was a whisper. "What do I have to do?"

He smiled. He hoped it was reassuring.

"Relax," he said. "The sensation will be foreign – uncomfortable, even – but don't let it alarm you. And don't fight it."

Sybella nodded tensely and squeezed her eyes closed. Ollivan took a moment to quiet his thoughts and banish his uncertainty. This was not like transporting, but all magic, he found, responded readily to courage. It would respond to Sybella's too.

He directed his power into the fingers that gripped her shoulder, and without hesitation, sent the smallest spark of it into her skin.

He knew it had worked before Sybella reacted. He could feel another force pull on his like a magnet, and shut his magic off abruptly. Sybella gasped, her eyes flying open. The water pitcher behind him shattered, but Ollivan paid it no notice. Sybella jerked out of his grip; a reaction Ollivan knew to be reflexive and not personal.

"Earth and stars," she breathed. She trembled like she had been dunked in icy water. She probably felt a lot like she had.

"Are you alright?"

She studied her shaking fingers, breathing hard. "I think so."

Ollivan put some distance between them, wordlessly moving the water glass out of her reach as he did so. She would not regain the ability to swallow for another minute or so. She would also be seeing spots and experiencing pins and needles in her limbs. "You'll feel like yourself very shortly, I promise. It's just shock."

"It... hurt, I think, and yet it wasn't *bad*. It felt like – like..."

"Power."

"Yes." Her eyes sparkled with it like she'd had too much champagne. Her formerly drained complexion was flushed. "You must teach me how—"

"No."

He should have been more afraid of this, but he had been so concerned with whether he could get her to trust him, he had barely considered whether he could trust *her*. He had tried to hint that the knowledge came with a cost. Of course it wasn't enough once she'd experienced it for herself.

She was looking at him like he'd insulted her, and Ollivan sighed and rubbed a hand over his face. "It is not commonly used magic because it will drive one mad. I believe it's because magic is unique to the one who summons it. My magic is not meant for another. I understand the appeal of the feeling, believe me I do, but you mustn't try to use it again." He waved an arm at the shattered pitcher on the console. "You did that without even calling your magic, and with only the smallest jolt of mine. It's dangerously volatile."

Sybella's eyes lingered on the shards of the pitcher, deep in thought. "How do you know so much about this?" she said eventually.

"Practice," he said darkly, and swiftly changed the subject. "What did the doll do to you, Miss Dentley?"

Her face shuttered, perhaps out of fear as she recalled the doll standing on the desk. "She pulled on my magic," she said, one hand unconsciously clutching just below her ribs. "I didn't call on it, but it rose anyway, and then it was escaping."

"Where?"

"Everywhere. Straight through my skin." She swallowed heavily, lip trembling, and Ollivan slid the water back towards her. "It was... it was as if she was extracting my *soul*, or my life force. Some essential part of me that couldn't simply be plucked free. I was frozen still. If I hadn't been, I'd have been pulled towards her along with it."

"And you passed out?"

"I was certain it was death," she said softly. "All my energy, all my strength. I thought that I would never... that it was over." She took a breath as if to continue, a flash of vulnerability crossing her face. Then her eyes darted away from him and she fell quiet.

Ollivan stood by the window, frowning out into the night. Rain had started to fall, blurring the slow trickle of carriages and pedestrians in the square. He didn't have long until he had to be home, but he could make time to see Sybella to her door, if she had the strength to transport.

"I wonder why the spell targeted you," he said, more to himself than Sybella. "I was in this room with the doll and it was so inanimate that I believed the magic gone." *Though perhaps that was only what it wanted me to believe.*

"Because I tried to destroy it," said Sybella. Ollivan saw the reflection of her head snap up in the glass, and swung round.

"What is it?"

"I forgot. I tried to destroy her. When she—" Sybella cut off, her eyes going wide. "She spoke to me. Oh, stars. I tried to destroy her because of what she said!"

She climbed clumsily to her feet. Ollivan was frozen with dread and confusion.

"Ollivan," said Sybella desperately. "The doll wants Cassia."

18

The clouds had rolled in and a steady rain was falling by the time Cassia climbed the steps of the Wending Place.

She longed to be able to transport, and suspected she was physically capable, even if her magic would not allow it. But Cassia did not mind being out in the rain, and especially enjoyed it at night. Rain was nostalgia in liquid form. Dry weather did not invoke the hazy impression of dry weather past; it was waking up every morning; it was eating lunch. Rain was being up past midnight and cinnamon loaves on the solstice. The smell of earth and iron, the sound of water knocking, just to let itself in without invitation; rain invoked the memory of every rain before it.

What Cassia *did* mind was being made to stand on a doorstep in anticipation of a door that may never open. She rang the bell thrice and heard it chime heavily from deep within the building each time. But that was not all she heard. Shouts and laughter punctuated the patter of rain; silhouettes cut through the yellow light shining from the windows in a frenzied dance. The Successors were there on the other side, creating such a raucousness that they couldn't hear the bell. *Someone* should be listening for it, shouldn't they?

She switched to pounding on the door, but after another five minutes had passed she tried the handle, cringing at her own boldness as the great old door swung open on groaning hinges and admitted her where she was not supposed to be.

Cassia had one foot inside when someone collided with her, gasped an apology, and spun away again before she could react, which she supposed was better than some curse for trespassing. The tingling brush of magic raised the hairs on her skin like the last time she was there, but this felt different. Fiercely alive. She held her breath. Was what they said about the Wending Place true?

A scream. Cassia's heart pounded as she spun towards to sound, one hand already reaching behind her for the doorknob, the way out. But it wasn't that kind of scream. The gaggle of Successors who burst from a doorway along the hall were laughing.

"I'm looking for Ollivan Sims," Cassia called to them as they ran past, but they paid her no notice. Their feet pounding the stairs joined the sound of abused floorboards from above; more Successors running from room to room, she imagined. But why?

Cassia drifted through an archway in search of someone else to ask and caught a snippet of chatter as two girls dashed past in the adjacent corridor.

"But the clue said *chord* with an *H*, as in music, not *cord* as in rope. It was a play on words!"

The scavenger hunt. She remembered Ollivan mentioning it to their mother. But how was she to find him among all this? Now that she was inside, the warm lighting she had seen through the windows must have been part of an illusion. A scarce few lamps glowed softly, their circles of light pinned in the corners as if beaten back by the shadows. The Successors were faceless shapes tumbling past her in the gloom. Any one of them could be her brother.

She would head to the President's Sanctuary, wait for him by the door, and hope the havoc ended quickly. How long could it take near-adults to play a simple children's game?

But when she turned to go back to the stairs, the walls had moved.

She almost collided with the dead end of the corridor inches in front of her. Cassia lifted a hand to touch it, her palm landing flat on aged burgundy wallpaper – solid, real – and she recalled more about the scavenger hunt. It was an annual tradition, and that meant it was woven into the fabric of the Society, and of their clubhouse. The Wending Place was more than involved in this hunt, it was the grand architect, and it had taken Cassia for a player.

How long did she have until Jasper was expecting her? They were meeting at Cassia's house. If she didn't show up on time, how long would he wait before he carried out his threat to tell her mother she'd attacked him?

It wasn't worth worrying about now. She just had to get the doll as quickly as possible and get out before the Wending Place played any more tricks.

There was a lone door at her end of the corridor. It had to lead her closer to the main staircase, so Cassia pulled it open – and almost tripped down the step on the other side.

But it wasn't a step. And that wasn't a white, plastered floor beneath her, it was a ceiling. She was in another corridor. Long, deserted, and upside down. Between her and the only other door at the far end was a row of ceiling lights on brass chains, stood on end like tiny streetlamps, oblivious to the pull of gravity calling on them to collapse. The objects along the walls – a suit of armour, a bust of one of the founding Successors on a mahogany stand, a shallow console with a vase on top – weren't concerned either; they hung from the 'floor' as though they had been nailed down. Still, Cassia leaned away from them as she navigated the ceiling lights. Nailed or fixed there with magic, if the Wending Place could turn a corridor on its head, it could drop a suit of armour on her at will.

As she passed a painting of a horse that appeared to hang like a bat, a flutter of paper caught her eye. It dangled from a string around the neck of the bust. A clue, out of reach, and in a corridor Cassia was certain hadn't existed five minutes before. Perhaps the scavenger hunt was more challenging than she imagined.

When she made it to the end and stepped over the threshold, she was no longer upside down, but neither was she inside the Wending Place. Cassia had found herself in a walled courtyard garden. There were no Successors here either, but still the sounds of the hunt drummed around her. Creaking floorboards, slamming doors, shrieks of laughter and surprise. She hadn't known the Wending Place *had* a courtyard, and as she peered around her, looking for another way back into the house, she wasn't sure it was a courtyard at all.

For a start, it wasn't raining. The constellations hung above her in the deep blue of a clear sky from horizon to horizon. What she had taken at first glance to be a bonfire was a fireplace, recessed into the wall between two dogwood bushes. Paintings hung along the brickwork, and when she moved across the patio, the stone slabs groaned like labouring hardwood.

Stranger still was the fact that her own shadow, thrown far across the courtyard by the trembling flames in the fireplace, was not alone. Silhouettes dashed across the bricks, stones that weren't stones creaked under invisible feet. Someone laughed, very close to her ear, and Cassia shuddered. She had read about glamours that revealed different things to each person who encountered them. She might be surrounded by Successors in an ordinary parlour, each person there under a different spell. Perhaps they could all see her. A breeze tickled her hair as someone ran past and, discomforted, Cassia raced across the courtyard to the door on the other side.

And then she was in another corridor, and rain pelted the windows, throwing pebbled shadows across a carpet that was, mercifully, underfoot. She jumped as a door to her right clattered open, and two girls tumbled out, breathless and giggling. One was adjusting the bodice of her dress as the other re-pinned her hair. They stopped short at the sight of Cassia, who averted her eyes from the mouth-shaped bruise over the first's collarbone.

"I beg your pardon, but I'm trying to find the President's—" Cassia began, but the girls burst into shrieking laughter, and before she could force her question upon them, they sprinted off down the corridor.

"At least someone's having fun," Cassia muttered as she peered into the room the girls had come from, drawn in by the sound of music. A vast mirror rested against the far wall, in which she could see the string quartet in the opposite corner, behind the door. Employing musicians to play in an out-of-the-way room seemed an extravagance for even the Society of Young Gifted Sorcerers, but when Cassia cleared the doorway and turned around, the musicians weren't there. Another illusion. She looked into the glass again and a violinist winked at her. There was a clue tied around the neck of her instrument, and it danced and spun as she dragged her bow across the strings. Drawn in, Cassia stood with her nose to the mirror and squinted at the slip of paper for a long moment, before deciding there must be another trick to finding out what it said. It was impossible to read.

At the end of the corridor she finally found a staircase, and she started up it gratefully. The echoes of the hunt were fainter here, though she was certain the way she'd come had taken her in a loop. A single sound punctuated the sudden hush: the creak and thud of a door slamming somewhere above.

"Ollivan?" she called up the stairs.

It was darker now, every shape looming and unknowable. A curtain, or the fall of a coat as its wearer stood silently, watching her? One of the house's famous draughts touched her skin, still damp from the rain, and a shiver rolled through her. She couldn't bring herself to call out for her brother again, and she couldn't say why.

She was watching her feet as she took the stairs, so she did not notice the movement beyond the banister until it was very close; a silent, steady motion as two shadows peeled apart. When she turned her head, breath held tight, they had already folded back together. She stared into the darkness for several endless seconds and waited for the movement to make sense. But the darkness was too thick.

And it did not dissipate as she reached the first-floor corridor. Cassia stood clutching the banister as her eyes adjusted, her breaths too shallow for the thumping of her heart, but she didn't dare to make a sound. Quick, light footsteps retreated somewhere behind her, making her jump, but when she swung round, she could see no one.

"Ollivan?" she said, but it was only a whisper. Could he be playing a prank on her? Well, Cassia was not a fool, and she could take a joke, but not tonight, and not from him. Cursing her brother, she marched confidently down the corridor after the sound of footsteps.

She was brought to a leaping halt when she reached the end. The corridor let out into another, at the far end of which was a picture window throwing impressions of the rain onto the floor. And before it, shadow stretching towards her, was Violet.

Her visage was hidden by the darkness, but her hair was unmistakably wild, the ringlets pressed into ragged shapes around her head. He had surely unravelled the spell by now, but he had placed her in a standing position, probably propped up to best startle her.

Cassia sighed heavily and started down the corridor.

"Heaven and earth, Ollivan," she grumbled.

"Ollivan is irrelevant to me," said the doll.

Cassia couldn't contain her gasp. She grappled desperately until she found a lamp and turned it high.

Violet was not propped against anything, but stood on her own, as she had inexplicably in the garden. Her head was gently turned in Cassia's direction, green eyes on hers.

"He bound you," she said. "In his jacket."

"Yes. But he could not perform his little spell without unbinding me."

"His... little spell?"

Violet's head turned, just a little. "It was an unravelling, I think," she said.

So it hadn't worked; whatever Ollivan had written to undo the Guysman had failed. Cassia's mind flashed with Ollivan unconscious in his office. She had to trap her somehow, or bind her. Cassia called upon her magic, but she already knew: if Ollivan hadn't been able to best his own creation, she had no chance of succeeding where he had failed.

But perhaps she could stall her. Perhaps, if she could keep Violet here, there would be time for Ollivan to recover, and bind her again.

"Where is he, Violet?" Cassia asked, attempting to sound casual.

"Somewhere." The doll's voice was disinterested and slow. "I was looking for you."

"For me? What for?"

"Because I want to help you."

At that moment there was a bang as a door was flung open. Cassia both prayed and dreaded that whoever it was would venture this way. But their footsteps disappeared in the opposite direction.

"Why did you call out to me in the junk room? Why did you ask me to cast a spell and wake your magic? Is it because Jasper wouldn't?"

Violet's porcelain face was blank, and yet the flash in her eyes made her look angry. "I didn't like that boy. He would throw things and scream when he was angry. And he stole me. But I saw you, and I knew you were different. That you and I could be friends."

At least Jasper also hadn't seen the danger where Cassia had failed to. Yet even as she released a breath, something twisted inside her. She and Violet *had* been friends, until Ollivan had swept in and taken that away from her. He had taken Jasper too, in a way.

"I want to help you, Cassia," repeated the doll. "But for now I need to escape here. Could you please open the window?"

Cassia shook her head and banished her sadness. She was taking slow steps backwards towards the adjacent corridor so that someone could see her should they come this way. "I can't."

231

"You wish to fix your brother's mistakes for him?" Her girlish, musical voice was weighed down with disgust. A disgust Cassia should not have let hurt her, coming from a stars-damned doll. But nevertheless, the denial was forced from her on a swell of shame.

"No—"

"Then don't."

"You hurt Jasper."

"Because he would have hurt you. I've watched him from that room you found me in. He's not your friend, Cassia. I am."

With an uncanny, vaguely macabre motion, one leg pivoted at the hip and landed before her. She was walking; clumsily, and without the joints and tendons of a fluid human body, but the doll was walking. "But I'm not your fault. Open the window. Let me go, and I could be Ollivan's downfall. I know that's what you want."

It wasn't – was it? Something in her responded to the words, the way her magic responded when she called. It wasn't possible that Violet could read her mind; Ollivan's magic – a Sorcerer's magic – could never have achieved such a feat. But then again, she didn't need to. She had told Violet enough to piece together that conclusion.

Cassia shook her head, but her conviction was wavering. "You're dangerous," she said.

"I don't wish to hurt anybody. I'm your friend, Cassia. You can trust me."

The words had a rightness that settled on her skin like a balm. Violet *was* her friend. Even attacking Jasper had been in her defence.

Footsteps landed at the top of the stairs.

"Try that way!" called a voice – Ollivan's – and Violet's porcelain face snapped to the corridor. He was coming their way, loudly but slowly. He was combing the Wending Place, flinging doors open and curtains aside in search of his creation. If Cassia called out for him now, he could transport here. He would bind Violet again and find a fail-safe way to destroy her.

And Ollivan would get away with it. Again.

Her brother had been handed magic, status, most of their mother's love; everything Cassia dreamed of. He had squandered and sullied it; he had cheated, stolen, hurt people, *killed*, and somehow the consequences slid off him. It felt like she was the only one to notice. Maybe that made her the only one who could do something about it.

So Cassia marched to the window, undid the latch, and pulled it open. She hesitated with her hands on the frame.

"You have to promise me that—"

But there was no time to extract a promise – no time to voice the thousand questions and hesitations dancing on the tip of her tongue – because footsteps were upon them. Cassia spun round just as Sybella Dentley emerged into the corridor.

"Cassia!" she gasped in alarm. Her wide eyes went to the window. When Cassia turned around, Violet was somehow stood on the ledge.

Sybella raised an arm to hit the doll with a spell. "Stand back."

Cassia leapt out of the way, but something stayed Sybella's hand. Violet, too, had raised a tiny arm. Her eyes glowed a dreaded gold.

"No—"

But Violet was not drinking Sybella's magic. She was attacking her with a spell.

233

The sparks crackled down the corridor. When they cleared, Sybella was gone. She had ducked around the corner, and emerged again unscathed and ready to fight back.

"Oh, stars," she said, her hand dropping to her side.

Cassia turned back to the window, but Violet was gone. They both ran to it and looked down, but in the dark and the rain, it was hopeless.

"Cassia?" called a second voice, Ollivan's, and then he was there too, alarm wrought vividly across his features at the sight of her. They both came closer than she thought necessary given she could hear them from across the passage.

"What are you doing here?" he said, eyes sweeping the corridor and hands ready to channel magic.

It was only then Cassia recalled her purpose. "Jasper. When Violet knocked him unconscious, she drained his magic somehow. He threatened to tell Mother I attacked him if I didn't give him the doll back." She would have to tell him that Ollivan had destroyed her.

"She's gone, Ollivan," said Sybella, before turning to Cassia seriously. "Are you alright? Did it hurt you?"

"Hurt me?"

"The doll was looking for you," said Ollivan. "She drained Sybella's magic too. Come back to the Sanctuary, quick."

They ushered her back down the hall to the Sanctuary, and shut and locked the door. Then Ollivan started pacing the perimeter of the room as he set a ward. In the light, it was clear that Sybella was pale and wan too. Sick regret filled her.

"That thing is wielding magic, Ollivan," said Sybella.

Ollivan spun, wide-eyed. "*What?* That's impossible."

234

Sybella looked to Cassia expectantly.

"It's true," said Cassia. "I saw her attack Sybella with a spell."

Right after assuring her she didn't wish to hurt anybody. Right after Cassia had set her loose to spite Ollivan. She went to the couch and sank onto it to stop the room spinning.

"Why was she looking for you?" said Sybella.

I want to help you, Cassia. "Strange as it may seem, I believe she's fond of me."

"Fond of you?" said Ollivan, as if she had just suggested they braise a leather boot with carrots and greens for dinner. "She can't be fond of you."

"Stars, thank you, Ollivan."

"We assumed she wanted to hurt you," explained Sybella, shooting Ollivan a look.

"Oh." That struck Cassia as a sensible assumption to make about a dangerous spell that had already attacked someone, and yet the sensible had eluded her at the crucial moment. *Fool.* "You don't have a drink of water, by any chance?"

In answer, Ollivan lifted the glass handle of what had probably been a vessel, but now clung to only a shard of the thing.

"Here." Sybella put a glass of water in her hand. Cassia hummed a thank you and took several long gulps before she spoke.

"I thought that she only drained Jasper because he was frightening me."

Ollivan's jaw was clenched tight. "She may have done, if indeed she's formed an attachment to you." He was pacing across the room. "And she drained Sybella because she tried to stop her. Neither means she's less dangerous."

"Ollivan, what in the earth and stars is this spell?" said Sybella.

His explanation washed over Cassia, like the murmur of people talking in the next room. *Dangerous.* She had known it, and still she'd helped Violet flee. Perhaps she was as consumed with resentment for her brother as he was with resentment for Jasper. Perhaps she wasn't so different from him at all. The thought made her shudder.

"Alright," said Sybella with surprising calm once Ollivan had filled her in. "So she's drinking people, instead of spells?"

"Unfortunately."

"And the ability to speak? To move?"

"She walks now," Cassia heard herself say, bringing a moment's ringing silence to the Sanctuary as the others no doubt pictured the horror she had seen first-hand.

"She was an ordinary enchanted doll before I performed the Guysman," said Ollivan eventually. "That original spell accounts for the talking. Her moving independently was yet another unintended outcome. The real danger, however…"

Sybella caught her eye with a long-suffering glance, and something in Cassia released as she remembered: this was not her fault. Sybella knew as well as she did that Ollivan and his dogged fascinations with magic and revenge at all costs had caused this.

"The thing about Guysman's draft for this spell, the thing that unfortunately didn't occur to me until too late, is that the vessel only absorbs magic."

"Yes?"

"But then what? Even when you mend a button, say, you burn magic on that action, but it doesn't just vanish. There's an

236

exchange: magic for new thread. What neither Guysman nor myself accounted for was what happens to the magic next. The Guysman vessel is not just a vessel for the spell – it must also be the vessel for everything it takes, all the magic it absorbs. When I started to think about the spell in the Otherworld, *that* was my main concern: that it would release it spontaneously in some kind of eruption. I don't know what the effects of that would be but I've theorised that all existing magic and magical peoples in the blast radius would be overwhelmed. That any magical infrastructure would fall apart. That people could even be harmed, if a blast of unchannelled magic were to hit them." He glanced then at Sybella, who grasped some meaning that was lost on Cassia. "But it appears the doll is not merely *releasing* the magic." He ceased pacing and rubbed a hand over his face. "She's using it."

Sybella was shaking her head. "Ollivan, that's... *impossible*."

"Spells do it all the time," Ollivan countered. Then he tilted his head in concession. "Alright, not in the way we do. But think of your grandmother's vanity mirror, the one that advises her on which hat to wear with which jewels and such. A clever, well-executed spell has the function to make independent decisions. It's not true sentience, but put it in something that looks like a person and it could appear to be."

"And because you neglected to tell this spell what to do with the magic it absorbed," said Cassia, "it decided on its own?"

Ollivan made no reply. It clearly pained him to have no response, but Cassia knew what it meant. Most spells that made independent decisions were designed that way; it was a function of the way they were meant to work. Absorbing magic, even if it didn't know what to do with it, did not automatically lend itself to using it. Unless the intention was corrupted in such a way that, somehow, Ollivan had commanded this doll to wield magic.

"Ollivan," said Sybella, "she jumped out of a window and fled into the night. She's loose, with her alarming new talents for moving, decision-making, and casting spells. And if she continues to attack people, isn't she just going to get stronger?"

Loose. Gone. Another wave of sickening regret overcame her, but she buried it under indignation and pushed off the couch.

"You have to tell Grandfather."

He stared at her, but it was as if he didn't see her at all. He wore that dogged look on his face. "No. I'll be arrested."

"As you should be! What in the heaven and earth possessed you play around with some shoddy, half-thought-out work of a madman? She's going to *hurt* people, Ollivan. Tell Grandfather. He'll respect that you've told him yourself. Perhaps he'll take that into account before he punishes you."

She didn't know who she thought she was fooling. Certainly not Ollivan, who shot her the look of derision she deserved. Then he turned his gaze on Sybella, his ex-love, his new partner. Sybella held his gaze for a long moment, indecision warring behind her eyes. Eventually, she lowered them to the ground. She could not, or would not say Ollivan should be spared.

"Ollivan?" Cassia prompted again.

"I won't," was all he said, and for maybe the first time in her life, Cassia pitied him. Pitied the wall of pride that would not be brought down, even for the smallest fool's hope of saving him from a fate that tormented him. She could practically see him withering inside.

"Then I will."

"Do what you must, but I would ask you to reconsider." His voice was low and steady, but belied by the edge of desperation in his gaze. "I underestimated the Guysman, as I've underestimated a great many things these last couple of years. But I do not underestimate my enemies twice. Jupitus will have no mercy for me, Cassia. And I know this spell better now. I can fix this, and no one else can. Just let me try."

She had already let him. She had given him one of the famous second chances she so resented her mother for, and a day later, the problem he had already sworn he would fix was worse.

Because of you.

No, because of Ollivan. This was his doing.

"Your curfew is upon us," she said. "You have until I get home to do the right thing."

Cassia did not look back as she marched from the office and back out into the rain.

*

She had walked to the Wending Place, but now she approached the guard point by Westminster Bridge, and asked one of the militia to fetch her a carriage. He disappeared on the spot. In less than five minutes, her grandfather's carriage pulled up. In twenty, she alighted onto the pavement outside her house.

Voices floated to her from the drawing room as the maid took her coat. Jupitus was there as well as Alana, but Ollivan's was most frequent. Disbelief, then irritation flooded her. He could not be confessing. She had not believed for a moment that he would. This damning affair was Cassia's to bring to them. He was robbing her of the chance to watch their faces as they discovered she was the only one who had seen him for what he really was.

But it was not a confession she could overhear. She stood beyond the light pouring from the doorway and listened as her brother recounted his day for them, minus any mention of the magic-sucking horror doll he had set loose on the city. He was fulfilling their grandfather's condition of his being allowed to stay in the Witherward.

Why was he bothering? He had already destroyed his chances of spending the next two years as a free man in Witherward. If Jupitus couldn't undo the magic of the Society charter, he would simply keep Ollivan in a cell until the protection expired.

Cassia's mother and grandfather thanked and dismissed him, and Ollivan bade them goodnight. When he stepped into the hallway, he was unsurprised to see her lurking there. He stopped, so they were face to face, and looked down at her for a long moment. Cassia met his stare defiantly, even as his expression ate into her very soul. Resigned disappointment. She would not have cared that it was coming from him, if only she didn't recognise that look. It was the look their grandfather had given her the night of her second failed initiation. It was the look her mother had worn when she demonstrated her magic for her upon coming home, and was found wanting.

Stars, she hated him. She would follow the enforcers the day they dragged him to the portal. She would watch them see him through and forbid him from ever returning.

He left her there without a word and slowly climbed the stairs, and that's when she realised: he had given his report because he still hoped she would change her mind. He took the stairs in favour of transporting to watch her a moment longer, in some misplaced hope that she wasn't about to ruin his life.

240

Let him watch, she thought as she moved towards the drawing-room door.

"How unexpected," Alana was saying, and Cassia paused. "That in spite of everything he shows the political acumen we had hoped for."

Cassia shot a glance at the stairs, but Ollivan had finally vanished up them. For the second time that evening, she questioned whether her brother had somehow mastered the Whisperer talent for mind control.

Jupitus, at least, still had some sense. "Do not get any ideas, Alana," he said sternly. "If he lasts two years without giving me cause – and I'm afraid I doubt that he will – then he'll be returned to the Otherworld. There is no political future for that boy here."

"I know that," said Alana, though her tone carried the hurt Cassia knew she had suffered over Ollivan's crimes. "I was merely commending his successes. Can I not do so? My son may be a criminal, but he is a lot of other things besides."

Cassia would have chosen this moment to interrupt, had the next word not been her name.

"Cassia, though. Father, I still think we ought to explore the possibility that she could replace him."

"There's nothing to explore," said Jupitus, without a second of consideration. "She's bright, she's quick-witted. She has the will for it, I'm sure, but she's not respected among the Sorcerers. Flaunting her poor command of her magic so publicly has damaged her. Her generation would never allow her to lead them."

"Has her magic damaged her," Alana said softly, "or have *we* damaged her? We've confined her to her role as a peacemaker, the effect being that she can be nothing more. Here, she's practically a Changeling, by association."

Practically a Changeling. She had been told that before, by Camden folk wishing to be welcoming. It did not impress her then, as it did not impress her now. *Practically a Changeling* was not a Changeling, but it definitely wasn't a Sorcerer either. She was neither.

She was nothing.

And her own mother agreed.

"She is a good girl," Jupitus continued. "She will continue to toe the line, and she'll do us proud when she's safely back at the Zoo, beyond everyone's notice. Soon, hopefully."

Jupitus's last statement was half request and half command. "Give her more time, Father. Another year. She could still find her footing. It will improve her character and perhaps settle her into her place here."

Cassia leaned against the wall and listened to her grandfather reply, though she heard none of it. They had said nothing she didn't already know. She was not liked among the Sorcerers. She was not respected. She was unfit for leadership. Ollivan was better. Also, that they believed her path was set, and she would go back to Camden. *Soon, hopefully.*

So why did it hollow her out to hear it aloud? Why could she say such things to herself and feel them fuel her, spur her onwards, and when it came from her family, it stilled her completely? She had known it was true, and she had known that they knew it too.

She wished she wasn't crying. She wished she didn't feel so foolish for how certain she had been only moments before; certain she held a victory she was about to deliver into their hands. What had she expected? A pat on the head? To hear that they were proud? No, if she went in there and told them about the Guysman, it would be about Ollivan, as everything was. She could not impress them by *toeing the line.*

She crept from her listening spot and up to her room, scarcely breathing so they would not hear her sniff, treading only where the stairs wouldn't creak; a quirk of her family home she had only mastered in the last two years. Ollivan had known these stairs since he was a child.

Her mother wanted her to have another year of chances to be a proper Sorcerer, but what good would it do? Would they even be proud of her if she succeeded? Or was it only what was expected, and not worthy of commendation? If Ollivan could get banished and still deserve praise, then Cassia had been labouring under a misconception. That toeing the line was how to earn her family's respect.

Well, Ollivan had earned their respect; their disappointment, yes, and in Jupitus's case, resentment, but their mother's respect at least was intact, and even their grandfather took him seriously. So Cassia would try it his way. She didn't have as much to lose here, and if they could do it, if they could fix this together, she would be a hero. A maverick, but what did that matter now?

When all else fails, spite.

She knocked softly on her brother's door, and there was commotion from the other side. It sounded like he was shoving something heavy under the bed. When it quieted, he beckoned her in.

Ollivan sat on the edge of his bed, his hands between his knees, as if she might believe he hadn't been up to anything. When he saw it was her, he relaxed and knelt on the floor.

The thing he had hastily hidden was a suitcase. He was escaping.

"Where will you go?" said Cassia.

"The continent," he said without looking at her, and commenced throwing things into his suitcase.

"Aren't you in a hurry? You won't find a ship leaving at this time of night."

"I'll probably get out of the city first. I've less chance of getting caught boarding a ship in Wessolk." He stopped and looked up at her warily. "I don't know why I told you that."

Then he truly looked at her, and stopped his frantic packing. "Why are you crying?"

She wasn't any more. She couldn't even summon the feeling that had brought tears to her eyes outside the drawing-room door. A new calm had overcome her, and into it had fallen all her foolish anxieties. There wasn't space for them any more, not where Cassia was going. She wiped the tears from her cheeks and looked her brother in the eye.

"I'll help you," she said, hearing a steel in her voice. "I'll help you stop Violet."

Ollivan had somehow convinced his sister not only to refrain from turning him in, but to actively help him. His next problem was convincing her it could wait until morning.

"What about this situation doesn't strike you as urgent?" she said when he asked her to vacate his room so he could get some rest.

"The size of her legs, for a start," he fired back. "Her inability to find, hold, or indeed read a city map for a second. I will eat the glass shards off the carpet in the Sanctuary if the thing has gone far by morning."

*

"What now, genius?"

Cassia stood with her arms folded and squinted at him in the morning sunlight. A thorough sweep of Drusella Square and the surrounding area had turned up no trace of the stars-damned doll.

The truth was, Ollivan had stalled because he didn't know what they ought to do now. He hadn't known the night before, and after lying awake until dawn, exhausted and wound as tight as a spring, he still had no idea how he planned to capture the vessel *or* undo the spell.

"Let's go up to the Sanctuary," he muttered, stalking past her.

"No." Ollivan stopped. "I'm not sneaking into that place ever again."

"You wouldn't be sneaking in. As the President, I can invite whomever I wish. Now let's get off the street before we're seen together." Cassia's folded arms dropped to her sides in rising indignation. "It looks suspicious! The last time we willingly associated you were four and I was interrogating your ragdoll for espionage... and now that I think on it, perhaps only one of us was willing."

"You sliced her arm off with a cutting curse," snapped Cassia as she stalked past.

He followed her to the Sanctuary, where Cassia spun to face him and leaned against his desk, her white-knuckled grip on the edge. "Let's try a locating spell."

Ollivan couldn't contain a snort of laughter. "We are in a house of immense magic, Cassia. Please don't desecrate it by calling some hack's half-thought-out and then disproved theory a *spell*."

"Ollivan—"

"Location is antithetical to everything I stand for. We may as well turn our hopes to the mysticism they pretend to practise in the Otherworld. I cannot understand why it ever caught on."

That wasn't entirely true. The way the history of an object and of everything it had come into contact with complicated the finding of it was compelling to Ollivan, the way it had been compelling to theoreticians throughout history. It suggested that everything left a magical footprint; that magic was part of the fabric of the universe, which was a cornerstone of its exploration.

As a way to find things, he would see it banned even faster than the work of Everard Guysman.

Location magic claimed that with a map and a marker of some kind, one could pinpoint the location of anything, including a person. The reality, however, was that locating spells only worked without failure or flaw when the Sorcerer performing one *already knew* where the thing they sought was, and was concentrating on it as they performed the spell; making the results when used for its intended purpose anything from misleading to utterly useless.

"You don't have to be so dramatic," said Cassia. "Would you at least *try it*?"

"Why don't *you* do the honours, if you're so married to the idea?"

She tensed, and when she drew breath to speak again, her lip shuddered. "Fine. Do you have a map?"

Of course he did. Maps of the city were almost as abundant in London as copies of the morning paper, and in fact one often accompanied the other. Having somewhere to mark the changes in borders during the night, and the no-go zones where skirmishing was active, could both save one's life and facilitate trouble-free route planning.

Ollivan spread a map of London over his desk as Cassia removed her earring and held it in a fist before her.

"What are you doing?" he said.

"It's a token," said Cassia of the earring.

"Very good. If you're going to waste both our time, at least do it with commitment," Ollivan said sarcastically. He rifled through the drawers until he found a stub of sealing wax and tossed it to her. "This spell is going to cast a net for anything related to the doll, including you. Something of yours in the mix is only going to amplify your influence. Didn't you know that?"

"Yes," muttered Cassia. She was trying to fasten her earring back in place but her fingers were trembling. "I wasn't thinking."

Intrigued, Ollivan stood back and let his sister perform the spell. She took her time, staring unblinking at the map for several seconds before closing her eyes and taking a deep breath. One would think she was preparing to step on stage and perform an aria.

Cassia dropped the sealing wax onto the map. It landed with a dull thud right below her hand.

"It didn't work," she said.

"Yes, I can see that." He had felt it too. Or rather, *hadn't*. No spark of magic had occurred as Cassia dropped the token. "What intention did you use?"

"*Find.* I know how to perform a locating spell, Ollivan."

"And were you thinking of—"

"Of course I was thinking of Violet!"

Ollivan raised his hands in surrender, but he couldn't stop his smile. "So this is the problem I keep hearing about."

"Hearing from whom?" said Cassia, her eyes wide.

"The Successors, mainly. Some of them were talking about your initiation attempt the night I came back."

She sank into a chair like the air had gone out of her. "Oh."

He could see what this conversation was doing to her, but his curiosity got the better of him. "Is that how it always goes wrong? Your magic doesn't pick up the intention?"

Cassia opened her mouth to respond – no doubt with a barb – but then halted. "What do you mean?"

Ollivan's eyebrows shot up. "Someone taught you how to use your magic over in the Changeling quarter, didn't they?"

Her mouth was a hard line. She looked down at her hands before speaking. "I think it might have been a poor substitute for actually knowing other Sorcerers. The others always seemed to learn the most about Changeling magic by playing together. I didn't have that."

She fired the last at him like an accusation. Ollivan chose to ignore it. He'd been seven years old when his sister was fostered in Camden; it was clearly not his fault that she grew up there.

"I'm sure there's nothing you missed about play that you couldn't learn yourself through practice," he said. He meant it as a comfort, but Cassia seemed to be immune to any attempt at kindness from him. Her mouth dropped open like he'd insulted her.

"If that's the case, then something dire is wrong with me."

"Well." It wasn't an invitation to comment, but stars help him, he couldn't stop himself. "I can tell you right now that it's psychological."

"Psychological?" Cassia said, eyes narrowing in suspicion.

"It's certainly not the strength of your magic, is it?" He laughed. "Stars, you'd have to be supremely untalented to not produce a single spark performing a *locating spell*."

She was on her feet so suddenly that Ollivan lurched back. She snatched his wrist and firmly deposited the nub of wax into his palm. "Just do the damn spell."

"I didn't mean—" he began, but she shot him a look that told him not to. He sighed in indignation. "Fine, but I want my objection to this farce noted for the record."

"Don't fret, Ollivan. I assume you object to everything until told otherwise."

Ollivan was quick-witted, so it was rare he had to ponder whether he was being insulted. It told him to tread more carefully around his sister. Perhaps they had more in common than he'd first thought.

He fixed the appearance of the doll in his mind, summoned his magic, and tossed the wax at the map. It tumbled and spun for a moment, before being pulled as if by a magnet to a street pressed against the south bank in the Sorcerer quarter. Ollivan bent over the map to look closer. Cassia came to stand by his shoulder and gasped.

"It must have worked. Why else would it lead us to such an unrelated location?"

"Why indeed?" Ollivan murmured.

He knew this street. Not just the street but the very spot, he believed. How it was connected to the Guysman, or even *if* it was connected, he couldn't say. "This is my very objection: we don't know. Jasper stole that doll from a child we know nothing about. Perhaps they lived there. Or perhaps the relative who handed it down to them did, since the thing is so old. But I'll be damned if I'm going to gallivant about because location magic told me to."

Cassia was full of arguments, but at that moment Sybella appeared across the Sanctuary and breezed towards them. She looked as vibrant and healthy as ever, and Ollivan sent up a silent thanks that the Guysman appeared to have done her no lasting harm.

"There were enforcers here," she said breathlessly, and Ollivan realised the flush of vitality in her cheeks was from alarm. His gut answered by twisting in on itself. "A Psi man was found unconscious in the square last night. Ollivan, his magic is gone."

"A *Psi*?" said Ollivan. He could hear the edge of hysteria in his voice. "That can't be."

250

"If Violet can drain Psi as well as Sorcerers, then…" Cassia looked at Ollivan, her face paling. "Anyone in the city could be in danger. And no one but a Sorcerer could be to blame for magic like this."

Ollivan ran a hand over his face. "Jupitus will wet himself with glee if he can pin an inter-faction incident on me. Who is this man? We should try and talk to him."

Sybella shook her head. "I don't know. Two enforcers came to the door and asked me to provide a list of everyone who was here last night. I tried to get more information from them by insisting it was for the safety of the Society members but they wouldn't tell me a thing. They were unusually circumspect. What do you think it means?"

Ollivan looked again at the map spread over his desk. "What's the date today?"

"It's the third of October," said Cassia. "What does that have to do with any of this?"

"Everything," said Ollivan, and then wished he hadn't. The date, the Psi man in Drusella Square, and the result of the locating spell aligned in a way he couldn't share with either of them. "I think I know how I can find out more. Tonight."

There was a pause. He watched Cassia slowly realise it was all he had to say. She made a noise of indignation.

"You have to tell me," she said, and Ollivan fought not to laugh at the petulance in her tone. She transformed before his eyes into a four-year-old, demanding things of him in exactly the same way. On the heels of his humour came a stabbing of something sadder.

"It's better if you don't know. But I'll report back what I learn right away."

"No! You can't pull me into this and then continue to keep secrets."

"This is dangerous, Cassia. Trust me —"

"If I haven't already made it perfectly clear, I *don't* trust you. But whatever stars-damned awful decisions you make from here onwards affect me too. I'm coming with you."

He was surprised by her courage, and impressed, but it made no difference. She didn't understand what she was asking. Better that she continue to believe him selfish and untrustworthy, so he flashed her a grin he knew would make her want to kill him and gave a small salute.

"You can try," he said, and then he was gone.

20

Cassia was going to kill him.

Ollivan would clearly disagree, but she had thought being in this mess together meant actually sharing what they knew. If something happened to Ollivan during whatever dangerous thing he planned to do that night, how would they ever stop Violet? He was the only one who knew the enchantment well enough to unravel it.

"I won't let him do this." She looked up at Sybella, who was wearing an expression of greedy curiosity. "What?"

"Oh, nothing. I'm just learning what it must be like to have him as a brother. Thank the stars my sister isn't yet a year old. I would hate to have to loathe her as you must Ollivan." She gave a small sigh. "Well. I have one thousand things to do and must be getting on."

"What? But we have to… stop him. Or help him."

Sybella raised an eyebrow. "Well, which is it?"

Cassia didn't know. She had expected stopping Violet to take her beyond the bounds of her respectable life, and maybe that meant letting Ollivan be Ollivan. But not if it got him killed and left Cassia holding the gun. She needed to get to where he was going tonight, and she needed help.

But Sybella was shaking her head before she could speak. "I helped him revoke his banishment," she said. "I didn't know what a truly terrible idea that would turn out to be. But it's done, and I helped, and if any of it gets out because his attack doll has run rampant across the Heart, I shall be very upset. That's why I came up here to tell you both about the Psi man, but now I'm done. I won't be involved any more."

She swept towards the door, her curls bouncing and her skirt swaying with her steps. Sybella moved as if she had never stumbled; as if the only way she could end up on the floor was if it were to come to her. Cassia envied her confidence.

"What *would* you have done?" she called before Sybella reached the door. "When you were together?"

"What would I have done?" She gave a laugh. "It's not a woman's job to keep a man out of trouble if that's where he chooses to be."

"You know that's not what I meant." Cassia tried to channel the other girl as she crossed the space between them. "Didn't you used to love him? Weren't you ever afraid he would push my grandfather too far? Or get *hurt*?"

Sybella's boldness faltered. "It wasn't like that," she said, her voice like a damning confession. "Back when the escapades were harmless, we were in them together. We used to sit outside cafés and cast glamours to taunt passers-by. Gold coins on the street. Bird droppings on their shoulders." Cassia could almost see the reflection of memories flicker across her eyes. "I knew when he started spending time with Jasper, but he was always the same old Ollivan around me. We didn't talk about magic."

"*Never?* Magic is all he cares about."

"He cared about *me*," she retorted, voice breaking, and Cassia sensed her opening.

"Then help me. Please."

Sybella laughed, brushing away her sadness like it was a dusting of snow. "Oh no. You shan't draw me into this by playing on my emotions. In two years, I'll be President of the Society of Young Gifted Sorcerers. In ten, I'll be High Sorcerer. One doesn't forge a career like that by abandoning the path to run headlong into trouble. I suggest that *you* think on the path you wish to forge also." She tilted her head to one side and squinted at Cassia. "You know, I've been looking for a young woman to mentor. Someone hoping to get into the Society and make the most of being a Successor. When I'm President I'll need to appoint a Secretary, after all, and I'd like it to be a woman, and someone who shares my values. I was imagining someone younger, but what would you say if I offered my mentorship to you?"

A mentor. Someone to help her get into the Society, not just tutor her for her mother's coin and her brother's secrets. Someone to usher her towards who she wanted to be and how she wanted to be seen. There was nothing Cassia wanted more. With the Secretary herself as a patron, she might finally win the good opinion of her peers. It would be her *angle*, as Lev Mallory had said. *The thing they can talk about instead.*

"I would need my future Secretary to be dependable, sensible," Sybella went on, drawing the words out meaningfully. "Someone the powers in the Heart would approve of. Someone who would reflect well on me."

So this was the choice: follow Sybella, or follow Ollivan. Was it too late to leave Ollivan to clean up his own mess? Perhaps not, but stepping away from their quest to stop Violet wouldn't be enough to absolve her. She would also need to turn Ollivan in.

She will continue to toe the line…

Cassia deflated. Sybella meant well. She was trying to incentivise her to extricate herself from this. She had identified Cassia's weakness and used it to manipulate her, if only for her own good. Sybella was a true politician, through and through.

"Thank you, Sybella," said Cassia, making sure Sybella knew she meant it. "But for better or worse, I have to find my brother."

Sybella shot her a small smile and turned again to leave. "At least I can say I tried." She had one hand on the doorhandle when she spoke again. "*But* if you're sure you're intent on trouble, I know the boys to help you."

2 I

Ollivan didn't go far. He had long known one of the best places to go undiscovered was the Wending Place library. Despite the library being a cornerstone of the Society's ethos, most members would sooner die of boredom than step foot inside. For most of the day, Ollivan ensconced himself blissfully in a corner from which he could see the door, with a volume on meteorological manipulation and a platter of sandwiches from the kitchen, .

In the darkest hour of the night, he went to the river.

There was a bite to the air, and the sky was perfectly clear. That was good fortune, astrologers said, as the stars turned fate in devious ways when they weren't being watched. But tonight, the ripples and whorls of the Thames caught flecks of moonlight, scattering them in an abstract pattern that illuminated the water from the north bank to the south.

Except in one spot. In the middle of the river, a patch of moonless, black water, thirty feet wide, was moving at a steady pace upriver, away from the docks and further into Sorcerer territory.

The glamour in use on the river had this single flaw; Ollivan had watched it many times to confirm it for himself. The ships enchanted with it made no sound and caused no disturbance to the current, nor did they catch the light like the water around them – but they did block it. Whoever wrought the disguise was either unaware of this flaw in their work or unable to correct it. Ollivan suspected the latter – water could be tricky – but so far it hadn't mattered. The ships docked only in the dead of night. Besides, there was enough magic operating in London at any given moment that observers were not in the habit of interrogating unexplained phenomena unless they had a reason to be suspicious.

Perhaps Ollivan alone knew what a perilous night it was to be on this stretch of bank. Be spotted, and he would be begging to have everything he had accomplished undone. He would be lucky not to be tortured before they killed him. That Cassia had demanded to go with him made him shudder. He held no guilt over leaving her behind without an explanation; his sister didn't know what she was asking.

He stood at the corner of a warehouse, where the hulking building threw a heavy swath of black into the moon's path, and kept his bad right ear to the wall. Two hundred yards down the lane was the spot that stars-damned locating spell had identified. Between them, a woman leaned against a lamppost and pretended to pick at her nails. Despite the chill of the evening, she didn't wear a coat, which was probably in an attempt to make her look like a working girl. It was where the resemblance ended, but if the brush of magic against Ollivan's senses was anything to go by, she had the aid of a distraction glamour. He doubted any passers-by would have time to doubt her line of work before they met with a pressing need to think about something else.

Such magic would not work on Ollivan, who had no trouble noticing the ship docked in the tiny quay behind her, for he already knew it was there. The glamour that had made the vessel nearly invisible on the river had been lifted to allow the smugglers to unload their cargo onto waiting carts, but the tiny mooring – a space only wide and long enough for one ship, and best navigated by Psi using magic to steer it in – was hidden between two buildings.

Buildings owned by Jupitus Fisk.

Doing business with the smugglers were half a dozen of his grandfather's most trusted enforcers, all of whom would recognise him. And if Jupitus ever learned that Ollivan knew of his black-market dealings, nothing he did to absolve or damn himself would make a jot of difference to his fate.

The Principles decreed a great many things that shaped life in the broken city of London, from what a person must do to live or work beyond their own quarter, to who was responsible for them if they married or bore children with someone of another magic. But none of the Principles carried as much weight or as great a penalty as those relating to trade.

The agreement decreed that all imports must come through the docks – in the Oracle territory of the Docklands – and be declared at the Trade House. And the High Sorcerer had probably been flouting that rule since the day he helped write it. The ships crept up the Thames and delivered poisons, artefacts and – Ollivan feared – slaves to his grandfather. It was an enterprise that had made Jupitus – already publicly one of the wealthiest people in the city – a lot richer than anyone knew. And one that would see the destruction of his empire if it came to light.

But this was where Ollivan might find his only clue about the whereabouts of his Guysman. He would rather be dead than suffer the consequences of failing to stop what he had started. As for the torture he would most certainly suffer until his grandfather could be sure he had told no one else – Ollivan chose to simply not think about it. It was how he achieved most ill-advised things, and it was yet to fail him.

The deal taking place down the lane would soon be over; the militia and smugglers were going about their work with practised efficiency and a visible dose of nerves. But he needed a more secure place to hide until then, and he knew of one. He had long ago discovered that the buildings disguising the little quay were façades; empty shells that served no purpose other than to hide the mooring between them. He transported himself into the nearest one, his arrival displacing a pallet leaning against the wall. Breath tight in his chest, he caught it before it hit the ground, but couldn't prevent the deafening groan of the floorboard as he did so. He froze at the noise, eyes peering out from the dark at the people on the wharf.

The nearest looked up and straight in his direction. Caldwell. An enforcer. Ollivan could do nothing but wait to see if he was caught. But the militiaman appeared to brush the sound off and went back to unloading the crates the crew were bringing down the gangplank.

It was a waiting game. About a dozen crates were unloaded, each containing boxes the enforcers loaded onto the carts. He couldn't see what they were buying, perhaps a range of goods, but no people at least; not from this particular ship. As he predicted, it wasn't long until money was changing hands. Ollivan clenched his fists to keep his fingers from tapping as he waited restlessly for the carts to leave. So restlessly that he paid no mind to his vulnerable right-hand side, the side of his bad ear. He had no idea he wasn't alone until the blade was at his neck.

"Do you want to play?" Gedeon says.

Yes, you want to play. The game is breathless and daring – one boy tosses the hoop as high as he can, the other turns into a bird and flies through it.

But you can't play, because you'll never have wings.

"How's this?" Gedeon makes Eliot roll the hoop across the lawn instead. He takes a run at it and dives through. The grass stains are atrocious. After two turns each, yours are worse.

Eliot won't take his turns. After three, he stalks off. When he's nearly at the house, you shout his name and whip the hoop as high as you can.

The sun blinds you as you watch the sky. When the flash of a raven streaks by, Gedeon, by your side, lets out a whoop.

You catch the hoop as Eliot lands, and it's like coming back down to earth.

22

Cassia watched her brother marched onto the ship with a blade at his back, and beneath her terror, felt a wicked stab of validation. She had been right to follow him.

It vanished almost instantly when she realised she had no idea what to do.

"We have to get onto that ship," said Virgil. The anxious crease in his brow belied his decisive tone.

They had climbed an exterior stair on the side of one of the warehouses for a good view without getting too close. It didn't help Cassia's nerves that Virgil had thrown a distraction glamour over them; every rat below her and every wisp of cloud above looked like one of her grandfather's militia coming their way.

"And do what?" Lev gestured to the tiny mooring a hundred yards before and below them. "Did the crew with the long knives and clandestine drop-off look like the type of folk we can politely ask for our friend back?"

Virgil fixed him with a deathly serious stare that said he didn't appreciate the wit. "He's not on a getaway to France, Mallory, those smugglers are going to kill him."

Lev groaned. "I *told you* we should have been keeping a closer eye on him."

"You said that already," snapped Virgil.

Cassia blocked out their bickering and tried to steady herself. This wasn't the backup Sybella had promised when she had given her an address.

*

Virgil Pike had shut his bedroom door on the raucous chatter of too many women and turned to face her, arms folded, brows riding low above his eyes. Cassia had to crane her neck to meet his stare.

"Explain it again," he said, and raised a hand when Cassia drew breath to begin. "Slower."

"There's an out-of-control spell at work somewhere in the city." Cassia paused to check that explanation for damning details and found none, but Virgil's expression said he was reading between the lines before she even mentioned her brother. "Ollivan and I are trying to stop it, and he's gone to try and find out how, but he's gone alone. He said it's dangerous."

Virgil was silent, but his gaze drifted away from her as if in thought.

"He wouldn't tell me anything else," she pressed on, "meaning whatever it is, it's bad news. And whether that means it could get him killed or found out by my grandfather, I don't know how to stop this enchantment without him. I came to ask for your help."

She didn't have the magic to be prepared for whatever she was walking into, and she was hoping Virgil would infer that without her having to say so. She mustered every ounce of her patience as he paced the length of his room ponderously. It was a simple space compared to the more lavish rooms she had spied in the rest of the house; rooms more in keeping with what the families she knew typically lived in. There was a bed, a desk and chair, a large wardrobe, and several bookshelves. Half of the space on them was taken up with pamphlets, rolled-up posters, and educational materials. The books he did own followed the vein of Goforth's *History of the Heart*; historical and political tomes that, here and there, strayed from Jupitus's approved sources.

"I prefer to give my money to worthy causes," said Virgil, noticing her taking in the space in which he lived.

"That's... noble," said Cassia, hearing the weakness of her words versus the power of Virgil's commitment. She wondered if she could strip her own room if she told her mother it was for charity, then felt shallow.

"Cassia, I love your brother. He's my oldest friend. And I don't want any harm to come to him. But you have to understand, if I gave myself to helping Ollivan out of every one of his own mistakes, there'd be nothing left of me."

Cassia heard what Virgil was really telling her, whether he meant to or not; that he could be persuaded. "The last time he made his own mistakes, Virgil, he came back on fire." He looked at her questioningly a Cassia shrugged. "Jasper. He has this vendetta against him. He says he's the reason he was banished."

Virgil blinked in surprise. "How?"

"He wouldn't tell me."

"And do you believe him?"

Cassia didn't think her answer was what Virgil needed to hear. "Do you?"

He sat slowly, as if the weight of the question dragged him down. His long fingers tapped absently against his knee.

"I think so. My best friend has a heart. He reminded me of that yesterday. I had forgotten."

Cassia would contest the claim that her brother had a heart, but now wasn't the time. "But you went looking for him, didn't you? In the Otherworld."

He smiled. "Because of Lev. He didn't need any convincing that Ollivan was innocent. He said we couldn't just abandon him there. And I think Ollivan knew that. You know he was working at Pendergast's?" Cassia nodded. She had rarely stepped foot in the Otherworld herself, but most Londoners knew the places in that other dimension where they could find one another. They had gotten word of what Ollivan was doing from a *passer-by*; an Otherworld dweller who brought news whenever they came through the portal. At the time, Cassia had taken a dark satisfaction in the fact her mother never made moves to visit him.

Now, for some reason, she was picturing Ollivan at that shop in a way her mind hadn't cared to before. He had stayed there to be found, and Lev and Virgil had found him. Their mother had not. Cassia hadn't either. An entire life lived, and all the acquired acquaintances and loved ones that went with it, and all but his two best friends had abandoned him.

Cassia wasn't sure why she cared, but she soothed herself with the knowledge that she was going looking for him now, with or without Virgil's help, and even if she only needed him alive to get rid of Violet.

"Please help me help him. You have a heart too, Virgil. You care about things." To demonstrate her point, she picked up a political pamphlet from the top of a pile near his bed and waved it at him. Virgil half rose from his seat, face frozen in horror, one hand reaching as if to take the pamphlet off her.

So Cassia looked at it. It was about the protection fees the Sorcerers paid to Jupitus; a tax of sorts, ostensibly to pay the militia to keep the Heart strong. Except that Jupitus had no real right to tax anyone, and enforced it with threats, intimidation, and violence. The pamphlet listed numbers of the quarter's poorest who had had possessions taken, parents beaten, families who had been reduced to even greater squalor by the protection fees. It pointed out that while Jupitus had made the Sorcerers the wealthiest faction in the city, that wealth belonged to the few; to those who could keep him in power.

"Goforth's *History of the Heart* is one thing," Cassia murmured, staring at the pamphlet in her hand. "Yesterday I would have thought I ought to tell my grandfather about this."

Virgil made a choking sound. "You mean to blackmail me into helping you?"

Cassia's head snapped up, and she heard the words she had said – almost to herself – the way Virgil must have heard them. "Oh stars, no! I'm sorry, I didn't mean that. I would never actually tell my grandfather something like this. I just meant that I would have agonised over not telling him for a week."

She had not been brought up among the Sorcerer elite. She had been brought up at the Zoo, where they valued their necessary and grudging alliance with the High Sorcerer, but criticised his iron fist and those who allowed his methods so long as they came with his trade deals. When she spotted small rebellions against him – a poster in an alley, a muttered criticism whispering past her in the market – she felt the same uncomfortable twist she did now, an old fear in one of its many guises: that she did not belong among the people who would overlook his methods so long as they themselves were in his favour.

266

But perhaps, she thought, looking up at Virgil, she was not as alone in this one thing as she imagined.

"Forgive me," he said, visibly relaxing. "I should have guessed any sister of Ollivan's would not dance on Fisk's strings. You know his faults better than anybody, after all."

Cassia looked at the pamphlet again and back at him, confused. *My best friend has a heart.* "This is why you're friends with Ollivan?"

"Well... yes, I suppose it is. It's how we bonded, anyway."

Cassia supposed she could see a vague link between Ollivan's refusal to abide by Jupitus's rules, and reasoned criticism of him as a ruler, but she had never thought of it that way. Ollivan's complaint with their grandfather was that he didn't let him do what he pleased.

She put the pamphlet back. "Look, Virgil. I will understand if you don't think much of me—"

"Oh, don't take the frown personally, he's like that with everyone." Lev Mallory shut the door with a gentle click and grinned at Virgil. "Everyone except me."

As if to illustrate Lev's point, Virgil shot her a dark warning glare. Cassia ignored it. "Lev, Ollivan has gone off to... do something dangerous, and I'm worried he's going to get himself hurt."

Lev's grin slid right from his face. Virgil cursed under his breath and let his head fall into his hands.

"Then we'll help him," said Lev. He drew breath to go on, but Virgil stood abruptly and stormed over to the wardrobe.

"Where are you going?" said Cassia.

"I know how this goes," he responded, pulling out an overcoat and shrugging into it. "Lev and I argue, I beg him not to let

267

Ollivan come between us, he says he doesn't want that either and then, suddenly, I'm doing exactly as he wants." He turned back to them, wearing his overcoat and his scowl. "But since this is an emergency, let's cut to it."

Lev crossed the space between them and kissed him firmly. When Virgil managed to break free, his scowl had eased. He turned to Cassia. "I don't suppose you have any idea where we find our troublemaker, do you?"

In fact, Cassia did have an idea. She had caught the disgruntled look Ollivan had shot at the map on his desk before he vanished. The locating spell he had so disparaged had hit upon a real connection to Violet's whereabouts.

"We're going to need a carriage. I'll explain everything on the way."

*

Now Cassia crouched on the platform against the warehouse, her fists gripping the railing and a sense of foreboding creeping over her.

She didn't understand what she was seeing and she wasn't sure she wanted to. Crates were being unloaded, but of what, she couldn't guess. Goods for trade were declared and bartered for at the Trade House. The presence of people she recognised as militia suggested the delivery was for Jupitus. But their plain clothing and hour of the rendezvous said there was something disreputable afoot.

She wanted to flee, and erase the memory of whatever was happening here from her mind. It did not bode well to know too much about her grandfather's less savoury activities. It especially did not bode well for *her*, whose ties to another faction meant she was considered untrustworthy at the best of times.

After the smugglers and militia had shaken hands, the carts departed. Cassia, Lev, and Virgil could do nothing but watch as, moments later, Ollivan emerged from one of the buildings that flanked the mooring, three Psi with a plethora of blades behind him.

Virgil was right; they had to get onto that ship.

"How many of them are there, do you think?" Cassia asked.

"A dozen."

The three of them jumped. Virgil let out a high-pitched scream that he tried to pass off as a cough when it transpired the words had come from Sybella. She had transported into being on the platform beside them, and was lucky Cassia had quashed the split-second instinct to push her down the stairs.

"Where *were* you?" said Cassia.

"Below," said Sybella with a casual air that turned to a pout when Cassia gave her a knowing look. "Yes, alright, so I don't want Ollivan *dead*. It's a very low level of regard: it doesn't make me a romantic."

Sybella could protest all she wanted; Cassia had been expecting her sooner.

"You managed to get closer?" Sybella nodded. "Is that building on foundations, or stilts in the water?"

"Come again?" said Lev.

Cassia looked between them. "Ollivan can transport," she said. "Even if the building is on the river, they came out of it onto the road and he still didn't escape while he could. Why?"

"One of those Psi must have had a hand on him," said Sybella. "You can't transport when you're in contact with someone."

"I know that," said Cassia tightly. She had no right to be testy, she knew. Sybella's explanation was the only one that made sense. And they were far enough away that perhaps it was true.

They descended to the ground, exchanging snippets of plans.

"If we damage the ship, they'll have to come ashore."

"What if they leave him to drown?"

"I don't think we want to be seen."

"We need a distraction," said Lev. "Lure half of them away and the odds are…"

He trailed off. All around them, the dark was giving way to a silver glow. Cassia squinted at the sudden brightness, but after a moment her eyes adjusted, and the source of the light revealed itself.

More weapons than Cassia could count pressed the four of them together as Psi emerged from the dark on every side.

"Congratulations," said the woman before them, the markings of her magic pulsing silver across her brow. "You lured half of us away."

23

Ollivan paused with one foot on the wharf, half a dozen disembodied blades floating at his back.

"I would much prefer if we could do this here," he said, leaning away from the knives as they encouraged him onwards. If he had not been distracted, he would have seen his captors' approach; behind him, the whorls across their brows glowed with every moment that they wielded their magic.

"Quickly, now," said the one in charge, tipping his chin towards the ship.

So Ollivan was to be at a disadvantage. Him, a Sorcerer over water, who could not transport to safety. Them, a crew of Psi aboard a ship in the thrall of their magic.

He straightened his jacket in a dignified manner and tried to ignore the blades as he walked down the wharf and climbed the gangplank. There were more smugglers on the deck, not all of them Psi. Someone had to be responsible for the glamour, after all. He took the small man with the wiry moustache to be their Sorcerer.

The woman with a wide stance and her jewelled hands on her hips was their captain. She was taller than Ollivan – at least six foot – and just as broad. The Psi fashion for wearing their hair pulled back from their foreheads – to better display the sign of their magic – had endured through the ages, and she wore hers in dirty blonde braids that circled her head and showed off even more jewels glistening at her ears. She had a prominent nose, straight and proud, and as she looked him up and down it was as if her nose moved first, like a bloodhound's, and the rest of her head was pulled along behind it.

Ollivan flashed her a winning smile. "Just the smuggler I was looking for."

Delphine de Magna issued a command with a nod of her head, and the knives holding Ollivan in place retreated. He felt his shoulders relax.

"Why so long, Sorcerer?" said Delphine. "We were starting to worry your banishment might stick."

"Ah, Delphine, you needn't have feared. The planning took a little time, that's all."

She nodded in bored assent and twisted a heavy gold ring as she regarded him. "Why are you spying on me, Ollivan?"

Ollivan tensed. He and Delphine had an amicable history, as much as was possible between a narcotics chemist and the ruthless crook who sold his wares for him. Having discovered her by spying on Jupitus, it was too good of a joke to sell his grandfather the drugs he made. Chemical-magical concoctions of his own design or adapted from the pages of the secret ledgers. Compounds that let Sorcerers manifest their dreams and nightmares in the form of a glamour, or brought on lucid and multi-sensory hallucinations of the taker's choosing. A smoke that brought on a sensation often described as music in the veins. A dangerous and unsettling tonic that caused an intense euphoria in the place of pain.

Those he didn't sell himself at the Wending Place or among the punters and fighters of his duelling evening, he supplied to Delphine. She in turn sold them to the High Sorcerer, whose agents distributed them throughout London, and quietly placed the profits back in Jupitus's pocket. So it was that no blame befell Ollivan that he didn't share with his unwitting grandfather, and Delphine's empire and wealth swelled.

But now, he could read every line of Delphine's suspicions as clear as the intricate marks on her brow. He had escaped punishment from the High Sorcerer, and now she had discovered him watching her movements in secret. Instinctively, Ollivan's magic reached for the ground, and he had to fight the sickening sensation that came with finding water instead. It was like losing one's balance at the top of a cliff.

"I promise you, Delphine, I wasn't spying. I was waiting for the militia to leave. You know that my grandfather can't find out I was here."

"So this is a social call?" She spread her hands, a wry smile creasing her face. "Isn't it polite to bring gifts?"

Ollivan reached into the inside pocket of his coat and produced a cloth-wrapped parcel that Delphine accepted greedily. Inside were packets of a sky-blue powder that could be dissolved in water and consumed to mimic the physical sensation of flying. It was addictive in large quantities, and caused a fierce malaise as it wore off, and yet it was enduringly popular. Ollivan had recovered this batch from a hidden stash, remarkably unscathed since his banishment.

"A gift," he repeated meaningfully. "Not an opening offer. This is only two hundred doses. I've turned over a new leaf, Delphine."

"Ah, the new leaf." She looked wistfully into an invisible distance. "I've turned over several myself. You come and see me when it passes."

She led Ollivan below deck and to the captain's cabin. The space had not changed since he'd last been there; its contents sparkled like their owner and would have funded the Heart for several months. A long glass display case along one wall was filled with jewels that would look out of place on anyone less important than an empress, though one wine-soaked evening the two of them had donned the entire collection. A pair of diamond-encrusted muskets were mounted on one wall. They had vanished from the personal collection of a Psi arms dealer, a merchant of war, nearly two years ago. The dealer had guarded all of his priceless possessions against any kind of psychokinetic burglary, but like many of London's elite, he believed the Principles were adequate in protecting him against theft from a Sorcerer. Ollivan had gifted them to Delphine after the particularly lucrative sale of a batch of his products.

She poured them each a drink in exquisite crystal tumblers and leaned back against the desk, studying him. Ollivan settled into a chair.

"I understand one of your people suffered an accident outside the Chambers last night," he said.

Delphine's eyes widened, and Ollivan knew instantly his hunch had been right. A Psi in Drusella Square the night before Delphine arrived, and a locating spell pointing him here. It could only be her representative, there to arrange the rendezvous.

"Oz," she confirmed, fingers tightening on her glass.

"Is he on board? Can I talk to him?"

"He is being *treated* in one of your infirmaries." Her emphasis left no room for doubt. Jupitus wasn't letting Oz go. "A goodwill gesture. Fisk wrote to the officials personally. Anything to make it look like he has nothing to hide."

The 'officials' were what Delphine called the Trinity. They were the three representatives of the ruling families of the Psi; the Underground's equivalent of High Sorcerer. Ollivan understood Delphine's frustration. She took no part in the dealings between faction rulers. To her, Oz was not a citizen of the Underground, he was a citizen of the under*world*, and it was inconvenient for the city rulers to be in Oz's business. In *her* business.

Ollivan twisted his glass in his hands. "And does Oz remember what happened to him?"

"A *magic doll* worked some enchantment on him and knocked him unconscious," said Delphine without missing a beat. "But of course, you already knew that."

Ollivan's head snapped up. "Did he tell my grandfather's people that?"

She shot him a derisive look. "What do you take us for? Oz won't speak to them if they keep him for ten years. Lucky we have someone in the infirmary to act as go-between."

"And what... state is he in?"

Delphine's scowl deepened. "Can *you* not tell *me* that? Do you know of this cursed toy or don't you?"

"I'm just trying to assemble the facts," said Ollivan. "I believe the enchantment might be... drinking people's magic. Is that what happened to Oz?"

Delphine was silent for a long time, and Ollivan could tell she was trying to decide if he'd told her enough to place blame on his shoulders. He readied an explanation.

"Oz cannot lift so much as a feather," she said, and Ollivan went cold. "He felt his body go weak and thought he would die.

When he woke, it was as if he was an Otherworlder. Not a spark of magic in him."

"Heaven, earth, and the damn constellations," breathed Ollivan into his hands.

"What sort of weapon is this thing, Sorcerer?" Delphine's voice was low and dangerous. "What kind of magic can steal another's? To wield such a thing…"

Ollivan couldn't read her expression, but he took a guess. "There's no money in it, if that's what you're thinking."

Her gaze hardened. "You know my rules. I'm not a killer – not for money, at least – and I'm not a slaver."

"That doesn't mean you wouldn't—"

"I trade in *goods*, not in lives. And these are people's lives." She smiled cruelly. "No, Sorcerer. We sail for the continent tonight. I won't be back in London until whatever evil you've unleashed is dealt with. This time I wouldn't mess with what you're in for all the money in the world."

And Ollivan would pay all the money in the world to be out of it. Oz's magic, gone. Was that what would have happened to Sybella if Ollivan hadn't helped her? He did not believe he could do such a thing for Oz. He did not even understand how a Sorcerer spell could absorb Psi magic. It was perverse.

"Can he get it back?" she asked him, an edge in her tone. A warning.

Ollivan met her eye. "I don't understand this spell," he said, though it pained him. "But I understand magic. If the vessel can take in Psi magic, it can release it too. Theoretically."

"And Wraith magic?"

He stilled. "Wraith?"

Delphine laughed. She had a cruel, grating laugh. Ollivan usually enjoyed it a lot. "It seems you can go straight, or you can know what really goes on in this city, but not both. Four of them, near the border."

"On the Wraith side?"

"Yes. They were picnicking, I think, or something else sweet, and they were found unconscious. There was a little on it in some of the evening papers. Fisk has kept the fact of Oz perfectly quiet, so no one has made the connection."

No one but Jupitus, if it was in the papers. "How do you know there is a connection?"

The underworld always knew.

"One of Isiah's people saw the doll." She leaned closer. "*Running*."

Even as he shuddered, Ollivan refused to let his mind settle on the word. He did not care to picture something he could see freely in his nightmares.

Delphine laughed again. "I understand from Isiah that his man's face looked as yours does now. He said he saw the thing slip down a drain."

"In the North? You're absolutely sure?"

"Of course I'm sure."

The vessel had traversed nearly the entire length of the quarter – had crossed the river – attacking people at will and remaining unseen. It – *she*, Ollivan found himself thinking, as the thought of her running forced its way into his head – had drained a *Wraith*.

And a Psi. How, he only wished he knew. But why, only one reason made any sense.

She was collecting magics.

There was a knock at the cabin door. "Enter," called Delphine.

A Psi crewmember stepped into the cabin. "More lurkers, Delphine," she said. "Four of them."

Delphine's most ruthless gaze cut to Ollivan, the full weight of her suspicion returning in a flash.

"Well, they're not with me," he protested.

"You have them?" The woman nodded. With another glare at Ollivan, Delphine's markings began to glow. The two long knives at her hips unholstered themselves and hovered by her shoulders. The gems in their hilts twinkled in the clara lamp glow as she spun them; a pretty threat. "See them in."

Ollivan just had time to fear that the captives were his grandfather's people before the reality became much worse. Cassia, Virgil, Lev, and Sybella were hustled into the cabin and arranged into a line before Delphine. Ollivan couldn't resist the urge to look over his shoulder, like one of Jupitus's spies might be clinging to the outside of the ship with their face to the window. This was wrong. This was everything he feared.

"Ollivan?" said Cassia.

Delphine rounded on him, accusation in her eyes. His friends took him in – whole and hale, with a glass of some expensive spirit in hand – with expressions ranging from confusion to disbelief. Virgil was the first to offer an explanation.

"We're here to rescue you," he said in a monotone.

Ollivan had thought he enjoyed this; lawlessness, peril, wreaking havoc right under the High Sorcerer's nose. Now, looking at the blades hovering near the necks of – he looked at each of them as he made a mental head-count – *everyone* he loved, he was astounded that he had ever seen the appeal. He thought he might faint.

"Sorcerer," said Delphine in a growl, and suddenly her blades were pointing at *him*. "Explain yourself."

"Would love to," said Ollivan. "Can't, unfortunately, except that it seems your lurkers are here out of concern for me. Sybella Dentley, Lev Mallory, Virgil Pike, and my sister, Cassia Sims." He gestured to Delphine. "This is Delphine de Magna. She's an old friend."

"You said it was dangerous," said Cassia, her voice small, and a sickening guilt swirled inside of him. She was here because he was; had followed him, as he had never really believed she would. He had said it was dangerous, and here she was anyway. What did that mean?

"I meant for *you*," he said. Was it the words or the rare gentleness of his tone that pulled her brows together that way?

"This is your sister, you say," said Delphine, prowling closer to Cassia. To her credit, Cassia held her ground, a proud tilt to her chin. "The High Sorcerer's granddaughter."

"He will kill her," said Ollivan firmly, looking Cassia in the eye. He needed her to understand. "If he even suspects she was here, or knew about you."

Cassia's expression faltered. She blinked at him in shock.

Delphine considered her a moment longer, then cast a cursory glance at the others. Her gaze finally came to rest on Ollivan.

"They're no danger to you," he said imploringly.

"I will choose to believe you," she said, her markings finally growing dull as she lowered her weapons and signalled her people to do the same. "But I leave it with you to impress upon them how much they will regret speaking of this to anyone."

"I assure you, Delphine," said Ollivan, looking again at his friends and trying to calm his panic at seeing them there in the smuggler's cabin, "I will."

"Good," she said lightly, picking up her glass. "You can get off my ship now."

Ollivan had no wish to hang around. He had a lead on the Guysman; a tenuous one, but it left no time to waste.

The crew cleared the way to let them leave, Ollivan bringing up the rear.

"If you decide to get out too, Sorcerer," said Delphine as he reached the door, "I could use you in my operation on the continent. I would set you up with a comfortable place, an extensive laboratory, freedom to experiment. Just come and find me."

Ollivan sketched a salute as he left, heart clenching at the feelings the offer stirred. This time yesterday, he would have laughed his refusal. He was moving forward, out of his old life and the trappings that had led him to the Otherworld. Everything was going to work out, if only he kept fixing one problem at a time.

He did not like how much he welcomed the offer of escape.

When the sound of the explosion fades to a ringing, you're sitting on the pavement, and there's blood on your hands. The window of the sweet shop is gone. Lemon drops and pebbles of glass decorate your dress.

You sway to your feet and stumble away from the melee of roaring wolves and Whitechapel guns. Adults run in all directions, too fast and too far above you to recognise.

But Hester's coat was red. She's gone, Gedeon and Fyfe too. You're not one of them so they've left you, and you stand in the street with the explosion still throbbing through your skull, and sob.

Someone grabs your shoulder and you try to run. But she tightens her grip and kneels before you, touching your hair, your shoulders, brushing glass from your skirt. Then she lifts you awkwardly in her arms. You're too big, but she tucks you into her red coat anyway, and carries you to safety.

They were half a mile away at the corner of Battersea Park – the moonlight striking the Thames but the trees casting them in shadow – before Ollivan declared it safe to speak. Sybella was fastest.

"You know smugglers." It wasn't a question.

Ollivan flashed a grin. "You didn't think I kept all my products for the Successors, did you?"

"I *suppose* I thought we had an understanding that involved you being a good little President until it was my turn, and yet here you are, leaving a business meeting with a pirate."

"I think a pirate is different," said Lev. "Just because she does crime on a ship, that doesn't make her a pirate, right, Ollivan?"

"She dabbles," said Ollivan, eyes still on Sybella. "*My* understanding was that if I died, you would become President, and yet here you are on a mission to save me."

"Don't flatter yourself. Cassia wanted my help. I'm here for her."

Four pairs of eyes turned to Cassia. Sybella's bored into her, imploring her to confirm the lie. Cassia had seen in the Sanctuary that Sybella's feelings for Ollivan were not neatly confined to the past.

"Can we talk about the more important issue here?" cut in Virgil, an edge of hysteria in his voice. "Enforcers. Smugglers.

Clandestine meets. Have any of you *read* the Principles? What in the heaven and earth happened back there?"

Ollivan rubbed a hand over his face. "A few years ago now, I was in the library at the Wending Place very late. I was looking out of the window, across the square, and I saw someone in a hooded cloak exit the Chambers through a side door. So I followed them." He shrugged. "I had my nose in my grandfather's business as often as I could. It seemed wise to know more than he thought I did. And the person was wrapped up in a cloak in the height of summer, meaning they didn't want anyone to see their face."

"Because they were Psi," said Lev.

"I followed them back to the Underground. To a hidden berth, and a smuggler's ship, and a whole beautiful, damning conspiracy."

Cassia heard only parts of the rest of his explanation. How he had continued to observe the enforcers and the ship over several months, tenaciously, until he had pieced the whole thing together. How he had discovered *other* black-market traders in London and beyond who dealt with the High Sorcerer; some in priceless artefacts with whom Jupitus matched buyers among London's elite, others in worse things: animals, human organs, *people*.

He answered every question, described every detail, everything but the one fact they did not need explaining; just how badly Jupitus was breaking the Principles. He had told her it was dangerous. Cassia hadn't understood.

"I went to find out more about the doll, and I did. Listen to me. Oz hasn't recovered his magic. And she's attacked four Wraiths now as well."

Cassia's stomach flipped. "She can't... *use* that magic—"

"No," said Ollivan without any conviction. "Stars, I doubt she can even hold their magic once she drains it."

"Then why is she bothering?" said Lev.

Ollivan's eyes unfocused and his brows pulled together as he worked through the problem like a sum. "It's possible she likes the taste."

"The *taste*?"

"All the spell is designed to do is drink magic. Sentient beings take pleasure in the things that are natural to them. Eating, sleeping, sex. And Violet's original enchantment mimics sentience. She wants variety."

Cassia scoffed. "You don't know what she wants, and you don't know what you really designed her to do. How do we *find her*, Ollivan?" He continued to stare into space, lost in a thought. "Ollivan!"

Ollivan blinked as he snapped out of his reverie. "She's going to go after another magic. It'll probably be Changeling or Whisperer, since those quarters border the North. She might be moving independently but she's still little bigger than a rat and probably no faster, and she'll likely have been hampered by a lack of easy victims overnight. With a little luck… we might be able to catch her in the act."

"Champion," said Lev, brightening at what sounded like a plan. "Then we split up. Half of us go to Camden, half to Whitechapel."

Ollivan said nothing for a long moment. "I don't want to drag any of you into this."

Sybella snorted. "Your words say one thing, but your face says another. You need our help."

Ollivan quirked a brow. "And you're offering it?"

Sybella folded her arms across her chest and shifted her weight. "If she's attacking people of other factions, this could have political implications. I want to inherit a *stable* ruling seat when I become High Sorcerer."

Cassia wasn't fooled. Ollivan knew Sybella better than her, so she guessed that he wasn't either, but he said nothing. Instead he turned to his friends.

"Virgil?"

Virgil sighed, that weighty sadness settling on his shoulders again. "Is it true this was all about revenge against Jasper Hawkes?"

Ollivan shifted his weight. "What do you know of it? For a matter of fact" – he turned on Cassia – "what do *they* know about any of this?"

"Your sister was looking out for you," said Virgil, his tone brooking no argument. "She came to us because she knew we'd look out for you too. And I don't need to know everything that happened between you and Jasper Hawkes to understand wanting revenge. I've thought about breaking his nose often enough. And his jaw. Perhaps a few ribs."

"Easy there," muttered Lev, smiling affectionately.

"Because the fact is, whatever happened that night, the night you, ah…"

"*Didn't* kill anyone?" said Ollivan, a note of challenge in his voice. Virgil didn't rise to it. He met Ollivan's gaze soberly.

"Whatever happened, your real friends wouldn't have let it come to that. But stars, Sims. I wish you could learn to control your temper. It would be so much easier to care about you."

285

Ollivan ducked his head. Sybella averted her eyes, and Cassia thought she saw them glisten with threatened tears. In the tension that suddenly pulled taut between them all, Cassia fought not to voice her admiration for Virgil and the hard, honest thing he had said. Her brother needed friends who would hold him to account. It revealed something intangible to realise he had them. People cared for him. They believed he had a heart.

But Lev cleared his throat, erasing the tension with it.

"So what's the plan?" he said.

Ollivan straightened, no doubt happy to have changed topic. "Delphine said the Wraiths were attacked just the other side of the border. If she's looking for Changeling or Whisperer victims, I don't think she'll go further than she needs to. Near the border to the North, somewhere with people." He looked up. The first light of a new day was turning the sky grey. The stars had vanished. "A commuter area perhaps. There's time for us to be there first."

"Marvellous. And then we can have our magic sucked out of us before we pass out," said Cassia, earning a scowl from her brother. "What exactly are we supposed to do if we find her, Ollivan?"

"I'm not saying this isn't dangerous," said Ollivan, "but we'll be in groups. You and I will go to Camden; Virgil, Lev, and Sybella to Whitechapel. We'll have numbers on our side, so corner her. There's no part of her enchantment that protects against good old-fashioned being torn limb from limb. Immobilise her, however you can, wrap her in a binding spell and get her to the Wending Place."

"And if she does drain our magic?" said Sybella. "I can take a couple of stunning spells if she's got them, but you said the Psi man hasn't recovered."

"Magic taken from a person is theirs, is it not? I can't vouch for how it feels to wield Psi magic and Wraith magic, but I do know magic bears the mark of the wielder. It responds to our wishes because it is ours alone." The others nodded their agreement, so Cassia nodded too, even as her ribs tightened around her heart; she didn't recognise the phenomenon Ollivan spoke of. "If the vessel is opened – that is, if the spell is destroyed – that magic has nowhere to go but back to those who wielded it."

Sybella narrowed her eyes at him. "You believe if you can unravel Violet, the victims' magic will be restored."

"It's a theory," he said carefully. "But magic obeys rules, even if one doesn't understand them, as is the case with this Guysman. This rule, however, I *do* understand. Yes, I believe the victims will get their magic back."

Theories, ifs, maybes. It was the most haphazard, reckless plan Cassia could imagine. If they had to wield their magic in Camden or Whitechapel, they would be breaking the Principles. Even if they didn't, and they could snatch the doll up in their hands, Violet's very presence outside the Heart probably constituted a breach, and that would befall them too. And suffering the consequences of all of the above might be the better scenario if Ollivan was wrong about drained magic returning to the owner.

But if they had a chance to catch Violet, they had to take it. Despite her misgivings, Cassia could think of only one amendment.

"I won't go to Camden." Ollivan raised an eyebrow in question. "I don't want to be recognised by any of the militia."

If she sounded petty, she didn't care. She had been granted an exception to use magic in the Changeling quarter when she had lived there, but it had been revoked when she left. If she had to risk the humiliation of being arrested for using her magic outside Sorcerer territory, she would rather it was in front of strangers.

"Alright, fine," said Ollivan peevishly. "You and I will go to Whitechapel."

"If you can get there, cross the guard point at Blackfriars," said Sybella. "There's a tram not far from there that will take you north."

"Thank you. We'll see you back at the Wending Place." Ollivan looked from Sybella to Lev and Virgil. "Earth and stars, will you please be careful?"

"We'll look after each other," said Lev, grinning. Despite his weak magic, he looked less afraid than any of them. He turned to Cassia. "You look after each other too."

And then they parted ways; Lev, Virgil, and Sybella doubling back to cross to the north bank, Cassia and Ollivan following the river east on the lookout for a hackney cab to take them to Blackfriars. A hint of yellow was starting to show above the skyline to the east.

"I think it's safe to say you've missed your curfew," said Cassia.

"Oh, don't worry about that. I already reported to Mother last night and went up to bed early. I said I'd eaten a bad prawn and feigned nausea to discourage her from bothering me for any reason. You know how averse she is to sickness."

"But—" She had so many criticisms that she hadn't even chosen one when she began speaking, and couldn't narrow it down to the most pertinent. She was in a dark mood; with Ollivan, with herself, with the mess of a night that had seen her captured by smugglers for no reason. *Of course* Ollivan had found himself among friends, because that was the type of luck that his worst choices brought; because when you were Ollivan Sims, you were more likely than not going to end up in the hands of smugglers who *liked you*.

He was watching her, she realised, a probing disquiet in his eyes. Cassia picked up her speed until she was marching ahead of him and could pretend he wasn't there.

All was silent between them for a time, and Cassia could be alone with her thoughts; thoughts that were sparking and smoking, and threatening to engulf her.

"Is something the matter?"

Cassia was suddenly certain she had just heard the four most infuriating words in existence. That he could ask her that. That he was so blissfully unaware of how awful he was. "I should have gone with Lev and Virgil."

"Pardon?"

"I said, 'nothing that would concern you.'"

A beat of blessed silence. "That's a bit unfair," he said. "Considering I don't know what it is yet."

She stopped and spun to face him. Ollivan staggered to a halt. "Fine. You meant it when you said Grandfather would kill me if he found out I knew about his illegal trading."

She didn't pose it as a question. Ollivan answered it anyway. "Of course I did. That's why you're upset?"

"You meant it… and you were right."

"Cassia." He didn't look remorseful, exactly, but a kind of sympathy crossed his face. "I know it's not an easy thing to hear, but I needed you to understand it."

"It's not that." She shook her head as she tried to think of what she meant. "I wasn't surprised. I mean, I *was*, but I was

289

only surprised that I wasn't surprised. And I was so… ashamed of myself. For never having realised it."

Ollivan said nothing. Then he, too, shook his head. "You've lost me."

Cassia was numb. She was too numb to talk about this. "Just forget it."

She tried to keep walking, but Ollivan grabbed her arm and stepped into her path. "No, wait, try again. You're upset with yourself for never realising that… Jupitus was dealing on the black market?"

"*No.*" The frustration was building. She was afraid she would cry. "I thought my fate was either being a disappointment to him or making him proud, and that my life would be better if he was proud, even if he was a tyrant. Even if I would rather have nothing to do with him, things would be better for me. But those aren't the only options. There's a version of my life in which he has me murdered, just like anyone else who might be a threat to him. And it's so stars-damned obvious.

"And *you.*" She jabbed a finger at him and he stepped back. "You knew exactly what he was capable of and you started *trading with one of his business partners.* You're not just courting his ire, you're courting his blade. And ever since the ship I can't stop thinking *why*? Why would Ollivan be so reckless? Why has he been such an unrepentant miscreant his whole life? I always thought it was arrogance, some foolish idea that you could outmanoeuvre him. Or maybe it was just who you were; bad and rotten, and incapable of following rules handed down by *anyone*. And now I'm thinking of what Grandfather is – because I refused to think of it sooner – and I'm terrified that I was wrong. I'm terrified that it's because… because you would simply rather be a disappointment to a tyrant than a source of pride."

Cassia hated herself, and she *hated* Ollivan. All her life, she had measured herself against her older brother and felt underappreciated, unseen, but at least *righteous*. But it turned out, even in his delinquency, Ollivan had still managed to be better than her. He hadn't been a coward.

She realised she was staring at the lightening sky so as to avoid his face. She couldn't bear to see the self-satisfied grin, didn't want to hear the teasing, or worse. But when she finally found the courage to meet her brother's eye, he wasn't smiling. He wasn't sneering. He looked sad.

"Welcome to the path of most resistance," he said.

"No," she growled. "I'm not like you. You're a murderer."

"Am I? Because another murderer told you it was so?"

She stilled. She didn't want to be taken in by any of this. She wanted to go back to believing him arrogant, and herself righteous. Just because she had new insight into how Ollivan had come to kill someone, it didn't mean she had to take his side. It didn't mean she had to believe him when he said it wasn't his fault.

"You don't have to be like me, Cassia. You just have to work out what you do want."

She laughed bitterly. "I don't get to choose what I want."

"You're right. You don't get to choose, not if you ever want your magic to start working with you. Your magic *is* you. It knows your real intention even when you don't." Cassia could do nothing but stare at him in confusion. His smile appeared, laced with self-satisfaction, and her stomach turned. "That's your problem, after all, isn't it?"

"My problem?" She didn't recognise her own voice; low and breaking with rage. Ollivan Sims thought he knew about why her magic was failing her; thought he was helping her. She stepped very close, so that he could feel every lick of her fury as she went on. "You don't know *anything* about it. So don't you dare to presume to tell me my problem."

She stepped around him and continued walking. At last they reached a main thoroughfare and hailed a driver still yawning as he began his working day. Cassia collapsed into the seat in exhaustion and relief. If she had to cross the entirety of London with Ollivan at her side, she would do it by the fastest means possible.

"Thank you, by the way," said Ollivan as they set off towards Whitechapel. Cassia glanced over at him. He was looking at his fingers, laced together in his lap. "You thought I was in danger tonight, and you came after me. I didn't think you would. So thank you."

Cassia had been clinging to her anger so tightly that it burst, seeping from her grip like whisps of cloud. She felt bereft without it; empty. *Ollivan* had made her feel empty.

"I didn't do it for you," she clipped. "I just need you to stop Violet."

25

Ollivan did not care for Whitechapel.

The territory of the Whisperers was a place unlike any other in London. The streets, the businesses and people were all of an ordinary sort, but the atmosphere was uncannily absent of an element he never even noticed the presence of elsewhere.

Whisperers read minds, including each other's. Though they were generally capable of speech, they claimed mind-to-mind communication carried a precision that spoken language could never achieve, so it was the preferred language of one-to-one business and conversation in their quarter.

It meant an atmosphere of silence louder than thunder. Ollivan likened moving through Whitechapel to trying to break the ice at a party, except the entire room waited on your joke. Every door that creaked on unoiled hinges was the awkward clink of a glass against someone's jewelled fingers. Every scuff of a shoe was a throat being cleared in the corner. Ollivan was never so aware of his own breathing as when they passed the guard point at Blackfriars without speaking a word.

And that was before they even boarded the tram.

"Two please," said Ollivan, pitching his voice low and still feeling as if he had screamed through a megaphone. He could feel the eyes of the few other passengers turning to ogle him. The look the conductor gave him said he needn't have broken the silence at all. He handed Ollivan his change without a word.

Cassia started directly for the rear with her chin tucked low into the collar of her coat and her eyes on her feet. Perhaps she thought the stares would be less at the back, but Ollivan doubted it; Whisperers did not readily move their faces, finding that minds conveyed emotion as well as they did meaning, but they were perfectly capable of twisting their necks to stare. Besides, the only cover they would have for the words they spoke would be the sound of the horses. He wished to be as near to them as possible.

"Let's sit here," he called to her. Cassia swung round, glaring like he could not embarrass her more if he started singing. She doubled back and dropped onto the frontmost bench beside him.

The wheels and horses started up a blessed rumble. The sun had broken over the horizon, and the sky was bleeding from purple to sunny blue. The tram was not as laden with passengers as it would be in another hour, the streets not as beaten beneath heels, but the day was beginning. Violet's potential victims were stepping out. Perhaps he should have done without Cassia's help and transported directly to where they were likely to find her. It wouldn't be the first time he had done so against the decree of the Principles; a bit of paper he had scarce little respect for. But he did not want to attempt this alone. Having tried to shake his sister from his tail once already, he was glad she was here.

Ollivan tried to oust the thoughts from his mind. He knew how to put up mental obstacles against a mind reader – a protection some Whisperers were willing to teach, for a price – but it was not an exact science. If any of his fellow passengers were nosy or suspicious enough, they might succeed in seeing his purpose in Whitechapel, and alert their militia before he was any the wiser.

294

He forced himself to relax, to let his thoughts dance lightly through his mind, intangible as smoke, instead of digging in and sprouting roots. Whisperers could grasp roots.

He drifted into a daydream of Virgil exacting his vengeance on Jasper, just as he'd described it; with fists instead of spells. He imagined Jasper spitting out his teeth, Virgil towering over him. It was a grimly satisfying fantasy, and yet absurd enough that he smiled. Virgil was bigger than Jasper, but he didn't have an ounce of real malice in him. He was good; gentle. Grinding Jasper Hawkes to a pulp wasn't worthy of him. Not like Ollivan.

I wish you could learn to control your temper. It would be so much easier to care about you.

The daydream transformed, and then it was Ollivan throwing a fist at the boy who had destroyed his life. *Blood on his knuckles. Blood on his face. Bodies packed around the ring. His opponent was on his knees, swaying like he was about to go down. One more blow would end it...*

Ollivan jolted as something gripped his arm. But it was Cassia, leaning close to speak. Her features were tight with concentration; she was trying to guard her mind from their fellow travellers too. "Are we to manage this without magic?" she murmured under the sound of the horses.

Ollivan had been running through scenarios since Delphine's cabin. All he needed was eyes on the stars-damned doll, and a chance to throw something over it again, and it would be done. In the better scenarios, they lay in wait in a likely spot, saw her before she saw them, and split up to crowd her from two sides. With any luck, she would be focused on her quarry – the Whisperers – and whatever sense he had for Sorcerer magic would not give them away. Perhaps one of them would draw her notice and have to take a spell or two before the other seized her. He would make sure it was him; he had been in enough fights that a bit of aggressive magic didn't scare him. And if they couldn't get close enough without returning fire? If they created a scene in front of the Whisperers?

"If I have to immobilise the doll with magic," he said, matching his sister's volume, "I'll grab her and transport out. Leave calmly. Don't give any sign that you know me. Head south and I'll find you."

Cassia made a face when he confessed he would leave her there, but appeared to see that it was the best solution. "And if I have to perform magic? I can't transport."

Ollivan opened his mouth to reply that she had no magic, but after the revelations of the night before, that seemed a cruelty too far. Besides, he didn't truly believe it. "I'll create a distraction. Slip away the first chance you see, and we'll follow the same plan."

Somewhere in the middle of his speech, he lost her attention. She was sitting straighter in her seat, craning to see around the horses. Ollivan was so used to a Heart level of background noise that he hadn't caught the rising commotion up ahead, but it seemed that just like the rest of the city, Whisperers did not panic in silence. Cries and shouts were coming from ahead.

Ollivan grasped the handrail above him and swung out of his seat to stand at the open front of the tram. They were nearly to Whitechapel's northern border; the area in which they had hoped wildly to catch sight of the doll. The morning was almost in full swing, and around the tram, people were beginning to swarm.

They were flooding in the opposite direction.

"Ollivan," said Cassia warily. She had come to his side, and she pointed to a steward – Whitechapel militia – who was hurrying another figure in the opposite direction to the tide. They wore the purple and white tunics recognised the city wide as the uniform of healers. "Someone's hurt."

"Maybe more than one."

The tram was banking left to take a detour, the driver shooting wary glances at the regular route, but half a dozen more healers and three times as many militia were centred on an office building down the street. Ollivan couldn't be sure, but he thought the dirty smudges on the white tunics was blood. Could that mean his wayward enchantment wasn't involved in this?

"Militia," said Cassia, her voice thin with fear.

"I saw them."

"No, *enforcers*. There."

She pulled Ollivan away from the front of the tram and back into their seats just as four people in the suits and gold pins of Jupitus's mob passed by. They were accompanied by even more stewards. Whitechapel had welcomed them there.

He met Cassia's eye, and saw his realisation mirrored there: they were too late.

"We have to get out of here," said Cassia near his ear.

Ollivan nodded, his mouth dry, and tugged at the collar of his shirt to let some cool air in. What if he was discovered here? What excuse would he give? It was worse than a trap laid by Jupitus; it was one of his own design.

"We split up," he said. "Stay on the tram until the next stop, then go to the Wending Place. I'll meet you there."

Cassia nodded, but her hand gripped his arm before he was fully out of his seat. She tipped her chin at a *second* group of enforcers crossing the road in front of them at a run.

Ollivan turned and made for the rear of the tram, keeping low. The Whisperer passengers were too engrossed with watching the action in the street to be curious as he slipped through the door and jumped into the road. The enforcers were coming into view on his left, so he spun right and kept pace with the tram for cover. They passed without looking in his direction; he watched them until they rounded the corner and disappeared.

By the time he turned to be on his way, it was too late to hide.

"Mr Sims." Selby. The enforcer and his comrades fanned out to block Ollivan's path. A wave of dizziness overcame him at the triumphant smirk on the man's face. "Your grandfather would like to see you."

Ollivan rallied to match Selby's grin with one of his own and feigned surprise. "Me? By all means, lead the way."

An iron grip tightened around his arm, but Ollivan barely felt it. As he was marched towards a carriage, he chanced a glance at the retreating tram. Cassia's face was pressed to the window, pale and wide-eyed. But Ollivan shook his head minutely, and she pulled away, turning stiffly to face forward, borne onwards by the horses.

26

Whitechapel was closing its borders to the Heart.

"Surely that's an overreaction," said Sybella, pacing the Sanctuary as Cassia leaned against her desk. Lev and Virgil were slumped against each other on the couch in an exhausted stupor. "They can't even prove whatever hurt those Whisperers is Sorcerer-made."

"The whole office full of people suffered nose bleeds as they lost their magic," said Cassia. "And it gets worse. You and Jasper were fine, Ollivan said the Psi man hasn't recovered his magic. Two of the Whisperers are in comas."

She had struck upon the idea to go home before coming to the Wending Place, in the hopes Alana would still be there and would have word of the goings on in Whitechapel. "The only blessing, at least according to what my mother knew, is that witnesses saw everything except the cause. Nobody actually *saw* Violet."

It was hardly reassuring when Cassia had feared exactly the type of escalation the morning had brought. This was not merely about magic and the victims of the Guysman. The more damage Violet did beyond the boundaries of the Heart, the more they risked civil unrest.

Yesterday, the news from Whitechapel would have seen Cassia marching right into Jupitus's office to confess to everything. Now, she doubted her own motives, let alone the mercy she would hope to receive for turning Ollivan in. They would pick at her story, make her recount everything that had happened since she had found the doll. They would interrogate Ollivan too, and probably Jasper. Somehow, eventually, her grandfather would learn that she knew of his black-market dealing. Then nothing her mother might say would protect her.

"If no one saw her, then there's nothing to link this to Ollivan," said Virgil. "Fisk can't punish him for it."

"*Shouldn't* isn't the same as *can't*," said Lev.

"Well it should be! If he tries to pin this on Ollivan, we'll hold him to account. We'll let it be known the city over that he's making Ollivan a scapegoat. Whatever happened to due process?"

Lev nodded sympathetically as Virgil gave up and sank back into the couch. "Except Ollivan *did* do this," he said. "Perhaps he's confessing."

Cassia snorted a laugh. "Ollivan is *not* confessing. And my grandfather won't be drawn into a dance trying to catch him red-handed. He'll wait for proof."

"And he'll find it," said Sybella. She chewed on her lip. "Sooner or later."

*

Cassia was returning home again, praying she would find Ollivan there and hear the excuse he offered the enforcers, when *sooner* became the likelier scenario.

She was cutting across the communal garden in front of the Sims' house when he stepped out from behind a tree as if he had been lying in wait. Cassia froze. Jasper's ultimatum had seemed like the smallest of her problems after Violet escaped, and it had all but slipped her mind. Now that he was in front of her, she wondered how that had ever been.

"Jasper—"

"Help me understand why I waited for hours for you the other night and you never showed up. I was worried."

If he thought that would work, he had caught her at the wrong time. Cassia huffed a sigh. "Something came up."

He waited as if he expected her to go on, but Cassia was still trying to think up the fastest way out of this interaction. "We made an agreement, Cassia. Where's the vessel?"

Could she admit that she'd lost the doll? Would that make it worse if Jasper decided to make good on his threat? Before she could say something she'd regret, Jasper stepped closer, a greedy glint in his eyes.

"How do you siphon off the magic?" he whispered.

"Beg your pardon?"

"I know what happened in Whitechapel this morning. And the North have confirmed that the Wraiths found unconscious yesterday have lost their abilities. But how do you extract the magic it absorbs for yourself? Is there another part to the spell? You have to show me how it's done."

For a moment, Cassia was speechless. "You think that I'm... setting Violet on people and then taking their power? Other magics included?" It sounded preposterous out loud.

Jasper scrutinised her, then plastered on a mild smile. "I'm getting carried away. Of course you haven't got that far yet. Just the vessel will do. I can figure the rest out without you."

Cassia landed on a reply that gave nothing away and still told him everything he needed to know. "I'm not giving you the doll."

His smile vanished, and he came forward until he towered over her. They were in a secluded corner of the garden, with head-high hydrangeas on three sides, and a line of trees separating them from the road. Jasper had caught her alone.

"Do I need to remind you that the Guysman enchantment is so far above your level of capability that the best you can hope for is not killing yourself?" he snapped. "I don't want to get you in trouble, Cassia, but I won't let you endanger whoever you please with magic you can't control. You'll give the vessel to me, or I'll tell your mother who's responsible for the stolen magic."

Again, Cassia heard his harsh words from a detached part of her mind, and yet she mourned the person she thought he'd been. As cruel and driven by foolishness as Jasper was, he still posed a threat to her. She only saw one solution, and it was a temporary fix: stalling.

"I understand," she said, letting her gaze lower in submission. "But I need a bit of time."

"You have until tonight," said Jasper. "Have the vessel with you at the ball."

"The ball?"

Jasper gave her a funny look. "Your grandfather's ball? Surely you were invited?"

Cassia was not only invited, she was obligated to be there; only she had been so consumed in chasing Violet that she was losing track of the days. "Of course. The ball, then."

"Is that a promise?" Jasper put on a more reasonable tone, but this time Cassia would not be led on.

"I promise," she said, and she hurried away before he could guess that it was a lie.

27

The Chambers of Alchemy was a public building, which was inconvenient for Jupitus Fisk, who cared nothing for his people. As such, he was forced to discourage their presence by inviting them to see their own deaths in the shine of the barred windows, the impossible black of the enchanted walls, and the needle-like spikes atop the surrounding wall. When the wind blew just so, one could even hear the screams from the cells on the lowest level. Sorcerers told their children it was just an enchantment; a warning.

Ollivan knew better.

Today, thankfully, he was escorted directly to his grandfather's office. It was a room designed with a different kind of intimidation in mind; one reserved for those who might have believed, before they stepped inside, that they were Jupitus Fisk's equal. A velvet carpet, the same shade of gold as the militia's neckties, cut across the naked grey stone of the Chambers' interior from the doors to the desk, like a long tongue conveying Ollivan into the acid belly of a devouring beast. Along the walls, opulence warred with more featureless, cold marble; Fisk's taste in paintings began and ended with *monstrously large*, much like his taste in desks, fireplaces, and chandeliers. The space was as cold and brutal as a prison cell, and more expensive than the emperor of Alkonos's throne room.

Ollivan took a seat before the desk to wait for his grandfather. After many minutes, the doors opened again with an echoing groan, and Jupitus Fisk began the long walk to meet him. The old Ollivan would have stayed in his chair, perhaps even propped a foot on the High Sorcerer's desk. The new Ollivan – the one who had enchanted then lost a highly destructive spell that was currently claiming victims all over the city – was on his feet before Jupitus could focus his weakening eyes on him.

If the old man would deign to. But he did not look up. He was wiping his hands on a cloth, which he passed off to the enforcer at his side, whispering something to her as he did. The echoes came to Ollivan from the corners of the cavernous stone room, but the words were too soft to pick apart.

As Jupitus skirted the desk and sat behind it, a crimson spot against the white of his cuff drew Ollivan's eye. The cloth, now being thrown into the fire, flashed pink and mottled before the flames consumed it.

"What's this?" said Jupitus at the shuttered, pallid look on Ollivan's face. "No quip about interrupting something? Or being next, perhaps?"

He had such a quip. He couldn't force it out.

"Another traitor," Jupitus went on. "One of the last of this particular revolt, I think."

Ollivan knew there were always plots, always enemies, and he knew they were bled and beaten. He tried to forget that he had seen it happen, but that single speck of blood on his grandfather's sleeve threw the doors to the memory wide open.

He had been ten years old. *Almost a man*, his grandfather said the morning he had collected him to take him to the Chambers.

Ollivan thought he was there to learn his grandfather's job, and he sighed and dragged his feet as he was led through the corridors. He was already disinterested, but his increasingly daring experiments in disobedience had planted in him the idea that he could only be punished for so long. He was not *almost a man*, but one day he would be, and the type of man he became was up to him, and not his grandfather.

And then they had descended a curling staircase, and the screams filled his ears.

"Come," was all Jupitus said when Ollivan stopped, backing instinctively into the wall. The enforcer behind him gave him a shove and they continued.

He registered the smell as pig's blood. The cook had let him help make black pudding the week before, so the scent memory was fresh. It had turned his stomach then; now it mingled with the screams until his juvenile mind caught up. It was not the blood of one person – the bare-chested and carved-up man shackled to the wall in the cell before him – but years' worth of victims, their life force imbued in the stone foundations of his grandfather's empire.

The things his grandfather said as he split the skin of the prisoner with long, elegant slices only came back to him later. Peace and prosperity was the responsibility of those with power, and this was power. That Jupitus Fisk mutilated his own enemies, rather than pass the task on to another, was a matter of principle. He wanted them to see the whites of his eyes and know who they had wronged, and what it had cost them.

Those were the sentiments Ollivan recalled, but it was too late to be fooled by them. For he had seen the look on his grandfather's face, witnessed the quiet serenity that overcame his entire being when he had a knife in his hand. He had never known a lighter side of Jupitus Fisk, but watching his grandfather dab blood from his neck, Ollivan had the unsettling and out-of-place realisation that this is what other children's grandparents were like; human, passionate, alight from within. It took torture to bring it out of him.

And so the High Sorcerer's lesson was lost, because the truth had been burned into Ollivan's ten-year-old mind.

"Is there anything you wish you tell me?"

He blinked. Jupitus was watching him patiently from behind his desk.

Ollivan took a deep breath, and in the moment it took him to collect himself, he pretended to be summoning his courage. "Alright, yes. Yes I do. Your décor is not doing much to recommend you. But I suppose to achieve both minimalist *and* ostentatious deserves some praise in itself."

Jupitus had very little reaction, but it gratified Ollivan to know at this point how hard he worked to appear unruffled by him.

"I am giving you this chance," said his grandfather slowly, "to own up to your part in this before my people discover it for me. It will be no help to you to lie."

It would be no help to me to tell the truth, thought Ollivan, studiously keeping his eyes off the blood spot on Jupitus's sleeve.

"Grandfather, I haven't the faintest clue what you're talking about. Have you run into some kind of problem? Is it one I can help with?"

Jupitus smiled, completely at ease. "That surprises me, given that it appears to have begun on the steps of the Wending Place."

Ollivan clicked his fingers. "Oh, you mean *that* problem. Yes, some attack or some such? I take it you haven't found the culprit? Have you questioned the Successors? I can promise you the bunch of fools will be no help whatsoever but at least—"

"Enough," said Jupitus. He didn't raise his voice, but his tone relieved him of the need to. "I will not waste my time asking what you were doing in Whitechapel at dawn, since we both know the answer already. But when I find the proof that you are involved in this – and believe me, I have put considerable resources to the task – you will be dealt with by the rulers of every faction whose people you have hurt, beginning with Lady Wrike. This is your second offence against the North, and this time the circumstances are not in the slightest bit mitigating. The faction rulers will enforce whatever punishments they see fit, in accordance with the Principles, and I will not interfere."

"I've assaulted no one," said Ollivan through gritted teeth.

"In the meantime, the Heart will continue to dissuade them all from charging us with this until a Sorcerer's involvement can be proven," he continued as if Ollivan hadn't spoken. "You will personally head up those efforts by making a sparkling impression on every one of them at tonight's ball." He turned his attention to the papers in front of him. "You are dismissed."

Biting his tongue so hard he could taste blood, Ollivan turned on his heel and made for the door. But it was then that his grandfather spoke again.

"I understand you've made Sybella Dentley Secretary of the Society."

Ollivan's step faltered. Blood rushed in his ears. He fixed his eyes on the door.

"Have you rekindled that courtship?"

"No," he answered too quickly, his voice hoarse. He did his best to smooth it over and turned to face his grandfather with a smile. "I cannot pretend I care a jot for my position as President," he said, drinking in the indignation in Jupitus's eyes and using it to fortify himself. "I needed a Secretary who would do their job *and* mine. Miss Dentley was the only willing candidate."

For the length of his speech, he pretended he believed that Sybella was nothing to him. In fact, he willed it to be true. If he played the role well enough, perhaps he could convince both of them that Sybella was inconsequential to him.

He had tried it once before, and he had lost her, so perhaps now it could be true.

"All the same," said Jupitus, "you would do well to consider my words of over a year ago. My daughter may try to stay my hand when it comes to you. She has no power when it comes to others."

And Ollivan was dismissed. He flung the door open with enough force that it slammed against the wall and set every militia guard on the other side bracing for a fight. In the antechamber, beyond his grandfather's wards, he transported out of there before he could write his own fate, once and for all, in his grandfather's blood.

"You won't come back."

Gedeon is smiling, but it doesn't touch his eyes. You reach for the words to reassure him, but they catch in your throat. Last night, you lay awake, head full of memories you haven't made yet. Memories of going home.

Then he leans close and presses his forehead to your temple, and the memories dissolve. You don't want to leave; you're not sure you ever did, not when you could stay like this instead.

But you can't, so you tear a gap between you.

Still, Gedeon smiles. He always does when he looks at you.

28

The grand hall at the Chambers of Alchemy, a fierce stone monument to her grandfather's nature, was enchanted for the night of the ball into something beautiful.

Bare grey stone gave way to gold-veined white marble. Living garlands of jade-green leaves and cerulean flowers wound their way around carved Grecian pillars and trickled down the walls. Long tables draped in gold held a veritable banquet, the crystal punchbowls winking in the clara stone light cast by bird-shaped chandeliers that seemed to swoop in flight overhead.

The grounds had also succumbed to magic. On one side of the ballroom, tall glass doors led to a terrace, then down into a garden enchanted from the militia's practice grounds, with reflecting pools, topiary sculptures, and plenty of dark corners for passionate encounters. The Chambers was the site of a long-maintained spell to banish the coal smog such a large city generated, and as such the air was just a bit sweeter there than anywhere else in London. Tonight, it was fragrant with flora and magic.

Cassia was in the usual spot she occupied at balls; against the wall, in the lowest light she could find, trying not to be seen or otherwise draw any attention. Usually it was to avoid being gossiped about by the people who didn't like or trust her; this evening it served the additional purpose of hiding her from Jasper.

She needed to get Ollivan alone and warn him about Jasper's threat; that they may be exposed tonight, here. But she may as well hope to enchant the entire ballroom to glow with the colours of the rainbow for all the chance of that happening. Ollivan had arrived with their grandfather, not long after Cassia and her mother, and had been paraded around the ballroom like prize livestock on a leash. Whatever had been discussed and agreed when he was summoned to the Chambers of Alchemy, it involved a great deal of kowtowing and charming the High Sorcerer's guests. Ollivan was currently talking with the Trinity, the three representatives of the ruling families of the Underground. She recognised the look on her brother's face; the broad, easy grin and steely, raging eyes. Jupitus's net was closing around him.

Cassia tested how that made her feel. Was she uneasy because she didn't wish Ollivan to be banished a second time, or because she feared her own punishment should Violet's chaos be traced back to them? Perhaps she should go to Jupitus at once, and beat Jasper to it. She could save herself, by giving her brother up.

Her grandfather was across the ballroom. She could circumvent the dancers spinning under the soft gold light of the chandeliers, skirt along the row of crystal punchbowls holding concoctions in half a dozen enticing colours, and ask his bodyguards to speak to him at once. Apologise. Explain everything. It was probably her only option.

At that moment, the announcer's voice rang out above the music.

"Hester Ravenswood, Alpha of Camden Town," he crowed, and the new arrival stepped into the ballroom.

Cassia felt a pang of something halfway between longing and homesickness as the space between them briefly cleared, and

Hester was framed in the doorway, flanked by her militia guard. She was dressed in a dark red gown, sleek and flattering, with little in the way of ornamentation; she had always cared little about fashion, and preferred a quiet salon to the grandeur and bustle of a ball. Her caramel blonde hair was swept into an equally simplistic chignon, and her shrewd hazel eyes scoured the ballroom in a decidedly unimpressed manner. When her eyes landed on Cassia, however, her expression twisted into a knowing smile.

They crossed the ballroom towards one another, and met halfway with a tight embrace. Hester was the first to let go, holding Cassia at arm's length to take her in.

"Your taste has certainly changed in the last two years," said Hester, eyes travelling over the excessive lace frothing around the low neckline of Cassia's blush-pink gown.

Cassia smoothed the front self-consciously. "My mother interpreted my love of flowers as an affection for all things feminine," she explained. "The chance to correct her passed a long time ago."

Hester gave her a probing, opaque look, the kind that made her wonder if she was being judged. "I'll send you some things," she said. "Or perhaps I should insist you collect them yourself. I expected you would visit us at least *once*."

Now she *knew* she was being judged. "I'm sorry," she said, avoiding the woman's eyes while she dug around for an explanation. "I've been awfully busy, what with my lessons."

"So your education is progressing well?" said Hester.

Cassia swallowed. She was remembering what it was like to be interrogated by Hester. In some ways it was much like the scrutiny of her family – her faults laid bare, her shortcomings named and categorised. In others, it was worse. Her family made her feel helpless and incapable. Hester made her feel responsible, and capable of better. She made her chastise herself without ever joining in. Once Cassia was feeling her worst, Hester offered kindness that she didn't feel she deserved.

"Remember this, above all else," she had told her once. "There is nothing you cannot do. Say it."

Cassia had, and Hester had tutted. "*Mean it.*"

It was the day she had decided to come back to the Heart. The day she had decided finding power in her magic was worth something, even if it took her further from the people she wished to call her family. It had seemed insurmountable, the task of separating herself from them to start from scratch so far behind her peers. But Hester had believed that she could. And so, she had.

"There is nothing I cannot do," she had repeated again, and Hester had nodded, just once, and that was the end of that.

She could not admit she had been proving them both wrong for the past two years.

"Getting there," she lied with a quick smile, before changing the subject. "Tell me, how is Gedeon?"

Hester's face twisted into a long-suffering sneer, and Cassia couldn't help but smile. Hester's cousin, Gedeon Ravenswood, was the rightful ruler of the Changelings, and was set to take over as alpha when he turned eighteen in a matter of weeks. Her heart had cracked a little to see he hadn't accompanied Hester this evening. She had spent a lot of the last two years desperately wishing to see him – her oldest friend, the boy she had grown up alongside and who had treated her as one of his own – and desperately suppressing that want. It would only bring her misery.

"I told him he must come tonight," said Hester, as if she read the direction of Cassia's thoughts. "He needs to forge his own relationship with the High Sorcerer if he is to maintain our alliance. But of course he was gone when I sent a wolf to fetch him for the carriage. He and Eliot have disappeared off somewhere, no doubt to cause trouble." She gave Cassia a knowing smile. "Of course, I had told him you would not be here, which was my mistake. You're so easy to miss at these things."

"I'm like you. I prefer quieter entertainment," said Cassia. "But my mother insisted."

"Well, if he had known, I know he would have been here. Any chance to see you."

Cassia felt a blush creep onto her cheeks, and cursed herself. But perhaps it was better that Gedeon weren't here. Yes, she would have wished for the chance to dance with Gedeon. Just ten minutes to catch up on everything that had happened in their lives since they last saw one another. But dance with the alpha-in-waiting of Camden with her own people looking on and whispering about her? And what else might he have witnessed this evening? She swept an eye over the ballroom for the hundredth time. Jasper was still nowhere to be seen. It did nothing to quiet the anxiety racing through her.

"Have you made a decision yet?" said Hester unexpectedly. She was not one for small talk.

"About what?" said Cassia, though she feared she already knew.

"About returning to the Zoo, of course."

Her eyes found her grandfather, still in conversation on the other side of the ballroom. Dancers and revellers passed in and out of view between them, and every time his ageing face appeared between them, Cassia felt watched. Hunted. A heavy sadness settled in her stomach as she braced herself to say the words she had never said aloud, for fear it would make them real.

"I'm not sure it will be my choice."

Hester's expression darkened, and she followed Cassia's line of sight.

"That wasn't my agreement with him," said Hester in a low voice.

"I know."

"And if you were to choose, which would it be?"

Cassia hesitated. It was partly that she didn't know the answer, and partly that she didn't like to entertain impossibilities. Hope and expectation had burned her one too many times.

"Cassia," said Hester, meeting her eye defiantly. Hester had a leader's voice, a quiet command that was hard to ignore. "If you wish to return to us, you need only say so, and I will make it happen. Your grandfather will see the sense in it, with a little persuasion. It's good for our relationship to have you at the Zoo. If you wish to remain here, I'm sure I can make that happen too."

Hester's words were the balm Cassia had craved and feared in equal measure. She couldn't help but trust in her, this woman who had taken her in, protected her, guided her for over ten years; this woman she looked up to above all others. She raged against the relief she felt at being told that she would look out for her again; that she need only say the word and her problems would be solved. Because it couldn't be true. The High Sorcerer was the one who had power over her, who had steered the course of her life to suit his ends. She had forgotten what it was like to trust

315

that someone had her best interests at heart, and yet, she did not wish to remember. That way only led to more disappointment.

So she nodded her thanks, but did not speak. She didn't trust herself to.

Hester was looking at her in that probing way again, her head tilted slightly to one side and back, like she was trying to bring Cassia into focus. "I can see that you're distracted, so I won't take up any more of your time. Enjoy your evening, Cassia. And I'm sure if Gedeon knew we were speaking, he would ask me to insist that you reply to his letters."

Cassia laughed at the scolding note to end the conversation; a dash of characteristic judgement to temper her kindness. For a scalding moment, Cassia's longing for the Zoo overwhelmed her.

And then Hester moved away to greet someone else, and from across the room, her eyes locked with Jasper Hawkes'. That other life skittered away like smoke on a breeze, and the problems of the present rushed back in.

Jasper motioned for her to follow him, and Cassia didn't see that she had a choice. She skirted the edge of the ballroom and followed him out onto the terrace, dodging a servant who tried to approach her with a message; whatever it was, this was more pressing. The music was nearly as loud outside, but it faded as Jasper led her down a set of steps until they were beneath the ballroom windows, under the arches of a covered walkway. Cassia suppressed a wry remark; if this place wasn't meant for secret rendezvous, then her name wasn't Cassia Sims.

Jasper leaned against the archway, his back to the garden, and looked her up and down. She glared back at him. She refused to give him the satisfaction of seeing her scared.

"What gave you the impression I wasn't to be taken seriously?" he said.

"Believe me, Jasper, I take your inability to listen and comprehend very seriously." His eyes lit up with ire, and he took a step towards her. Cassia forced herself to speak more carefully. "Stars, Jasper, it's not in my power, or anyone's, to simply give you the Guysman. Besides, having the thing anywhere near you wouldn't just be useless, it would be dangerous to you. It's as if you've forgotten what happened last time."

Jasper scoffed. "I remember that I tried to touch you and your little plaything incapacitated me. That you would even think of claiming that you don't know how it works and didn't at least *attempt* to control it shows you take me for some kind of fool."

This conversation certainly had her thinking as much. Cassia rubbed her temples and tried to think of a way to get through to him. One kept coming to mind, but she couldn't tell if it was a good idea, or if she was just tempted by the thought of telling Jasper everything she thought of him.

"Why did you offer to tutor me?" she blurted, her mouth making the decision for her.

Jasper was momentarily confused, then an unfriendly smile spread across his face. "Why do you *think* I did?"

"I don't know," she said. "I think maybe you wanted to lure me into whatever sick games you and Ollivan used to play. Or maybe it was more mundane than that and you just wanted to get to his notes. But I do know that you used me. You let me believe we were friends – could be *more* than friends, even – and now you're trying to blackmail me. I don't have the stars-damned doll, Jasper, but if I did, and I could control it, and I could hand that control over to you – why in the heavens do you think I ever would?"

Jasper was unperturbed. He shrugged. "Because I will ruin your life if you don't, perhaps?" He took a step towards her, crowding her against the wall. Cassia held her ground and summoned her magic. "I will take this whole affair to your grandfather. How you snapped after you failed your initiation a second time. How you saw Ollivan's return as an opportunity to finally win some power for yourself. How he helped you create the Guysman to win you magic you could never have dreamed of, at the expense of anyone you chose."

Cassia shook her head, her mind spinning at the manipulation. "And you think my grandfather would believe you?"

Jasper's smile was slow and ice cold. "He believes every word I say."

Cassia didn't know what that meant. She only knew she could not stand here a moment longer and entertain the whims of this boy. He knew too much, but he couldn't bargain with it the way he thought. Cassia couldn't do as he wished. She couldn't make this better.

She might as well make it worse.

She didn't think, she only loosed the spell she had readied at her fingertips. It hit Jasper in the chest, audibly knocking the wind from him. He grunted as he was shoved backwards into the arch.

It had worked. Her magic had done as she asked – and now Jasper was sneering at her like she was about to pay for it. Through the heady rush of power, fear crept back in.

And then Jasper grinned. She remembered he'd been drawn to Ollivan once, that they'd been part of some kind of duelling

318

evening together. Perhaps a little fight was exactly what Jasper wanted from her.

"It wasn't just about Ollivan," he said, something wistful in his eye. "I wanted to do what no one else seemed able to – get to know you. You were always so removed from the rest of them. So above it all. I thought we were alike.

"So answer me one thing." His face reminded Cassia of the old Jasper. The false version she had known before Violet. "Tell me if there was ever a chance for us, before all of this. If you ever thought of me the way you knew I wanted you to."

Cassia saw the opportunity open up, a chance to buy herself a little more time by pretending she felt what Jasper wanted her to feel. She knew it was possible to manipulate someone like that; to play on the sympathies of a romantic prospect, whether innocently or not. It seemed to her sometimes that everyone was doing it. Perhaps she had done it herself, when she fastidiously avoided the topic of Jasper's heart so that she could keep him as a friend.

But this. This required her to flirt. It was another thing she had no skill at. But if she simply began, then perhaps the words would reveal themselves to her.

"Not at first," she said haltingly. "But of course I've thought of you that way. Hadn't we grown close? How could I not?"

She thought she'd done alright; a little dry, a little awkward, but perhaps the latter worked in her favour. She allowed herself a little spark of relief when Jasper's face softened and he took a step closer. Then he took another, and fear seized her. Would he try and kiss her? Should she let him, to maintain the fiction? So much rested on what Jasper's goodwill might change.

And yet, she couldn't. Not if it bought them more time. Not even if it saved Ollivan from a cell. She wouldn't kiss him when the thought made her shudder. So as Jasper leaned in, she put a hand firmly on his chest and held the space between them. She met his confused gaze, and let him see in hers that this would never happen.

Jasper didn't react as she imagined he would. He didn't replace his softer expression with a sneer, didn't issue another threat. He only looked at her sadly and put more space between them.

"The trouble you and I could have caused together," he said with a plaintive smile, and then he was gone, and Cassia leaned against the wall, her heart pounding.

It took her a moment to collect herself, before she followed him back to the ball. She could still fix this for herself, if not Ollivan. She could go to Jupitus now, before Jasper had the chance.

Cassia took stock of the room. Ollivan was dancing with Sybella, his face bent towards hers, her eyes glassy and searching his. Their grandfather was talking with Hester near the windows; Jasper hadn't seen him yet. She could get there first, *maybe*. Or she could get to Ollivan, warn him of what was about to happen. They might have a few moments to put a story together.

And then Jasper saw the High Sorcerer, and Cassia's choices vanished. Without a moment's more hesitation, she crossed the room directly towards where Jupitus and Hester were in conversation.

The band played a soaring waltz to accompany the dancing couples she wove around, Jupitus coming in and out of view as she battled her way through them. A scream went up – no, a shrieking laugh, as a female guest reacted to some anecdote or joke. The music of chiming glasses filled every remaining gap in her senses, but Cassia's focus narrowed to the conversation by the windows. To what she was about to do.

"Miss Sims!"

The servant from before was in her path once again, his tone and expression insistent. Had he been trying to find her again this whole time? Cassia craned over his shoulder. Jupitus was still there. He was twenty paces away now.

"Please, Miss Sims, someone is asking for you outside," said the servant.

"I'll be there in a moment," she said, not meeting his eye, already stepping around him. He snatched a hand out to grasp her arm, and in shock, she spun around.

She couldn't read the servant's expression, but there was unease there, boarding absurdly on terror. "I fear that this is urgent, miss," he said.

"Who is asking for me?" she replied impatiently. "Can't you let them in?"

The servant shook his head emphatically, and whispered something she could not have guessed. "I fear to."

Cassia felt his fear, but only for a moment, for above the noise around them, Hester's commanding voice rang out.

"Of course, High Sorcerer. Don't let me keep you."

Cassia turned slowly, dreading what she would see.

Jupitus was excusing himself from his conversation with the alpha in order to attend to someone else. Jasper led her grandfather from the room, his bodyguards in tow.

She was too late.

29

"Another drink, Miss Vallance-Crowe?" said Ollivan, summoning a server to top up their glasses.

Carolina Vallance-Crowe was a bored drinker, he had found, so he had been doing his best to bore her while keeping her in champagne, and the strategy had bought him some relief, at least from one of the women before him.

They were the Trinity, the rulers of the Psi; a council of three members each ostensibly representing one of the ruling families and wielding equal influence. But a generation ago, a son of the Vallance family and a daughter of the Crowe family had conspired to join their bloodlines, and bought their descendants majority influence in the Underground. As a result, the second member of the Trinity was Carolina's twin sister, Euphemia. The third – the least drunk and most bothersome – was Thaddea Arden.

"And what of the theory that it's some kind of toxin?" said Thaddea. At least that explained the handkerchief she kept putting to her nose, and the smell of purifying xandita seed.

"I can assure you, Thaddea, the Heart are exploring all possibilities thoroughly," said Ollivan.

"I understand the effects are getting worse," Euphemia cut in. Ollivan had barely finished his sentence. "Nose bleeds. Comas. We've begun recommending our people stay indoors as much as possible."

"Prudent, perhaps, but there's no cause to panic. We have every reason to believe those affected will make a full recovery."

Ollivan took a long drink from his own champagne and used the opportunity to scan the room for an escape. He had been unwillingly ensconced with the Trinity for over an hour now. And though he held no hope that the countless hovering enforcers would allow him to escape altogether, he was desperate to relieve himself and find a bite to eat. There was braised pork on the buffet table. Ollivan had big plans for it.

Lev and Virgil were dancing; Cassia was pressed against the far wall like she hoped to disappear right through it, which Ollivan guessed might have something to do with the pink lace concoction she was dressed in; a gift from their mother. Sybella stood with some friends under the light of one of the chandeliers. Still accounting for his own feelings, she was the most radiant woman in the room in a frothing muslin gown, gold ribbons at her waist and adorning the gauzy tiers of her skirt. They played off the notes of gold in her hair, and she seemed to shine. Ollivan pushed down the sinking misery in the pit of his stomach and astutely avoided her eye as she turned around. She was not a viable option to appeal to for rescuing, not after Jupitus's renewed threat the day before.

"I myself wonder if it might be worth consulting an astrologer," Thaddea said.

"Oh, always worthwhile," agreed Ollivan emphatically, knowing the Psi to be a notoriously devout woman. "The stars granted us our gifts after all; who is to say they cannot decide to remove them?"

"That is just my thinking. But if, after all, it turns out this *was* the doing of one of your own—"

323

"Miss Arden," said Ollivan, pulling on his most congenial manner. "If this tragedy was indeed caused maliciously by a Sorcerer under my grandfather's rule – and I must remind you we have no evidence that that is the case – you know as well as I do how they will be dealt with." He leaned closer. The other two ladies bent their heads closer too, though Carolina swayed slightly as she did so. "But between us, if Jupitus Fisk was the ruler responsible for deciding your punishment, would *you* risk such a thing as a breach of the Principles?"

Thaddea met his eyes conspiratorially. Ollivan had judged alluding to his grandfather's bloody reputation to be just what she craved in terms of reassurance, and he had judged right. The Psi ruler smiled at him, and exchanged glances with her council-members.

Ollivan could sense that his work with the Trinity was done, but before the lurking enforcers could whisk him off to sweet-talk the next anxious important guest, Sybella appeared beside him.

"Misses Vallance-Crowe, Miss Arden," she said, performing a small curtsey. "I hate to interrupt, but Mr Sims promised me a dance."

"I did?"

"You did."

Ollivan kept his expression neutral, and scanned the room yet again. His grandfather was engaged in a conversation some distance away. Hadn't he been hoping for an escape? And how could he politely refuse?

"Will you excuse me?" he said, offering his arm to Sybella and handing off his champagne to the server, to whom he made a gesture to stay near Carolina and her glass.

One dance. They were colleagues. It was to be expected. There was no risk.

And so Ollivan led Sybella into the centre of the dance floor, placed a hand on her waist, and pulled her close. His heart gave an appreciative thud; he cursed it to the Otherworld and back.

"You're welcome," said Sybella to his chin. He was staring out across the top of her head; a picture of perfunctory, polite dancing, nothing more.

"What am I thanking you for?"

"Saving you from those women and whatever boot-licking your grandfather has sentenced you to," she said. "You were engaged with them for over an hour."

Ollivan risked a glance at her face, and was struck by how familiar a collection of freckles could appear in such close quarters. An astrologer could not know the night sky better than Ollivan knew Sybella's freckles. "Perhaps I was enjoying their company."

"Ah, yes, imaginary toxins fascinate me too."

"And you were eavesdropping?"

"Don't be too flattered," she said. "I was passing by. And knowing you, you're lucky I whisked you away before you said something to land you in hot water."

"How hot, exactly? Because you know I'm prone to a chill."

She failed to mask a laugh, and Ollivan returned it with a smile before he could help himself. His posture had grown loose; his hand on her waist too firm and familiar. He snapped out of it at once, shooting a glance towards where Jupitus was—

Was now looking their way.

He schooled his expression back into indifference, and tilted his chin upright. Sybella was saying something more, but she trailed off at the change in him. Was the silence that followed sharp and terrible, or was his own anxiety making it feel so?

It was a peculiar kind of torture – one he doubted even his grandfather could concoct – to dance in awkward silence with a partner he used to laugh with. He could feel Sybella's own cold disappointment with the situation, and he couldn't even be gratified that she felt anything about it at all. He longed to study her freckles again, to feel everything he had felt the last time he'd held her like this. Instead he was putting distance between them, and he hated himself for it.

And, earth and stars, he hated his grandfather.

Jupitus was now at the side of the dance floor. He was in conversation with one of his advisors, and yet he stood side-on to the man, so that he faced Ollivan. He needed to end this. He would make an excuse and excuse himself and—

"You won't ever change, will you?"

He was looking at her again, and his own roiling sadness was reflected back at him. Sadness, and accusation.

"I beg your pardon?"

She smiled sadly. "This is just as it was before. You, here, but not really. Your mind was always on something over my head."

Ollivan held her away from him, so he could see her face fully while he explained how unfair her accusation was.

"How could you say that? Yes, granted, I am caught up with my books and my discoveries a great deal of the time, but, Ellie" – he paused at his own transgression, but she didn't correct him – "when I was with you, you had every bit of me. Always. Don't you dare say you remember it differently."

326

"It *was* like that, for a long time." Sybella was now the one whose expression was carefully blank and posture rigid. "But I couldn't keep your attention, could I?"

"I was always present," Ollivan protested again.

"Until you weren't." She searched his face, and must have seen his confusion plain there. "You really don't know what I mean, do you? You didn't even notice yourself pulling away."

"I never—"

But he did. They spun, and over Sybella's head, his grandfather's face came into view once more. Ollivan felt his rage begin to simmer in his stomach. Funny, it felt so much like magic when it first ignited. Only, Ollivan had the full mastery of his magic.

"That's it, isn't it?" he said flatly. "That's why you left me."

Ollivan had always been able to call his grandfather's bluff. Alana stood between them, a buffer that shielded him from the worst of Jupitus's harm. Alana was intelligent, she was popular, she had support in the faction that he himself had cultivated for her. She was the perfect second who could become the perfect adversary, and Jupitus was not fool enough to believe his people weren't starting to look to her as old age crept upon him. He needed his daughter's support, and there was only one way he could lose it forever: threaten her children. Yes, there were circumstances in which he had more to lose than her support – like the future of the Heart, should the other faction leaders find out about his black-market trading – but while all Ollivan threatened was his ruthless reputation, Alana was her son's stalwart defence.

A few months before Ollivan's banishment, Jupitus had struck upon a solution. He had struck upon Sybella.

It was so simple. So foolproof. The High Sorcerer summoned him to his office one morning and commanded, with a smile on his face, that Ollivan cease embarrassing him, or Sybella Dentley would meet with an accident. He disposed of inconvenient people all the time. What was one daughter of a moderately well-thought-of family, who happened to slip into the river when walking home one night?

It was too much power, Ollivan had decided. How dare he even think of wielding it against Sybella? He couldn't let him win. There had to be a loophole, a trick, for Ollivan was smarter than his grandfather by a mile. Nothing so simple as brute force would make him concede. He had just needed time. Time to think and scheme; time to see all the angles and find his grandfather's weaknesses. Time when Sybella was kept safe by being kept at arm's length. If Jupitus believed their love affair had ended, he had no power over Ollivan once again.

That, he saw now, was how he'd lost her.

She was watching him now, as they continued to spin about the dance floor. She was waiting for him to say something, and Ollivan could feel his mouth opening and closing as he tried to form an explanation he could live with. Back then, he couldn't bear the thought of Sybella seeing him bested by the old man, and he couldn't bear it now. Not when he *knew* the solution was just out of reach. He could not tell her his only options had been to see her harmed or give her up.

"Ellie," he lamented. "Why couldn't you have given me time?"

She snorted. "Time for what? To complete everything else you were striving for before we could be together?"

328

"No. You ended things without even giving me a chance to explain."

"Oh, earth and stars, no one ever lets you explain, do they, Ollivan?" She pulled her hand from his and stepped away. They had stopped dancing. Now they were only stood in the middle of the floor arguing. "You're so misunderstood. Why won't everyone just stop complaining and start digging?"

"Digging?"

"Through all your faults to get to the truth of you. The work it takes to forgive you time and time again – do you have any idea?"

Ollivan's head was spinning. Jupitus had vanished, reassured that there was nothing between them for him to ruin. There was no time to defend himself. A harried server appeared at their side.

"Excuse the interruption, Mr Sims," the man said. His voice was elevated with anxiety. "Do you know where I might find *Miss* Sims? It's rather urgent."

Ollivan murmured that he didn't know where his sister was, and dismissed the man without so much as looking at him. His eyes were firmly on Sybella.

"What are we really talking about here?" he said in a low voice when the server dashed off.

She shook her head in disappointment. "Do you find it so impossible to believe I meant exactly what I said? Do you have that little self-awareness?"

"The Guysman wasn't my fault," he ploughed on, ignoring the further barb. "I lost my temper one evening a year ago, but I don't think I ever meant for it to be awoken. Cassia's the one who—"

"I cannot *believe* you."

"But I'm sorry, Ellie." He cut to the end before she could cut him off any more.

She stopped, though Ollivan didn't think the abject surprise on her face was entirely warranted.

"Excuse me?"

"I'm sorry that you got hurt by it. But I'm not going to let that happen again." He moved closer to her. "I'm going to fix this. I promise."

Sybella searched his face, her expression unreadable. After a moment that stretched on for eternity, she shook her head. "As I said, Ollivan." Her voice was quiet and sad. "You're never going to change."

She spun and walked away. Ollivan made to follow – this wasn't done with; not until they understood one another, and right then he understood exactly nothing – but someone blocked his path. Their hand closed around the skin of his wrist.

It was an enforcer, in his gold tie and gold pin. There was another gold pin on a chest beside him; Elodie, one of Jupitus's inner circle, and at least two more behind. It was a whole squadron. The dancing had stopped around them, though the music continued.

"Come with us," said Elodie, and the others surrounded him.

On instinct, Ollivan tried to tug his hand free from the enforcer's, and in response, something pierced his skin. He gasped. The man was wearing a ring with a small lance on it, a commonly used device for taking prisoners who could transport. A Sorcerer could not transport when in contact with another's skin; the second individual grounded them in place. In Ollivan's experience, the lance would be an inch or so long, and it was now buried searingly among the dense veins of his wrist. Pull away from the enforcer's grip on him, and he would tear them open.

He had been taken prisoner.

They moved him through the ballroom, watched by the revellers, and out into the hall.

"Is this about my dancing? I know it's not my strong suit but was it truly *that* bad?"

No one replied, but the man gripping his wrist tugged on it, and Ollivan gasped. He was leaving drops of blood behind them on the stone floor.

They took him to the adjacent room; some kind of meeting room, judging by the long table in the centre. There were more enforcers here, and Jupitus, stood with his back to them, looking into the mirrored surface of the window and the black night beyond.

Ollivan saw his face reflected in the glass, suspiciously calm and relaxed, along with another figure, one who stood behind Ollivan, near the door. He had missed him as he entered, but he turned now and met his eyes.

Jasper. He lounged against the wall, hands in his pockets, his face a mask of wretched glee.

The net had fallen over him, and instinctively, Ollivan checked his collection of knives with which to cut through it. He could stun the enforcer and remove the lance from his wrist, then transport. It would take but a moment – he could cast the spell and fling his hand off him in almost the same movement – but it risked heavy bleeding, and transportation required a calm he did not currently feel. So did a well-aimed stunning spell, for that matter.

He could create a distraction; aim a spell elsewhere, buy enough time to get the upper hand on his captor, and use him as a hostage to get out of the room. Jasper was at his back, however; Elodie and another enforcer also hovered near the door. He was too surrounded for such a gambit to work.

He could go for broke, bring the ceiling down on all of them, dive under the cover of the table while everyone else was still processing what he'd done. There could be deaths though—

And then what? He forced his fists to unclench and his magic to quiet in his abdomen. There was only one thing he could do, and that was explain. Anything else he could not come back from.

Jupitus had turned and was watching him with casual interest. Ollivan was loath to believe the old man could see every thought passing across his face – he did not know him, not at all – and yet his quiet amusement suggested he at least knew what Ollivan knew; Jupitus had won.

"Where is the Guysman now, Ollivan?" he said calmly, with every expectation of being obeyed.

"Who is Guysman?"

Jupitus nodded. "Let me tell you what's going to happen. My people are going to take you downstairs, and you're going to go with them quietly. You'll have some time. A cell is a remarkable space in which to think, you'll find. Take as long as you need. When you're ready, you will send for me, and I will come. Then, you will tell me the truth, from the beginning, including where you have hidden this abomination, exactly how you made it, and how it can be destroyed. Do you understand me, Ollivan?"

Ollivan searched for the right words to defuse this, but he found none. He found nothing. Only panic.

"It was never meant to be awoken. Cassia—"

"Ah yes. You have involved my granddaughter in this too. What part has she played in this? Does she need to be dealt with as I will deal with you?"

So Jasper hadn't implicated Cassia fully, and now Jupitus was testing him. What had Ollivan even been about to say in his panic? That the blame lay with her? That the whole thing had been an accident? Would either help his case?

"She played no part," he said, aiming a defiant look at Jasper. "If Hawkes has told you otherwise, it's a lie."

Jupitus looked at Jasper then, and something passed between them. From his place in the middle, Ollivan couldn't catch the complete silent exchange.

"One thing I cannot wrap my head around," mused Jupitus, "is how even you would conjure something so… *wrong*." He stepped close, so that Ollivan was forced to square up to him or shy away. He chose the former. "To drain magic from the magical. This is some unique evil you have brought into the world."

The blow of the old man's fist took him by surprise, whipping his head around so that he saw, through watering eyes, Jasper lift a hand to his mouth to hide his delight. Ollivan licked up the blood from around his gums and spat it at him, allowing himself a moment's gratification when the boy recoiled in disgust.

Then his grandfather grabbed him by the hair and wrenched his head to face him.

"There is only one punishment fit for you," he spat, face inches from Ollivan's. There was glee in his pale eyes, the kind he wore as he carved up his dissenters. Ollivan flashed back to being ten years old; to watching his grandfather come alive as he sliced a man to ribbons. "Before you disarm the Guysman, you will suffer it. I'll have your magic for this, you miserable whelp."

"No." Ollivan tried to force back his next word, but failed. "*Please.*"

A scream. For a long moment, Ollivan believed it to be coming from his heart. But then a second cry joined it, and a third.

It was coming from the ballroom. A mounting panic was tearing through the guests.

Jupitus dropped him to the floor just as the lamps began to flicker.

30

Air. Cassia needed air.

She pushed through the crowd and back out onto the terrace, where she drew in shaking gulps of cool air, leaning against a stone urn on the corner of the balustrade. The music and talking just beyond the doors seemed a mile away.

Would they banish her? Surely not, when she explained the full story. Yes, technically, she had awoken some evil, centuries-old magic while making bad decisions in a place she was not supposed to be, but the whole thing had been an accident. Her mother would make Jupitus see that, even if his wrath was immense.

Or would she? Cassia had a new fear of her grandfather, one she wished she could rebury and never think of again, but couldn't. What if Violet's victims never recovered, and the other faction leaders demanded she pay with her life? How far would Jupitus go to negotiate an alternative? Where did she fall in his list of valued possessions?

"There you are."

Cassia jumped. She thought she recognised that voice – light and childlike – but when she followed it, a woman was ascending the step from the garden. She wore a hooded cloak that fell to the floor and hid her face entirely, and she moved with a peculiar gait, like the parts of her worked independently from one another. Unnerved, Cassia backed into the corner.

"I asked for you at the door," said the woman, "but they wouldn't let me in."

This was the person who'd been asking for her, the one who had conjured fear in the doorman?

"Do I know you?"

She lifted her head, and the light from the ballroom fell across her face. It was porcelain. Her mouth did not move as she replied, "Do you not recognise me, friend?"

"Violet."

The name was a breath forced from her paralysed throat. Gone was the porcelain doll Cassia had lifted from a shelf in the Wending Place. The thing before her had the same eyes in the same mild, expressionless face, but was more like an articulated mannequin. She had Cassia's height and build – and her hair; Violet's once rigidly styled locks fell in loose waves from her hood. In the back of her mind, Cassia wondered if she looked as wild as this mannequin with her too-green eyes and her long, black hair.

"I have much to tell you," said Violet.

She flickered, like a candle flame, and then she was no longer in front of the doors, but right before her. Cassia bit back a scream. It was shock, she told herself. She was not afraid. This was an opportunity.

"How did you do that?" she said, forcing herself to sound calm.

"That was the Wraith." She tilted her head to one side, and Cassia was reminded of a puppet lolling on its strings. "His magic was the strangest, I think. It made me feel so... light. And watch this."

She lifted a hand. Violet's hands had also been porcelain when Cassia had found her, and they were still. But now she had mechanical joints at the wrist and knuckles, and she used them to extend one finger and point to the urn on the balustrade.

"This was from the Psi," she said as the urn was wrenched from the balustrade with a grate of stone. It only hovered for a moment before it began to glow orange from inside. Cracks appeared in its surface as the solid stone burned, and within a few seconds, the urn had disintegrated and vanished, leaving nothing but a wisp of smoke.

Violet was not only casting spells; she was wielding other breeds of magic too.

"But that's not what Psi magic does," said Cassia, struggling this time to keep the tremor from her voice. "They can't destroy anything that way. And Wraiths can't move like you just did."

"No," agreed Violet, and her eyes appeared to flash. "The magic is changed within me. When one touches another – Sorcerer, Wraith, Psi, Whisperer – there are new colours. New notes. I cannot read minds, but I can do this."

She looked to the windows, and for a moment nothing happened. Then the nearest guest turned towards them, unseeing, his eyes clouded over. He dropped his glass, and it shattered at his feet, drawing his friends' attention. The nearest was close enough to catch him when his eyes rolled back in his head and his legs crumpled beneath him.

Cassia realised she had covered her mouth with both hands to hide her horror.

"What did you do to him?" she said.

Violet sighed. "I drank his mind," she said dreamily. She flickered again, like she was not quite solid. "His name is Londus. He designs trains. His mother died three weeks ago. I have gathered so much wisdom and history since I found those Whisperers. I have seen so much of the world. They taught me to be wary of Oracle magic, that I might not like it."

Was that why two of the Whisperers hadn't woken up? Londus was limp in his friends' arms as they shook him. His eyes were open, but they looked at nothing. His mouth was slack, like a dead man's.

"You told me you wouldn't hurt anybody," Cassia said. She could no longer mask the horror; she no longer wanted to.

"I said I didn't wish to, not that I wouldn't. But this is what it takes."

"What *what* takes? Why are you doing any of this?"

She tilted her head again in that macabre way, and Cassia resisted the urge to squeeze her eyes shut like a frightened child. "For us."

No. Cassia leaned back against the balustrade, suddenly dizzy.

"For you and me, Cassia. I found the solution." She took Cassia's limp hand in her cold, mechanical one, and Cassia shuddered. "Your brother gave it to me, unwittingly. I watched him give magic to another, as I will give all this magic to you, and more. I've been collecting it for *you*."

Cassia snatched her hand away. "*No*, Violet. Thank you," she forced herself to add. "But I can't take magic from another. It's not the solution."

Violet gave a tinkling laugh. "But it is. It's the solution to everything. I've seen your world now, and I've confirmed my suspicions. The people of this city claim to worship the stars, but it is a self-deceit. The only thing they worship is power. *Magic*. Until magic is yours to command, they will never see your worth as I do."

338

Cassia could not argue with any of Violet's conclusions, except one. "All the same, you're hurting people. It's wrong. It's not the way to get what you want."

Violet laughed again. "You believe that now, yes. You would know better if you had felt the power that I feel; if you had what I want to give you. It's so, so beautiful, Cassia. And it's yours, by right. You must be yourself, in all things, as must we all. *This* is who you are meant to be."

Violet reached a hand towards her, and it brushed her shoulder. Cassia wrapped her fingers tightly around Violet's porcelain forearm and yanked it away. The doll-woman's eyes flashed, her head jerking in surprise... or anger.

"Violet, please listen. I won't be respected for earning magic this way. I would be a villain." She had to make her understand. "You would humiliate me."

Beyond the windows, a disruption had brought the dancing to a stop. There were enforcers in the centre of the room. Another wave of fear consumed her as Cassia approached the window. Ollivan was at the centre of the militia. As she watched, they began leading him away.

"A villain," said Violet pensively, making Cassia turn. She too was watching the drama unfold inside the ballroom. "You wish to be the hero instead."

"I—that's not what I meant."

"For one to rise, the other must fall."

"Violet," Cassia begged, but Violet's eyes were still on Ollivan as he was led from the room.

"They compare you to him. I understand now."

She stepped around Cassia and opened the door to the ballroom.

"No!" Cassia lunged to stop her, but Violet flickered as she stepped inside, and then she was across the floor in pursuit of Ollivan. Her hood caught the air and fell away. Those who saw her jolted in fright, and then laughed as if whatever spell had animated a porcelain woman was part of the entertainment.

The laughter broke the spell that was on Cassia too, and she pushed away her fear. She could fix this before it got worse. She could right her wrongs before she had to answer for them in front of the High Sorcerer.

Your magic knows your real intention, Ollivan had said. It had obeyed her once this evening when she truly needed it. Perhaps that's what he'd meant. And now her need was even greater. Cassia could pretend the fear coursing through her was power. She could be who Violet thought she was, without her help.

She stepped into the ballroom. Violet was halfway across the floor and moving fast; there was nothing for it but to draw in a lungful of air and shout.

"Violet!"

The band stopped. The room went silent. Cassia summoned her magic. "Stand aside!" she commanded the crowd, raising her hands so they knew what she intended.

A corridor opened as the alarmed party-goers cleared a path, moving faster when those near Violet caught sight of her and finally registered the danger. Screams went up, but Cassia blocked them out as Violet came into view, stood alone in the centre of the room.

There was no chance to second-guess herself. Cassia poured her magic into her fingertips and readied the intention in her mind.

Burn.

The flame burst into life at Cassia's feet and raced in a line across the marble floor. It engulfed Violet in an inferno. More guests screamed. Militia guards poured forward, but there was nothing for them to do. Violet was already burning.

And then she wasn't. The inferno winked out, and everything was black as Cassia's eyes adjusted. It only lasted a second before she could see what she'd achieved.

Nothing. Violet stood as she had before, undamaged, as the glow of the fire seemed to withdraw into her. Her eyes burned gold as they found Cassia's across the room. She drank the spell up as she did the magic of her victims.

"Thank you," she said.

It was Cassia's only warning before the nearest enforcer threw up their hands to launch an attack, and Violet raised hers in return. Flames poured from her fingers, and as they swept over the young enforcer, his screams were lost in the cacophony of terror that erupted in the ballroom.

People ran for the doors. The space around Violet emptied of bodies as guests pressed together to get away from her – and around Cassia too. She was suddenly alone in a circle, fearful and outraged eyes burning into her. For a second she didn't understand it, and then she realised: she had given Violet this power, and Violet had thanked her. Not only was this Cassia's fault, it looked intentional.

"I didn't – I'm not…"

There were faces she recognised staring back at her. Kiva. Patience. Gale Garner was backing away from her in horror. The room was spinning. She was going to faint.

And then there were people at her side. Two of them slid their hands into hers, another stood at her shoulder. Was this it? Were the enforcers taking her captive?

"Friend of yours?"

Lev. He unleashed a shaky grin as their eyes met, and gripped her hand tighter.

"Why isn't she a doll any more?" said Sybella on her other side in a tone of feigned lightness.

"*That's* Violet?" said Virgil. He muttered a curse. "Of course this is about Ollivan."

"Not *everything* bad has to be about Ollivan, Virgil," said Sybella. "But yes, this happens to be."

"It's not," said Cassia in a whisper. "It's about me."

"You cannot hurt me," Violet announced to the room. Her voice was eerily calm, and yet it rang out above the din. The fire she had spelled had gone out. Cassia avoided thinking of what that meant. "There is no magic I cannot make mine."

As if to demonstrate her point, she raised two graceful, mechanical arms towards the chandeliers. The lights flickered; not just the chandeliers but all those along the walls and on the tables. Then, as one, they went out entirely. The darkness was absolute. Faces turned to the windows and the city beyond. Violet had drained the magic of every clara stone as far as the eye could see.

Those brave or foolish enough to stay and watch the horror unfold – Sybella, Lev, and Virgil included – ignited flames in their palms, but the darkness around Violet would not give to the light. It shrouded her in shadow; Cassia could barely make out her face as she closed false lids over her glassy green eyes. "The magic here is old. Sweet. So many spells, so many enchantments, I—

342

There is one. Something… remarkable. Oh." Her voice took on the tone of her smile, even as her face didn't move. She opened her eyes. "What is *that*?"

Her eyes glowed gold as she drank in whatever she had found. Cassia pressed closer to her friends, tensed in anticipation of… *something*.

It began with fog, grey and impenetrable, rolling from Violet's skirts and filling the ballroom. Then it crept in from the open doors to the terrace. Cassia squinted out into the night. The peculiar fog was rising from the ground and filling the air.

"Bitter," said Violet, as if to herself.

"The smog spell," said Virgil. "She's done something to the smog spell."

In panic, the remaining enforcers began raining a litany of spells down on the porcelain woman. They had no effect other than to fuel the burning glow behind Violet's eyes.

"Stop that!" screamed Sybella with frightening command. "She's drinking magic, you fools! You'll only make her stronger!"

For a beat, the spells stopped, before a dozen enforcers with torches barrelled into the ballroom, the High Sorcerer at their centre.

The place was illuminated like a firework, light bursting from the mirrors, the chandeliers, the gilt detailing adorning the walls. Violet shrank back, and for a moment she appeared vulnerable.

It was enough to convince a man who always responded with force that she was.

"Enforcers!" Jupitus screamed. "Destroy it!"

"Wait!" said Cassia, but her voice was drowned out by another shouting the same; Ollivan, trailing behind the mob. He was

343

clutching one wrist. Blood trickled through his fingers. He spotted them across the ballroom.

"Run!" he bellowed.

And then she lost sight of him as the enforcers battered Violet with even more spells. She stood in the centre of the ballroom, besieged on all sides, and stretched her arms wide, welcoming the magic they poured into her.

"We can't stop her," said Cassia. "We have to get out of here."

Sybella nodded brusquely.

"But Ollivan—" began Lev.

"Will meet us," said Sybella as she pulled them towards the terrace doors. Cassia had to trust her. "I know where."

31

At first Ollivan didn't notice that the lance was no longer in his wrist.

He lay on the floor, jaw throbbing from his grandfather's blow, forgotten the moment the fog began to pour from under the door. He ignored it, his mind turning over his story, his explanation, the fix to this bind.

He went over everything in his head as the lights flickered and stuttered out. It was a moment of blind anger, over a year ago. Jupitus knew why he resented Jasper, even if he didn't believe the explanation. To perform a spell that hadn't worked the first time, centuries before, even in the service of revenge, was not in itself an unforgivable crime. And that was all he had done, wasn't it? A little bit of bad magic.

He had planned to correct the slip-up, and he had months' worth of notes on the unravelling spell to prove it. Penance, regret, awareness of the issue and a willingness to solve it; they were all there on paper. No, he had not told Jupitus of the issue; but first, he hadn't known what would come of the spell – hadn't even known that it would work at all – and second, he was the only one with enough knowledge to undo it. Jupitus had said so himself.

If not for the screams coming from the ballroom and the fog gathering heavily outside, he might have had a chance to share his explanation.

He climbed to his feet, filed his defence away, and followed the sounds of chaos, knowing what he would find. Guests flooded past him in the entrance hall, hurrying in the opposite direction. He could hear but not see their finery – the rustle of taffeta, the clip of heels, the shiver of jewels – under a chorus of gasping breaths and muttered questions, all amplified by the unpunctured darkness. He reached into one of the lamps lining the corridor with his uninjured arm and lifted out the redundant clara stone inside. It didn't hum in his palm the way clara stones were supposed to, the latent magic calling to like. He called his own magic and enchanted the stone to *light*. Nothing happened. The stones were not just turned off: they had been drained of their power.

The Guysman had done this. It was what he had intended of it, but not like this. When he had last encountered the doll, she had shown no skill for draining spells, only people. This was a talent that she had *developed*.

Tossing the clara stone aside, Ollivan proceeded to the ballroom, the darkness growing denser as he approached. He had a half-formed plan, one centred on brute force, applied with a mix of magical and non-magical means. And his dinner jacket, once again, to bind her if he had the chance. Hopefully Jupitus would be there. Hopefully he would see Ollivan take care of this and all would be restored.

But his jacket, Ollivan soon realised, would not help him this time.

How his Guysman had become *this*, he had no idea. Those who hadn't fled –mainly Successors; too young and invincible to think of self-preservation – were pressed to the walls of the ballroom, gaping in horrified fascination at the scene in the centre. Jupitus and a dozen enforcers were there too, having gathered flame torches to light the spectacle. In the middle of the floor was a woman of artificial parts; porcelain arms, screws in the joints of her elbows and fingers and wrists. But the thing's face was the same. This woman was the doll his sister called Violet. She flickered in and out of being like a shadow.

"Enforcers!" shrieked Jupitus. "Destroy it!"

Ollivan had half a mind to let them try; perhaps they could weaken the Guysman or throw it off before he swept in and ended this. Then there could be no doubt what his grandfather and the Heart owed him.

Unless more people were hurt.

"Wait!" cried Ollivan as the enforcers loosed two dozen spells, but they ignored him. The flashes of magic were near blinding, but he squinted through the glare at their target. Violet stood unmoved by the onslaught, with her arms spread, like she was welcoming it. She was absorbing their directs hits just as she had sucked the magic from the clara stone lamps, and it made Ollivan's blood run cold. What became of all that magic once it was hers?

And then he found out, as the enforcers' spells were turned back on them. The militia in front of him were blasted off their feet, and Ollivan threw himself to the ground with everyone around him. A body landed on the marble beside him with a sickening crack. Another met with a window and came to earth in a shower of broken glass. Ollivan looked for his grandfather, but the old man had transported, or been whisked away. Jasper had likewise fled. He was contemplating a similar exit, his magic rising to make it so, when another power gripped him.

The room fell silent. The fighting stopped. Ollivan's magic had answered his call, but now something intercepted it, ripping it from his grasp even as it flowed through him. He struggled, his instincts begging him to disappear, run from the room, transport, anything but this. Anything but his magic. It was abandoning him – reluctantly, painfully, but going all the same. A pressure crushed his skull and hot liquid trickled from his nose. He fought the terrifying urge to let it end, all of it, let the Guysman take his life with his magic. He didn't want one without the other.

And then the power holding him released with such speed and force that the air rushing back into his lungs burned. He chanced a look at the vessel; she had turned towards the garden.

"Cassia?" she said, her voice high and childlike. Ollivan realised he had never heard her speak. She flickered again and was gone, like a candle winking out. Or a Sorcerer transporting.

He reached for his magic, despite the fear of what he might find. His grandfather was right about one thing, he could not deny: how could he have brought such an evil power into the world?

But it was there, and Ollivan could not have stood if he tried, for his magic rushed to him like a faithful friend, embracing him in trembling arms. It was weak, like it might be after injury or exhaustion, but it lived on, and he knew in a way he couldn't explain that it would regain its full strength. The Guysman hadn't completed its work.

Feet pounded the ballroom floor around him as the enforcers sprung to action. The danger having passed, Jupitus was nearby and screaming orders again, but the only words he heard were *arrest him*.

Ollivan closed his eyes, feigning unconsciousness to buy himself a moment's pause. He pulled his explanation back to the forefront of his mind, and tore it up.

Jupitus would not listen. He had proved as much before. And now his small mistake had swollen beyond anything he knew how to control, making matters even worse. He would be taken into custody, and tossed in a cell. Perhaps he would even be quietly killed. Perhaps he would prefer that.

But no. He could not submit himself to that fate. He could not quit. The solution was always there. With a chance to think, to scheme, he could discover how to undo the Guysman.

A foot landed near his head, and another just above, and he sensed someone lean over him to lift him up. His magic felt fragile as he coaxed it to his fingertips, but it was intention that mattered most, and Ollivan's was steadfast. He pushed down the weight of his heart and his pride and focused on it.

With a flash, he opened his eyes and loosed the spell with both hands, stunning the enforcers with enough power to knock them backwards.

Then Ollivan poured all his focus into his destination and, with the last of his magic, he fled.

They sprinted across the Chambers' garden to the nearest gate. The fog had smothered the moonlight, so that they could barely see the path or each other. Sybella, Lev, and Virgil conjured flames, and Cassia followed their light, the sounds of their breathing, and the crackle of gravel underfoot. Stones tore through her delicate slippers and into her skin, but she couldn't feel it. All she felt was shame. She had had a chance to stop Violet, and she had failed in front of everyone.

She and Lev were trailing behind when the sounds of fighting from the Chambers abruptly vanished. They both stopped and looked back, foreboding creeping over Cassia and raising the hairs on her arms.

"What happened?" said Lev, gasping for breath. He looked over his shoulder. Sybella's and Virgil's lights were disappearing in the fog. "Hey, wait!"

Something smothered his cry, shrinking his voice to a whisper, and Sybella and Virgil continued to run.

"Lev, do you feel that?" said Cassia, her voice hoarse and breaking. Magic. It had been thrown over them like a blanket. "I… I don't think they know we've stopped."

The two bobbing flames vanished in the fog. A heartbeat later, Lev's went out too.

"Lev—"

"I can't… my magic won't—"

"She's here."

Cassia felt her presence like a breath on the back of her neck a second before her gaze swung to a third outline in the darkness. She groped for Lev's hand.

"Lev—"

"Lev has left us," said Violet. "It's temporary. I don't want to hurt your friends."

Cassia's eyes groped in the darkness, passing over the spot where he stood several times before she saw him. Everything was varying shades of black, and he stood so very still. His arms rested at his sides. His head hung slightly like he was sleeping.

"Lev." She shook him and he swayed slightly, but didn't react. Were his eyes open? His face was a featureless black shadow, even as she stood inches from him.

The darkness shifted to her right as Violet came closer. Cassia was out of words, beyond begging. The best she could do was not cower as Violet leaned close to speak softly.

"You would stand in my way when I'm trying to help you?" She sighed sadly. "It's alright. You don't understand. But you will. When I have brought this city to its knees before you, you will love me."

Magic shivered along Cassia's senses. Sleep rose up like a wave and dragged her down, and a different kind of darkness descended.

33

The floor of the President's Sanctuary welcomed him with a light groan. Ollivan marvelled that it didn't give way entirely. He had never felt so heavy.

Shafts of grey moonlight were all that lit the Sanctuary, the Guysman having destroyed the clara stones here as well, but soon these grew diffused and began to fade. Curling fingers of fog caressed the windows, searching for a way in. How and why had she conjured the fog? Ollivan couldn't coax his mind into tackling the question; he could only lie there.

It was the type of helpless inaction he usually despised, but he had been forced to do so many things tonight that he passionately resented, he couldn't bring himself to care. He was weary, and he wanted more than anything to dress the wound on his wrist and have someone tell him it would be alright.

That would be inane, of course, but he longed to hear it all the same. Ollivan was a fugitive; a man who had attacked his own people's militia and fled from his leader's 'justice'. Mentally, he added 'find vindication for *this*' under 'stop the Guysman'.

One problem at a time. The first was to get up off the floor.

He was yet to accomplish this when a series of cascading thuds sounded beyond the Sanctuary, growing closer, and the door swung open with a great force. Ollivan readied his magic to whisk him away again – how quickly he was exhausting the places he could run to – when the scent of lilies filled his nostrils and Sybella grabbed him by the lapels.

Of course; he had come here because it was safe. No one but the two of them could open the door.

"Oh, stars, Ollivan. Are you hurt?" Sybella demanded of him.

Ollivan raised his head. She knelt at his side, Cassia and Virgil hovering behind her, the latter with a flame in his palm. "Only all the way down to my wretched soul."

"What?"

He sighed, and presented her his injured arm. "I suppose you can start with my wrist."

Sybella held it tenderly in both hands as Virgil brought his flame closer. "This?" she said. "This is why you're on the floor?"

"Oh." He snatched his arm back and let his head thunk back against the carpet. "No, I'm on the floor for cover. The Guysman can do spells, don't you know? Did you close the door?"

"And bolted it," said Virgil. "Does that make a difference?"

"It can't hurt." Ollivan pulled himself up and crossed the room to draw the curtains. They would look for him here, sooner or later, but he didn't want to announce his presence if Virgil's flame was visible through the fog. "The Guysman's gone again."

"We heard," said Sybella. "The square is swarming with people. News was crossing it as fast as we were."

"And Lev?" Three blank stares. "Where is he?"

Virgil frowned and looked over his shoulder. "He's right—"

But Lev was not in the Sanctuary, as Ollivan could have told them the moment they arrived. Something tugged at his suspicion. How did Virgil lose the boy he was so fiercely protective of?

"He ran to check on his parents," said Cassia. "I'm sorry, I forgot to tell you."

"*When?*" said Virgil.

"As we were crossing the square. You and Sybella were ahead of us and he just… peeled off."

Virgil frowned. "They do live very close. But why wouldn't he tell me?"

Sybella had rummaged through the Sanctuary and found a couple of candles, which she lit by holding them to the flame in Virgil's palm. When she was done and Virgil's hands were free, the two of them set about bandaging Ollivan's wrist with Virgil's handkerchief and the gold ribbons from Sybella's dress.

"Are we going to talk about the fact that Violet is eating up *enchantments?*" said Sybella as she fastened the ribbons. "I thought you said that wasn't how she worked."

"It wasn't how she *appeared* to work. It seems, among everything else I've accomplished, I've cast an enchantment that knows when to hold off playing its trump card. But let's catalogue what we've seen her do."

"Shoot flames," said Virgil.

"Beg your pardon?"

"You were otherwise engaged for that part," said Sybella dryly, "but it's true. Cassia tried to set her alight and Violet just absorbed it and turned it on an enforcer."

Ollivan's brows rose in surprise, and he grinned at Cassia. "But you managed the spell? You can toast mannequins now?"

Cassia did not return his smile. "*Mannequin?*" she said distastefully, before choosing a different complaint. "I'm not entirely useless, whatever you believe."

"I didn't say – never mind. And she's assassinated the clara stones, I see."

"The smog enchantment too," said Virgil. "Or at least I think that's what happened. She was talking about old magic at the Chambers, and something about it being bitter."

The smog enchantment – of course. There was an old spell, first cast at the Chambers, that kept the air across London sweet and fresh, no matter how many coal fires burned. Ollivan sank slowly onto the couch; he was too exhausted to work his mind and his legs simultaneously, and his mind was starting to whirr. "And now she's producing this fog."

The Sanctuary fell quiet, or perhaps he blocked everything else out. It was a minute or so before he realised Sybella was saying his name.

"Ollivan?"

He turned his thoughts into words and continued to follow them aloud. "She drank up the clara stones and now there's a kind of darkness hovering around her. She drank the smog enchantment and now she's producing it. She absorbed Cassia's fire spell and half a dozen other things when they were deployed to defend against her and now she's using them to attack. It's the reverse of what was intended."

"But how is she doing it?" said Virgil.

"The enchantment I was trying to cast was meant to activate when Jasper hit it with some magic, and then ultimately ruin his life when it led someone to the ledgers and the banned spells. The problem was that I didn't specify what became of the magic once the Guysman drank it, which left room for it to interpret my intention to decide for itself." He looked at each of them in turn, but they didn't appear to be following him. "At the heart of it, I wanted to turn Jasper's magic against him."

Sybella's eyes widened as she began to catch on. "And now Violet's turning our magic against all of us. Earth and stars, Ollivan, next time you're rage-casting, could you try being a bit more specific?"

"How does any of this help us stop her?" asked Virgil.

Ollivan sat back on the couch. "We get her to absorb something that will hurt her when she drinks it."

"Like what?" said Sybella.

"Like another Guysman."

It was precisely the reaction he expected his words to have; silence.

"Excellent," Sybella said. The word dripped with sarcasm. "My little sister has an enchanted doll we can borrow."

Ollivan shook his head. "I'm not talking about another doll, just a variation on the spell that will drink Violet's magic in a way we can control."

"Oh, what an idea!" Sybella's smile was almost believable but her voice was an octave higher than normal. "That's all we needed all along – to control the Guysman. Who could have figured it out but you, Ollivan?"

He raised a hand. "I know how it sounds."

"*Do you?* Because you're still speaking."

"Sybella, think about it," he implored. "We can't hurt her with any spell but her own. Hit her with an unravelling of any kind and she'll just absorb the magic and turn it to her own purposes somehow. Put any kind of weapon in front of her and she'll suck

356

the magic out of that too. So if we present her a weapon with an enchantment *intended* to be absorbed—"

"Like a pill," said Virgil slowly. "Something designed to work from the inside."

Ollivan nodded. "She's drinking spells and turning them on their heads, so we give her something that's doing the same – absorbing magic – and it will cancel the original enchantment out. It'll neutralise her."

"Or make her twice as powerful," said Sybella.

"There's a chance, yes."

"You can't do it."

It was Cassia. Ollivan scowled at her, and she only shrugged.

"The first Guysman didn't do what you intended," she said. "Even Guysman himself never completed a version of the spell. What makes you think you can enchant this version you're suggesting?"

"You're not very nice today," said Ollivan. "Or should I say, you're more objectionable than usual."

Cassia's lips thinned further and she folded her arms, but made no response. That neither Sybella nor Virgil jumped to her defence told him he wasn't the only one who had noticed. But he brushed his sister's snippiness off and answered her question.

"I failed with the first Guysman because I was more concerned with revenge than with magic. I had no business casting spells, let alone untested ones, with such little research. This time, my approach will be different. I can conduct some tests. The three of you can help me edit the draft." He drummed his fingers slowly on his knee. "But magic has a mind of its own. We all know this. I've dedicated my life to its study, and even I can't guarantee this will work. But it's the only chance I can see. Does anyone have any other ideas?"

Sybella shook her head. Cassia continued to stare stone-faced at him, but something like apprehension was tugging at her brows. For that, Ollivan couldn't blame her. What he was suggesting was exceptionally complicated, but the problems and solutions were already beginning to arrange themselves before him in an orderly fashion. He felt energised.

And then a second round of pounding footsteps filled the corridor beyond the Sanctuary. Shouted commands were volleyed up and down the stairs, and several indignant cries as the enforcers dared to manhandle any Successors who had taken cover in the Wending Place.

"How many do you think there are?" said Sybella as someone began trying to break down the door.

Ollivan shrugged. "Over a dozen just failed to detain me across the square, so hopefully at least twenty-five. That would truly make me feel special. I should like to imagine them all squashed together in the corridor."

"Come out, Mr Sims," said a voice from the other side of the door. "You'll only make things worse for yourself. We have a dozen experts in unravellings. We can find a dozen more."

"Tell them all I hope their careers survive the Wending Place," Ollivan called back.

There was another resounding thud, and this time the door groaned in its frame.

"They'll get in eventually," said Sybella.

"Nonsense. The enchantments on the Wending Place have held for hundreds of years."

"But has anyone really tried to break them? Your grandfather is going to throw everything he has at getting in here."

"In case you're not clear," added Virgil, "everything he has equals hundreds of thousands of Sorcerers who'll do as he commands, and as long as it takes."

It pained Ollivan to admit it, but his friends were right. No one living knew the nature of the spells cast on the Wending Place, but it was like breaking a code. With enough magic thrown at the door, sooner or later they would hit on the right intention. All of that assuming Violet didn't simply spring back up and drain the old house dry.

"Perhaps there's somewhere else we can hide?" said Sybella meaningfully.

Ollivan swallowed. There was a room above a temple a mile east, one Ollivan had returned to all too often from his narrow bed at the boarding house. Sybella blushed as she saw him remember it. But...

"Not secret enough. I won't go anywhere they could trace us to." Ollivan went to the desk and retrieved a small stack of hazel wood paper. "I have an idea that will get us out of the Heart. We just need a few hours to work out this Guysman."

"I'm not coming," said Virgil. "I have to find Lev and see if he's alright. I still don't understand why he would just disappear on me." He shot a look at Cassia.

"And I've no hope of getting out of here at all," said Cassia with a shrug. "I can't transport."

Ollivan had forgotten, and the reminder hit him with an accompanying wave of dread. He couldn't understand how Cassia was so calm; she was trapped.

But perhaps there was something he could do.

"Listen." Ollivan addressed his plea to the walls and ceiling. He ignored the glances exchanged in the corner of his vision. "I know we've not been together long, you and I, but don't try to claim you aren't fond of me. I heard those well-timed rattling groans at the election. Thank you, by the way, for that."

"Ollivan—"

"And there's really only so much you can do about the door, I understand that. But if we truly are friends, perhaps you could do me a favour and show me another way out of this room." A lull in the pounding on the door conspired to amplify the silence that followed. "Please?"

More noise in the corridor, then a shuddering boom that flashed green around the doorframe. It rattled the old house so severely that plaster dust rained down on them, and for a breathless moment, all eyes were on the ceiling.

So Ollivan could not say exactly when the wall opened up. The disguised door had swung wide, and a draught trickled up from inside, catching Sybella's hair and making her turn.

"Oh, stars, it actually worked."

They crowded together in the doorway. On the other side, steep, narrow steps wended down into perfect darkness. They were worn smooth; ancient. Cobwebs stirred in the corners.

"But the billiard room is the other side of this wall," said Virgil. "This shouldn't be."

"You think the might of the Wending Place is confined by the laws of physics?" said Ollivan, caressing the wall. "You insult it."

"I don't think it's safe for Ollivan to be on the streets, no matter where this lets out," said Sybella. "Cassia, you ought to take the tunnel and meet us."

"No." Cassia was frowning down into the tunnel, lost in thought. "I meant to say, not right away. I don't want to risk leading anyone to you. Besides, I don't think I can help you with this spell." She looked at the clock on the sideboard; it was nearly dawn. "Let's meet at dusk. Does that give you enough time?"

Ollivan and Sybella exchanged a look, and Ollivan shrugged. "It ought to. Where shall we find you?"

"Hyde Park. By the statue of Drusella. Do you know the one?"

He nodded. "Dusk in Hyde Park. We'll work out a plan of attack for Violet then. She seems to have some attachment to you. You'll be useful."

Cassia's expression soured. "Useful?"

Ollivan winced. "Stars, I didn't mean—"

"Forget it. We don't have time."

Without a farewell, Cassia picked up her skirts and started down the secret stairs.

"Odd," murmured Virgil.

"What?"

"She didn't take a candle."

Ollivan peered down the steps after his sister, but they had lost her to the dark.

34

It started as a hum, burrowing into her sleeping mind and nudging her awake.

But Cassia didn't want to wake. She resisted the humming, and the light that coaxed her to open her eyes. There were horrors in the waking world, things she would have to face when she arose.

And then the humming grew louder and clearer, until it wasn't a hum at all but a million smaller sounds that she couldn't place. Snaps of air? The billowing of sails? And rising slowly above it all, were those... *screams*?

Cassia jolted awake, her eyes flying open. She was outside, under a cloudy grey sky, and above her flocked thousands – hundreds of thousands – of crows. It was not screaming she could hear, but the cawing of the birds as they sang of their frenzy. Their wings roared. Cassia knew rationally that she need not be afraid – they were passing by – but her heart knew no such thing, and it hammered in her chest like the beating of so many wings.

And then they were gone, their black forms vanishing in the fog long before the sound of their wings and their cawing.

At last, she became aware of her body, her surroundings, her last memories in the vast and empty dark. She lay on the gravel where Violet had left her. Somewhere beyond the fog – so dense that the ground stretched no more than two yards before being swallowed by it – the sun had risen. Virgil said Violet had broken the smog spell, which made sense. That spell *was* old, and it was cast and maintained at the Chambers. But Violet's fumes were not quite coal smoke; what she had created had a faint sickly, rotting scent, like dying flowers.

Cassia climbed carefully to her feet, brushing tiny stones off her skin. They left deep bruising impressions in her arms; some had cut her. What magic had Violet used, that she had slept for hours on a bed of sharp rocks and not even wanted to wake?

There was a crunch as the gravel shifted. Cassia turned. A little way away, another figure was waking on the ground.

"Lev." She ran to him. "Are you hurt?"

Lev lifted himself up on his forearms. His eyes were half closed from sleep. "I dreamed of birds," he said. "And Virgil. Calling for me."

"You didn't dream the birds." Cassia looked around her again. Somewhere out there was the vast training ground behind the Chambers. "And I doubt you dreamt Virgil either. He wouldn't have a hope of finding us in this."

"We were... following Sybella."

Cassia remembered, and it suddenly struck her how alone they were; Virgil couldn't find them, Sybella hadn't said where they were going.

"Violet did something to you," Cassia told him. "Lev, I swear I wasn't helping her in the ballroom. I was trying to stop her. I don't want her to do any of this but she won't listen."

Briefly, and with heavy emphasis on her lack of control over the situation, she filled him in on what Violet had said the night before; of her plan to amass power on Cassia's behalf.

When I have brought this city to its knees before you, you will love me.

"She's doing all this for *me*." She felt the horror of it all over again as she said the words aloud. The fleeting rush of the spell working when everyone was watching. The slow realisation that her peers were gaping at her in horror. There had been a voice in her head, irrational and wild, demanding she take it back, make it stop, when she knew full well it was too late. Even now, she wanted to shy away from the memory; if only she didn't look at it – didn't play it back like a nightmare that haunted you after you woke – perhaps she could scrub it from her memory altogether.

But she couldn't erase it from the minds of everyone she knew. It was a permanent and immutable blight that would stain her forever, perhaps the proof of everything they already believed; that she did not belong among them.

Lev got to his feet, and similarly picked gravel from his battered skin. "Is it strangely quiet?"

On one side, the fog was a little darker. Cassia squinted until the straight edge of a roof materialised. The Chambers of Alchemy loomed before them. So that way was the river, and that was the direction they had been running. They hadn't got far. Lev was right; for the hub of the Sorcerer quarter, it was far too quiet.

It probably wasn't wise to go back inside when Jupitus's people were surely looking for her, but she didn't know where the gate to the training ground was; they could grope around it forever and never find their way out.

"Come on." She moved closer to Lev – she would not lose anyone else to this fog – and they headed for the dark shape of the Chambers.

They made contact with a hedge first, and were forced to follow it until it met the corner of the building. It wasn't long until they found a guard entrance, the door of which yielded when Cassia turned the handle and opened it into the deserted corridor.

"So much for the guard," said Lev.

The fog had found its way inside, but here it kept low, so that they waded through frothing shallows that stirred with every step. Eventually, whispers of life in the Chambers began echoing off the stone walls, and they crept along with greater care. If there were enforcers here after all, the sooner they found their way out into Drusella Square, the better.

But it wasn't enforcers they found in the room they emerged in. Some were guests from the ball, still in their finery, their curls collapsing and outfits creased. Others wore the white and purple of healers. Among them, two dozen thin mats were laid out across the floor, each bearing a patient. Their unseeing eyes pointed at the ceiling or straight through the loved ones who hovered over them. Some groaned faintly; another nearby was making sounds that were almost words, but no words that Cassia knew. Several twitched or struggled faintly, as if under attack by a force she couldn't see. An effort had been made to clean up the blood, but on every face Cassia looked into, a tell-tale crust around their nostrils said they had suffered in the same manner as the Whisperers the previous morning.

Had Violet only drained their magic, or also their minds? Could they recover from such brutality?

"What are they doing here?" whispered Lev. "They could have moved them to an infirmary."

"Unless they couldn't. What if the infirmaries are full? What if this is just the beginning?"

Lev paled. "The enforcers. If Violet's tearing through the city, that's why there's hardly anyone here."

Cassia shook her head faintly. "What can they do? She'll drain all of them."

She spotted someone she recognised, and shifted behind Lev and out of their line of sight.

Selleck. He was a Camden wolf, one of those based at the Zoo to guard Alpha Hester, her lieutenants, and the Ravenswoods' seat. He had accompanied the alpha last night as part of her guard.

And now he knelt over one of the mats, dabbing at the brow of another wolf who lay there. Anika. Cassia had known her for years. She had entertained her children sometimes while the militiawoman was on shift. Now she was near comatose – her eyes rolling vaguely in their sockets, her mouth horribly slack – and Violet had Changeling magic.

"The crows," she said aloud, causing Lev to frown. She thought back to the stone urn Violet had lifted psychokinetically, and then burned from existence; to Londus, the party guest whose mind Violet could take but not influence. Had Anika's magic manifested in her as an ability to generate new forms entirely? If so, it was a blessing that Violet had rejected the idea of drinking an Oracle. What chaos could be wrought on all of space and time with that kind of power?

"I have to find Virgil," said Lev. "He'll be looking for me still. Come with me. If he's with Sybella, perhaps they've found Ollivan too."

Cassia nodded. She didn't need to be persuaded to stick close to Lev. Jasper had revealed all; she had nowhere else to go but to Jupitus, followed by the cells beneath their feet.

35

Ollivan's brilliant hiding place was a renowned pub in the Underground called The Height of Deception. The owner was away and the building would be locked up, giving them ample space and privacy to put together their second-chance Guysman.

Though Sybella already knew of the place, they did not transport straight there, landing instead in one of Ollivan's well-worn safe spots; the nooks and crannies of another quarter where he knew he could transport in and out and get away with it. Ollivan had done a great many audacious things in his life – transporting outside the Sorcerer quarter among them – but even he was not so daring as to magic himself straight into a building owned by Delphine de Magna.

As he stuck his head out of the alley to check the coast was clear, Sybella sniffed haughtily.

"I don't do that any more."

"Do what?"

"The thing I just did."

"Transport?" said Ollivan. "Why ever not?"

"Break the Principles. That's the first time I've used magic outside the Heart since we broke up. And the last."

"Oh, Ellie, I'm devastated for you." He grinned. "Do you remember the games we used to play? Who dared to cast the most conspicuous glamour in a crowd?"

"Please stop. I feel dizzy to think of it. I can't believe I never feared what your grandfather would do to me if we were caught."

That sobered Ollivan. She didn't know the half of what her grandfather might have done to her for loving him. "It's this way."

The Otherworld had an Underground, a series of narrow train tunnels that made Ollivan pity their lack of imagination and debilitating lack of magic. He had missed *this* Underground, the territory of the Psi. It was a sprawling maze of pale stone carved from the earth, bridges and staircases winding throughout to connect the many levels. Endlessly discoverable and stunningly cohesive, the Underground was both a playground and a work of art.

In daylight hours, it was illuminated by a centuries-old spell that mimicked the rising and setting of the sun above. Right now, it was nearly invisible.

"She got the clara stones down here too," said Sybella, looking out over the balustrade of the bridge they had landed on. Someone had thought to place oil or gas lamps on some of the staircases, but Ollivan doubted there were enough non-magical lamps in the entire city to light every step in the Psi quarter.

"It'll be morning soon. Just watch your step."

The Height of Deception was tucked up against the cavern roof, forming the very last three storeys of one of the colossal towers that reinforced the cave. They crossed the enormous bridge – lined with tightly packed shops and cafés, their bright awnings tucked away and doors bolted – and climbed several winding stairs before the pub rose before them.

"I loathe this quarter," complained Sybella, craning over the edge of the wide parapet surrounding the pub and looking down through the warren of other layers to where the wide boulevards at the cavern's lowest level lurked in the dark, hundreds of feet below. "One can barely get a carriage anywhere. It's undignified."

Ollivan was hardly listening. He risked a small flame in his palm and checked his watch. "Dawn has come and gone."

Sybella turned, the flame catching the flecks of gold in her eyes, as well as the alarm. "Heaven and earth."

It was Sorcerers, of course, who had enchanted the Underground to grow light with the sun, as part of an agreement made centuries ago. If the original spell couldn't be restored, Jupitus was in a very strong position to negotiate its reinstatement. What would light cost the Psi?

Ollivan couldn't let it come to that. He would find a way to restore the enchantment himself if needs be.

They spelled the door of the pub to unlock without a hitch, but spent several minutes more checking for other traps against intruders. There were a couple of predictable magical alarms, but nothing sinister. This was the Underground, after all, where the best defence of one's valuables was hiding them. A Psi could rob an empty pub without ever stepping foot inside.

When they were finally in, Ollivan locked the door behind them and reset the alarms. Then they pulled a sofa near the fireplace in one corner of the bar and magicked a flame into being.

"You think we'll be safe here?" said Sybella.

"As safe as anywhere. If Jupitus had any way of linking me to Delphine, I would have been dead long ago."

"Ollivan?"

"What?"

"You're bleeding." She nodded to his wrist. A trickle of blood had escaped Virgil's handkerchief and was snaking along his little finger. "You need to put some pressure on it."

"It's too tender."

She scooted closer. Ollivan offered her his wrist, and with confident fingers, Sybella redressed the wound. A silence fell. Ollivan knew where her thoughts were going right before she voiced them, and his stomach clenched.

"What happened at the ball? I thought Jasper was only threatening to turn Cassia in."

Ollivan rubbed a hand over his face. "Well he made sure not to leave me out. He probably realised there wasn't much value in getting her into trouble, whereas Jupitus has been champing at the bit for evidence of my wrongdoing."

Sybella shifted uncomfortably. "You and Jasper were friends, once."

"I thought so too."

She hesitated again. "You told Lev and Virgil that Jasper was the reason you were banished."

He nodded, and his heart began to race. Just the thought of saying what was in his head, what he desperately needed people to know, triggered a terror so vast he wasn't sure he could cross it.

"Nobody believed me," he said, leaning back against the wall. Sybella left the silence open for him, so he drew a series of long breaths, told himself to expect the worst, and forced himself to speak. "The rules at the club were simple. You won the fight if your opponent stepped from the ring or conceded. If either of you incurred injury in the process, that was to be expected, but to use lethal force was forbidden." He laughed humourlessly. "I don't believe the organisers were all that intent on protecting our lives, just the enterprise. Someone dying, their family asking questions, militia investigating; it would have been a good way to get the whole thing shut down and most of us charged with breaking the Principles, sooner or later.

"We rotated locations, to spread the risk. It was treacherous for everyone involved, but the infractions would not be so bad if one was caught in one's own quarter. Everyone else there was using their magic beyond their borders. That month we were in Sorcerer territory. If we had been anywhere else, perhaps everyone would have questioned the sense of me killing someone with magic. Perhaps I would have been believed when I said it wasn't me." Ollivan leaned his head back, his eyes on the ceiling. He had played the what ifs over and over in his mind for the last year. Whenever he wondered if Jasper had planned his betrayal all along, the location of the duelling evening was evidence that he had.

"I drew a Wraith named Jonas Benn. A vicious bully. He was almost banned several times before that night for causing too much damage." He put a finger in his right ear and jostled it around, like he had done compulsively a thousand times before. "He cost me my hearing in this ear the last time we'd fought. Punched me in the head and knocked me out. Everyone knew our rematch was going to be heated. I started with the upper hand. His technique was brute force; I managed to keep him at a distance with a volley of small cutting curses. I was trying to tire him out by making him dance around the ring avoiding them.

"Then he got under my guard, threw a punch at my head. He was aiming for my ear again. He knew he'd made a weakness the last time we fought and now he wanted to break it open.

372

He missed his mark, thank the stars, but I came away from that punch with my cheek torn open." He gestured to the scar along his right cheek, badly healed in the Otherworld, without the help of Sorcerer medicine. "He was wearing a ring. I saw it after the punch – I think he wanted me to. An ugly thing with a raven's head on it, but the beak was a blade. Weapons were against the rules for Wraiths, Sorcerers, and Changelings – one had to use one's magic, and their magic alone – but it was too late to call him out for it." He sighed. Some masochistic urge told him to tell the full story, unedited. The version with his own mistakes and flaws included. It was a test of sorts. He needed Sybella of all people to believe him, even with the full truth.

"I was angry," he said softly. "And I had things in my arsenal he wouldn't know to expect. Spells to whisper voices in his ear, descriptions of his family being slaughtered. Something that conjures moths in the victims' lungs. I started hitting him with it all. He was coughing up blood, on his knees when—"

He cut off, restless. "I should tell you about the fighting ring. It was marked in paint on the floor, but the spectators would pour over the boundary. Money was changing hands so everyone wanted to get ringside. If you didn't have another person's blood on you by the end of a fight you weren't in, then you didn't have a very good view. Sometimes the crowd would have to get out of the way or push you back into the centre. If someone touched you as you fought, there was nothing strange in that. That's the important thing to know.

"Jasper had bet money on me. So when I was ready to end the thing – knock Benn out – when I had raised my hand to direct the spell, he put a hand on my shoulder and squeezed, and for a split second, I thought nothing of it." Ollivan could still see the whole night in vivid colour; could almost feel the wrongness grip him, grip his magic, as it reached for his fingertips.

"But it wasn't encouragement." He looked to Sybella, begging her to understand.

An age seemed to pass before her eyes widened. "He jolted you," she said.

Ollivan nodded. "Do you remember what that was like?"

"I had no control of it." Her voice had dropped to a whisper. She knew; she understood. She *had* to understand.

"No, but if you had been performing a spell at the time, it would have been amplified. Beyond what you had intended, and maybe with effects that were beyond you to help."

"What was the spell?"

Ollivan's breath caught in his throat. He hated to be thinking of that night; it stirred emotions far worse than anger. Or maybe that wasn't why he was choking up. Maybe it was the sudden presence of Sybella's hand in his.

"It was a... it was a wind spell," he said. "I just wanted him to fall out of the ring."

Sybella pressed her eyes closed. When she opened them, tears glistened in the corners. "You weren't even trying to hurt him any more."

"But I did. I couldn't control it, couldn't have stopped it. Perhaps if I had expected the blast of power things might have been different. He could have survived a strong gust of wind with cuts and scrapes. But the shock of it, the *sharpness* of it... it made a blade out of my spell. I pierced his heart with a stars-damned gust of air. And not a soul there knew the nature of what Jasper had done."

"How did Fisk find out?" said Sybella.

Ollivan clenched a fist. "Jasper told him. It was a set-up from start to finish. The night, the opponent – one everyone would believe I had lost my temper while fighting – and telling my grandfather everything."

"But why?" said Sybella.

Ollivan didn't know for sure. If he had, he could have seen it coming, and guarded against betrayal. But he had theories. "Jasper introduced me to an entire way of life. Drugs, brawls, dangerous spells, they all had one thing in common; the practice of magic. He lived for the debauchery and the danger; for inflicting pain and suffering. It didn't matter how a certain narcotic worked, or the mechanism of a banned spell, so long as it funded his vices or did something awful. It's no way to excel at something. But *I* excelled. I was his protégé and I was better at all of it than he had ever been."

"He was jealous?"

"Constantly." He fixed his gaze on Sybella. His hammering heart was finding a calm he had not known in over a year. "I was just too focused on the magic to see it. I was too focused to see anything."

Her held her gaze until she ducked her head to wipe her tears, but he saw something at the last moment; something that reminded him of the days before he had destroyed them with his own hubris.

"Now you know what a stars-damned fool I was to use that same spell on you the night Violet drained your magic."

Sybella shook her head. "That wasn't the same. I wasn't spellcasting. And nothing bad came of it."

"I still knew better. It was foolish to take that risk with you. Please forgive me, Ellie."

She froze, head tilted gently to one side. Her eyes narrowed shrewdly. It was as one corner of her mouth tugged upwards into a wry smile that Ollivan froze.

"Now hold on a moment," he began.

"Beg your pardon, but I don't think I heard you right."

"Don't make a thing of this."

"Ollivan Sims *apologises* now?"

"I have always apologised," said Ollivan fiercely, startling her. "When I'm at fault. But I will not be a scapegoat for the likes of Jasper Hawkes. I won't accept blame just because everyone is telling me to. Not when I know the truth."

Sybella's humour evaporated, replaced with something softer. "Of course you shouldn't be held responsible for Benn's death." Her words were careful; the things she wasn't saying rang as loud as each word she did. "Nor do I hold what you did for me against you either. You don't need to apologise for the channelling. I would have begged you to if I'd known it was possible."

Ollivan had not imagined that begging was in Sybella's repertoire; but then again, he would have claimed it wasn't in his own. Faced with the threat of losing his magic, he had also learned different.

"Did you know that every High Sorcerer for the past hundred and thirty years was first President of the Society of Young Gifted Sorcerers?" she said suddenly. She was the one now staring into the fire. "Your grandfather was both at once. And then *I*… I failed my initiation three years in a row, and now I have one chance to be President before I age out, and no chance at all of winning."

Ollivan had leaned back into the cushions, but he pushed himself upright. "What are you talking about? You're the Secretary. Former secretaries win the presidency all the time. Wasn't that the whole point of blackmailing me?"

"It was the *idea*, yes," she said, narrowing her eyes at him. "But we're off to a rollicking poor start, for one thing. While I should have been dealing with the mounting stack of members' business on my desk, I've been consorting with smugglers and otherwise finding this Guysman business rather time-consuming. And besides, it turns out the members believe you only gave me the position because we're involved."

After a year, it still took Ollivan's heart a moment to recognise that the present tense was a fiction; a rumour. "But we're not involved."

"Quite."

He turned his face towards the fire, feeling foolish. It was nothing other than what he'd expected to hear, and yet he couldn't deny he had wanted something else when he stated the obvious.

"But now that you're the most interesting gossip of the season, everyone seems to think I'm riding on your coat-tails and have taken you back."

"Need I remind you the most interesting gossip of the season was marched from the dance floor by militia last night in front of everyone? What good am I to your reputation?"

"Perhaps wider society takes your grandfather's view of you – in public at least – but the Successors love a scandal. They voted you their president *because* they think you murdered someone, not in spite of the fact." She huffed a sigh. "But what they won't tolerate is a shameless social climber. I'll never win an election.

I just wish I could find a way of breaking it to my parents that being Secretary hasn't played out like we all hoped it would. I can't bear to hear them making plans about my future as if they finally have reason to be proud of me."

This was the bittersweet, familiar territory Ollivan realised he had wanted, and now wished to banish. Soothing the damage Sybella's mother and mama did with the pressure of their expectations were memories he could do without.

"I know you can be hard on yourself, Ellie, but writing off your tenure as Secretary after only two weeks is a new level, even for you." She looked up sharply, and he held her gaze. "So the Successors don't see you as president material. Prove them wrong. You have time. You can still be the most obnoxiously effective Secretary those cretins have ever seen."

Sybella gave a weak smile, but then she hugged her knees to her chest. "Perhaps you're right," she said. She sounded anything but convinced. Ollivan cursed himself. He used to be able to convince her. "But since you channelled your magic into me, I'll always know what I'm trying to succeed without. I've never felt power like that. My magic has always been… adequate. I work so hard at it, and it shows. But when your hand was on my shoulder, and your magic touched mine, I realised all at once why people covet it the way they do." She looked at him desolately. "I'm fighting an uphill battle, and now I can't ever forget it. Respect is easier to come by with magic like yours. If I had your magic, and my ambition, I would be usurping Fisk as we speak." Ollivan opened his mouth to protest, but she cut him off. "I don't resent you for it. I know you too well to begrudge you not wanting what I want. Being High Sorcerer would be the death of you, Ollivan. I shudder to think of you manoeuvred into the role by your family, but… well. I just hope you don't begrudge me wanting it."

Ollivan turned her words and feelings over in his mind, but he couldn't undo the knots; the fallacies.

"You will be a formidable High Sorcerer, Sybella. I know wholeheartedly that it's in your stars." She softened, the weight of the pressure she was carrying eased, if only a little; if only temporarily. "But magical power is not what you need. It won't buy you social status, or popularity, or the things you need for politics."

She laughed humourlessly. "Oh, Ollivan. Yes it will. Do you think" – she lowered her voice, despite them being alone – "that your grandfather's fading power would be whispered about the way it is if it didn't matter? And look at *you*. You're nothing but trouble, while Cassia is the perfect dutiful daughter, and still your family favours you over her."

"*Favours me?*" Ollivan leaned towards her, unable to believe what he was hearing. "They banished me. Because they refused to believe my version of events over Jasper's."

"You didn't tell them the whole story though, did you?" Ollivan paused, and he could see in Sybella's eyes that she'd seen what she expected. "What did you say to them, to explain Benn's death?"

Ollivan rubbed his face, then frowned into his hands. "It would only have made matters worse," he said in a whisper. "If I had told them exactly what Jasper had done, it would have led back to the rest of the banned magic we were meddling in."

"But it would have exonerated you of the murder," pressed Sybella.

"You wouldn't be saying that, if you had been there." Ollivan kept his gaze on his fingers; concentrated on rubbing them to banish the memories of that day. "The sheer glee with which he took my life to pieces and handed the wreckage back to me. He just wanted a reason, Ellie. He would have twisted whatever I said into a worse crime, not a better one, if he even listened at all.

"And when he turned to my mother and asked her if my banishment was fair… she couldn't even look me in the eye as she said yes."

The fire snapped like twigs underfoot, the low rustle of the flames a soothing drone to amplify their silence. Sybella shifted in the corner of his vision, paused, as if second-guessing, and then shuffled closer, so that they were sat side by side. In the warmth of the flames, the lily scent of her perfume engulfed him like sleep.

"I'm sorry too," said Sybella, forcing Ollivan's eyes up. She was so close, leaning into his shoulder to speak softly. "I shouldn't have asked you if you did it, that night at the Wending Place. I already knew."

Ollivan smiled. "It's easy to say that now," he said. "You didn't sound like you knew at the time."

"I was afraid that I'd never really known you," she whispered, so close that her breath brushed his neck, and Ollivan felt hollowed out. That was his fear as well. That all that was left when she ended it was his broken heart and an impression of something that had never truly existed; like waking from a good dream, and having to live forever in a reality a little greyer for it.

"He threatened you," he blurted.

Sybella pulled back a little and blinked up at him. "What?"

He needed her to know. Nothing about them was real if it wasn't the truth. His pride didn't matter next to this.

"I had stolen from his vault," he said in a rush. "Again. I don't know if he knew about the other times but I'd taken a lot that night and I was caught red-handed. It was quiet; only a few enforcers were there. I was brought to his office in the middle of the night. I thought he was trying to avoid the embarrassment of everyone finding out how easily I was stealing from him. But he had a plan. A new idea to keep me in line, one he was so certain would work."

"Me." Sybella stared into the middle distance; the hand that had been reaching for him as the truth spilled out fell to her side. "He couldn't hurt you, because of your mother, but he—" Her fist gripped a handful of her taffeta skirt. "He would have disappeared me. Mother and mama would never even know what had happened."

Ollivan took her shoulders in his hands so that she was facing him. "I would never have let that happen."

He knew, with every fibre of his being, that that was true. If it had come down to it, he would have done whatever Jupitus asked of him, even become Alana's heir and given his life over to defending the Fisk–Sims rule. He would have died slowly of loathing and resentment and never made a wave. It never came to that, because she had ended it, and their estrangement made her worthless to Jupitus's gambit. Yet a guilt gnawed sharply at his stomach when he thought of how it had all played out. He had not risked her life, but he had risked her affection.

He looked into the fire, and not at her, as he recounted for her how he had come to be absent, distant, how he had abandoned her before their relationship ever ended. He hadn't found a solution in time. He had failed her.

"Ollivan," she said slowly when he had finished. His name sounded like a reprimand, delivered through gritted teeth, and when he looked at her, there were tears welling along the line of her lashes. "You could have told me."

"Could I?" he challenged. "Could you have been understanding if I told you that we had to be apart because I couldn't give in to him? I love you, Ellie—"

"Ollivan—"

"*Loved*, then. If it makes you more comfortable. But I couldn't let him use that – use *you* – to put me in a cage. Not if there was anything I could've done to help it."

Her expression had shuttered at his free-flying confession of love, and Ollivan pulled himself to his feet to find some pens and paper. "We should draft this spell," he said.

She was still quiet when he returned and held out a pen to her. Sybella's fingers closed around his slowly, then squeezed tight. "It's not what you chose that upsets me," she said. "There was a time you let me in on your plans, before Jasper. However much trouble we would be in, we were in it together. It's partly my fault. I started taking my future seriously, and it changed how you saw me."

"That's not true," said Ollivan fiercely, even as he turned it over in his mind. Sybella's growing focus on her political future; Lev and Virgil falling in love; teaming up with Jasper. Had he been losing the only people he felt truly cared for him? Had he channelled that hurt into his resentment for his grandfather and his own future? Sybella was right; before his diversions had turned darker, she and not Jasper had been his willing accomplice. There was a reason her parents hated him – Ollivan had been a bad influence. But had he changed enough to leave Sybella behind, or had they grown in opposite directions, and forged the gap between them together, but alone?

A new pain found a weak spot in his heart and burrowed in; the fear that their love story was not one of heroes and villains, danger and wild passion, but of thawing affections and intimacy leached away slowly, like a draught under a door. In front of the fire, with Sybella beside him, her fingers around his, he had felt closer to her than he had dared to dream he would ever be again. But how did two people pick up where they left off if the loose thread was frayed and worn to nothing?

Sybella's hand slid from his, and she ducked her head to collect some paper from the pile he had brought. She shook off any emotion she had been feeling and squared her shoulders.

"Let's fix this," she said with renewed resolve.

She did not mean what Ollivan wanted her to.

36

The Mallorys lived on a curving street of identical white houses, which Cassia and Lev were forced to navigate in fits and starts. Every few paces, new shapes materialised from the fog in front of them; residents hurrying from doors to carriages, suitcases piled on the pavement. People were fleeing.

"Father," Lev called suddenly. A couple loading a cart looked up, and Lev broke into a jog.

"I'll wait here," Cassia said as Lev's edges grew soft and he became a grey shadow like all the others. Her grandfather's people would be looking for her; if she could avoid anyone who might become a witness, she would.

Lev appeared to infer this. She caught only snippets of the conversation, but she couldn't miss the moment their heads turned her way.

"A friend from the Society," she heard Lev tell his parents.

From the Society. It was the obvious thing to say and a harmless lie, so why did it make her feel invisible?

The Mallorys exchanged words about Virgil, and their voices grew louder as Lev shook his head. *I have to find him, I can't,* and *I'll follow* all reached Cassia's ears. Lev embraced his parents, then stood on the pavement and watched until the cart vanished.

Cassia joined him. "They're leaving you here?"

"They're going to my grandparents' house outside the city," he said, his voice strained with emotion. "My uncle's joining them tomorrow. I promised I would follow with him once I know Virgil's alright."

"And they just accepted that?"

"They weren't happy about it, but it's not up to them." He chewed his lip and peered uselessly into the fog. "Virgil's dropped by twice. They said he's frantic. Someone told him I was coming here last night, amidst all the Violet chaos."

"If this is where he thinks you were going, perhaps we ought to wait for him to come back," said Cassia.

"That's my thinking too. Besides, I'm starving."

Lev let them in and they went straight to the kitchen, where they pillaged what the Mallorys had left behind; some bread, butter and jam. The clock on the wall said it was late afternoon; they had been unconscious and lost in the fog for most of the day. Lev brewed a pot of tea, and they sat quietly at the kitchen table sipping it and picking at the food they'd longed for. Neither of them voiced what Cassia knew they were both thinking; life as they knew it was crumbling to ash.

"How are you?" Cassia looked up warily, and Lev broke into a smile. "I wish I was making a joke, but I'm asking in earnest. You looked like I should. After the ball..."

Cassia expected herself to flinch at mention of the ball, but she felt nothing. "These last two years," she began softly, "I've slept, eaten, and studied magic. I've worked myself ragged to feel like a proper Sorcerer. It was all to get into the Society. I don't think it started that way. I'm not sure how or when that became the goal, because it was only when I failed at it the second time that I realised there was nothing else I wanted; nothing else *to* me." She risked looking up at Lev, and he nodded. "I wanted the Successors to be impressed by me. And then last night... out of nowhere, I pulled off the strongest spell of my life in front of all of them."

Lev smiled weakly. "It was quite something."

"It was everything I'd wanted." Unbidden, the appalled faces of her peers sprang to her mind. Kiva, Patience, Gale; others had been there, so many of them, and the memory filled their faces in for her too. "And it was the solid end of any respect they might ever have had for me. Everything I've chased is... out of reach." She swallowed the lump in her throat and took up her teacup. "Suddenly I'm not so sure it was ever about magic. Maybe I just don't fit in."

Lev's fingers strummed softly against the table. He couldn't stop himself looking to the door every few minutes. Cassia was beginning to think she had lost his attention somewhere in her speech – that it had been too vulnerable, too serious – when he broke the silence.

"When I was a child, the only thing I wanted was to have been born with my mother's magic instead of my father's. I had this idea in my head that it would have been whole. Stronger." He shrugged. "I had no reason to believe that, I just wanted to be something, *anything*, other than what I was. I hated being a weak Sorcerer, and I hated my parents for having me. I said the vilest things. Accused them of being traitors to their people, told them I wished I'd never been born."

As he spoke, Cassia's shame engulfed her. "Lev... I didn't think," she spluttered. "Forgive me, I didn't mean—"

"It's alright, Cassia," he said, grinning. "I'm only trying to tell you that I understand. Magic felt like it was everything, and no matter what my parents said, it was so, *so* hard to stop feeling that way when… it's true." The smile slipped off his face. "Magic is how this city divides us, how it judges our worth. It shouldn't be that way, but it is."

"So how did you get past it?"

"My parents. They had so much patience with me," said Lev. His fondness for them dripped from every word. "They're the ones who finally showed me what else matters. My father's a very talented Sorcerer. He was also Society Secretary, you know." He laughed. "Which is probably the only reason I ever got initiated with that stars-damned awful dancing enchantment."

"That, and your winning personality," said Cassia.

"That too. But my father's family haven't spoken to him since he told them he was marrying a Whisperer. His magic hasn't helped him there. His friends tried to dissuade him from it, so he lost them too. The High Sorcerer's protection fees are double for households with non-Sorcerers." He said this to the table, and Cassia was glad she didn't have to meet his eye. She could not change who her grandfather was, but she could still feel ashamed of him. "My parents chose each other, and sometimes their life is harder for it, but I was never permitted to see that growing up. All I knew was that I had everything my peers did, and I was loved. They're proud that their son is of two factions, and they haven't been ashamed of my magic for a single second. And that's so much more valuable than what anyone else thinks."

Lev was right, and his perspective had humbled her – and yet her heart felt heavier than ever. She didn't have Lev's family. To be proud of who she was would be to defy them. An aching wave of homesickness overcame her, but it was not for her mother's house.

A door slammed in the hall, followed by a shout. "Lev?"

"Virgil!"

Relief became laughter as the boys collided in the doorway of the kitchen. Virgil broke the embrace briefly to kiss Lev hard on the mouth, then the nose, then the top of his head.

"Where in the heaven and earth have you—"

Virgil broke off as he saw Cassia standing awkwardly by the table. "Hello."

He looked from Lev to her and back again, concern mounting. "What happened?"

"Violet happened," said Lev. "She knocked Cassia and me out in the Chambers' garden last night. I think she enchanted you too, so you wouldn't notice we weren't following."

Virgil shifted his weight. He put a hand on Lev's shoulder, but his eyes didn't leave Cassia's.

"Virgil?"

"Cassia said that you'd peeled off to check on your parents as we were leaving the Chambers last night," said Virgil without looking away.

"Um." Cassia, in her confusion, ran his claim through her head a second time. "No I didn't. I haven't even seen you since last night."

"We've been together all day," said Lev slowly.

Virgil crossed the room in two long strides and scrutinised her face.

"I'm not a Changeling," she said, her fear mounting when she realised he was searching for the minute twitches that gave their magic away. The other tell-tale sign was the eyes; Changelings couldn't change their eyes. Cassia let Virgil peer into hers and confirm their vivid green tone.

"Wait," said Lev, eyes wide. "You were with a Changeling disguised as Cassia last night? Who? *Why?*"

Cassia gasped. "Not a Changeling. Violet."

Violet had already shown she could change form, and now she had real Changeling magic. A false face need not twitch, and even if she couldn't change her eyes, hers were already so like Cassia's.

Nausea swept over her. She had seen Changelings impersonate her before; as a child, she'd been endlessly fascinated and entertained by the magic of her friends at the Zoo. But this was different. Violet had taken her identity.

Virgil leaned against the table, looking shaken. "We were with her. She was right there."

"Why would she pretend to be you?" said Lev.

"I don't know but… she wants to ruin Ollivan. She thinks he's in my way."

"In your way?" said Virgil, bemused.

"You mean *kill him*?" said Lev.

"I don't think so. She's trying to make me look…" Violet's plan started to align right in front of her eyes. "Stars, she's going to turn him over to Jupitus disguised as me. She's trying to turn me into a hero."

Very slowly, Virgil lifted a hand to cover his face. "Oh, stars. She knows Ollivan's plan. You – *she* was right there as he explained it."

Ollivan had a plan. The words gave her a modicum of hope, which vanished just as fast at the knowledge that Violet knew it. "She's with them now?"

Virgil shook his head. "She made an excuse to meet them later. Dusk, in Hyde Park."

"It's a trap," whispered Cassia. She looked at the clock. It was getting late. "When is dusk?"

"Well it's—" Lev scrambled to the window. It was dark, but it had been dark all day. The fog gave nothing away. "I think it's now."

A bell echoed through the house, and they all jumped.

"The door," said Lev, as whoever it was let themselves in.

They must have known what they would find, for they wasted no time. Before Cassia had even known to hide, two men bearing her grandfather's pin had entered the kitchen.

"Miss Sims, there you are," said the nearest with an insidious smile. "We've been door to door over half the quarter looking for you. Then one of the neighbours said they saw you hovering by their fence."

The street outside had been full of people. They must have passed right by her while the Mallorys were talking. Why hadn't she been more careful?

"Your grandfather has requested you be brought to him immediately." He stalked towards her, as the other warned Virgil off with the crackle of a spell at his fingertips. "He's worried sick."

"It's alright," said Cassia to Lev and Virgil, though it was anything but. It suddenly all felt so inevitable, but she'd been expecting some sort of relief to come with it. As it was, she had never wished she could transport more; she would become a fugitive in a heartbeat over facing Jupitus.

But she didn't want Lev and Virgil to know that. So she held her chin up as they escorted her from the room, sparing Virgil a whisper as she passed him.

"Go. Now."

At the door, Cassia looked over her shoulder, but Virgil was already gone.

37

Ollivan was lost in his craft.

A lot of Sorcerers bored quickly in the face of complex spells. Detailed and lengthy discussions of the virtues of certain word choices – *consume* or *absorb*? *Hold* or *retain*? *Delay* or *defer*? – diagrams scrawled to keep track of a myriad of small, crucial intentions. But Ollivan lived for this. Designing spells, working out the kinks, anticipating every way the magic might get tripped up by unclear intentions, and then smoothing it into a perfect, concentrated bit of magic; it made him feel like he held the instructions to the universe and had been handed a pen with which to amend them.

To be rewriting the world with Sybella pushed him into ecstasy.

"Any mention of *removing* magic will scupper the whole thing, I reckon." He was pacing, a bacon sandwich clutched messily in one hand. They had pilfered the food from the Wending Place before they fled, and cooked it in Delphine's kitchen. "I think that was Guysman's main error."

"Right, because it's unnatural," said Sybella, tapping her pen in a staccato rhythm on the arm of her chair. "It has to be about the transfer. But Ollivan—"

He ceased his pacing and looked up at her.

"We need to fix your main errors. Violet absorbs magic. You managed that part fine. We need to dictate what the new Guysman does with it once it's drained her."

Ollivan took another large bite of his sandwich. A drop of grease ran down his hand, and in following it he noticed he had bled through the makeshift dressing on his wrist. He pulled the fabric away from his skin and peeked beneath it; the bleeding had stopped. He untied the sodden handkerchief and threw it into the fire.

"I've thought long and hard on this," he said between mouthfuls.

Sybella waited several beats for the rest of his thought. "And?"

"And I don't know what the answer is."

"Oh. Well," said Sybella with exaggerated cheeriness. "It's not like it's important."

"Violet drains the spell from our vessel – we'll make it something dangerous-looking, to encourage her to see it as a threat and want to suck out its magic—"

"Enchanted sword?" said Sybella, eyeing an ornate, gleaming cutlass above the fireplace. "We could make it glow red for that extra magic feel?"

"Good idea. And then our new Guysman wakes up when it comes into contact with the old Guysman, and Violet's neutralised. It will stop her from absorbing magic, but we need to drain off the magic she's holding back into our own vessel – this lovely cutlass—"

"*Glowing* cutlass."

"—to be sure she can't harness any of it." Ollivan took up pacing again, completing two more laps of the room before he spoke again. "And then what?"

"I asked you first."

"Do we design some mechanism so that a person whose magic Violet has stolen can reabsorb their own power if they come into contact with it?"

"It does sound next to impossible when you put it like that."

"*Or.*" Ollivan paused for dramatic effect. Sybella, all too familiar with his dramatism, flinched in trepidation. "Do we design the new Guysman not to hold the magic at all, but to release it from the doll as it takes it in? Like a conduit."

"You mean… into the *atmosphere*?" She was still a long time, mouth open as she prepared to speak. "Ollivan. Isn't that exactly what you were afraid of Violet doing? We have no idea what the effects would be. It could be cataclysmic."

"You're right," he said hastily. "I was just thinking out loud." He dragged his feet along his pacing route, but couldn't contain what he wanted to say. "But aren't you curious?"

"Oh, earth and stars," muttered Sybella.

"My theory was that the stolen magic might return independently to those it was taken from," he hastened to explain. "Don't you want to see such a thing happen? When will the world ever see such an experimental opportunity?"

"And what about everything else Violet is harbouring? Not all the magic she's taken in has come from a person. What happens to all that raw energy from the spells she's dismantled?"

Ollivan grinned. "There's no way to know unless we test it out."

Sybella did not return his grin. "Flash me that smile all you want. I'm not letting you leave this pub with a spell that looks like that."

"But—"

"No." There was no give to her. Her jaw was tight and her eyes were fierce. "Think of something else."

Sighing, Ollivan turned to the clock above the mantle. "We don't have much time."

Sybella returned to tapping her pen. Ollivan, sulking, lost his will to pace and leaned against the wall.

"The important thing is disabling Violet," said Sybella. "We can design the Guysman to *contain*" – she wrote the word down to draft a new verse of the spell – "until we can develop a new spell to release the magic safely. As long as the intention is watertight, we shouldn't end up with something that starts using it itself." As an afterthought, she added, "We should make absolutely sure that cutlass isn't already enchanted."

Ollivan tilted his head back and stared at the ceiling. "How do we release all that magic?" he said, mostly to himself. "If we don't know everything that's in there, we can't plan for its redistribution."

"It's a problem, I admit. But it's not a good enough reason for what you're thinking." Ollivan looked at her, and his expression of disappointment made her soften. "You'll have a chance to conduct tests on this new vessel. There must be ways to uncover what interests you about it without blowing up half the city in a magical supernova. But can we please solve your last problem before we make a new one?"

One problem at a time. Sybella was right. Their priority was disabling Violet. What happened after that could wait.

In between the discussions of wording and intention, they tested a series of smaller spells; miniature Guysmans designed to absorb and hold the energy of a particular spell one of them would perform; conduits formed from Delphine's treasures and furnishings to move raw magic around. Among the missteps and near misses – at one point Sybella managed to confuse a teapot into stunning her with her own spell instead of capturing and holding it – they began to form something Ollivan was confident could work. An enchantment to be cast on a vessel, one that would lay dormant until absorbed by another spell. When Violet absorbed it, the original spell would be disarmed and the stolen magic would be sucked from her and into the new Guysman vessel. There was only one snag they couldn't smooth over.

"Violet absorbs magic selectively," Sybella said. It was getting late, and they were exhausted, but she had three sheets of hazel wood paper in her hand that contained the final product. "She can choose to drink something or leave it alone. We can tempt her by making the vessel look like a threat, but how do we guarantee she'll take the bait?"

"We don't cast it," Ollivan replied.

Sybella's brows shot up. "I beg your pardon?"

Ollivan rubbed a hand over his face. "The only safe approach is to cast the enchantment at the moment we need it. If she sees us cast the spell, she'll assume it's an imminent attack and try to neutralise it."

"But—"

"But she'll try to neutralise *us* before we can manage it, I know."

Sybella flicked through the pages, eyes alighting on the countless addenda and conditions stitched delicately throughout the main intention. "This is the most complex enchantment I've ever seen," she said warily. "And you want to cast it live, in front of its target, before she drains your magic?"

"What I *want* is for you and I to hide in this pub and craft devilishly tricky enchantments together until we're old and grey." Sybella blushed. Stars, it had been so long since he'd made her blush. "But yes. It's the best way."

"Are you sure you can manage this? You haven't slept." Her gaze flickered over him. "And you're overwrought."

Overwrought was a polite choice of words. Ollivan had been channelling a deep well of fear and resentment into their work for the past twelve hours, and now they were done, those emotions had nowhere else to go. This spell was his only chance at vindication. Even if he succeeded, he faced the task of painting himself as enough of a hero that his previous transgressions – which now included disabling two enforcers and fleeing from custody – could be downgraded to a slap on the wrist. He wished he'd been nicer to his mother since he returned; she could be a valuable ally or his worst enemy in deciding the treatment he got at the end of all this. A few weeks ago, the thought of grovelling had been anathema. Now he wondered how he could have been so prideful.

"Ellie, if I'm not given a chance to speak in my defence," he said, "you must do what you can to help Cassia. Tell any lie you must to paint her as innocent in all this."

Sybella's mouth quirked sceptically. "I thought this was all her fault. What changed?"

What had changed was that Ollivan had disabused his sister of the belief that their family's respect was worth striving for, and instead of feeling like he had freed her, he had made something she had suffered for meaningless. Growing up, he had thought of his sister rarely, and when he did, the way she was raised had seemed like a thing that had been done to *him*; the firm proof that the expectations his family placed on him, she would not be burdened with. That Cassia had been happy at the Zoo and valued by her guardians was all the proof he needed that her life was easy, while his was being made a hell.

But he understood now how she had been conditioned for duty by the exact same mechanisms that had conditioned him for rebellion. He had never blamed himself for his values, and therefore he could not blame Cassia for hers. She would not have stepped so willingly into *his* life if hers was what he imagined. She was looking for a way out, and the escape Ollivan had offered had led her here, to the biggest mess of either of their lives.

He could not undo what Cassia had learned, but he could get her out of the rest of it, and then he would see her forge her own path, regardless of what he believed she should do.

But that was not the answer he gave Sybella. Those feelings strayed too close to an admission of wrongdoing, to a version of himself he didn't wish her to see. "It doesn't help me for her to go down too," he said. It was getting late; up above, the fog would have begun shifting through darkening shades of grey. "We should go."

"Perhaps you should rest first," said Sybella.

Ollivan shook his head. "There's no time."

"I can't cast this spell if the moment comes and you're not fit," said Sybella, but she stood, the spell clutched in her hand anyway.

"You won't have to," said Ollivan. He stood before her, and saw his own exhaustion reflected back. "Or rather, you won't get a chance. If I can't pull this off on the first chance, we'll probably be out of time."

"Oh," said Sybella in a mockery of someone reassured. "I wonder if she's advanced to killing people yet."

Killing people. The thought stirred Ollivan's frayed emotions into a nauseating frenzy; a kind of burning ache so fierce he couldn't look at it, nor even explain it. It took him a beat to muster a light-hearted reply. "Here's hoping it'll be fast."

And then Sybella kissed him. It was brief, too brief, so that he was more aware of the aftermath than the kiss; the lack of her lips on his, rather than their presence.

She kept her face close to his, but didn't kiss him again, and Ollivan was too afraid that she would pull away if he tried.

"Just in case it's *too* fast," she said softly, and then the contact was broken. She straightened and squared her shoulders. "Let's go and meet the others."

*

They landed just south of the park. If something had gone wrong – if Cassia or Virgil had been found and the details of the rendezvous forced from them – Ollivan and Sybella might have a chance to spot any lurking militia and flee.

But the streets of Kensington were deserted.

They stopped every few paces and listened at every corner, but no sound betrayed the presence of another soul out there in the fog. It was no mystery why; Ollivan hadn't appreciated how impenetrable, how still, how *uncanny* it felt to be caught in it until now. He could not feel a lick of magic and still, somehow, impossible colours danced in the corner of his vision, only to dissolve when he looked at them. Shadows would pass, sometimes engulfing them, before being carried away like on a non-existent breeze. The fog smelled sweet and earthy. It reminded him of rotting rose petals.

It was still a few moments until dusk when he and Sybella reached a gate near the southwest corner of Hyde Park, less than one hundred yards from the statue of Drusella and their meeting place. They stood a little way from the gate, eyes tracking endlessly through the fog and ears sharp to their surroundings. Were there no enforcers on the streets, looking for him? Was there no one to pass by with soft footsteps, causing him to hold his breath and fear his downfall?

Sundown approached and his sister did not. A shattering of glass caused them both to jump and swing round. Ollivan grabbed Sybella and pressed them both back against the park fence as, steps away from them across the street, the black shape of a man crawled from a broken shopfront. With his arms full of stolen wares, he ran off down the street, his steps hidden beneath the undulating of a metal vase or plate he left spinning on the cobblestones.

Ollivan was clutching the cutlass – their vessel for the new spell – but he handed it to Sybella as he approached the shop; he would need his hands free if he had to defend himself. But no one was inside. Pans and jugs hanging from the ceiling swung ominously in the wake of the break-in, but none of the spells shopkeepers relied on had sprung into action. No ropes or chains had shot from the walls to capture the trespasser; no enchanted bells chimed incessantly and unnaturally loud. The wards that enforced glass and doorways usually emanated a faint pink glow, but the shop lay in darkness.

There was another store – a tailor's – a little further down. On closer inspection, someone had raided this one too. The entrance had been forced, the frame in tatters and the lock hanging from the door. It swung with a creaking of iron as Ollivan pushed it open. There were no wards here either, which meant only one thing.

Violet continued to grow in power.

And she laid London to waste as she did.

Sybella made a *psst* sound to get his attention and Ollivan swung round, magic at his fingertips. Sybella shook her head, and pointed into the park. A single light shone through the fog from the site of the statue. It bobbed as it was swung in one direction and then the other, searching for them.

"Come on," Ollivan murmured, taking her hand as they stepped through the gate and into the open expanse of the park.

Each step was like a mile, Ollivan scanning the fog with eyes and ears. Every bench and tree looked to his wracked nerves like a figure, but still the lone lamp called to them from beneath the statue, and no one stepped out of the fog.

"If we're separated," Sybella whispered. She did not finish her sentence, but he knew what prompted her to start it. It was the same irrational foreboding that slowed his steps.

"It's alright," he said, to himself as well as her.

They were ten paces from Cassia now. Virgil was absent. Had he not found Lev yet or were they just running late? He could not think of harm befalling Lev, not now; he had to stay focused on the plan.

Three paces.

"Ollivan!" bellowed a distant voice. Virgil. He was nowhere to be seen. "It's a trap! Run!"

Cassia turned, and Sybella gasped. The lamplight illuminated not his sister, but Elodie, Jupitus's advisor, her vulpine features twisted into a grin.

Sybella wrenched her hand free from his. She turned to him, tried to convey something, and he knew what it was – a Sorcerer could not transport while touching another – but a particular fear had risen above the others and frozen him to the spot. Sybella vanished; she still believed that he would follow. But Ollivan could not.

He turned on Elodie.

"Where is my sister?" he growled.

A small hand closed around his wrist and he jerked, pivoting. Cassia. His sister was right at his side.

"What is this?"

Cassia smiled, but it wasn't a smile Ollivan recognised, and at that moment, he knew.

"A trap for the villain."

He sucked in a breath as the lance of Cassia's ring punctured the still-tender flesh of the earlier wound.

"You – betrayed me," he gritted out, hearing his own voice as if from far away. This couldn't be happening again. It couldn't.

"No, Ollivan." A voice called from out of the fog, low and grating.

Ollivan swung wildly around, and in response, Cassia's hand tightened on his wrist. During his flash of confusion, bodies had transported into the square all around them. They advanced, enforcers with their hands braced before them, magic crackling at their fingertips. And at their head, his cane tapping out a death march as the fog seemed to clear around him, was the High Sorcerer.

402

"You betrayed us all," he finished. His mouth was a hard line, but the fire in his eyes burned with satisfaction.

A second hand grabbed Ollivan's other arm and yanked it behind him, and then he was in chains. The spindle of iron on his sister's finger never left his flesh. He met her eyes as they were bundled together towards the street into a carriage. Ollivan saw their grandfather in those eyes; fierce, triumphant, and brimming with loathing.

"I should have known," he said.

"Yes," said Cassia, and she turned to the window as the carriage set in motion. "You should have."

Cassia thought she was being taken to the Chambers of Alchemy, so when the hulking black compound emerged from the fog and the carriage didn't slow, a sneaking sense of wrongness overcame her.

Ten minutes later, they pulled up outside her grandfather's house instead, where she was hustled inside and shut away in the room she had sometimes slept in as a small child, before she was sent to the Zoo. The two beds had been hers and Ollivan's. The rocking horse by the window had been broken in a fight over whose turn it was to ride it. Cassia pushed it tentatively and it scraped forward on the faulty mechanism, unmended after a dozen or more years. Ollivan could have fixed it with magic if he'd wanted to, but though he couldn't ride a broken rocking horse, neither could Cassia, and he had settled for that and wandered off to find something else to destroy. At the time, she had believed it the height of cruelty; an early sign of what he would eventually become. Now, looking back, he was just a child being childish.

There was no clock in the room, so she had little sense of the passing of time. She tried the door at intervals, as if she hoped to discover someone had corrected the error of locking her in. She dozed a little, but she was too alert to every sound to properly rest. There was nothing to entertain her except a chest of children's toys; unfortunately, Cassia was thoroughly done with such things, and so eager to keep them locked away that she repeatedly unfastened and refastened the clasp on the chest, like she was keeping prisoners of her own inside it.

It was a long way through the night before a key turned in the lock, and one of Jupitus's servants appeared in the doorway.

"Come with me."

She rose from the bed on which she'd been sprawled and followed him down the stairs.

Jupitus was waiting for her in the dining room, his back to her and his hands clasped behind him. Supper for one had been laid out on the long table; bread, cheese and cold meat, and a glass of water. Cassia had not thought of food or drink once during her hours of imprisonment, but now her stomach growled a greeting at the plate.

The servant left them, and her grandfather turned to face her.

"You must be hungry," he said, nodding to the food, and Cassia fell upon it without further preamble. The bread wasn't fresh, and the cold cuts were not today's either, but she hardly cared. She forgot her grandfather was even there until the plate was half empty.

When she looked up, Jupitus watched her keenly, his expression unreadable, and Cassia remembered her circumstances; Violet. The ball. An imminent punishment for falling in with her criminal brother. It hardly felt real. She couldn't fully believe she had done those things, made those choices.

"Your brother has told me everything, Cassia," said Jupitus from across the room.

Cassia tried to hold her head up, but her bones felt unsteady, and she sank down in her chair. She should not have eaten so

405

quickly; her stomach clenched with the threat of bringing it back up.

Jupitus crossed the dining room, slid the chair opposite her out from under the table, and folded himself into it. He had to brace a hand on the arm to lower himself, and he failed to mask the couple of deep breaths he needed when he was seated. Her grandfather had had so much grace once. It must have been agony for a man like him to witness his own decay; a decay no amount of power could hold at bay.

"He confessed to stealing literature that was being kept safe at the Chambers, and using the notes therein to create this enchantment," he went on. Far from stumbling over the words *kept safe* and the untruth they told, his tone was so smooth and confident that Cassia almost believed him. "And he told me that you stole the enchanted doll to take its power for yourself."

That lie did not ring true to Cassia. The emptiness of the room announced itself at that moment; she and Jupitus were alone. Cassia could suddenly feel her heart beat like it was trying to break free of her ribcage. She was shaking her head, but she couldn't find the words to cry foul before he continued.

"… that you enabled this sentient doll to harvest the magic of this city and its people with the belief that there was some way of channelling it into yourself."

"No."

"When you found this to be impossible, you came up with another plan." His eyes bored into hers, and Cassia couldn't blink, as if he held her in a trance. "To feed this tool of yours Changeling magic, and have it impersonate you to create the illusion of power."

So many inaccuracies. Cassia's wretched mind could not summon the words to refute them, nor stop them tumbling over one another as she tried to catalogue them. She hadn't stolen the doll, she had found her. Magic *could* be channelled, according to Violet, and Ollivan knew it.

"Please, Grandfather," she begged. "It was nothing like that. I didn't mean to awaken the spell. I thought she was an ordinary enchanted doll. Ollivan enchanted her to appear so until she absorbed her first bit of magic. I didn't know!" Hot tears were running down her cheeks and it took her a moment to realise they were from fear. "And she's not my tool. I can't control her. She has an attachment to me, yes, and she tried to tempt me to join forces with her. I think she *is* doing all of this for my benefit, but I didn't command her to! I tried to get her to stop. You have to believe me. Ollivan is—"

Lying. He had betrayed her. This had all been a terrible mistake; awakening the Guysman, letting Violet get away, trusting her faithless, wicked brother. She couldn't believe her own stupidity. She deserved whatever blame he had managed to place on her. Cassia's tears came hot and fast, and she buried her face in her hands, defeated. Abandoned.

"Calm yourself, girl," said Jupitus. At some point he had come round the table, and he laid a firm hand on her shoulder. "I was testing you."

Cassia spluttered, a sound somewhere between disbelief and relief. She stared up at her grandfather through watery eyes, expecting to see some guilt there, or tenderness. But there was none. He was well practised in this type of interrogation, and she was just another enemy falling apart under questioning.

"Testing me," she said flatly. She caught the handkerchief he unceremoniously tossed at her.

"I needed to see what you would confess to under duress." He paced away from her, as if she was forgotten. It was several moments, and Cassia's tears had given way to a numb disbelief before he spoke again. "It is true, however, that this enchantment is impersonating you. It helped us arrest your brother, and now it has disappeared. It continues to wreak havoc across my city. We have Ollivan, but the damage he has wrought continues."

"You mean... he still doesn't know how to stop it?"

Jupitus turned. "He hasn't confided the method in you," he said, his disappointment revealed in the metal edge of his tone.

Cassia scrambled for something helpful to say, something that might redeem her in his eyes. Virgil had spoken of Ollivan's plan but casting her mind back, he hadn't given any hint of what it was. "I'm sorry," she said, feeling small and pathetic and helpless.

Jupitus's expression remained black, but he raised a lazy hand to calm her. "I believe the Guysman woman knew of a method. Of course, she didn't reveal it to me, but she knew I was suspicious. I believe that's why she's vanished again."

So Violet was still out there, perhaps still wearing Cassia's face, and with advanced warning of whatever plan Ollivan had come up with. Had Jupitus known she wasn't Cassia while dealing with her? Had he played her game – even let her go – for the prize of catching Ollivan? *The damage he has wrought*... Cassia had once let Violet go free to hurt her brother. Perhaps Jupitus was not above doing the same.

"He'll bargain for his freedom," said Cassia as the realisation came to her. "He'll see this whole city laid to waste if he doesn't get what he wants."

"He will try."

Cassia met his eye and shuddered. It was not her grandfather who had issued the threat, but a man braver people than her had cowered before, begged at the feet of. He was a man of precise and unfeeling steel, as clinical as the edge of the blade with which he opened his enemies' throats.

And he had Ollivan.

A mess of feelings twisted inside of her. The whiplash of her brother's betrayal still battered her. "Did he really say any of those things you accused me of?" she said, her voice small.

Jupitus didn't miss a beat. "Did he try to lay the blame at your feet? You know your brother well enough, Cassia. Of course he did."

It wasn't that she didn't believe him; the shift was subtler than that. It was that she knew he would have said it either way. That it didn't matter what Ollivan had or had not done. This man's hatred for his grandson meant he would never let him win. What else did it mean?

"Did he really murder Jonas Benn?"

Jupitus's reaction was not so smooth, but perhaps that was the surprise of the question. She wasn't sure what she had expected or wanted from asking it; certainly not a truth she could believe. But she didn't need one. She had always known her grandfather was ruthless. But she had come to realise something new: that he was unfair. That he would hurt even those he should love if they stood in his way.

Or damaged his reputation.

"Of course you do not wish to talk about what *you* have done," said Jupitus. He let his eyes fall to the floor and shook his head sadly. "Cassia, my dear. What possessed you?"

She's not respected among the Sorcerers. Flaunting her poor command of her magic so publicly has damaged her.

She swallowed. "I thought Ollivan and I could handle it on our own. Things just got out of hand."

Her grandfather sighed. "I fear your mother and I have failed to teach you true responsibility. You have been home with us for nearly two years now with no goal. No real purpose."

No purpose? "I... I'm here to learn Sorcerer magic," she said.

The look he gave her dripped so much condescension that she flinched. "And what has that come to? I think it's time to assign you a real endeavour. Something that will challenge you."

Cassia waited in silence, feeling like a child trying their hardest not to be noticed by their governess. It sounded as if Jupitus was finally demonstrating some real faith in her as something other than a dutiful granddaughter. And yet, given the circumstances, Cassia was anything but grateful. She was terrified.

"I've secured an ambassadorship for you."

"You're... sending me back to the Zoo?" said Cassia. Her heart sank at being dismissed from her own people's territory, like having her here had been a failed experiment, but it beat harder to think of seeing her friends again; of returning to a place she was comfortable once.

"No," said Jupitus, smiling in a way that promised fangs. "If we're to maintain peace, I need representatives across the city.

Not every faction has been amenable to the suggestion, but some have been very enthusiastic."

"Another faction?" Cassia's voice trembled. Bile rose in her throat. "Which one?"

"The Docklands."

The room spun. Cassia gripped her chair. "What?"

"The Oracles are expecting you at the temple imminently. You will pack your things and leave tonight."

The Oracles. The Docklands. Cassia had never been there. Few non-Oracles had. It was not a part of London frequented by those who had any other choice.

"I don't want to live in the Docklands," she said, hearing her own voice crack in desperation.

Jupitus drew a slow breath and took her in. It looked like satisfaction. "The decision's been made."

"Send someone else." She was desperate not to cry again – he would think her petulant; a child incapable of making her own decisions – but she could feel the burn of tears behind her eyes. "Please."

He rubbed his chin thoughtfully, and Cassia could have fallen to her knees to drive her desperation home. "The decision is mine," he said. His eyes gleamed. "And I'm sending *you*, Cassia."

"*No—*"

"It's done."

Cassia's mouth snapped shut. She had stood, she realised, but she was leaning heavily on the table. Everything she knew about the Seer – the leader of the Oracles – and her temple in the Docklands flashed through her mind. It was a regime of religious zeal and paranoia, led by people in possession of a magic so volatile it frequently drove them mad. She knew of no outsiders who had joined their court. They seemed the last faction to agree to host an ambassador – and the last place on earth she would ever wish to go.

"How did you arrange this?" she said through gritted teeth. "What lengths did you go to to ruin my life?"

"You're acting like a child," said Jupitus, bored.

"You could punish me however you choose. Why choose *this*?"

"It's not a punishment."

"*Liar.*"

Jupitus's eyes flashed, and Cassia froze. He was angry, but underneath was triumph. He was enjoying her losing control of herself. This was exactly what he wanted when he handed down this judgement. He had measured her perfectly, and hit upon the worst thing he could do to her; send her somewhere she would never belong, would never find a place.

She pulled her spine stiff and choked back her sob, meeting her grandfather's greedy stare with one of steel. She could not let him win *this* – her anguish – as well. She folded his handkerchief neatly, dabbed the tears from her eyes with dignity, and tossed it down onto the table. She fought the consuming urge to continue to fight him, knowing what she did now; that he was incapable of backing down. She wouldn't be her brother, an unstoppable force battering into him until everything around them was in ruin.

Jupitus, however, had a final word to deliver.

"They won't grant you special dispensation to use magic in their territory," he said. Cassia halted on her way to the door. "You will have to do without."

She heard what he had not said in so many words: *you are not a Sorcerer any more.*

She had failed.

Perhaps it was to torture herself, but she asked him something she feared she already knew the answer to.

"How did you know Violet wasn't me?" she said, without turning to face him.

He released a breath that might have been a laugh. "That thing transported right into my office."

A piece of magic, like so many others, that Cassia couldn't do. She straightened her shoulders and left the dining room without another word.

39

No magic existed that could prevent a capable Sorcerer from transporting. The only remedy was to render them *in*capable.

Pain was distracting. It made the focus required for transporting impossible to attain. Broken bones were the usual method, because they became excruciating in the instant before transporting, as if the universe was pressing on one's weakest parts in order to fold the body through the space between atoms. It encouraged the victim to pull helplessly away from the spell at the last second, or risk tearing themselves to pieces with their pain-shattered intention.

Perhaps the High Sorcerer wished Ollivan to suffer more, or perhaps he wanted plausible deniability should Alana accuse him of torturing her son, as Ollivan was submitted to a pain that left no marks, one he recognised but had believed lost.

It was a spell.

Elodie's pain spell was not as strong as the one Ollivan had once used, judging from the way Jasper had screamed when they had discovered and tested it on each other. Nor was it as strong as Jasper's, whose magic Ollivan had once withstood for exactly fourteen seconds before surrendering. The pain Elodie inflicted was steady and feverish, like influenza, causing him to writhe and sweat to bloom all over his body. It was not enough to make the wound at his wrist – left unbandaged to bleed onto the stones beneath him – fade from notice; it was a constant sting against the throbbing ache everywhere else.

But it was enough. Ollivan could not even approach the level of focus it would take to flee, or attack, or even think up a more inventive method of escape. Nor could he curse his grandfather, Jasper, his treacherous sister. He simply lay there, shifting, never at ease, never relieved.

For how long, he didn't know. There were no windows in the cells beneath the Chambers to announce the passing hours, and even if he could have summoned the will to speak, he doubted his captor would deign to offer him the time. But after what could have been hours or days, the barred door yawned on its hinges, and his pain intensified as someone plunged a lance into his wrist once more.

"Up," said a voice, and the agony receded, leaving a feeling of such relief that Ollivan shuddered. Now that someone had a hold on him, Elodie had relinquished her magic. He braced a palm against the floor and pushed up carefully, like the wrong movement might bring the pain flooding back.

Jupitus stood beyond the bars of the cell, Elodie beside him. She, too, was sweating lightly, the exertion of maintaining the banned spell clear in her weary features. Two more enforcers – one of whom held him with the lance – hauled him to his feet and deposited him in a chair. It was only when he lifted his head with shaking muscles – nausea threatening at the remembered pain – that he saw who else was there.

Jasper leaned a shoulder against the stone wall and watched with an expression of intense interest. Of course; he must have told them of the pain spell. Had he asked for a reward for turning Ollivan in, or was watching him suffer enough? Yet more enforcers hovered nearby in the gloom, rounding out the High Sorcerer's guard.

"So this is why you've returned," said his grandfather. "To exact your revenge."

Ollivan forced his cockiest smile. "So you agree I'm owed vengeance?"

Jupitus nodded to the enforcer with the back of Ollivan's neck in his meaty hand, and the man wrenched his head back by the hair. Ollivan hissed.

"I *did* want revenge," he said. "I set the trap a year ago, the last time we were here. You didn't go to such extreme measures to hold me the last time. But I came back to make a fresh start."

"You were given one," said Jupitus. "In the Otherworld."

"Let's not toy with each other, Grandfather. There was no life for me there. That's why you sent me, is it not?"

Jupitus advanced into the cell, until Ollivan – still in the enforcer's grasp – was forced to look up at him.

"I've put it behind us." Ollivan laughed. "There were just a few things I needed to clear up before you and I were friends again."

"Ah, Ollivan." He couldn't see the old man's hands, but he knew he clasped them behind him in a pantomime of restraint. But the High Sorcerer's hands were never clean. "Do you have any idea how much effort your mother and I have gone to, trying to keep you on the right path?"

The work it takes to forgive you time and time again – do you have any idea? Ollivan thrashed against the hands on his arms and tugging at his hair.

416

"What you don't understand, my boy, is that I have only ever wanted what was best for you," he went on. "At first, that meant a career like mine. The chance to shape the future of this city. When it became clear that fate was not in your stars, I settled for your safety. I tried to keep you out of trouble, by any means necessary. Your mother begged it of me. So I tried to appeal to your human nature; to the capacity I saw in you to protect. To cherish."

Ollivan could have turned to flame. The desire to reach out and turn the pain spell on his grandfather was so strong that his magic rose, unbidden and opportunistic. His fingers stung as tendrils of it escaped; the air crackled and Jupitus stepped back.

"You threatened to murder Sybella," he growled.

Jupitus's face was grave, remorseful; a lie. "Sometimes the things we're forced to do for those we love are hard for them to accept. We can only hope they don't seek to punish us for trying." He looked around, his eyes resting on each of those present in turn. "But you have punished all of us, Ollivan. You've endangered this entire city trying to hurt me."

Ollivan laughed. "This was for *him*." He jerked his head at Jasper, still lurking in the dark of the corridor. "You know about our experiments now, I assume. He told your lackey how to perform a pain spell, didn't he?" The thought of having the pain spell inflicted on his grandson must have been pleasant, for a slow smile crept onto Jupitus's face. He glanced at Jasper, who grinned back. "Did he tell you about the rest of the banned magic? About everything we stole from this very building?"

"Mr Hawkes has told me nothing. But I know we do not *ban* magic, Ollivan. Magic is a gift from the stars. It is sacred."

"Then perhaps you ought to know how much *sacred* magic your forebears suppressed."

"Now, *suppression*," said Jupitus, nodding sagely. "Suppression is another matter. No magic is out of bounds." He smiled. "But some must be reserved for only those who would use it rightly. *You* are a perfect example of why."

Ollivan's breath was coming fast. "You knew."

"About the history of my own office? Come now, my boy, for all your faults you are smarter than that."

He *was* smarter. He had been so sure the dusty and decaying boxes he and Jasper had found under decades' worth of detritus were unknown to any other living Sorcerers; that their hands were the only ones that had been on them. Or maybe, in his hubris, that was what he'd wanted to believe; that he possessed magic known to no one else on earth.

"You had another copy," he said as the realisation landed. "You've had knowledge of those spells all along."

"A perk of the position." Jupitus shrugged. "And eminently useful. One can inflict pain with a knife or a chain with perfect effect, *physically*. When that fails, however – say, on someone too unimaginative and headstrong to believe that I can best them. There is a psychological effect of magical pain. The knowledge, as it courses through someone, that anything is possible with magic. That perhaps there is no limit to their agony. That perhaps I could torture them forever and their body would remain undamaged; that they wouldn't die."

The threat was blatant, and yet Ollivan's whirring mind had moved past it to more important things. Ollivan's fierce gaze slid past his grandfather to the boy still lurking against the dungeon

418

wall; the one whose reputation defended the convenient lie that Ollivan, and not him, was a killer. The boy his grandfather had always spoken of so highly.

"You knew of the channelling spell," he said. "You knew that he—"

Jupitus prowled closer, until his patient, curious expression filled Ollivan's vision, inviting him to think harder. As the realisation dawned, Ollivan tried to jerk away, but he couldn't. He wanted to kick out, to spit, to roar, but his mind could not make the connection with his legs, his mouth. All it could do was crack open and fill with the one thing that mattered.

That Jasper had framed him for murder because his grandfather told him to.

"There was no other way," Jupitus said mildly, seeing Ollivan piece it together. "You refused to learn that your actions had consequences."

"They weren't my actions!" Ollivan yelled. He strained again against the hands holding him firm, and they gripped tighter, bruising flesh and setting his scalp on fire. He welcomed it; it fuelled his anger.

"Stealing? Fighting? Making drugs?" Jupitus snorted. "These things weren't you?"

"I've never killed anybody," he gritted out.

"No, Ollivan. What you did was worse." His breath gusted hot and rancid on Ollivan's face. His voice was low and dripping with poison. "You threatened my rule. You revelled in the fantasy that you were stronger than me, and you did it in front of my people and my enemies. You tried to damage everything I have been building for over fifty years, when I had been building it *for you*.

419

So I did what you forced me to do, Ollivan. I *removed* you." His breath was coming faster in excitement. Spittle flecked Ollivan's skin. "I could not kill you, as clean and final as that would have been, because however you died, your mother would know it was me. I needed due cause to put you in the Otherworld. And so I *made* due cause." He straightened. His mouth was a snarl but his eyes glistened with glee. "Do you know how, Ollivan? Do you know how I managed to destroy you the way you tried to destroy me? Because I am stronger than you are. This is my world you are living in, and you are here by my grace."

He had known about the duelling club; known that Sorcerers were breaking the Principles beyond his territory and other factions were breaking them in his. He had known about the banned magic – suppressed it himself – everything Ollivan and Jasper had used to wreak havoc and cause pain. He had done nothing, and so Ollivan had believed there was nothing he could do; not until he threatened Sybella. But that had been a minor game to him, and Ollivan had tied himself in knots in the belief that if he won the round, the board was his.

And then Jupitus had had a Wraith killed. He had broken the Principles he had helped to write and upheld with fierce control; had thrown away the rule book.

Because he could. Because Ollivan couldn't stop him.

Everything Ollivan had been fighting for; everything he had done – stealing the election, tackling the Guysman in secret. His prize had never existed. His place here, his life, was not on the other side of stopping Violet and falling in line. Because the only person who could give it to him was the one who had taken it away.

"It was your mother who went to Jasper to implore him to make you see sense," said Jupitus, retreating a comfortable distance. "But I saw something else in the young man she brought to my house." He looked over his shoulder, and the shared smiles were gone now. He looked Jasper up and down with a sneer. The boy had enough sense to look uncomfortable. "Dissent. Dissatisfaction. An ease with undermining authority. He reminded me of you. I suddenly understood what you saw in one another. So I persuaded him into a bargain; immunity for stealing and using the ledgers, in exchange for helping me be rid of you."

Ollivan studied Jasper as his grandfather spoke. Had he ever been in the dungeons before? Had he seen the High Sorcerer interrogate someone? Or was his look of mounting trepidation a sign that he was considering the situation he had put himself in for the first time? Jasper was intelligent, but he was also self-important, and that was enough to convince a tool that he was an ally; enough to manipulate him.

"And what are the terms of your bargain now?" said Ollivan. He did not need to fake the grin that spread across his face as he pushed his point home. "Now that you failed."

Jasper snorted a laugh, and looked Ollivan up and down pointedly. "I put you in that cell, Sims."

"Actually, my sister did, in the end."

"I turned you in." The look Jasper darted at Jupitus warmed what little was left of Ollivan's soul. "I told the High Sorcerer of the Guysman spell."

"And can you destroy it?" said Jupitus levelly. He did not deign to look at Jasper as he asked the question.

Jasper summoned some indignation, pushing off the wall. "I already told you I can't. The spell is an original, he only based it off Everard Guysman's." Jasper stepped closer to Jupitus. "I fulfilled my end of the bargain."

With half a look, Jupitus signalled the enforcers along the wall, and two of them stepped forward. The blood drained from Jasper's face as they seized him, and he struggled futilely, an instinct Ollivan could understand. The enforcers threw him back against the wall, out of the way, and held him there. With a sigh that was almost boredom, Jupitus turned his attention back to his priority prisoner.

"Ollivan," he said. "Mr Hawkes, as he freely admits, has been no help in this matter." Jasper opened his mouth again to protest, but the anticipation on Ollivan's face must have convinced him of how bad an idea that was. "The Guysman enchantment. Your work is a blatantly Sorcerer creation that is terrorising the people of this city and straining the peace. You will tell me how to stop it."

Ollivan gasped a laugh. When Jupitus put it like that, helping his grandfather almost sounded like a reasonable ask. Then the metal lance in his wrist tugged, a fresh jolt of pain shot through him, and he remembered this was not a conference on how to stop a mutual threat. It was an interrogation. The smell of blood permeated the cells, like the threat of his own potential torture.

"Ollivan," said Jupitus with a sigh, as the moment dragged on and Ollivan didn't answer. "You are still my grandson. You should feel lucky that that still affords you some privileges. Were you anyone else, I would slide blades along your bones until you told me what I needed to know. As it is, I will offer you this: cooperate

422

now, and I will consider leniency when I decide how to move forward from this."

He emphasised the word *consider* – no promises, no mercy, no suspicious breaks from character – but it was not enough to sell the lie, nor was it intended to. Ollivan knew there would be no leniency now. Jupitus knew that he knew it. What he really meant was disguised in the brazen way he delivered such impossible hope; *you have no choice. You have lost.* He had Ollivan the way a horse trainer had a broken gelding.

And so Ollivan told him everything he wanted to know.

When he was finished, a fresh-faced enforcer was brought down to replace Elodie, and before the spiked ring was finally removed from his wrist, nauseating pain swept over him once more. Ollivan was finally free of restraining hands, and he was left to slump out of his chair and find the floor alone. He was not so consumed with misery that he would miss what he knew was coming next. Raising his pounding head off the cold stone, he peered through the bars as his grandfather retreated, sparing another minute gesture for the enforcers and their captive; the boy who had only played his part in destroying him.

Jasper had just enough time to scream as, without ceremony, an enforcer drew her blade and dragged it across his throat.

"I'm so tired." Your voice breaks. Your fingers tense around the fragile petals of the snakeskin; your newest treasure. "I'm so tired of wishing I was a Changeling."

Hester's eyes go wide. "Earth and stars, Cassia. Then stop."

Stop? She may as well have plunged you into icy water. It's what you get for expecting comfort from her.

But when you surface, the truth remains. You can't make yourself a Changeling. But who might you create if you wanted something else?

You both know what you have to do. "Promise me if you go that it won't be running away," says Hester.

"Not running," you say, your thumb caressing your new specimen. "Shedding a skin."

40

Someone had packed Cassia's things already.

Two trunks – the only belongings she had brought with her from the Zoo – sat waiting in the hall, ready to go with her on her second exile. It was a scene from the day she arrived, fifteen and near breathless with hope. Had she gathered nothing new since then? Some magic books she wouldn't need any more, and some dresses she would rather not wear. It was like they were erasing her being here at all.

"A carriage will be here on the hour."

Cassia spun. Her mother leaned in the drawing-room doorway, a glass of something hanging from her fingers. She did not meet Cassia's eye. "So Father tells me."

She never called him 'Father', not to her children. It was always 'your grandfather' or 'the High Sorcerer'. But Alana had a faraway look in her watery eyes. Cassia felt a searing stab of guilt and hoped it was just the drink that had made her mother look like that. She dug around for something to say.

"I didn't mean for any of this," is what she settled for, feeling weak.

Alana smiled, but it was more of a grimace. "Are you sure you didn't?"

Cassia flashed back to a night that felt forever ago, when she had lingered outside this very door and listened to her family dismiss her. Had Alana known she was there? Did she know the motive that had pushed her daughter to spurn both her help and her approval?

Alana didn't wait for an answer. "You know, when I was your age, I had a sweetheart in the North."

Cassia straightened in surprise. "You did? A Wraith?"

"A *Wraith*," Alana confirmed, lowering her voice to a whisper and grinning.

"Did Grandfather know?"

The smile slipped. Alana's eyes dropped to the floor. "He found out, yes. I suppose I had wanted him to. I don't think I really liked the boy. He was a bit of a bore. All we ever did was ride an open-top carriage around the park and take tea. Awfully old-fashioned. I wanted to kiss under cover of moonlight." Cassia had never known this side of her; fun, energised. It made more sense that she had fallen for Cassia's flighty, irresponsible father. "But that was the year Father started training me in earnest to be his second. I would disappear with my Wraith every time I was supposed to be at an enforcer's meeting. That's what he minded; not that I was seeing a non-Sorcerer. That I wasn't turning into what he'd wanted from me."

This was not a history Cassia had ever known. "But – you've said you always wanted to be his heir."

"I have," said Alana. She left the doorway and sidled towards Cassia. "But I had to push back all the same. I was testing his limits. It's what children like you and me – and Ollivan – have to do; find the boundaries of our cage."

Alana was in a cage? A mess of contradictions pummelled Cassia's thoughts. Her mother was Jupitus's *ally*, especially when it came to her and Ollivan. How could she second him when she knew what it was like?

"What did he do?" she asked. "When he found out?"

Alana's hand drifted up to brush the curve of Cassia's cheekbone. Her eyes glazed over. "He had me beaten." Cassia swallowed. The walls of the cage around them both seemed to press in. "I came home from the North one evening, and the house was locked up. The guard on the door said they were fumigating the hall, due to vermin, and I needed to use the kitchen entrance. As I was making my way, two men stepped into my path. The next thing I knew, my head was hitting the wall." She lifted the mass of curls on one side of her head. A silver scar crept across the hairline above her temple. "That's the day I got my second's badge. They left it on my chest after they knocked me out, in case I had any doubt about what was happening."

She came closer and gripped her daughter's shoulder, and Cassia blinked back tears, the fresh wave of hopelessness that overcame her.

"I know what he is capable of," said Alana, and this close, Cassia could smell the liquor on her breath. "And I *fear*... I fear what he would do if I tried to usurp him. I can't risk my children like that. I didn't inherit his courage, or his ruthlessness." Her voice grew so quiet Cassia had to lean closer. "Our best defence is that he continues to believe that I did. It's the only way I have of tempering him. It's the only way I have of... saving my son."

Her face crumpled, and she swayed on her feet. So this was why Alana was drinking; because Ollivan was somewhere in the cells under the Chambers, leverage to both his mother and his grandfather.

427

Cassia wanted to pull away; wanted to run to her room and lock the door against the vulnerability of her mother. But she no longer had a room to run to, and her mother had nowhere at all.

The sound of horseshoes and wheels on cobblestones approached in front of the house. Cassia's carriage had arrived. Alana's watery gaze drifted to the trunks by the door, then back to her with new urgency.

"He's fading, Cassia," she said, fingers digging into Cassia's shoulder once more. "Do you understand? It won't be long." She lunged at her and planted a rough kiss on her forehead. "Just hold on."

And then she was gone, back into the drawing room where she became a shadow in the dim light of the candles. A servant was already removing her luggage to the carriage when Cassia turned around, but next to the last remaining trunk was another item; a rose sapling, in a jar of soil. She had had one left of the pre-prepared practice bunch she made before her ill-fated initiation. Had her mother included it with her belongings, or a servant who had packed her things and didn't know how else to deal with a jar of soil? Cassia had no use for it. As her final bag was delivered to the carriage, she picked it up and placed it on a nearby console, out of the way.

She was on the steps before she went back for it; she wasn't sure why. Perhaps she was merely delaying the fate she walked towards. Perhaps she wanted something to remind her that she had been a Sorcerer in the Heart once. She focused on the glass in her hands instead of the house she was leaving as she made her way back out and the door shut with a click.

The driver held the carriage door open for her. He was an Oracle, Cassia realised, her stomach plummeting. She was not even past the border and she belonged to them now. It brought her to an unwilling halt, unable to lift her foot onto the step into the cab.

The Oracle man – who had previously been scuffing his feet against the cobbles, disinterested – looked up at her quizzically when she paused. Under his cap, his head was wrapped in bandages – as was his neck – but the recent burns crept out around the edges. Cassia didn't have time to ask what happened to him before his head jerked and his pure white eyes widened. She stepped back, alarmed, but he made no move towards her. His fingers tightened on the handle of the carriage door and, though it was hard to tell, his eyes moved rapidly from side to side.

And then it ended. He blinked, and looked at her oddly. Cassia stiffened. He had Seen something; something related to her. A future threat? A way towards a *solution* to all this? She suddenly recalled another recent vision; something about power and harm, and confronting herself. She was sorry to find it still sounded like nonsense.

"What is it?" she hazarded, unhopeful of a meaningful answer.

Sure enough, the Oracle only shook his head. It was not their way to share their visions with non-Oracles, at least among the faithful. The man mumbled an apology and gestured to the carriage.

Cassia didn't see that she had a choice. She climbed the steps into the carriage, closing her eyes as the door shut behind her and the sounds of the outside world were muffled. Her mother's words about cages haunted her like phantoms lurking in the corners of the dark cab. Cassia reached overhead and turned up the oil lamp to banish them, but it only brought the four walls closer. She couldn't bring herself to look back at the house as the horses started a trot and it glided away beyond the window.

A sob escaped her. *It won't be long.* And then Alana would ascend to the position of High Sorcerer and liberate her? What if Alana met a challenger, and someone else succeeded Jupitus instead? Her mother's guise of ruthlessness – her role as a perfect model of her father – might not withstand the instability of a shift in leadership. It only took a little pressure in the right place, the curtain would fall, and she would be ousted. And then what would become of Cassia? Of all of them? Would the fight be bloody? Would Cassia meet a worse fate than a lifetime in exile in the Docklands? Alana's best bet was not to succeed her father at all, but to lend her support – and quickly – to the next most popular candidate.

She would write a letter to her mother, tell her the danger did not end with Jupitus's death, as she believed. She knew what it was to convince yourself you were something you weren't; to hold on to the farce stubbornly when it only caused you harm.

But no. She laughed bitterly at her own pride. Her mother, like the High Sorcerer, believed her incapable. Unfit for politics. Why would Alana, who had been preparing to lead her entire life, listen to Cassia's fears about this? There was nothing she could do.

She gripped the jar with the rose cutting between two hands. It felt like the only thing she had left to lose; a pathetic jar of soil that would never bloom. She had to fight back the thoughts she had drilled into herself; the intention she had worked so hard on that pushed to the forefront of her mind when she looked at the cutting, like muscle memory. Her magic stirred within, ready to act on the will she hadn't directed it with yet.

She put the jar beside her and turned away. The magic quietened inside her. Yes, she wanted to use her magic one last time before the chance was gone maybe forever, but she couldn't bear the thought of humiliating herself a final time.

You have no one to humiliate yourself in front of.

The champagne sparkle of magic bubbled forth before she had even finished the thought, ready and eager. It leapt with her breath every time the carriage wheels volleyed over a bump in the road. Stinging tears sprung to her eyes. It was as if her magic didn't understand; as if no one had told it what was happening. They were being removed to a place where Cassia and her magic would grow estranged. And now, of all moments, it wanted to be her friend when she needed one.

"Fine," she snapped, grabbing the jar once again. In answer, the power within her swelled, so that she was racing to hold the intention in her mind before the spell burst from her unformed. Her hands shook on the jar as power coursed to her fingertips. Reflexively, she held the jar out at arm's length and leaned away. There was no time to think.

"Bloom and grow!" she shouted in her panic as magic raced from her fingertips into the jar.

She didn't realise she had closed her eyes until she was opening them again, afraid of what she might find. Something she had never experienced before had taken hold; her *magic* had taken hold; had gripped the intention she had given it, ripped it from her and made her nothing but a conduit.

And the cutting was growing.

It was stretching out of the jar and sprouting vines, some that cascaded over her arms and others that stretched for the roof of the cab as if seeking the sun. Green buds unfurled and became mature leaves before her eyes. The stalks filled the cab and grew robust, until the jar was ripped from Cassia's hands. And just in time too, for the roots were also spreading. The jar shattered as they broke its confines and snaked across the floor.

But the roses.

Each flower burst into being with a sigh, like squeezing the air from a down pillow. So many Cassia could barely see a vine. Velvet soft, blood-red petals stroked her arms, her hair, and her cheeks, collecting her tears. The cab filled with their perfume, mingling with the magic in the air to tickle Cassia's nose. They shuddered with the movements of the carriage, dropping petals into her lap.

She couldn't understand it. Why now? Why here? Still the fizz of power tingled inside her, mellow and satiated but ready to swell at her will. Her hands still shaking, she reached out to grasp a rose head between her fingers. The stalk was firm and thick with thorns, and it wouldn't come away easily.

Sever.

With a gentle snap, a cut appeared in the stalk, and the rose was free. Cassia held it before her, unsure.

"B... black?" she said, only belatedly aware she was speaking her intentions again, her confidence slipping. Her question was answered by another question, a gentle nudge from inside that told her to try again.

Black.

Starting at the tips of the petals, black seeped through the rose. Cassia sighed. So did her magic. Her friend when she needed one.

Your magic is you. It knows your real intention even when you don't.

Ollivan had tried to tell her. He had failed to make sense to her because he hadn't truly understood the problem. He hadn't understood that Cassia knew exactly what she wanted.

It had never been about magic. Cassia's intention, infecting nearly every spell she'd conjured since she set her sights on the Heart – just as Ollivan had infected Violet – was to belong. To be seen to be a worthy Sorcerer. She had tried to wield her magic like a tool, not to conjure and enchant, but to impress her peers and win respect. Well, that was lost, along with her home, her friends and family, her freedom. She had no hope of finding her place in the Docklands, let alone of becoming who she wanted to be. She had been stripped of the chance; stripped of any claim of belonging to the Sorcerers.

And yet her magic remained. It heard her when she called. It responded with resistance when she pressed on it, or accused it of showing her up. It had been trying to tell her all along.

She was a Sorcerer of the Heart. It wasn't a social position or a ticket to join a club. It was pure magic.

Her mind went back to the ball, to the blaze she had conjured effortlessly. She had thought her magic answered her because it sensed her need. But her focus on the moment had simply stripped the intention to be *seen* away, and left her free. The same had happened when she attacked Jasper; all she'd wanted in that second was to get him away from her. Her best spells had been the ones when being a *real Sorcerer* had been furthest from her mind, but the yearning for acceptance over magic had mostly been there. In her desperation and foolishness, Cassia had thought they were the same thing.

Her tears flooded her vision and ran freely down her face. "I'm so sorry," she whispered, her face pressed to the roses. And something inside her responded; a flash of power that enveloped her being and warmed her throughout. She laughed, crying even harder.

An entire library of spells flashed through her mind; everything she had mastered in theory over two years of intense and endless study. Glamours, for instance. At the very thought of glamours, her magic stirred, waiting for an intention it could grasp onto. Cassia designed the first glamour that came to mind: *fill the cab with music. Strings. Soft ones. Play something bright. Don't let it be heard outside.*

As she fashioned the intention, her magic gathered the details and held them together, so that when she uttered the single word of the spoken spell – *strings* – it was with perfect confidence. As if from far away, a joyous melody filled her ears and swelled. It was a tune she had never heard before. It sounded like roses.

This was what strong magic did when used right, she realised. It understood you. Precision was only partly in maintaining a strong intention and a focused mind, both things Cassia excelled at. The rest was talking to your magic, and being heard. She was not one mind, and yet she wasn't two. Her magic was a part of her, like her heart and lungs, her laugh, her dreams. It was like she was seeing herself for the first time.

The carriage jolted as they went over a hole in the road, announcing itself and where it was taking her. She couldn't let this happen. She couldn't live with a decision her grandfather had made when he was underestimating her; when *she* was underestimating her. Now that she had found her magic, she would not give it up.

Just like Ollivan.

She suddenly knew why all this was so important to him. The idea of being forced to the Otherworld and only performing magic in the shadows was anathema. She had to get out of here. She would find her brother – break him out of the cells if need be – tell him he had been right, that she understood him now, and solve this once and for all. She didn't need to prove herself to every Successor and member of high society in the Heart, but she *did* need her grandfather to see that she was more valuable to him at home.

Cassia fought through the tangle of roses – her skin catching on thorns and tearing open – to peer out of the small carriage window. First, she needed to find a way out of this cab without the driver noticing, preferably before they hit the border to the Docklands.

But they were not heading for the border. At least, not any guard point Cassia knew of. They had moved east, and now it looked like they were travelling due north, towards the river. For a moment, the fear that her grandfather had duped her – that she was not being sent away, but disposed of – gripped her. But—

The driver. His flash of Sight as she was getting into the carriage.

Cassia's stomach plummeted. She wasn't being assassinated, at least not by her grandfather. But this Oracle had an agenda of his own. What had he Seen? That she was a threat somehow? That his own future was best served by kidnapping her?

She could transport.

Her magic wanted to, and Cassia tamped down on it like slamming the lid of a box. For an endless moment, she feared it would simply *happen*, that her magic would take control again and she wouldn't be quick enough to stop it. She tensed, squeezing her eyes closed, but the tide receded, and she was still in the cab, and whole.

Transporting was too risky. Those who never struggled with their power still trained for months with exercises Cassia had never got far enough to even begin. Whatever her magic longed for, she had to find another way out of here.

But before she could think of one, the carriage slowed, and she was jolted into the thorny mess of roses as it stopped entirely. She dared not make a break for it, not when she didn't know what was out there. Instead, she pressed back into the chair and readied a spell to fire when the door opened.

Someone made an exclamation of surprise. The roses shuddered on their stems. Then two hands parted the flora, and the Oracle driver's face appeared from through the vines.

Cassia's hands flew up in warning. "I'll stun you," she said.

"No need, miss," he said, eyeing the inside of the cab like he had a thousand questions. "I'm only doing you a good turn."

"A good turn how?" She didn't lower her hands. Her magic bubbled at her fingertips.

"*What* is going on in there?" said an exasperated voice Cassia recognised. "Are those… roses?"

The driver made an attempt to clear the vines aside so she could get out, but only succeeded in tearing his shirtsleeves and also himself.

Recede, instructed Cassia, and the roses parted themselves to clear the door of the carriage. The driver gestured for her to climb out and – still poised to defend herself – she did.

Her relief at seeing Sybella lasted two seconds, before Sybella shot a stunning spell at her and knocked her off her feet.

*

"You treacherous! Miserable! Rat!"

With every word, Sybella pummelled Cassia with another stunning spell, but after the first, Cassia had gathered her wits and thrown up a shield. She was still so delighted to be using magic properly that she lay on the damp ground marvelling at the delightful, tinny sound of Sybella's attack as it bounced off the protective bubble.

Sybella gave up after that.

"That's new," she snapped, gesturing at the bubble. "So you cracked magic and now a little loyalty is beneath you?"

"Are you going to attack me again if I get rid of this shield?"

"I'd like to, yes."

Cassia remained where Sybella had thrown her, unable to keep her hands up to maintain her shield and climb to her feet with any sort of grace. The Oracle driver came into view near her head. "You said you were doing me a good turn," she accused. She raised her head higher and addressed Sybella again. "Is this about Violet disguising herself as me and helping my grandfather catch Ollivan?"

"How stupid do you think I am?" Sybella, in her ire, aimed another futile stunner at the shield. Then she quieted for a long moment. "She disguised herself as you?"

"Yes."

"Then where in the heaven and earth have you been?"

Sybella folded her arms, and Cassia took the chance to drop her shield and get to her feet. The carriage driver had deposited her in front of a stone arch, but between the dark and the fog, Cassia couldn't tell where it led, or why Sybella would be there.

She explained how Violet had knocked her and Lev out, how they had woken up and gone looking for Virgil, and that with his help they'd realised Violet was impersonating her.

"We realised she was luring you and Ollivan into a trap. Virgil was trying to get to Hyde Park to intercept you. But I suppose he didn't make it."

Sybella shook her head. "Not in time. The park was full of enforcers. I didn't see what happened. I thought we could get out of there in time, so I transported here." She pointed up past the arch, but whatever she wished Cassia to see was lost in the fog. "This is where we used to meet to… be alone. It's where I come to temple. There's a room up there under the roof where we would… well. I tried to tell him to meet me here if we got separated, but I wasn't sure if he understood me." Her mouth formed a round pout and tears brimmed in her eyes. "I've been waiting in case… in case he managed to escape. Why did *you* come here?"

Cassia turned to the driver, who was still turning his cap, faster and faster. "You said you were doing me a good turn by bringing me here." He nodded. "Why? What do we do now?"

He shook his head. "I'm afraid I don't know, miss. I only Saw you and the young man thanking me for it, and I owe him a kindness."

"What young man?"

The Oracle gestured to his cheek. "He has a scar, right here."

"*My brother?* Why would he—"

If Ollivan thanked this man sometime in the future, it likely meant this Oracle was either in the Chambers' cells – unlikely – or Ollivan was out of them.

438

"He helped me, you see," the driver went on. "I was injured in that distillery fire and he dressed my burns."

Sybella's eyes widened in understanding. "I sent him to help at the hospital," she said.

But Cassia had lost interest in the *why* part. She knew what they had to do next. "We have to get Ollivan out of those cells. He has a plan, doesn't he? He knows how to unravel Violet?"

"*We* have a plan. And we're not going to unravel her. Ollivan and I spent all day drafting another version of the Guysman spell, one that will absorb Violet's magic when she absorbs *it*. Sort of like an inoculation against maniacal evil." She bent down and picked up something at her feet; a shining gold cutlass. "It's our vessel," she said when Cassia raised an eyebrow at it.

"Another Guysman?"

"I know, but it's our best shot. But we have two problems. First, Ollivan's locked up in the Chambers."

"We'll remedy that."

"And second, Violet knows the whole plan. She was with us when Ollivan announced the idea, pretending to be you."

This didn't concern Cassia as much as it appeared to concern Sybella. "Then we'll have to take her by surprise. I have an idea." She turned to the driver. "Can you take us back to Drusella Square?"

"Uh—" He looked over at the carriage. A small carpet of red petals had collected below the door, out of which the rosebush had burst. Cassia waved her hand and it receded to a small plant inside the cab. She wasn't ready to part with it entirely.

"Come on. And leave the sword," she said, and she and Sybella hurried to the carriage, the driver climbing up behind the horses.

Cassia's mind was churning with plans, her veins coursing with terror, as they set out in the direction she had come.

"Cassia?" said Sybella, breaking her out of her thoughts.

"Yes?"

"Do you hear music?"

4 1

The enforcers started torturing Ollivan in shifts.

After enough hours of the pain permeating every inch of his being, blurring his vision, pounding on his skull, and bringing bile to his throat, they no longer had to keep the enchantment up at all times. Jupitus probably enjoyed the fact that Ollivan could be left to his own devices in a flimsy stone and steel cell for an hour or two and wouldn't escape.

It wasn't for lack of trying. The first couple of times his captor eased off the pain spell, Ollivan exerted all his energy in trying to achieve enough mental presence to transport out of there. But transporting demanded too much from him; how to channel his magic, how to visualise where he was going and the way he was meant to tug on the earth to get himself there. He had performed transportations thousands of times, and he knew all of this like it was second nature. But blocking his pain – his physical pain, let alone the torment of his battered emotions – was like digging a familiar tool out from under a pile of debris after an earthquake. He was as likely to tear himself into several pieces as escape.

Time continued to pass without him grasping it, but throughout the minutes and hours that he lay there, noise built around him; people above in the Chambers, rumbles and booms from beyond the stone walls. He drifted in a fever dream of London crumbling around him, Violet roaming the streets, untouchable, his grandfather's enforcers closing in…

Then the noise was closer. He opened his eyes to sparks, then lurched upright as the wall by his head exploded, leaving a crater and showering stone on him.

The next spell found its mark in the enforcer guarding him, and the man crumpled to the floor with a groan. The strength of his agony waned.

Ollivan was still. He would recognise that silhouette forever more, and be taken back to Drusella's statue at sundown. To the last time he trusted anyone in his family.

Cassia walked the length of the corridor coolly and knelt in front of the cell, so they were at eye level. Hesitantly, she wrapped her hands around the bars so she could lean closer.

"What could you possibly want from me now?" Ollivan hissed. She had brought back to life something he had been struggling to summon since his grandfather's visit and the incessant, weakening pain since; fury. Always his strongest tool. It stoked the fire of magic inside him, swam through his veins. Suddenly the risks of intentions getting away from him didn't matter. What did anything matter? If his own spells destroyed him, at least he would take her down too.

Cassia looked over her shoulder. There was another woman in the dungeons. "Perhaps you should explain," said Cassia to the figure, who approached and knelt beside her.

"No," rasped Ollivan. "Ellie, you haven't."

Everyone. He had lost everyone. They had all allied against him.

"You have to listen to me, Ollivan," said Sybella. Her eyes had turned glassy at the sight of him; the sweat drenching him through, the trembling caused by simply trying to hold himself up. "Lev and Virgil are creating a distraction but we don't have much time."

She had something in either hand. In her left was a small potion bottle that she passed through the bars to him. It was a vitality tonic, a short-term cure for the symptoms of injury, illness, and fatigue. At least, that's what it said on the bottle.

In her right was a key; one of the long, iron keys that hung by the entrance to the cells, by the looks of it. She fumbled with it in the lock until the cell door clicked open. Ollivan glanced again at the guard Cassia had taken out and began to wonder.

"Drink up," said Sybella as she came into the cell.

"How can I trust you?"

Sybella recoiled, and looked between him and Cassia with a dangerous expression. "Given the circumstances, I'll choose to forgive you for such an insult."

Ollivan's voice was low. "Now that I think about it, you left me behind in Hyde Park awfully quickly."

Her mouth opened and closed again, the tears in her eyes gathering with new ones. Her reply was a whisper. "Stars damn you, Ollivan."

Cassia swept into the cell and stood between them. Bracing himself against the wall for support, Ollivan climbed to his feet. It would be easier to defend himself – or flee, if he got the chance.

"Violet is impersonating me, Ollivan. She separated us all as we were leaving the ball yesterday and took my place. I'm not sure how. Partly Changeling magic, I imagine, since she has that now as well. But I didn't hand you over to

443

Grandfather, *she* did. She thinks she can make me powerful by making you weak." She paused thoughtfully. "Although, I did get the hang of my magic, and you're in a cell, so perhaps she's on to something."

He hadn't registered that Cassia had used her magic to stun a guard unconscious until now.

"What changed?" he asked her.

"I started wielding magic for myself." She snatched the vitality tonic from his hand, unstoppered it and shoved it back at him. "I suppose you have no reason to believe a word I've said except that I'm here now, breaking you out of custody, and Sybella's been waiting outside her temple for you for hours."

Her temple. There was a room up a staircase off the observatory. They had spent whole nights there sometimes; some of the happiest nights of Ollivan's life. It was always their meeting place, when they didn't want her mother and mama to find them. It was where she'd been trying to tell him to find *her*, in the park. Where she had hinted they should go, before they chose the pub instead.

He dared a glance at Sybella, and forced himself to see all of her pain for once. Pain he had caused.

"Forgive me."

Sybella was still for a moment. Then she crossed the cell in four long strides, took his face between her hands, and kissed him. It was fierce and commanding, and Ollivan had nothing left. He leaned needily into her embrace, and when she wrapped her arms around him tightly, he let her take his weight. "I'm not here to stars-damn betray you, alright?" she whispered as she steadied him on his feet. "I'm here to get you out."

444

Speechless, Ollivan only nodded.

Cassia cleared her throat. "Um, I'm here too. In fact it was my idea."

Ollivan knocked back the vitality tonic, relief coursing through him along with strength as it took effect immediately. It was as if the last few hours hadn't happened; no screaming, no aching bones, no nausea. He could no longer feel the wound on his wrist, which was growing swollen and hot. He would pay for it all later when the tonic wore off and his ills came rushing back, but in the meantime, he would escape.

"The enforcers are combing the streets looking for Violet," said Cassia. "There are even militia from the other factions helping. Don't they know she'll obliterate them if they succeed in finding her?"

"No," said Ollivan as he stepped out of the cell. His jacket hung from a hook down the corridor, and he made for it, relishing the feeling of his own sure and steady steps. "They don't. They think they can disarm her with an elaborate unravelling."

"*Why?*" said Cassia.

"Because I told them they could."

There was silence. Ollivan shrugged into his coat and did what he could to make himself presentable.

"You lied to them," said Cassia. "Why?"

Ollivan scoffed. "It's what he deserves," he muttered.

"Ollivan—"

"Where are you going?" Sybella cut in.

"France, probably," he said.

Cassia looked like he'd slapped her. "You're not going to stop this."

Sybella laughed, but it was uncertain. "He was joking." She looked at Ollivan. "Of course he's going to stop this."

Ollivan focused on a spot just to the left of her face. The feel of her lips on his still lingered.

"Jasper killed Jonas Benn because Jupitus told him to," he said. "It was a set-up so he could banish me."

Cassia looked between Ollivan and Sybella. "*Jasper* killed him?"

Sybella put a fluttering hand to her mouth in shock. "Oh, Ollivan."

He didn't want her pity. He couldn't bear the violent way it twisted in his gut. He turned to Cassia and explained as briefly as he could. "He knew of the banned magic, and he promised Jasper his immunity for using it if he framed me. He just wanted rid of me."

To Cassia's credit, she barely showed surprise. "He *wrote* the Principles. How is he so content to keep undermining them?"

"He doesn't care about the Principles, Cassia. All he cares about is *power*, and he'll destroy anyone and anything he has to to keep it. Now the whole city is going to see what that's bought him."

Cassia's hand shot out and gripped his. He tried to pull away but she held fast, his blood seeping between her fingers. "Have you seen them? The victims, with their eyes glazed over and their faces covered in blood? She's causing some kind of coma. What if the only cure is for them to get their magic back?"

Ollivan suspected that *was* the only cure, and he shut down the pang of guilt it caused him. Because he had tried, he had tried so hard, to save London from Violet. To do so again – to do anything other than escape – would see him thrust back in the cell he had just been freed from. It would mean banishment at best, execution at worst. If it was cowardly to turn his back, then he was a coward, but he was not the one who had got them here. His grandfather had made an enemy of him, when what he'd needed was an ally. That was politics, wasn't it? It was about negotiation.

"Run," he said to them both. "Get out of the city and warn as many people as you can on the way."

Sybella dropped her gaze, but not soon enough to hide a disappointment that crushed Ollivan's soul. Cassia, on the other hand, stared at him, eyes wide.

"If the enforcers find her, she'll kill them," she said, her voice low.

"Good."

Cassia released his hand, her features slackening in shock. He was free to make his escape, but his surprise at his own reaction paralysed him. He wasn't a killer, nor did he want to stand by and let people be killed. Perhaps there was a way to head off the enforcers he had sent after Violet on a fool's errand, and then escape before they—

"He was right about you all along." It was Cassia, her voice soft and breaking. "You really are a monster."

Heat flared in Ollivan's chest; magic or fury, he wasn't sure. Sometimes he thought they were one and the same. *A monster.* His little sister thought so too.

"As I said." He took several steps backwards, out of her reach. "Run."

Then he thought of his destination, pulled his power to him, and disappeared.

42

Run.

Cassia and Sybella did the opposite. They stood in stunned silence in the gloomy cells as the world fell to pieces around them.

Cassia felt hollow and heavy at the same time. She was a fool for having come here; for believing the solution to all this rested with her brother. She had known who he was from the start; selfish, proud, incapable of taking responsibility. She shouldn't have let it surprise her that he would abandon them – the whole of London – to face an avalanche he had started.

Sybella was the first to break the silence.

"I suppose this has scuppered your idea, whatever it was." Her voice was thick with unfallen tears, and her arms were wrapped tightly across her chest. Cassia was not the only one who had put her faith in Ollivan.

"It has and it hasn't." Sybella looked up hesitantly. "We don't need Ollivan for the ambush, just enough bodies for a distraction."

Sybella nodded. "Lev, Virgil, and I can get you that. If every Successor we can find will do?"

"They'll do. As for the spell…" Cassia hesitated. Did she really mean what she was about to say? Something had changed today. Even now, her magic danced through her at the lightest mental touch, eager and ready to manifest her intentions. She wasn't Ollivan. She didn't have his natural ability or his nearly two decades of experience.

But Ollivan wasn't here.

"Sybella, how well do you remember the spell?"

"Remember it?" Sybella reached into her coat pocket and emerged with three sheets of neatly folded hazel wood paper. She offered them to Cassia, who took the pages delicately, like they might sense they were in the wrong hands and crumble to dust.

It was long. The hazel wood paper and the wielder's magic would do a lot of the work of binding the complex wording into a single command, but they would still need to know – and *focus* on – all of the various parts.

Power thrummed in her abdomen. Her magic wanted it. Or was that arrogance? The wish to be a hero?

She looked up at Sybella. "You're not going to tell me this is beyond me?"

Sybella shrugged. "I know for *certain* it's beyond me," she said. "And anyone else other than… anyone but me will have to learn it by heart just as you will."

"But what if I'm just not powerful enough?"

Sybella snorted. "I dare you to ask the man plucking rose thorns off the ceiling of his carriage that question."

Two years of mounting doubt and frustration had left a wound that would not heal any time soon. It was impossible to Cassia that she could have the power to do this. Impossible, and yet completely right.

Sybella nodded to the paper in Cassia's hand. "How soon can you learn that spell?"

Cassia's hands shook, but her heart beat steadily. "How long have I got?"

*

She sent Sybella with Lev and Virgil to fetch reinforcements. Then, taking one of the oil lamps from the corridor above the dungeons, went to find a blood-free corner in which to memorise the spell.

The Chambers of Alchemy was nearly deserted, all of her grandfather's people having been sent out to maintain the peace or seek the Guysman. The enchantment on the grand hall had been removed, or perhaps expired, but the detritus of revelry and carnage remained. Browning flower petals littered the grey stone, and an upturned banquet table had scattered the shards of glasses and serving bowls among them. Crows picked at the food.

Cassia found a large storage room for spell and potion supplies and cast a ward over the door to give herself privacy. The room was unlit, other than her stolen lamp, but its lack of windows was an advantage; all the better to keep her focused on the spell and not the chaos reigning outside. Fighting and looting filled the streets. The peace had broken down, if the thundering sounds of explosions was anything to go by.

She sat on the floor with the hazel wood pages in her hands, reading and rereading the spell, and trying not to think of the enormity of what she was trying to do; the weight resting on her shoulders. When she pushed those thoughts away, she found herself thinking of Ollivan.

Was it possible for a heart to break for someone and *by* them at the same time? Sybella had explained Ollivan's version of events the night Jonas Benn was murdered to Cassia, Lev, and Virgil in

450

broad strokes – detailing the channelling spell he had also once used on her – and Cassia had dismissed them. Her brother was cold-hearted and vengeful; he lied and tried to twist his mistakes into someone else's; and he was not above someone else dying for his version of justice, for he had abandoned all of London to an inevitably bloody fate.

And then they had found Jasper's body.

It had been laid out in a corner of the dungeons, only half covered by a sheet, as if nobody had the time or care to deal with it. Virgil knelt to close his eyes and cover him fully.

"I didn't wish this for him," he said, seeing their curious looks. His eyes brimmed with tears, but his hands shook with rage. It was another atrocity the High Sorcerer would never pay for.

The others had been slow to understand why he was dead, but Cassia wasn't. Her grandfather groomed people; for power, for service. Alana and Ollivan as rulers, her as a faithful pawn. It was easier to build someone into what he wanted them to be than find the perfect tool already formed. Jupitus had groomed Jasper for dirty work and found him willing, useful; he must have been testing the boy's continuing usefulness over the last year. He had helped to maintain his image, even hiring him to tutor her.

And then Ollivan had returned and upended it all. In the tug of war between her brother and grandfather, Jasper became a liability, a loose end, a tool gone blunt. Now, in death, Ollivan's enemy had become his vindication in Cassia's eyes. Jasper was dead because Ollivan was innocent.

Of this crime, at least, she thought bitterly as she prepared to save the city without him. She hoped to have an hour, she had told Sybella. One hour with the Guysman she and Ollivan had written.

"And then I'll fetch you?" Sybella had said.

Cassia shook her head. "There's no need."

She was expecting another. All she had to do was wait.

An hour had not yet passed, and Cassia was rehearsing the enchantment in her mind when she was suddenly no longer alone.

The crow stood by the door, which had not opened to let it in. It tilted its head and watched her with curious black eyes. A message? No, she realised as the crow turned its beak towards the door. A summons.

Cassia folded Ollivan and Sybella's spell and tucked it into the belt of her coat. There was no time or space left to doubt herself, her plan, her magic. She reached out to her power for comfort and it responded, enveloping her in warmth, lending her confidence. So she opened the door and followed the crow out.

Another waited outside. Along the hall, another. It was not one crow to guide her, but a breadcrumb trail. They grew in number as she walked, hopping about her feet, darting suddenly from perch to perch, cawing to one another – or to her. Were they some perversion of Changeling magic? Animal mind control? Were the birds even real, or some kind of glamour? An uncanny magical charge clung to the air, growing stronger as she reached the lobby. *She* was close; Cassia could feel it.

The grand front doors swept open by invisible hands as Cassia approached, and the fog poured in. She braced to step into it, but it parted around her, revealing a trail of scattered crows curving west, towards the bridge. The fog had taken on an otherworldly purple hue, pulsating with pinks and oranges in a light that seemed to emanate from everywhere. Through it, the hulking shadows of buildings were breathing, expanding and contracting in an undulating wave. The night sky rolled by, stars tilting across the heavens one hundred times faster than they were meant to, and in the wrong direction.

Not mind control, Cassia realised. Violet was not doing this to her, but to the world.

Cassia crossed the square, catching glimpses of silhouettes in the streets leading off it. People running. Buildings on fire. Had Violet attacked them, or had the Londoners done that, tearing themselves and each other apart in terror? How many of these people had lost their magic? A fear Cassia hadn't appreciated before – a fear of Violet's power – engulfed her. She couldn't lose her magic; she had only just found it. And if she failed, she would. She and everyone else remaining.

The bridge and the river were indistinguishable from everything else until the path before her opened around half a dozen enforcers. They crouched in terror against the balustrade either side of the mouth of the bridge. One was sobbing. Another stared slack-jawed into the fog at a nightmare shape flitting back and forth. Cassia had noticed the strange, flitting shadows and chosen not to think about them.

The trail of crows led between the militia and onto the bridge – towards the thickening darkness at its centre – but Cassia stopped by the balustrade.

"I need a book of matches," she said.

The enforcers stared as if they expected her to disintegrate like the rest of reality around them. When she didn't, the nearest reached into her coat pocket and tried to hand Cassia some matches, but dropped them from her trembling fingers. Cassia caught them.

"It would be best if you wait here," she said, pointlessly. The enforcers weren't going anywhere.

The opposite bank was invisible, so that the bridge stretched over the water into an abyss. As Cassia stepped foot over the Thames, the crows amassed around her took off as one. She covered her head in the sudden maelstrom of beating wings. An instant later, they had disappeared into the night, and Cassia was left alone.

Almost alone. Cassia had known, by some indefinable instinct, that she would choose the bridge. It was right by the Wending Place, but a much better trap; even if Cassia had the nerve to try, no Sorcerer could transport over water.

Each step took her further from safety, the world on land growing quiet, then disappearing from view. Neither bank was in sight when the thicket of darkness at its centre widened, swallowing the whole width of the bridge. The fog that had previously parted around her closed in, until darkness and mist had blurred into an impenetrable midnight cage.

She had taken the light, and now she created darkness; destroyed the smog spell, and now she generated a peculiar mist of her own. She existed to twist magic against those who wielded it, and she cared not a bit that the single boy she had been intended to ruin was lying cold in a dungeon.

Cassia extended one hand. *Burn*, she willed, and a flame no bigger than a taper's sparked to life at her fingertips. She and her flame became a bubble of light, a beacon, and everything beyond grew even blacker, so that her enemy was right upon her before she knew she was there.

Cassia's insides flipped. Her own pale face hovered before her, detached, dark hair and clothes blending in with the shadow.

You must confront yourself, girl, or you damn us all. Suddenly Cassia understood. It wasn't her the Oracle woman had Seen causing harm with her immense power. It was Violet. She could have been looking in a mirror, except that Cassia could feel the terror painted on her own features, and the ones looking at her were expressionless and static. A doll's.

And then Violet smiled.

Her lips pulled back from her teeth and her maw widened in an imitation of something human that made the hairs on Cassia's arms stand on end. She drew back, and shot a look over her shoulder, but she could see nothing in the blackness; not the end of the bridge, nor her friends and their distraction.

"I knew you would come," said Violet.

Her voice was not Cassia's; it was the doll's. That high and friendly lilt that now made her shudder.

"How did you ever fool them?"

A pale hand swept between them, spellcasting over Violet's own face. "There is nothing I can't do," she said, voice crumbling and re-forming as something deeper, smoother; as Cassia's own.

"Is it Changeling magic?" Cassia asked.

Violet's head tilted to one side; not like a person's, like a puppet's. Like a wooden screw was loose on one side of her neck. "I can't tell. It has all melted together. It's delightful."

"It wasn't fair of you to pretend to be me. That's not something a friend does." It sounded pathetic – a slap on the wrist for putting a flame to a whole city – but if Violet was doing all of this for her, maybe she could appeal to those feelings.

But Violet was unmoved. "Friends share. I like this body. It's beautiful."

"And Ollivan? Did he need to believe that *I* was the one who betrayed him."

Her green eyes flashed, no longer glass but real and alive, and Cassia's. "He needed to know your power. He was but the first."

"Why not just kill him?"

"Cassia," she said, an admonishment. "I don't desire to kill anyone, or even hurt them. In fact, I find it quite unfortunate that my magic has the effect it does on those I take from."

"Then why—"

Violet's hand shot out and snatched Cassia's free one. Cassia gasped, the flame at her fingers snuffing out as she lost concentration.

"This is how we take the world," Violet said. "You know that fear is power, but once we have the power, we can use it as we wish. It doesn't have to look like this. It could be beautiful."

She made another motion with her hand, and the screams, the flames; the carnage beyond the bridge was amplified.

"I can do *anything*, Cassia. *We* can do anything. These squabbling, hate-filled people in this hate-filled place. I've seen it all now, this city. And I'm so much more than them. And you…" Her grip tightened on Cassia's hand. "You're not their tool. They want you to remain in a box they built for you, but with me, you can show them their mistake. You and I could make this city a paradise, like all the High Sorcerers and alphas and petty, small rulers could not. *You'll* be the child your mother respects. You'll be the most powerful person in this wretched city." She grinned with her puppet's maw. "And you'll love me."

Cassia swayed on her feet, her heart fluttering. Her numb fingers wrapped around Violet's.

"You can do anything?" she whispered.

"Anything."

"Like get rid of the fog? And this darkness?"

Violet went preternaturally still. It appeared she did not breathe, despite inhabiting a form that was human.

"Show me," Cassia said. "If you can do anything, then I want to see how it could be. If you want me to trust you, then prove it."

Her eyes flashed – with magic or anticipation, Cassia wasn't sure. But she nodded, and releasing Cassia's hand, spread her arms slowly.

Light split the dark; blades of sun burning through the fog and widening, until clear sky appeared between shafts of shadow. It was golden, bleeding into pink in the east; sunrise. Another effect of Violet's unnatural magic, or was it time for the dawn? Cassia had lost track, but it didn't matter. She blinked in the light and looked to shore. The enforcers' faces emerged shakily above the barricade; on the other bank, the Changeling forces breathed as well. And beyond them both, the swell of fog Violet had brought upon them rolled away on her command.

Cassia's breath left her in a rush of awed relief, but she was suddenly exposed, the hazel wood paper spell tucked in her belt on show. Her hand went to it self-consciously.

Violet gave it a pointed look. "I heard your brother's entire plan. You could never have fooled me."

Cassia met her eye as she took the hazel wood paper out and brandished it between two fingers, noting Violet's lack of reaction. Cassia had never posed a threat to her.

But Violet did not pose one to her either. She had held fast to the belief that the two of them could work together; that the very reason she existed was to help Cassia grow. She had once been just an enchanted doll, after all.

So Cassia stretched her arm over the glistening expanse of water below, and let the pages go, to be pulled under by the current.

43

Ollivan found a man with a cart and the popular new desire to leave London, and paid him nearly everything he had for the privilege of crouching among the man's belongings. He would catch a boat from Wessolk and head east, as he'd previously planned.

But while Ollivan-the-runaway was eager to watch the boundaries of the city disappear behind him, Ollivan-the-Sorcerer was fighting the urge to take his chances on the streets and witness the unfolding of...

He couldn't describe it. The fog had taken on an iridescent sunset hue. A woman running past spontaneously transformed into a swarm of dragonflies and back again before collapsing in shock, or something worse. The ground was crumbling away behind the wheels of the cart, and something Ollivan feared was blood was bubbling up from below before hardening into an ordinary-looking road once more. In his drug-brewing days, he had been diligent about safety-testing everything he produced – a smorgasbord of mind-altering substances – and yet he had experienced nothing as hallucinogenic as this.

He had theories. Ideas about what the interaction of various magics might produce. So little was known about the hypothetical science of transference – harnessing and wielding the magic of another people – and all of the research was concerned with the *how*, and not the *what*. Changeling power infected with

Sorcerer magic could perhaps turn a woman into several hundred dragonflies, for example. Whisperer magic that had 'escaped' into the atmosphere might account for the murmur of distant voices coming from every direction. But combine it with Psi power, and Wraith power, and channel it through a vessel that was never meant to wield *any* magic; it seemed the Guysman had become something the fabric of reality couldn't sustain.

It wasn't worth it, he told himself, closing his eyes against the temptation of an upright piano that was floating along the street changing form; one second, it was made of solid gold, the next ice, then maggots feeding on rotting fruit. He had a notebook in the bag he had thrown together upon fleeing the Chambers; once he was safely crossing the Channel, he would make some notes on a new version of the spell, one that would allow him to run some experiments. Experiments that would hopefully result in dragonflies, or a malleable piano, but minus the ruination of a city.

He wished he wasn't leaving Sybella behind. He had no say in the matter, and the look on her face when Cassia had said what she did brooked no doubt; she wasn't coming with him, not now, not ever. But she was smart and resourceful. Her mother and mama were too. They knew a sinking ship when they saw one and would get out unscathed.

As for his sister.

Monster.

So there was something in him capable of being let down still. After Jasper, then Jupitus; his mother's spineless apathy and Sybella's empty admissions of regret, *still* he could be surprised in the most brutal of ways. And once again, he should have known.

Cassia had *barely* consented to stopping the Guysman with him, and had chafed at every turn. When it all came down to him in a cell, bleeding and broken, and whatever she had wanted from this broken with it, of course she had abandoned him.

Monster.

His pride roared furiously at the accusation, but his heart felt heavy and raw. For the first time in their lives, he and Cassia had been together in something. He hadn't been lonely for a sibling in childhood – at least not the sibling he had – but now it turned out she wasn't in fact spoiled, or entitled, unintelligent or unambitious, and a loneliness had seeped in.

The monster he thinks you are.

That she had looked at Jupitus, and looked at him, and decided *Ollivan* was the monster was anathema to him. Senseless. And Ollivan hated senselessness. He wanted to pack Cassia up alongside his notebook, add her to his list of problems to solve, figure out where the mistake had been made. One thing he did know, however, was that any bond he had thought was growing between them had been in his head.

The cart bounced over a hole in the road and Ollivan winced, motion sickness threatening. He tried to train his gaze on the distance – south, towards the river – but the choking fog was so thick he could only see as far as the park fence that ran parallel to the street.

And then a rush of warm air rushed past his face, and the fog with it.

"Earth and stars, what now?" said his companion as the horse startled; he crooned some reassurances at her, and snapped the reins to speed up their pace.

The fog was rolling away, though the pink and orange tint to the atmosphere remained. Dawn. It had been the dead of night only moments ago.

Ollivan climbed to his knees. The wind that took the fog had come from the direction of Drusella Square and swept in every direction so that, as he watched, the air cleared in an ever-expanding circle until the fog had left the city entirely. Cheers went up; more screams, too, as the extent of the chaos was laid before them. They were still in the Heart, but a band of Oracle militia were crossing the park; at a run, now that the fog was gone, and armed for battle. The sound of gunfire from behind him, to the north, followed by the blur of fast-moving bodies passing by, announced that the Wraith militia were also in Sorcerer territory. Plumes of smoke decorated the dawn sky; breaking glass, screaming, and what might have been explosions echoed from near and far.

This was London with its fragile peace in tatters; everyone for themselves. They were weak, but at least their enemies were weak too. Might as well take the chance that another faction's militia had been hit hard by the Guysman.

The only word Ollivan had for it was chaos – and chaos had been exactly what he wanted. As his stars-damned luck would have it, his own enemy was no longer here to take the blame.

His companion pulled sharply on the reins and Ollivan was thrown forward as the cart stopped. The fact he had never been to the port town, coupled with the distance, made transportation a risk, but as he rubbed the new bump on his head, he reconsidered.

"Will you be driving like this all the way to Wessolk?" he said, clambering back up.

But the driver had climbed down from his seat and disappeared in front of the horse. Curious, Ollivan vaulted the side of the cart and followed him.

A boy lay in the path of the horse, wide brown eyes staring up at them but seeing nothing. He was around six years old, and though he was moving, he wasn't conscious. His small body lurched with the motion of someone falling in their sleep; painful-looking, whole-body twitches. One elbow had cut open where he was slamming it repeatedly into the ground.

The cart owner backed away, but Ollivan shoved him aside and knelt by the boy, taking his head lightly between his hands. Blood had gushed from his nose and now it seeped between Ollivan's fingers.

"I'm here, I'm here," he murmured over and over. "You're alright."

It was a lie, but as Ollivan held him and waited and prayed that the fit would pass, he needed to believe it. For this was what Cassia had described, the worsening effects of Violet's magic. He had been so confident that returning people's magic would return them to health, but for the first time he doubted himself. If this was caused by the *act* of stripping their power – a trauma injury, rather than a symptom – then was the damage already done? What if it wasn't, but no one hit upon a way to shut down the Guysman?

His mind went to the hazel wood paper pages in Sybella's pocket. Had she shared them with anyone? Had Jupitus been delivered the solution without driving Ollivan to his knees? No – Sybella would be dismissed as party to another trick of Ollivan's. She would have expected that outcome and never gone to Jupitus in the first place, even if she found it in her to get past the High Sorcerer threatening to have her killed. Nor would she attempt the spell herself.

But Ollivan could end this.

It wasn't right that it would almost certainly see him arrested, but perhaps that didn't have to be a defeat. Perhaps it could be an act of defiance. Jupitus had tried to cast him as the villain. Jasper had helped. They had pressed the need for vengeance upon him, and he had taken it with fervour. He had thought surrender played into their hands, but it was hatred that had gotten him here. And now the city was burning.

Just as he had planned.

Ollivan scooped the boy up and put him in the back of the cart, rearranging the man's belongings to cushion him and placing his own bag under the boy's head.

"Find a hospital," said Ollivan, "and take him there."

"But—"

"You have all my money" – he dug the rest of what he had out of his pockets and pressed it into the man's hands – "and I can get you more. Just do it."

"I'm not risking my life to—"

Ollivan took him by the shoulders. "Your life will be fine. I'm putting an end to this."

Because Ollivan was not a monster. But he had done a monstrous thing.

A last-ditch bid for freedom started to formulate in his mind. Without wasting another second, he summoned the remainder of his energy, fixed his mind on his destination, and transported to his fate.

44

Cassia leaned over the balustrade and watched the churning water of the Thames swallow Ollivan and Sybella's spell.

For a second nothing happened. She could feel Violet's delight emanating from her in the form of waves of fizzing magic. Because Cassia had given her no reason to doubt. She had set her loose upon the city. She had thrown the spell into the Thames.

And she had told her friends to watch for it.

Violet's head twitched to the bank behind Cassia a split second before a barrage of spells fell upon the bridge. They were not aimed at Violet, for her magic would only drink them up. She could drink these too if she wished, but it would require her attention. It would give Cassia time to act.

They came from the north bank too, crackling lightning and arching flames; blazing flashes of coloured light. Cassia squinted through the onslaught. Among the Camden wolves, Sorcerers crouched behind the barricade. The Successors. They had shown up for her. Lev and Virgil would be there, Sybella on the south.

Now was her moment. The spell she had thrown into the river was Ollivan and Sybella's. The one she produced from her pocket and set alight now was her own, written on hazel wood paper taken from the storeroom in the Chambers.

It was based on the original, with one essential and risk-laden difference to account for what Violet was expecting. In the crucial moment, with the pressure of the city's fate pressing down on her, Cassia found the presence of mind to channel the words on the hazel wood paper into one clear intention: *drink*.

The paper curled and blackened. Violet's head snapped around, eyes darting between the spell and Cassia's own. She was panicking, just as Cassia had planned.

But she didn't act. To drink this spell would be folly. The first spell was designed to hurt her only after she absorbed it – surely this one was the same, was it not?

It was. But it would not look it. As the spell began to work, sparks crackled, lashing out. Like the original spell, this was another pretty distraction, and a signal of something unknown, designed to put Violet's defences up and make her cautious. It worked – Violet took several steps back, hands raised and ready to act. Meanwhile, Cassia's Guysman entered the intended vessel.

It entered *her*.

It started with a warming all over her skin. She couldn't see the spell seeping into her, but the sensation was enough that she felt like she could; red and roiling, and passing into her like she was made of air. And a sense of wrongness; a resistance that didn't come from her magic, but from her very being. She had expected this, had steeled herself against it, pressing her eyes closed tightly and focusing on the intention, and not the *wrongness* filling her up. If all went to plan, she didn't need to hold the spell in herself for long, so she held firm and purred reassurances to her magic.

It wasn't enough. Far from the spell growing too much for her, it began to disintegrate. Her magic gripped it tighter, but the tendrils spun loose. It understood the intention – the spell was watertight, her power told her – but she wasn't strong enough to wield it. The Guysman was dying within her, before it ever found its mark.

A weight landed on her shoulder. Cassia's eyes sprung open, expecting to find Violet upon her and her plan done for. But Violet was a distance along the bridge, backing away from the electric lights of Cassia's spell, her eyes darting every which way in anticipation of its magic.

A spell of some kind had wrapped around Cassia; a glamour? The weight pressed down – no, squeezed – and she looked over her shoulder.

Ollivan.

He *had* wrapped them in a glamour, one he must have used to sneak onto the bridge, the Successor's distraction adding another layer of protection.

His eyes met hers and his hand squeezed again, communicating something, and then Cassia understood. She didn't have the power.

But Ollivan could give it to her.

She was risking so much already, but her carefully planned attack was crumbling within her and it was all about to be for nothing. So she nodded her consent. Her brother nodded back, just once, and then everything went white.

She was invincible. The power rushing through her was like nothing she had ever known. At once, her magic snapped onto the spell, the understanding innate. The Guysman took form, a well opening up inside her. *What else*, her magic hummed. *What else do you want? Fame? Immortality?* The power at her disposal could do anything, and the world was opening up before her and offering itself.

No, Cassia replied. Because the well had no bottom, the sides had no grip, and everything around her was tilting into it, pulled by the force of what she had done.

Only a second had passed. Ollivan released her, but the Guysman did not. Her magic had taken what it needed from him and the spell was manifest. Where moments before the challenge had been catching a spark, now she was trying to quell an inferno.

Magic in unknown and grotesque shapes tried to force its way into her – Whisperer, Psi, Changeling; spells and enchantments that weren't her own, that tasted foreign and poisonous – and again, her being rebelled. It was wrong. It was agonising. And yet alongside all her fear and horror and pain, it was ecstasy. Power she should never have known belonged to her now. She could not control it – Whisperer magic became nonsense sounds and nightmare images, Changeling shifting was melting her bones and wringing her flesh – but for a short while she could touch it all. She could be what no one before her had ever been. If Ollivan's meagre jolt of power had made her invincible, now she was a god.

Dying, but a god.

She opened her eyes to find she was on her hands and knees, and a storm of magic moved in a cyclone around her. *This was meant to happen*, something told her. *Drink it all*, said another voice. But she couldn't. She couldn't control a thing. She could only descend quickly towards her own end. Hopefully not before whatever she had been trying to accomplish was done.

There was a hand on her again, this time gripping hers. She pulled away. No, she *thought* of pulling away and her magic did the rest, flinging the hand off her. Its owner screamed something. Her name.

468

Cassia's gaze met a pair of eyes she recognised, steel grey and wild. It was her brother, kneeling beside her on the bridge. He took her hand again, and this time he placed it on his shoulder. He wanted her to do something, but any more words were lost under a lightning crack of magic in the storm she had made. That was good, at least. She had made it to cause confusion, hadn't she?

The beautiful agony built towards a crescendo, and Cassia didn't want it to stop, but she didn't want to die either, and she could feel the stars beckoning her into oblivion. If she could temper all this power somehow…

Stolen magic continued to pour into the bottomless well she had opened, but her own power was still there, and it cradled her now, telling her what to do; coaxing her to relinquish control and let it do what it knew it could.

So Cassia let go, trusting in her magic as it funnelled away some of the power that was destroying her – and poured it right into Ollivan.

His eyes went wide. His mouth froze in a silent scream. In the clarity it afforded her, Cassia tried to pull away, but he held her hand to his shoulder in a vice-like grip, and her magic whispered reassurances below the cacophony in her mind. It wanted rid of the intrusive power she had welcomed in, and it siphoned it into her brother until he was sagging, trembling, onto the ground.

Like all pain, it was endless, and yet only a few moments had passed since Cassia completed her spell. A few moments before the waterfall of power tumbling into her and through her stuttered, and the weight of the magic she couldn't stop drinking began to abate. At first she feared that she had channelled it all into Ollivan, but he too lifted his head, the wildness rekindling in his eyes.

And then the storm around them was receding too, and as Cassia came back to herself, she remembered why she had made herself a vessel for the Guysman. The risks she had calculated, the role she had played. Because Violet had known Ollivan's plan. There was nothing they could make her absorb once he had inadvertently laid it all out for her. But faced with a danger she didn't fully understand, Cassia had left her with one choice: to drain the spellcaster instead.

As Cassia's magic waned, so did the cyclone of harmless smoke and flashing lights around her, and through it, her own face and body appeared, a delicate hand extending towards them, her head tilted gently to one side, as if she was listening. None of the overwhelming force of the spell she had consumed showed on her face. She had been designed for it in a way a Sorcerer was not.

But a frown appeared, as if the music had turned discordant. Her hand dropped to her side.

"Oh."

Violet's eyes glowed gold, and Cassia tensed, moving closer to Ollivan as he did the same. They crouched against the balustrade, leaning into one another for any safety or comfort they could find there as the golden glow intensified, until Cassia was forced to shield her eyes.

A blast threw her into the air – and then it held her there. Violet's stolen power had exploded from her and formed a bubble, encapsulating the bridge and those on it in pure magic. Cassia was floating somewhere in the realm between ethereal and solid, her body having been absorbed into its surroundings, for everything was magic. She was aware of everything, though she had no eyes with which to see, no hands with which to feel, and no mind to explain it to her. What little form she had was shifting rapidly. She was gas. She was paper. She had feathers. And she could feel another mind, one whose particles brushed against hers, and whose thoughts came to her like words whispered under a blanket in the dead of night, when they were six and four years old.

You came back.

Yes. Foolishly, I thought you needed me, said Ollivan.

But I did.

Is that so? You didn't even use my spell.

But I used your magic. The spell was dying without you.

His reply didn't come in words, but Cassia could feel him puff up like a preening cat.

Cassia?

Yes?

This spell. You didn't tell it what was to happen to the magic it released, did you?

Ah. I was a little short on time. That's bad, isn't it?

Hard to say. This bubble situation is nothing like what I was anticipating. Out of curiosity, can you feel your limbs?

Cassia felt around in the aether. *Sort of, if I concentrate on them. But they don't feel a part of me.*

I'm not sure they are, currently. I think the universe is trying to recalibrate to accommodate the magic before it sets it free.

So this will stop, eventually?

I hope so.

When?

I suppose we'll have to wait and see. Are you alright? he said.

Oh, I'm fairly sure I'm mortally wounded.

Don't be so dramatic. You're fine. You have to be.

Why is that?

Because when this bubble bursts and I have legs again, I have an arrangement with a certain smuggler to make a break for it.

Delphine?

Oz. He's very grateful that I broke him out of hospital. I'm going to work for them on the continent. I have quite an aptitude for stealing, did you know?

I'd heard rumours, yes.

I wish I could stay and nurse my little sister back to health, but I'm afraid it would probably cost me my neck. I'll have to trust you'll be fine instead. I'm sorry.

That's alright. You couldn't nurse a houseplant. Are you alright?

An ethereal laugh. *Ah, Cassia. I haven't been alright for such a long time. But I'm going to be.*

They floated through the magical aether in companiable silence, perhaps for a minute, perhaps a century.

I'm sorry too, said Cassia.

What for?

For calling you a monster.

Oh, that? I'd forgotten all about that.

Cassia had the sensation of passing through time the way a Wraith passed through solid objects, and wondered which Wraith's magic she was encountering. Whether she had met them. Whether they would get in back.

Will you do something for me? said Ollivan.

Something else, you mean?

Yes, I suppose I do. Can you tell Mother I coerced you into all this? Sybella, Lev, and Virgil too. Jupitus will be forced to accept it, coming from her.

Alright.

Alright? That's it? You're not going to fight me on it?

I don't want to fight you on anything any more. It's been such a waste, Ollivan.

The other psyche surrounded hers; gentle, soothing, and Cassia became a bit more solid.

Did you have a message for Sybella too? she asked him.

Ollivan's thoughts turned ruminative and sad.

Tell her if she wants to see me, she knows where.

The bubble shuddered. At its centre, Violet was an inferno of gold light, blades of which erupted from her and pierced the bubble's surface; just a few at first, but growing in number until everything was light. At last, it burst, and Cassia's world exploded a second time.

She was unafraid. Some of this magic was hers, and when she felt it rejoin with her – rekindling in the place inside her where it formed – she knew she was safe. Her head cracked against the bridge as she became whole. The sky above rippled as all the stolen power disseminated. Would those further from the blast recover their magic as easily as she had done? Did it know how to find home?

She rolled onto her side and pushed herself shakily off the ground. A gold light continued to pulse further along the bridge, but each flare was weaker than the next. At the centre was a figure on the ground, small and immobile.

Cassia looked around her as she crawled towards it, but there was no one on the bridge but her and the figure at the centre of the light. Panic fluttered inside her. Had Ollivan been injured? Had he failed to come back from whatever had happened to them?

The thought left her mind when she reached Violet. The light was dimming, and the doll was still, but her head rolled slowly in Cassia's direction as she came to kneel over her. Her glass eyes still followed her movements.

"My hair," she said. Her mouth didn't move. Whatever magic had made her into a woman, there was no trace of it now.

But her dress looked new, and her hair was the same. It hung loosely around her tiny, porcelain face, the way Cassia wore hers. The tight curls of two decades ago were gone.

"It looks beautiful," said Cassia.

But as the light receded, Violet's dress returned to what Cassia had accidentally made of it. The hem shredded before her eyes. The silk grew mouldy. When the light was only a shimmer in her green eyes, Violet's hair transformed too, the dated ringlets crushed and frizzed from a day spent wrapped in a sodden jacket. Cassia felt a surge of guilt; she had promised to style it for her.

"Really?" asked Violet, bright hope in her lilting tone.

"Really."

Cassia forced herself to watch as the magic withered and died. She laid a finger gently against Violet's porcelain hand. Did she feel pain? Cassia hoped not. As futile as it seemed, she sent up a prayer to the stars to watch over her. A crack – the one she had magicked from the doll's face – appeared with a quiet snap, and it was over.

Cassia sat back and turned her face to the dawn. A single small boat cut through the water below, heading east, away from the bridge. She squinted at the figure standing at the stern, but he was already too far away.

45

Ollivan waited for a day in the attic room of the temple.

He mainly slept, the vitality tonic he had downed having worn off on Oz's boat, around the time the Psi had called on his magic and opened a hidden tunnel to whisk them underground. There was a ship heading to France under cover of darkness, and Ollivan aboard it. He had lost his belongings, and no need under the stars would make him risk transporting home to fetch more money, so he was continent-bound with nothing but the bloody shirt on his back.

Whenever the despair of that future threatened to pull him under, he would watch the street through the arch that led to the temple courtyard below, and content himself with the knowledge that London would recover. From what he could glean, everyone who had lost magic to the Guysman had got it back, and those who had suffered the worst – like the boy he had found in the street – were expected to return to their old selves. Being rejoined with their magic had had a physiological effect no one could have predicted. It was almost that magic itself – whether Sorcerer, or Wraith, or Whisperer – was healing, or its absence ailing. Ollivan longed to find out – to stay here at the site of the event and learn what he could – but he had escaped the bridge with his freedom, and that was something he wanted more. It would have to be enough.

And it would be, if only—

One glance, and the archway was deserted. The next, and she was there. The shape of her was as familiar to him as his own, even under the moonlight. His longing compelled him to join her at once, but his future without her told him to wait, commit this to memory.

An owl hooted, and Sybella's face turned towards the moonlight, towards him. Ollivan grasped his moment, and transported down to join her.

"You're just in time." She jumped, curls bouncing as she spun to face him. A range of emotions flashed across her face, but settled on relief. She had been afraid of missing him. "My ship leaves at midnight."

"Well, it's not like it was easy for me to get away," she sniffed, folding her arms. "The President of the Society of Young Gifted Sorcerers has very few spare hours in the day."

"My congratulations."

She shrugged and looked out into the street. "It's not like I was voted in."

"More fool them. You'll be excellent."

He could feel a pounding from inside his chest; a furious fear of missing his chance to say everything he needed to, so strong it stifled any words at all. Was that why Sybella was silent too?

"And what will you be?" she said eventually.

Ollivan smiled his boldest smile. "All kinds of trouble."

She gave him a look he had never deciphered; it meant either *give me strength* or *I'm so in love with you it hurts*. Maybe it meant both.

"You could come with me," he said, already knowing her reply. But he couldn't help it.

Sybella quirked a brow. "I could," she agreed, "but I won't. I want to see my sister grow up. And I would have to write off any political future altogether."

"They have politics on the continent too, you know."

"True, but I hear there's much less chance of getting overthrown and murdered once you leave London, and that sounds terribly tedious." She smiled. "Don't look so glum. You've lost me once. It won't kill you to lose me again."

"Care to make a wager?"

She laughed, but her eyes had filled with tears. Ollivan pulled her to him and buried his face in her hair. Her arms encircled him. Her cheek rested against his shoulder.

"When I'm High Sorcerer," Sybella said, her voice muffled by his jacket, "I shall issue you a pardon."

"You should hire Lev and Virgil to manage your campaign. They're awfully good."

Sybella pulled away slightly and looked up into his face. Ollivan's thumb drifted over her cheek.

"Is there any use in telling you to be safe?" she said.

"None at all."

"Alright, then."

They fell into silence. The only movement was the rise and fall of their chests as they breathed each other in, and the swooping of an owl's wings as it took flight to give them their privacy.

This was not the night with Sybella he had longed for. But he had been hers, and he had lost her, and he knew the difference. In his perfect world, he stayed by her side as she took the city, and she stayed by his through it all. But this was not a perfect world. It was the Witherward, the world he had chosen. And he had

477

righted his wrongs – well, most of them. And the girl he loved, loved him too.

And there was magic.

They stood in the shadow of the archway, invisible to the city healing softly all around them, and for the first time in his life, Ollivan considered himself truly lucky.

Your scream gutters out with a wet, hiccupping sound, and in the beat of quiet you realise it's over. The carriage has pulled away and Mama and Papa have dashed back into the house, heads slung low, clutching each other.

A lone figure witnesses you leaving. His small, chubby hands are white as they pound the windowpane, over and over, mouth open in a wail. You watch him until the house vanishes from view.

The next time you see each other, too long has passed.

4 6

Cassia lay on her bedroom floor in a wash of colour.

She had enchanted the full spectrum of the rainbow onto the windowpanes; red bleeding into yellow, yellow bleeding into green, each pane a different shade, so that the colours danced over and around her in a coordinated riot.

She had been so weak for days – unable to read, or walk in the garden, or do much other than rest and watch the sun move across the walls of her room. As soon as she gained a modicum of strength back, she had devised a way to entertain herself. She could barely move from the floor any more, but it was not for lack of strength. She thought she might never need to read a book to entertain her ever again. She had magic.

There was a knock at her door, and Elodie entered. Cassia raised herself onto her elbows and stared her down until she started speaking.

"The High Sorcerer is ready for you," she said.

Finally. She had asked for a meeting that morning, and been told to stay at home and await a summons.

"Let me get ready," she said, standing and walking towards her closet for her coat.

"He's downstairs," said Elodie.

That was unusual. Why had her grandfather come to her for the first time in her life?

"Alright." She doubled back to her bureau, and amended a message she had waiting there, which she handed off to a servant to be delivered. Then she followed Elodie's instructions to meet her grandfather in the drawing room.

Jupitus sat in a wing-backed chair, facing the garden. As Cassia approached, her eyes landed on his hands. His knuckles were white as he gripped the arms of the chair, and Cassia's stomach plummeted. She had been readying herself to command this meeting since she knew they had to have it. Faced with her grandfather's ire, some of her courage deserted her.

"Grandfather," she said, breathing a sigh of relief that her voice did not break and her greeting carried across the room.

Jupitus leaned out of his chair to turn to her. "Come here," he said, and she obeyed.

Someone had placed another chair opposite his. Cassia looked at it, then looked at her grandfather.

She had thought it strange that she'd heard nothing of him or from him during her convalescence, but she had dared not ask. Perhaps he had simply been busy tackling the aftermath of Violet. But now he was meeting with her at her own house, instead of at his seat of power at the Chambers, with his bodyguards lining the room and his view of the city behind him. And looking at him, Cassia understood why.

He was dying.

His shoulders were straight. His eyes were clear. But his hands didn't relinquish their grip on the chair for a single moment. *Lest I see them tremble*, thought Cassia. His pale skin no longer held fast to his bones, but wept like wax around his eyes. Had he grown old all of a sudden, or had he simply been such a behemoth in her mind that she never noticed?

He motioned to the chair a second time, impatient, but Cassia didn't take it. She laced her fingers in front of her and squared her shoulders.

"I wanted to talk to you," she said.

"Not so fast." He put too much venom in his words. A miscalculation. It was too forced; too desperate.

Cassia knew what he wished to say.

"I don't know where Ollivan is."

"I expected you would say as much."

"It's the truth."

"I don't doubt it." His eyes bored into hers, and Cassia bit the inside of her cheek. Last time they had faced off, he had banished her to the Docklands. "What I find harder to believe is your mother's story that all the blame for the near destruction of our city lies with him."

He broke into a coughing fit that fractured the end of his speech with spluttering breaths. It triggered a deep and rattling discomfort in her, and she looked about for an attendant, a bodyguard, someone to strengthen him, but like the last time, they were alone.

She might as well say what she needed to say, and get out.

"Why did you never make me your heir?"

He squinted at her, head tilted like she wasn't making sense.

"I didn't know you had political ambitions," he said. A question, not a reply.

"That doesn't matter to you. Ollivan never did." She may as well play all her cards; she had nothing left to lose. "And even

482

after you had a Wraith killed to frame him, you never considered me as an alternative."

A muscle twitched in her grandfather's jaw, but otherwise he was very still. It reminded Cassia of a deer realising a wolf watched it from the undergrowth. He had been caught grazing, when he should have been running for his life.

But Jupitus didn't see it that way.

"It's admirable, my girl, that you set your sights so high." Condescension dripped from every word. "But ambition or none, your brother showed a flair that would have been well placed for inheriting my role someday."

"And me?"

He smiled; it wasn't friendly. "You don't need me to tell you any of this. You know you do not fit in in the Heart."

Cassia took a moment to marvel at her own reaction – or rather, the lack of one. It was true. She didn't belong here, and she did not need the High Sorcerer to confirm that for her. But that fact didn't hurt her. Indeed, it showed her the path ahead.

"But at least I can be counted on to *toe the line*," she said slowly. "Isn't that right, Grandfather?"

He regarded her, a realisation creeping onto his face. Ollivan was gone. Alana wasn't speaking to him, the enforcers whispered. And Cassia had started to suspect her father had got out while he could. Jupitus's tried-and-true methods of intimidation had failed on the Sims. Perhaps his own blood was tougher than he had ever given them credit for. And now he was dying. He could not afford the one safe bet he thought he'd laid to curdle into an empty hand.

"It seems you never understood my purpose in the path I

chose for you," he said. "Do you not know why I encouraged your parents to foster you to the Zoo?"

"To strengthen your alliance with the Changelings. To break down our people's prejudices. But I know what that really means." She tilted her chin up. "You think that I don't understand this game like the rest of you. But I grew up in a ruling seat just like Mother and Ollivan. It just wasn't *this* seat. I was a gift to the Zoo, a symbol of goodwill. A glorified hostage."

Jupitus shook his head, chuckling. "So you don't understand, as I thought," he said. "You were the opposite, Cassia. A spy."

He dragged the word out temptingly, the way one would entice a bored child with a make-believe role to keep them occupied.

But Jupitus *had* spies in Camden, just as she knew Camden had them here. He had never asked her once about her life there, other than to confirm she was behaving and reflecting well on him. And if that had been her purpose, why allow her to come home and abandon the post? Why relegate her to the Docklands?

"Don't you see? You are crucial to my rule here." He held her gaze fiercely, like if he blinked his spell would be broken.

But he had no spell over her.

"Crucial," she repeated. "Then I suppose it would harm you, if I refused to be your pawn."

Jupitus laughed openly. His fingers unfurled from the arms of his chair and interlaced in his lap. In the interim, they trembled. "Refuse? My girl, you have no such power."

Cassia tilted her head to one side, and wondered how it had taken her seventeen years to learn what Ollivan had always seen; the value of resistance, even when your options were limited.

She had never bucked against her cage, believing it to be sturdier than her; afraid she would bruise.

But there was always weakness. Sometimes you just had to rattle every last bar to find it.

"Miss Sims."

The servant's voice barely carried across the room. He was stood in the doorway, eyes darting nervously between her and her grandfather. "You have a, ah, visitor."

Cassia smiled. "Please see her in."

Watching her grandfather struggle with his confusion – the sudden lack of ability to control the situation – was equal parts sad and thrilling.

The quick snap of her boots preceded Cassia's guest into the room.

"I'm not too late, am I?" said Hester Ravenswood by way of greeting as she marched across the room. "I did try to sit tight and wait for your message, but my dearest cousin has flown off somewhere and left us all in disarray. The *Zoo* is an awfully apt name for that place this morning. Jupitus." Hester halted before the High Sorcerer's chair. Her gaze swept over him. "I hope you're well," she settled for, her tone raising no questions.

Jupitus gathered all the composure he could muster. "Hester. I'm disappointed you did not elect to tell me you were coming. I always wish to know when important members of other factions are in my territory."

"Yes, well, this is rather pressing," replied Hester, supremely unbothered by the implied threat in the High Sorcerer's words. She shot a questioning look at Cassia, who nodded. "Jupitus, I'm afraid I know all about your indiscretion with the Wraith a year back."

"I beg your pardon?"

"You had a Wraith killed, did you not?" Hester said impatiently. "By the name of Jonas Benn? I've harangued a handful of witnesses who between them can piece the whole thing together." She produced a piece of paper from her bag and waved it about, but did not offer it to the High Sorcerer. "Something about a very inventive, very volatile bit of corporeal magic."

When Cassia had told Hester the entire story and what she hoped to do with it, the Changeling had promised to find enough evidence to cause Jupitus some trouble with the Wraiths. It wasn't until Hester was laying out every detail – the buried ledgers, the channelling spell, the incriminating existence of Jasper Hawkes' dead body – that Cassia realised she hadn't dared to hope. How had Hester built such a complete case against him in just a few days?

The High Sorcerer's breathing grew laboured as fury overtook him. "You are playing a dangerous game here, Miss Ravenswood."

Hester waved a hand. "Oh, Jupitus, don't be so dramatic. I've set the stakes a lot lower than you could ever dream. In fact you should be thanking me. Let Cassia come back to the Zoo – on her own terms – and I make the whole thing disappear."

It was too good an offer to refuse. At best, the murder coming to light would mean a much costlier negotiation with the North. At worst, it would lead to outright war. Jupitus was fighting to keep his expression blank, but his eyes narrowed like he suspected a trick.

"Sending her back to us is what you would have done anyway," Hester went on. "I'm only suggesting you leave her be after that. Emancipation, shall we call it? She no longer belongs to you." Hester gave her an appraising smile, and tears sprang to Cassia's eyes.

"Am I to believe that's all you want?"

Cassia laughed, and they both turned to her. "I beg your pardon," she said through her giggling. "It's just that of course you don't understand, Grandfather. Whatever you try to claim now, I've never been of any value to you, so you don't believe I could be of any value to anyone."

That was his flaw, the fatally fragile bar of the cage he had put her in. He cared nothing for what he could not use. Jupitus had sent her to the Zoo as a pawn, and the Zoo had made her family.

"I've already packed," Cassia told Hester. They did not need to wait for her grandfather's consent. He would give it, because Cassia had proved once and for all she was worthless to him.

"Excellent," said Hester brightly. She was already marching away when she threw her parting comment over her shoulder. "A pleasure as always, Jupitus."

Cassia gave him one last look, and followed Hester without a word. She doubted she would see him again.

She meant not to.

*

Cassia held her mother tightly for the first time in her life, and promised to call upon her once in a while. Alana seemed a bit bemused by it, and by the way Cassia told her meaningfully that she would be sending her an important letter. She planned to convince her mother not to contest her father's office when he was gone; to slip from her own cage and down a path of her choosing.

Then she picked up her potted rosebush – which was thriving – and carried it out to the carriage. She was going to magically propagate a whole garden. Hester had already promised her a patch of space at the Zoo.

Sybella, Lev, and Virgil were waiting for her in front of the carriage.

"I knew you would leave," Sybella said, watching the footman load Cassia's bags onto the back of the carriage. Hester waited inside, studiously staring out the window and pretending not to listen. "It's a shame. I really think we could have been close friends."

"Politics is all about having friends, Sybella," said Cassia. She lowered her voice. "Perhaps I shall be a lieutenant in Camden someday, and then when you're High Sorcerer, we'll be colleagues."

"A Sorcerer lieutenant of the Changelings?" said Virgil. "You're strange, Sims, but you're not *that* strange."

Perhaps he was right, but Cassia would find a way to be useful to the Changelings. Not to earn her place among them, but for herself. She would build a life she had chosen.

Sybella reached into her pocket and started unwrapping the handkerchief she produced. "I brought you something."

She placed the object in Cassia's waiting hand. It was a Successor's pin.

"But—" Cassia weighed the pin in her palm. "I haven't earned this."

"Of course you have. I'm reliably informed by an insufferable schemer, who once had cause to learn the Society charter from front to back, that presidents are at full liberty to award membership for *feats of astonishing magic*. Initiation or no initiation. The rule hasn't been called upon in decades. The unsurprising truth is, most spoiled, overprivileged legacy children aren't actually all that *gifted* at magic." She gave a little wave. "Take it from one who knows."

"*Two*," corrected Lev. He mimed his mirror bit from his initiation again.

"Welcome to the Society," said Virgil, squeezing her shoulder.

Cassia gripped her roses tighter, and allowed herself a single moment of triumph. Then, she handed the pin back. "Thank you, Sybella. Truly. Don't take this the wrong way, but I don't want to belong to the Successors."

To her relief, Sybella laughed. Lev pantomimed offence with a hand on his chest. Virgil only smirked.

"Perhaps you're strange enough after all," Sybella said, and kissed her on the cheek.

Cassia embraced her friends and said her farewells, marvelling at how she had carved *something* here since awakening her brother's spell. And she had mastered her magic, just as she planned. It only made her all the more sure of leaving. She was not slinking back to Camden with her tail between her legs; she was going home a success.

Cassia waved from the carriage until they were out of sight. Hester sat next to her, Cassia's rosebush between them.

"How did you do it?" she asked. "How did you find the evidence to threaten him?"

In answer, Hester took out the paper she had waved at the High Sorcerer and handed it to her. It was a letter, detailing in lengthy technical descriptions the mechanics of the channelling spell that had killed Jonas Benn. It laid out Jupitus's desire to be rid of his grandson to protect his image, his use of Jasper to do it, and the end Jasper had met when that usefulness expired. It then named several Changelings who frequented a travelling duelling evening and may be convinced to provide Hester with colour and context in exchange for immunity.

It was signed by Ollivan. The last paragraph expressed exactly what he wished Hester to do with the information.

"He had the same idea as you, about emancipating you." Hester looked out the window and sniffed. "I'm not surprised. Now that it's all settled I don't mind telling you that I can't imagine how you ever considered staying in this place."

Cassia reached past the rosebush and grasped Hester's hand. The woman arched a curious brow at her – she was not the affectionate type – but didn't pull away.

"I thought my family was here," said Cassia.

All her life, she had been focused on who others wanted her to be; on the ways she could squeeze and break herself until she was a shape that fit. Nothing she did had worked. She was part Sorcerer, part Changeling. *That* was her place in the world. She couldn't change it for anyone, not even herself. But she could practise not wanting to. And she could hold those who didn't ask it of her with her whole heart.

They jolted to a stop at the Camden guard point. Among the wolves at their posts, two men waited for the carriage. The first leaned casually on his cane, and tipped his hat to her when their eyes met. Cassia's mouth formed Aelius's name as she felt the sting of tears.

The second was not a man at all. Cassia didn't recognise him even as he clambered into the carriage after Aelius. She was distracted by one of the wolves. He stood away from them, his face a mask of stone, and though his gaze slid briefly to hers,

490

he pretended not to have seen her at all. His disdain stung for a moment. Then Cassia looked back to her friends, who were beaming. Her own face cracked into a smile as Fyfe threw his arms around her. Such gangly, awkward arms; stars, how he'd grown. When he spoke, his voice was muffled by the crook of her neck, where he had buried his face like a child.

"Welcome home, Cassia."

ACKNOWLEDGEMENTS

My first thanks again are for my extraordinary agent, Zoë Plant, for holding my hand and cheering me on through the infamous second book experience. I could not have done this without you. Thanks also to the tireless work of agent's assistant and good girl, Rhubarb.

To my editor, Cat Camacho. Thank you for helping me wrestle this (sometimes unwilling) story into existence, and hone and sharpen it into something I could be proud of. Thank you David Lancett and your second editorial eye, for proving the adage that two heads are better than one. Also, the rest of the exceptional and hardworking team at Titan, including Fenton Coulthurst, Lydia Gittins, Julia Bradley; and Julia Lloyd for your extraordinary work on the cover. I didn't think you could top *Witherward* and yet you have! Thanks *and* apologies are due to Louise Pearce, my copyeditor, who had to contend with the election maths scene. I am so sorry. It took me a dozen passes and I am never writing anything like it ever again.

Thank you to my parents, who tell every friend, acquaintance, and person they pass on the street that their daughter is an author (and who were also roped into election maths). To Sam and Ellie, who send me every snapshot of my books in the wild, forward every kind message, and listen to every distressed voice memo. I can't imagine doing this without any of you.

To Jack, for disgusting levels of encouragement, among thousands of other things I have to live with; love, patience, laughing until I cry. Frankly, you're embarrassing yourself.

I am immensely grateful to the friends and family who have met this journey with such support and enthusiasm, and to the online community of other authors who have shared in my excitement and celebrated my successes.

I have left this thank you for last, not because it's the least important, but because my gratitude is so stunning that I hardly know where to begin. To the readers – a lot has changed in the process of publishing. Things I used to daydream about, I now have to remind myself to stop and celebrate. Success is a moving target. Dreams get bigger. But thinking of you overwhelms me every time and I don't think that will ever change. That you are out there, buying and borrowing my books, talking about them, *reaching out* to tell me they meant something to you, brings me unbelievable happiness. Thank you. I hope I get to keep writing for you, and hope you'll stay to see what comes next…

ABOUT THE AUTHOR

Hannah Mathewson's untamed creative streak led her through acting, music, drawing, and a desire to make films, before she narrowed in on writing. She studied Film and Television at the University of East Anglia, and worked in various jobs in cinemas, libraries, and archives while pursuing writing. Rich fantasy title *Witherward* was her first novel. She lives in Oxfordshire and tweets @HannahOClock.

For more fantastic fiction, author events,
exclusive excerpts, competitions, limited editions and more

VISIT OUR WEBSITE
titanbooks.com

LIKE US ON FACEBOOK
facebook.com/titanbooks

FOLLOW US ON TWITTER AND INSTAGRAM
@TitanBooks

EMAIL US
readerfeedback@titanemail.com